D1326060

ADVENT

ADVENT

James Treadwell

HODDER &
STOUGHTON

First published in Great Britain in 2012 by Hodder & Stoughton
An Hachette UK company

1

A CIP catalogue record for this title is available from the British Library

Hardback ISBN 978 1 444 72846 0
Trade paperback ISBN 978 1 444 72847 7

Typeset in Baskerville by Hewer Text UK Ltd, Edinburgh

Printed bound in UK by CPI Group (UK) Ltd, Croydon, CR0 4YY

Hodder & Stoughton policy is to use papers that are natural, renewable and recyclable products and made from wood grown in sustainable forests. The logging and manufacturing processes are expected to conform to the environmental regulations of the country of origin.

Hodder & Stoughton Ltd
338 Euston Road
London NW1 3BH

www.hodder.co.uk

ADVENT

If a man could pass through Paradise in a dream, and have a flower presented to him as a pledge that his soul had really been there, and if he found that flower in his hand when he awoke – Aye! and what then?

in the notebooks of S.T. Coleridge

One

A December night 1537

On a wild night in deep winter in the year 1537, the greatest magus in the world gathered together and dismissed his household servants, wrapped himself in his travelling cloak, took his staff in one hand and in the other a small wooden box sealed with pitch and clasped with silver, and stepped out into the whirling sleet, bound for the harbour and – so he expected – immortality.

All but the city's most utterly forlorn inhabitants had been driven from the streets by the bitter weather. The remaining beggars and strays were fully occupied with their struggle to survive until dawn, so the magus walked uninterrupted through alleys of filthy slush. Nobody so much as saw him; any lifted eyes would have been stung by the icy rain, which felt as if it blew from every direction at once. Nobody but one.

Some thirty paces behind him, a figure followed, bone-thin as the stray dogs and ragged as the beggars. It looked like little more than a jumble of sticks and scraps of cloth that should have been scattered at once by the ferocious wind; but seen more closely (though nobody saw), it was a woman, gaunt, weather-beaten, but steady. Her eyes were fixed on the man's back and never turned away no matter how the sleet blew.

Beneath his cloak the magus kept a tight grip on the box. Inside it, padded around with wool, was a calfskin pouch pricked out with marks of warding and asylum. Inside the pouch were two things: a small oval mirror in a velvet sheath, and a ring that appeared to be carved of wood, though it was not.

Inside the mirror was a share of the magus's soul. Inside the ring was all the magic in the world.

He came out of the alleys and hurried as best he could along a broader thoroughfare by a frozen canal, where the wind was at last able to settle on a single direction and roar at full force. He was not afraid, exactly. Since mastering his art, he had seen far more than any other living man, and outgrown faint-heartedness. Still, the things he carried were infinitely precious to him, and he was eager to be away, across the sea in England.

Even in the foulest weather, a falling tide and a wind blowing seawards kept the wharves from being entirely deserted. He had to break stride to pick his way through the lantern-lit clusters of carters and watermen clumped alongside creaking hulls. That was what made him glance around and so for the first time notice his pursuer.

His fingers closed tighter on the box.

'Johannes!'

Her voice made a space for itself in the air, slicing between the weather's din and the clattering and flapping of the ships. He halted, his back to her.

The moment she caught up with him, the wind stopped. Instead of sleet, snowflakes fell, gathering on his hood and shoulders. In the abrupt silence he felt in his ears the guilty hammering of his heart. The rest of the world around them had gone still. The two of them stood as if alone in the snow, as they would again, long, long afterwards, in their last winter.

He sighed and closed his eyes. 'How do you come to be here?'

'Johannes, turn.' She spoke in Latin, as he had.

'I know what I will see.'

'Then face me.'

He neither turned nor answered.

'What you took from me,' the woman said, 'you must now return.'

At this his eyes blinked open. He pressed the box tight to his heart.

She stretched out an arm towards his back, hand open, and held it still. 'You cannot bear it,' she said. 'Save yourself.'

Still without facing her, the magus raised his voice. 'I did not look for you to be here. Let me go.'

'Look for me?' He had never heard her angry before. He had not thought her capable of common passions. The ice in her voice cut as keen as winter. 'You never looked for me. No more can you dismiss me. But if you do not turn back, I will go, Johannes, and the end you fear will have arrived.'

For a few seconds neither spoke. The snowflakes made white shadows on the trimming of his cloak and thawed into cold drops on her upturned face.

He set his lips tight and took a step forward.

She gave a despairing cry, instantly drowned out by the return of the wind. In an eye-blink it hurled away the flecks of snow and spun them into the freezing murk. He looked around, but the ragged woman was nowhere to be seen. She at least had kept her word and was gone.

A voice bellowed, 'Master John Fiste!'

It was how he had given the captain his name. The vessel and its crew were English. He shifted round to put the wind at his back and saw a mariner beckoning and, beyond that, the harbour light glowing through a sparkling curtain of sleet.

Still holding the box tightly concealed under his cloak, he followed the man aboard.

Some hours later the wet abated, and because he had urged haste and paid them extravagantly, the ship put out to sea. The wind was strong but steady, and the crew made light of it. But as dawn approached it grew into a storm. All that day it swept the carrack unrelentingly westwards, far past the port where Master John Fiste had expected to begin his life again. When at last they were close to being propelled altogether out of sight of land, with no sign of the storm relenting, the captain resolved to risk an approach to the lee of the English coast, hoping to enter the great harbour at Penryn. As they neared the estuary, the wind squalled capriciously, the ship was blown onto reefs, and captain, crew and passengers were drowned, Master John Fiste and the rest.

For all anyone knew, the greatest magus in the world had stepped out of his house alone one winter night and vanished. In time, most came to say that he had sold his soul for his art and been called to a reckoning by the devil, snatched off without a trace. It made a good cautionary tale for a more sceptical age. Believing Johannes in hell where he and his practices belonged, even wise men barely troubled themselves with the fact that all the magic in the world had gone with him.

Part I
Monday

Two

GAVIN STOKES FIDGETED in his seat and willed the train to move. Outside the window his mother stood on the platform, waving and smiling weakly. He was worried she was about to cry.

He didn't mind the actual crying; he was mostly used to it. What he was afraid of was that if she fell apart right at this moment, she might change her mind about letting him go. His father had taken their trolley and was already heading off towards the Heathrow Express platform. Gavin saw him turn his head and say something to her over his shoulder, something that made the corners of her mouth tremble even more, and just at that moment, soundlessly, the world outside the window twitched and began to slide away.

'Take care of yourself, Gav, love,' he just about heard her shout. She took a few steps along the platform, but she couldn't catch him now. 'I love you!'

'Love you, Mum,' he mouthed back, without saying it. His father was out of sight already. A moment later and she was gone as well. The train was leaving them behind, gathering speed as if it too couldn't wait to get away from them and all the rest: home, school, London. It was taking him about as far away as you could go without leaving England altogether.

He pulled his bag down onto the table and dug through it until he found the envelope he'd taken that morning from his mother's desk. The night before, he'd dreamed that he'd gone into her room, opened a drawer, dug around and pulled it out. That was how he'd known where to find it.

She had torn it open. He unfolded the two sheets of paper, briefly surprised to see the tiny, thread-like handwriting. But of course Auntie Gwen wouldn't use a printer; she wouldn't have one.

My dear Iz, [there was no date or anything]
Hope you can still make sense of my writing, I know it's been a while. I'm truly sorry to hear about your troubles, but so, so glad you wrote to me! I think about you all the time, believe it or not, really I do. Being able to help now is like a gift to me. I'm really sorry I just can't come to London for a whole week with work and things here but *I have another idea, please listen, I really want to do this for you and Nigel and for Gavin too. Why doesn't he come to stay with me down here while you two are away? Think about it. Please! He's nearly grown up now, probably more nearly than I am (guessed what you're thinking didn't I Iz?)* [Here she'd drawn a little smiley face, and drawn it very well: it had Auntie Gwen's rather long chin and longer hair, and was winking.]

I'm sure he'll manage the journey down. You said he seems just the same as always so there can't be anything to worry about for a few hours on a train. I can meet him at the station in Truro so he won't even have to tune in enough to do the change.

I'd be just so delighted to have him stay here and maybe it will do him good to get away for a bit. [He grinned. Neither Mum nor Auntie Gwen could have begun to imagine exactly how good he was feeling.] *This is the kind of place that really might be perfect for him. And he and I always got on well. I know it's been a while since I've been up but I still send him those postcards sometimes so he won't have forgotten all about me.* [The grin turned to a frown. He'd never had a postcard from Auntie Gwen, or not for years anyway.] *It's not the ends of the earth here, there are good people around to help if anything happens. I know how much you and Nigel must be looking forward to your trip, really, why not let me do this and you can just not worry for a few days?*

To be honest there may not be anything to worry about anyway, you and I know what Gav is like, it's probably just something the school people hadn't seen before but for us it would just be Gav being Gav! Wish they'd told you what it was though, that seems so unfair, it makes it so much harder for you. Iz I really wish I could be there and just give you a big hug. Please try not to get upset, I know, easy for me to say, but I've always known there was something special about your boy, in a good way, the best. [Gav paused and for a while thought of nothing at all, while the city's weed-strewn margins swished by.] *Anyway, please think about it, no I mean please* do *it, give yourself a rest and me the pleasure of seeing my nephew and Gavin a break too. It's a bit short notice but it'll work, all you have to do is write back to let me know and just tell Gav I'll meet him on Monday at 16.48 at Truro station. It really isn't that easy for me to get to a phone – you and Nigel must find it hard to believe – but anyway, the post* does *work fine* [here the writing reached the end of the second sheet and had to cramp itself even more and turn up the side of the page.] *oops no room, I love you Iz, peace to N and G, write back quickly! XO G*

The cross-stroke of the last 'G' was lengthened out into something like a tiny dragon's tail, its arrowheaded tip just squeezed into the top corner of the sheet. He was staring at it but not seeing it.

It had taken him a lot longer than weird Aunt Gwen to work out that there was 'something special' about him. For all but the last few of his fifteen years he'd had no idea. The special thing, it turned out, was that some of the things that happened to him weren't supposed to happen. Some bits of his life were allowed – nobody minded them. Others weren't.

Learning the difference between them had been a miserable experience. He'd had no idea there was anything wrong until everyone started telling him about it, and even then it didn't really make any sense to him. Distressingly, it was apparently the parts of his life he liked best that shouldn't actually have been happening. He'd begun finding out about this a few years ago, around the time he'd switched schools. The first symptoms of the change were in the way his parents talked to him. Instead of 'Oh, really?' (with a smile), it became 'Oh, come on, Gav' (with a frown). Then it was 'Gavin, I think you're too old for this now.' (For what? he'd asked himself. For what?) Then it was 'Look, Gav, you've got to stop all this', and then 'I don't want to hear about this rubbish and frankly neither does anyone else', and then worse, until the night he'd thought his father was actually going to hurt someone. That night was when he'd finally grasped that the rules of his life had changed for good, without warning, without anyone asking him or telling him why.

He'd got up that night and gone along to his parents' room because Miss Grey had told him Mum was dead.

Miss Grey hardly ever said anything at all. Never, really, unless you counted when he was asleep, and even then the things she said were a bit strange and confusing and hard to get hold of, the way dreams are, though he always felt he understood what she meant. But that night, for once, the words had been quite clear: *The sun rises on your mother's grave.* He woke up straight away, worried. He knew his mother couldn't actually be dead or have a grave because she'd been listening to the radio as he dozed off – he'd heard it downstairs – but he couldn't help feeling anxious. He sometimes dreamed things before they happened, and those dreams always had Miss Grey in them. So he went along to their bedroom and opened the door.

'Mum?'

Rustling bedclothes and then Dad's head popped up abruptly. 'Gavin? What the bloody hell are you doing?'

'Is Mum OK?'

'What? Christ, what time is it?'

'Mum?' But his mother hadn't answered, and he couldn't hear her breathing. All he could see was a dark lump in the duvet, like a mound of earth. He panicked and switched the light on.

'Ow! What are you . . . ?' Bleary and blotchy, his father cringed from the light, but for a horrible few moments Mum hadn't moved at all and Gav had been utterly certain he'd dreamed the truth again. His first thought was that now he'd be living alone in the house with Dad, an idea of such deadly horror it made him screech.

'Mum!'

And then of course the lump had moved and she had pushed herself up, messy and fogged with the confusion of sudden waking. 'Gavin? What's wrong?'

He started to cry.

His mother sat up and beckoned him, smoothing her hair. He climbed over the bed to her. 'Oh, for God's sake,' his father grumbled, and she kept saying, 'What's wrong?' halfway between anxious and exasperated. 'What's wrong now?'

'I thought you were dead.'

'Jesus Christ.' His father fumbled for the bedside clock, pulled it to his eyes, groaned.

'What? Gav, Gav! Silly boy. Whatever gave you such a horrible idea?'

And because this had all been four or five years back, and he hadn't yet learned what he wasn't allowed to say, and also because he'd been scared witless for the awful seconds before she'd woken up, the truth came out.

'Miss Grey said. She said my mother was dead.'

His father slammed the alarm clock down on his bedside table hard enough to break it and shouted, 'I've fucking had enough!' which was terrifying because until then Gav had thought swearing was just a naughty joke. Even more terrifying was his mother's reaction. She'd frozen, gone white like someone caught in a searchlight, and then instead of holding her arms out to Gavin, she sort of shrank in on herself, her eyes inexplicably fearful. His father was bellowing at him to get out, bellowing and swearing and thumping the table, and as Gav scrambled back to his own room he heard the shouting go on behind him beyond the slammed door, until in the end Mum shrieked, 'I haven't! I haven't!' so loudly that they must have realised the racket they were making because they stopped, leaving Gav sitting bolt upright in his bed, perched stiff as if trying not to fall.

Even before that night he'd begun to understand that his parents didn't like him talking about Miss Grey. It annoyed them that they couldn't see her. That was fair enough once he thought about it, though they needn't have felt bad since no one else could see her either, as far as he could tell; but then that had always been true, so he didn't see why it should bother them all of a sudden. When he'd been smaller, he'd often listened to them laughingly explaining about his imaginary friend, if he'd happened to mention her to someone. 'Oh, that's his imaginary friend.' It was, he learned, the proper term for someone like Miss Grey. Other children had imaginary friends, or at least some of them presumably did, although he soon found out that he didn't know any. Also, none of the kids he did know liked being asked about the subject, though that made sense to him because he didn't like being asked about Miss Grey either.

It was a bit tricky explaining about her since she didn't behave at all like other people. He guessed this was probably the point about imaginary friends. They were secret, special. The only person he'd ever known who really liked to talk about her was Auntie Gwen, and Auntie Gwen liked it so much Gavin found her eagerness a bit embarrassing, and usually tried to change the subject.

'Is Miss Grey her real name?'

Um, it's just what I always call her, you know, like the people who look after you instead of Mummy at the school were called Miss Sandra or Miss Mara so I thought she was like that, except she didn't say her name so I made up Miss Grey 'cos she's quite grey.

'What games do you like to play with her?'

Um we don't really play games, we just sort of—

'Does she tell you stories?'

Oh yes! Well, sort of.

'What kind?'

You know. Funny things. Um anyway it's not really like telling stories. Can we get an ice cream before we go home?

'Can you see her now?' (Miss Grey smiled a little and shook her head.) No. I like plain Magnums.

After the horrible night with the shouting and banging, Gavin became much more wary of mentioning her to anyone. He was angry with her, for the first time. He thought she'd lied to him about Mum, which made the shouting her fault, not his. It was weird and disturbing, anyway, because he was used to her being right about everything. Also, something had happened between his parents, not just the screaming. Even the next morning he could feel it wasn't right. When they spoke to each other the silences between had a funny crackle to them.

His mother sat him down the next day for one of her serious conversations. Did he understand that he couldn't say things like that? Didn't he realise that it upset people? Mummy and Daddy love you very much. And: 'Gavin, you do understand that Miss Grey isn't real, don't you?'

'Yes, Mum.' Yes, he did. 'Real' meant the things Mum and Dad were interested in: newspapers and cricket and the carpet and money and all that. 'Not real' were the things they couldn't see and didn't really have any interest in, like stories and Miss Grey and the inside birds and the funny people he sometimes caught glimpses of. He'd learned this distinction early on and accepted it, like the difference between red and blue.

'Well, then, do you think maybe it's time to say goodbye to Miss Grey?'

Gav was old enough to know immediately that Mum meant something more than what she'd said. Obviously her question was stupid, since you only said goodbye to someone when they were going away, but he didn't say that out loud. As always with the serious conversations that you had to sit down for, she was actually talking about something completely different, some other unspoken issue involving mysterious unhappiness and blame. He knew from experience that if he made the wrong guess as to what the real subject was, she'd either start crying or send him off in that particular way that made him feel like he'd done something horrible.

'I just think you're too old now to spend so much time playing a game like that.'

He got it in a flash. He was supposed to become a different person. She wanted him to get more excited about carpets and newspapers and money. She wanted him to be more like Dad. She was telling him to 'grow up'.

'So, can you try not to talk about her any more? All right? Gavin? Would it help if we wrote her a goodbye letter? Perhaps we can think of all the adventures she's going to have now. Places she can go instead. She might like not being stuck in London.'

He nodded, because silent agreement was the best way to end the serious conversations as quickly as possible, but secretly he thought this whole plan ridiculous. Miss Grey wasn't at all the type to go on adventures. She wasn't like someone in a book.

'You're not going away, are you?' he asked her, the next time he saw her. They were standing on the railway footbridge he crossed on his way back from school, in a sullen drizzle. She looked at him with her almost-sad face and held her hands out, cupped, gathering a puddle of rainwater. She bent and blew gently on the water, then opened her hands a fraction, letting it trickle away onto the tracks.

'Please don't,' he said, feeling sick. 'Please don't leave me with Mum and Dad.'

She made the cup again, but this time held it up over his head. He leaned back to see what she was doing and flinched as she dribbled the rain over his mouth. When he licked his lips there was a dark taste, a lonely taste, but despite that he was reassured. Though she never said a word except in dreams, he understood what she meant most of the time, like he understood some other things that didn't speak, and he knew that she was promising he wouldn't have to 'grow up' at home without her, even if the darkness and loneliness were coming.

Unfortunately the growing-up happened all by itself, whether he liked it or (as was the case) not.

As the months and years went by, Gavin stopped pleading with her not to leave him. He stopped speaking to her at all. He stayed away from the empty quiet corners, the lanes behind back-garden fences and the mud and scrub of the towpath along the river, those untended nooks and crannies of the city where the things that weren't supposed to happen most often seemed to happen. He was learning, rapidly, that they weren't just against his parents' rules, but broke some other set of rules as well, some huge body of law that didn't only apply at home but was mysteriously in place everywhere else too: school, on holiday, parties, anywhere that people gathered. He had a feeling the regulations would have been relaxed if Auntie Gwen had been around, but Auntie Gwen never came to stay any more, because, he gradually discovered, she wasn't invited. Perhaps she was as illegal as Miss Grey. He couldn't guess. No one ever explained the system to him.

The imaginary-friend idea had to be discarded. Apparently that was just a silly thing little kids did, on a level with Mum's stupid idea about writing Miss Grey a letter. What was she, then? A ghost? Boys at school talked about ghosts. There were stories about them, lots of them: he read all the ones he could find. None of the things in the stories sounded anything like Miss Grey.

'How do you know ghosts don't exist?' he asked one evening at dinner.

His father put his glass down and went very still. Gav had thought he was being clever, finding a way to talk about Miss Grey without actually mentioning her, but it was immediately evident that Dad had sussed him out, and Mum knew it too. The funny crackle appeared in the air over the table.

'Well,' said his mother carefully, 'it's science, I suppose, isn't it? I mean, we know the world works a certain way. There's all those ways you can prove that certain things must be true and so you know ghosts can't be. Like going through walls. Appearing and disappearing. They're just not possible.'

'Derek says he's seen one.'

'Lots of people say they've seen one,' his father said.

'So they're just wrong?'

'They're just idiots,' said Dad, at the same time as Mum said, 'People can think they've seen something, but we know they actually can't have. Not what they think they saw. So perhaps Derek imagined something or, I don't know, saw something in a weird light or—'

'Or he's an idiot.'

'Nigel, please. Or maybe he likes telling stories.'

'Oh yes, I forgot that one. He could be a liar instead of an idiot.'

'For God's sake, Nigel.'

The crackle got so loud Gavin thought he could actually hear it in his ears, as well as in his fingertips and stomach and the skin of his cheeks.

'Anyway,' his mother went on, fiddling with the stem of her wine glass, 'people only believed in things like that because they didn't know better.'

'So how do they know better?'

'By going to expensive schools,' said his father. 'Though it's obviously not working for Derek.'

'I give up,' she said.

Gavin sat and ate until the crackle got so bad it was hurting and then went to his room.

The next time he saw Miss Grey – it was three or four days later, at school; she was standing holding her drab cloak tight around her, in a far corner of the visitors' car park, watching him – he tried knowing better. Even though he could see perfectly clearly that she was there, as usual, he decided to know that she wasn't. It was like trying to know the cars weren't there, or the trees behind them. It was like persuading himself that he didn't exist.

So that was how Gavin began to realise that there was something special about himself.

At the same time that the real things – home, school, his mother and father, being eleven and then twelve and then thirteen – got worse, the things that weren't real got worse too. His dreams started to change, in confusing ways. Sometimes he longed for Miss Grey to come back into them, because in dreams he thought she could touch him as well as say things to him, but sometimes he dreaded it because the darkness and loneliness had come closer. He still occasionally had the sensation of dreaming things that were going to happen, but now instead of simple things like a fox in the garden or a hailstorm or Mum losing her glasses, the dreams were full of dark birds with beaks the colour of fire, or smoke hanging over a city, or an Eskimo girl tending a dying whale on a cold beach: things that couldn't happen, and yet the feeling that they were real and waiting for him was even stronger than in the old come-true-tomorrow dreams. There was a change in Miss Grey too. It was like she knew he was trying to get rid of her and now it was her turn to plead with him not to leave. He found it harder and harder to remember on waking the words she'd spoken in his dreams, but at the same time it felt more and more urgent that he listen. The more he tried to ignore or forget whatever it was that was different about himself, the tighter it pressed in on him.

'Go away,' he said to Miss Grey, one February afternoon. It was twilight. She was squatting on the concrete coping at the edge of the towpath, trailing her fingers in the river: the tide was very high. He'd planned to just walk past, but instead he marched right up to her. He saw the way the silty water eddied around her hand, making little whorls and troughs, just the way science said it should.

'Just go away. OK? Leave me alone.'

Without looking at him, she picked up a twig and lowered it gently into the water. The falling tide was running steadily, sucking its burden of leaves and litter downstream, but the twig did not move. Tiny wavelets broke over its tip, as if it was anchored. Miss Grey picked up another, longer stick. She turned to look up at Gavin as she placed the second twig beside the first. Then she spread her fingers wide above the river as the current took hold of them both and carried them away together.

'I don't care,' Gav said. 'Forget it. I don't want to go with you. I don't care any more. I just want you to get out of my life.'

A dog sniffed at his trousers. He jerked round and saw the jogger who went with the dog. She stared for a second as she splashed past.

'Why are you doing this to me?' he hissed, when the jogger was out of earshot. 'Why me? Why can't I be like everyone else?'

She lifted her hands from the water and shuffled round to the muddy earth where Gav stood. He watched as she began to stroke the mud, erasing the mess of footprints, her small, rough hands quickly becoming caked black. When she'd made a smooth patch as wide as a sycamore leaf, she picked up another twig and dug a little curved furrow in the mud.

'Forget it,' Gav said, and walked past and went home.

But he couldn't forget it. That was his whole problem. Try as he might, he couldn't know better. So the next time he went down to the towpath, a day or two later, he stopped at the place where she'd squatted. There, among the churned mud and gravel, was the tablet of smoothed earth, and in it a word had been engraved, like writing in the sand on a beach.

COME

Gavin stared at it for a long time. Then he stamped his shoe into it.

Time weighed on him. He no longer spoke to her at all, ever. His dreams were a whirl of turbid darkness lit by fire, full of prophetic voices clamouring in alien speech. He was fourteen and miserable. The expensive school did its work and he at last knew that Miss Grey should not exist, that she was impossible, that the fact that he kept on seeing her was like an error in a calculation, a tear in the canvas of a painting, a misprint. He understood that if he tried to explain his life to anyone, the only thing they'd be able to think was that there was something seriously wrong with him. There was, surely, something seriously wrong with him. But because it had always been there, it was impossible for him to imagine how it was wrong.

And as for these things happening *in a good way, the best* . . . Gavin pushed his aunt's letter back into its envelope and scrunched his eyes shut for a moment, wincing at the memory of his conversation with Mr Bushy the week before last.

He'd eventually decided to ask someone what he was doing wrong, someone as unlike his father as he could find.

It had not gone well and now here he was.

The train, he realised, was slowing.

He tossed his bag onto the seat next to him, stretched his legs under the table as far as he could in the hope of obstructing the opposite seat too and pretended to be asleep. He felt the stop. Big doors clicked open and clunked shut; voices filled the carriage; luggage slithered into overhead racks. The sounds all seemed to pass him by, and once they were thrumming along again at full speed, he opened his eyes.

To his irritation, an old woman had managed to sit down in the window seat opposite, not put off by his protruding shoes. She was leaning her chin in her hand and gazing out of the window, but she caught his look reflected there and gave a very brief smile, enough to make him feel like he had to sit up and pull his legs out of the way. This was a kind of defeat, which irritated him even more. She wasn't actually an old woman, he now saw – middle-aged (to Gavin, at fifteen, this meant anything between three and four times his age), but with old-fashioned-looking hair that was all grey, and a floppy brown jumper. The smile had been quick and sharp.

Better get the earphones in, he thought, and reached into his bag. The woman didn't have a paperback or knitting or photos of her grandchildren or any of the other things Gavin imagined middle-aged ladies occupying themselves with on trains – no luggage at all, he noticed, let's hope that means she's not going far – so it seemed best not to leave open any possibility of conversation. He fitted the earphones, slumped in his seat again and stared out of the window, adopting the hard and indifferent face that he used on the way to and from school.

Used to use.

Nothing that might have belonged to home was in sight. No streetlights, no houses, no people. A low, dull sky lay over winter fields and stubbly hedges. As the dour landscape rolled past, he began trying to imagine how far he was from his parents. He checked his watch every half-hour or so until he guessed he'd come to the exact moment when they were being lifted off the earth, no longer attached at all to the country where he was. They'd probably be almost as relieved as him to have escaped. Mum would be worrying, but she'd never be able to say so, not for a single moment of the whole week. ('I am *not* going to let that boy spoil our time together.') Auntie Gwen didn't have a computer or even a phone. She lived in one of those knobbly green fingers at the very outer limits of the map. The most his mother had been able to make him promise was to find somewhere he could get reception every day or two and leave messages back at home. He pictured her having to slip away from Dad, smuggling her mobile into a bathroom so she could ring to check them. A couple of years ago that kind of thought would have upset him. Now he just let it go, sent it away with his parents. Once he'd realised they didn't want to know about his unhappiness, he'd stopped caring much about theirs.

The landscape grew rougher at the edges as the journey wore on. The track passed under hillsides where the fields ran out near the top and patches of scrubby brown rose above them. This was nothing like what his family called the countryside, which meant the bit around where his other aunt – Dad's sister – lived, just far enough away that going there for Sunday lunch took absolutely all day, but near enough that they thought it was reasonable to keep doing it. The country around there looked as if it had been assembled out of accessories from Gav's old train set: barn, fence, tree, cow, telephone box, placed indiscriminately over a green cloth with a few ripples in it. What Gav saw out of the window now couldn't ever be shrunk into plastic miniatures. London felt very far away, and now, for certain, his parents were in the air and gone (he looked at his watch again to make sure, but it had stopped), and his week of freedom was properly under way.

After a long while they came to another station. He thought about faking sleep again, but the woman opposite had pulled a book out of her handbag by now, some sort of nature guide, and was safely absorbed in it. More people left the carriage than joined. Gavin knew from the maps that he was reaching the point where England began to taper out, thinning into the sea.

And there it was: the sea. It took him by surprise. It was suddenly right by the tracks. There was a narrow strand of beach, where a few well-wrapped people had stopped their walk to watch the train go past, and beyond that, nothing: a huge, calm, open plain of emptiness mirroring the underside of pencil-grey clouds. On the other side of the train, cliffs the colour of grimy brick rose like walls.

For the first time since he'd been on the train, he thought about having to make the return journey, in just a week's time; having to go back to it all.

The train swooshed into a tunnel and, abruptly, Gavin was staring at the inside of the carriage in the window. He'd been captivated by the sea, his guard was down, and he realised too late that his eyes were accidentally directed straight at the reflection of the woman opposite, and hers, reflected, were directed back at him.

'It always makes me jump,' she said.

He cursed inwardly. He'd made it this far without getting trapped in some pointless conversation with a stranger and didn't want to spoil the rest of his precious time on his own by starting one now.

'Mmm.' He didn't know what she was talking about and didn't care. He looked down at his lap.

'It's the best bit of the journey, though. The sea and all the tunnels. I always remember thinking that once you got past here you were properly in the southwest.'

'Oh yeah?' He made himself sound as uninterested as possible and reached across into his bag to fiddle ostentatiously with his phone, but it didn't stop her.

'I used to love those journeys on my own when I was a girl. Just watching out of the window. There was nothing worse than when some old bore opposite wanted to talk.'

He reddened, more angry than embarrassed. 'Hah,' he grunted, with a forced smile.

'Are you going to Cornwall?'

A direct question. No way he could brush it off.

'Truro, yeah.'

'Ah! My stop too.'

Great. 'Oh right.' He was stuck with her the whole way. He opened a game on his phone, in the hope of demonstrating that he had better things to do than listen to her chatter, but it made no difference. She pulled a tube of mints out of her handbag and picked off the foil.

'Are you on your way home, then? Polo?'

'Er, no, thanks. Nah, I live in London.' He cursed himself again. That might have been his last chance to cut this conversation off before it really got going and he'd said more than he needed to. He'd blown it.

'Hmm. It hasn't been home for me since I was a girl, but I suppose it is now. I'm going native, as you see.' She tapped the cover of her book. It was called *A Field Guide to Cornwall's Wildlife*. He didn't understand and didn't want to. 'You've been before? Family in Truro?'

If she'd obviously just been making small talk, he might have kept on grunting rudely and then clammed up, but there was a patient curiosity in her questions that he couldn't seem to escape. 'Nah, not properly. When I was a baby, once. Think we went to a beach somewhere.'

'Oh well, this is better really. Summer has its uses, but a beach is a beach is a beach. I always try to come back in autumn or winter. The wind and the rain. It's not the holidays yet, though, is it?'

The possibility of a reprieve flashed in front of him. Perhaps the truth would do the trick and put her off. He met her eyes and tried to look belligerent.

'Not yet. I got kicked out of school.'

For a moment it looked as if he'd succeeded. 'Oh,' she said, looking down and up quickly. Then she sat back with a huge smile. 'How funny! Me too.'

He must have gawped. She leaned forward, right across the table, grinning a grin that belonged on the face of a conspiratorial teenager. 'Never mind. I'll shut up now. Good luck to you.' She patted the back of his hand and, still smiling, picked up her book and sucked her mint.

He looked around the carriage, wondering about switching to another seat. She didn't look like a crazy person. Quite the opposite, in fact: there was a brightness in her expression that made her look younger than the rest of her appearance suggested she was, and an air of subdued amusement that reminded him slightly of Mr Bushy, who was the cleverest person Gav knew. Maybe that was what stopped him from getting up and moving, though he told himself he was being an idiot, that she might start up again at any moment. But there weren't lots of empty seats. He might end up stuck next to someone just as bad.

He'd just about managed to relax again when she blinked up from her book and looked out at the hills, frowning slightly.

'We're still a while from Plymouth, aren't we?' she said, apparently to herself.

Taking no chances, Gavin slumped right back in his seat and half closed his eyes.

She craned her neck to peer up and down the line. 'I'm sure I haven't seen Ivybridge go by . . .'

The train was slowing; that was what had bothered her. As it braked to a crawl, the noise of its passage grew suddenly louder, and the windows went black. They eased deeper into the tunnel and stopped.

A group of kids at the far end of the carriage did a mock-spooky wail, 'Oooo-ooooo.' Gav turned up the volume on his music.

He didn't hear the details of the driver's apologetic announcement. Something about a temporary electrical problem. The kids groaned in chorus.

Abruptly the lights in the carriage all went out. At the same instant the music in Gav's ears stopped dead.

There was an instant of complete darkness and silence, and then the carriage filled with little shrieks and giggles and conversations starting up too loudly. There was no light at all, not the slightest glimmer. Gav felt across to his bag, wondering if his earphones had come unplugged. They hadn't. He pulled them out of his ears. His hands felt sweaty.

A hideous cry erupted out of the dark.

Otototoi!

Gavin cringed, his raised arms invisible in front of his face. The scream had been right on top of him.

Otototoi! Otototoi! Popoi! Popoi!

He was nauseous with terror. The hum of nervous chatter in the carriage continued, though the appalling shouts ought to have crushed it. He jammed his hands over his ears and cowered. At that moment some-one further down the carriage switched on a torch. There was a mass *Ahhhh* as the wobbly white light appeared.

The woman opposite was staring at him, her face in shadow.

In the seat next to her another woman was sitting, and Gavin knew at once that it was Miss Grey. He knew her by the silhouette of her tangled hair and by the shape of her cloaked shoulders and her thin arms braced on the table in front of her. He knew her by something else as well, the intimacy of fifteen years; he felt her close to him like his own reflection. But he'd never seen her indoors before, and beyond his dreams he had never seen a word come out of her mouth, barely even a breath, let alone the full-throated inhuman howl of madness that she threw out again.

'*Otototoi!*'

Gavin couldn't stop himself flinching. He was acutely aware of the eyes of the woman opposite. Shame burned him. He tried to shift round in his seat and fold his arms, as if all he'd been doing was getting comfortable. It was plain that no one else had heard Miss Grey's deranged howling. No one but him was haunted; no one but him was cursed. He had no idea what he'd done to earn this new punishment, or why she now had the power to pursue him inside and scream in his ear. He glimpsed a terrible future in which she wouldn't stop until she'd driven him out of his mind, properly crazy, as Mr Bushy obviously thought he already was.

He hugged himself tight and screwed his eyes shut.

The carriage lights came on.

Gavin tried to focus on his breathing. Don't look up, don't say anything, don't meet anyone's eyes. He was afraid that if the nosy woman asked him what was wrong, he might slap her.

'Ladies'n'gennlmun,' began an announcement, 'thizzizr driver speakin, we dopologise for 'zshor'delay, uh faulznowbin fixt'n' we'll beyonrway veryshor'y than'you.'

The train crept into motion.

'Come.'

It was Miss Grey's voice. He recognised it from his dreams and yet he'd never properly heard it before, not the actual sound, the disturbance of the air. 'Come.' A woman's voice, as rough and grey as she was, yet with a strength to it, the way her stillness always seemed alarmingly strong. It wanted to prise his eyelids open.

'He comes. They come.'

Oh God, he thought. Not now, not here. Don't look up, he told himself, clenching his teeth. Just don't look.

'The feasters gather.'

He didn't dare move or scream. He was sitting at one end of a train carriage with people all around him, ordinary people, the other kind. There was nothing he could do.

'The destroyer and his gift. It has begun.' The words sounded like they were being spat out of her throat. As the train picked up speed, they seemed to rhyme with the clackety-clack of the rails, insistent drumming gibberish. 'An open door. A closed circle. The sky is open. Drop down, drop down. His mother's sister is flown. His mother's sister is gone. His father is named destroyer. He will bear no child. He will bear my burden. It hurts. It hurts! *Otototoi!*' Now it was not a rattling scream, but part of the babble. 'He comes, he comes. The gift, the burden. Truth hurts. *Iew, iew, ohh ohh kakka.* Come. Come.'

There was a clumsy rustle opposite. The irritating woman was getting up. Gavin stole a look to be sure and out of the corner of his eye saw her squeezing past the seat in which Miss Grey had appeared. Miss Grey pulled her knees up out of the way, under her cloak. No one was looking at him. Gav raised his eyes cautiously and saw that the woman's eyes were red and her face drained of colour. She stumbled past the luggage racks and out of the carriage.

Miss Grey stared at him, arms round her shins, mouth open but emptied of its freight of meaningless words.

'Come,' she said.

He couldn't make himself accept that he was seeing her here, under bland electric light, her calloused and filthy bare feet perched on the edge of an upholstered seat. She looked like an escaped extra from a mediaeval costume drama. Under her dark grey cloak she wore shapeless rags. Her bird's-nest hair was grimy, soot-black. Only in her face was there something vividly, terribly actual, something unfeigned.

'Come,' she said again.

Gav glanced around. No one seemed to be looking his way. The couple across the aisle were absorbed in a crossword. He leaned across the table.

'Go away,' he said, between his teeth. His cheeks were burning.

'Come,' she repeated. She was like a bird. Her eyes had that opaque glitter. The word sounded meaningless when she uttered it: just a squawk.

'Please,' he said. He stared into her face, between the shrouding curtains of her hair. He was afraid he was going to cry. 'Leave me alone. I can't take it.'

Her head jutted forward. 'You must take it,' she said. 'You must take it. Come to me. Take it.'

The sliding door hissed. Without taking her eyes off him, Miss Grey leaned right back and pulled her knees tight, and the nosy woman wriggled back across in front of her to the window seat.

Gavin didn't know where to look. For a moment he'd been sure Miss Grey really had been talking to him, telling him something, when he'd least expected it. In his turmoil of stifled misery he'd barely taken in the words. He turned to the window, cradling his head in his hands, and saw dismal terraced suburbs beginning to appear on the lower slopes of the hills. Get a grip, he told himself. Get a grip.

The train was slowing again, coming into a larger town. A few people stood up and began putting on coats, gathering by the end of the carriage. Their chatter and commotion made him feel fractionally safer and he risked a glance around. To his surprise and relief, he saw Miss Grey getting up from her seat.

'He comes,' he heard her murmur. 'He comes. They gather. This night you go free.'

She eased among the small crowd waiting to get off. The train pulled in. He watched as the press of people carried her out of the carriage. No one was aware of her; she slipped like water into the spaces among them. He pressed his face to the glass to see if he could spot her coming out onto the platform, but she'd disappeared.

He felt himself calming down.

The carriage was much emptier as they left the station behind. Outside, daylight was fading. There couldn't be too much more of the journey to go. It occurred to Gav that he could probably find a pair of seats to himself now, where he could sit alone and try to get himself back together.

He was just about to act on this thought when he felt fingers on his wrist. The middle-aged woman had leaned across close to him. 'I'm sorry,' she said in a low voice. 'I know I said I wouldn't bother you, but there's a little thing I feel I should do and it ought to have a witness. It's rather embarrassing. I'm not usually this batty, I promise.'

He was too dumbfounded to answer at all.

'It has to be just here, as we go over the bridge. It'll only take a second.'

He looked out of the window, helplessly following her gaze. They were riding on a viaduct above the streets, leaving the station behind. The winter afternoon, already dim, was darkening fast. Clouds had sunk and were becoming a fog.

'I'd like you to hear a promise I'm going to make myself. It makes it more official. Bad luck for you that I happened to take this particular seat, hmm? Or something.' She was talking too rapidly for him to agree to this aloud. 'Anyway, I hope you don't mind. I really will shut up after this.' She extracted a small bottle from her pocket, unscrewing it as she spoke, and poured a little of something that smelled almost but not quite like whisky into the upturned cap. 'Ah, here we are.' The town fell away and the train began passing between bulbous steel girders. Gav saw a broad river far below. 'Right. Here goes. Are you listening?'

He couldn't think of anything to do but nod.

'Right. Good. I, Hester Lightfoot, earnestly and solemnly swear never to cross back over this river again so long as I live.' She swigged the contents of the cap. 'On pain of death. There, that should do it. Thank you. If you ever happen to see me east of here again, please feel free to . . . oh I don't know, push me under a bus or something. Would you like a sip?'

The train began to pick up speed, burrowing through the fog.

'No . . . thanks.'

She screwed the cap back on. 'Thank you for putting up with that. That was the Tamar. That river. West of it is all Cornwall. I'm coming home, you see, so I thought I'd make it ceremonial.' She tapped the open page of the book in her lap. 'Like the choughs. We're coming back, for good. I'm Hester, by the way, obviously enough.' She stuck out her hand.

The chuffs? Now Gavin was certain he was sitting at the same table as a lunatic. Grab your bag and move, he told himself, but with her hand right there in front of him he couldn't.

'Gavin,' he said, shaking, furious with himself.

'Nice to meet you. They say King Arthur's soul went into a chough after he died.' She lifted the book onto the table and pointed. 'For a long time they left. I think people assumed they were gone for ever, but they returned to Cornwall a few years ago. I'm taking them as a good omen.'

Gavin looked down. His vision swam.

The picture Hester had her finger on showed a black bird with a beak the colour of embers and legs of the same vivid ruddy orange. He felt suddenly dizzy. The image was an echo of his dreams, the terrible ones of darkness spotted and streaked with fire and alive with battering wings, a piece of his night world torn out of him and thrust under his eyes. Hester's words rang weirdly in his head: *Good omen, good omen.*

'Are you all right?'

She had closed the book. He shook his head and rubbed his eyes.

'Yeah, fine.'

'I'm sorry. I—'

''s OK. Forget it.'

She studied him with disconcertingly steady interest. 'All right, then. And now no more madwoman business. I promise.' She put one finger to her lips and leaned back in her seat.

Gavin wasn't sure how far he could trust that promise, so he closed his eyes, inwardly swearing all the while that if ever he was blessed enough to find himself on another long journey by himself, he'd take a fat book to bury his head in. She was as good as her word, though, which was fortunate, because he found it hard to do a convincing impression of going to sleep. He was so afraid Miss Grey might reappear on the train while his eyes were closed that he couldn't relax at all. After a while he stopped trying. His phone appeared to have run out of power, like his watch, though he'd charged it that morning. There was nothing to do but gaze out of the window, nowhere else to look.

Tight valleys ghosted past in the darkening fog. They stopped at stations that seemed almost abandoned, platforms sunk down in a bank of wet slates and brambles or overlooked by the backs of dreary houses. After a while he heard the announcement that Truro would be the next stop. Most of the few remaining people in the carriage were gathering up belongings. He took his bag and went to stand by the door. Someone had pushed the window down. The wheels hissed loudly and the chill air smelled of wet bark. There was almost no light left in the sky.

He saw Hester Lightfoot join the queue by the door, but she seemed to have lost interest in him. In fact, there was an oddly blank look on her face, as if she'd lost interest in everything. Her lips moved a little; she was talking to herself soundlessly. When the train stopped with a slight jerk, she nearly fell over, muttering as she grabbed the luggage rack.

Gavin stepped down to the platform, looking around quickly for Auntie Gwen. The station clock showed they were only a couple of minutes late. People hurried, mostly silently, towards the exit, on their way to somewhere more welcoming. He didn't see his aunt, so he followed the flow out through a ticket hall to the street.

A few cars idled in front of the station, but none of them contained Auntie Gwen. The mist that swallowed headlights and rear lights up and down the road might as well have marked the edge of the world.

He went back to check the platform again. A clump of people had formed at the far end, most of them school kids, though he noticed Hester Lightfoot there as well. He wanted to avoid the other kids almost as much as he wanted to be out of sight of her, so he sat on the least illuminated bench he could find and waited until the last of the passengers had scurried away.

Minutes passed. No Auntie Gwen.

The night and the cold closed around him.

Three

GAVIN HAD MADE two more trips out of the station to check the road when he returned to the bench to find the crazy woman standing beside it.

'You look like you've been stood up,' she said.

He was about to slip behind his usual no-it's-OK-I'm-fine routine, until it occurred to him that when she was so obviously right, denying it would sound stupid. Besides, he'd been waiting for more than twenty minutes and was beginning to wonder what he was going to do.

'Looks like it, yeah. It's my aunt. Being late, it's her thing.'

'Your aunt, did you say?' An odd frown wrinkled her face for a moment.

'Um, yeah.'

'May I ask . . . is she a maternal or paternal aunt?'

Gavin hesitated, suspecting some sort of odd joke, but Hester seemed to mean it.

'My mum's sister. Maternal aunt.'

'Ah. Idle curiosity only. Is she coming a long way, then?'

'Not sure. I've never been around here before. Dunno where her place is. It's, um . . .' and he unzipped his bag and dug out the letter again. 'Here,' he said, holding the back of the envelope under one of the grimy platform lights so they could see the scribbled address.

'Pendurra! Goodness me, how very grand.'

Grand? he thought. Auntie Gwen?

'That's a bit of a journey. Mind you, most places are a bit of a journey from there. Are you related to the Urens, then? How inexcusably nosy of me, I am sorry, but then after badgering you on the train I've already made an idiot of myself so I might as well keep at it.'

'No, no, I'm not . . . Er, Aunt Gwen's not from here, she came to live here a while ago. I think she's like a housekeeper there or something.'

Hester Lightfoot looked past his shoulder for a moment and then her eyes widened. 'Oh yes! Yes, someone told me once that her name was Guinivere. Small woman, always dresses in black, lots of bangles, rather . . . distinctive character?' Gavin was nodding. 'I should say I don't know her myself,' Hester went on. 'Everyone says she's very nice, just not the norm for that corner of the county, it's a little more predictable . . . But anyway! Isn't that odd? I know your aunt, almost. I don't think anyone knew she even had a family.'

He'd wished her away over and over on the train, but now Gavin found himself quite relieved to be talking to her.

'Looks like she forgot about her family this evening, at least,' he said.

She was obviously so amazed to hear him make even half a joke that she examined him doubtfully before chuckling.

'Hmm. Well, I'm sure you won't mind me saying, but she does have a bit of a reputation. It's probably entirely undeserved. I suspect the locals think she's unreliable just because they've seen her wearing purple lipstick. Did you try ringing her?'

'Nah. She hasn't got a phone.'

'Of course not. Have you checked to see if she left a message?'

It would never have occurred to him, and he admitted it.

She went into the ticket hall, and he heard her talking through a partition to the one person on duty. She took longer about it than he expected and eventually he went in after her.

'. . . So if she does show up you can let her know that I've given him a lift already? . . . Hester Lightfoot. Here – I'll write it down' – she found a pen on a string and the back of an abandoned ticket – 'and my number too, but if she comes, you can just tell her Professor Lightfoot picked him up. All right? . . . Thanks very much.' She pushed the ticket through the window and turned back to Gavin. 'No message for you, and I don't see why you should have to hang about here in the cold when I'm going the same direction anyway. I hope you don't mind. We just have to take the branch line a few stops and then I can drive you round to Pendurra. It's only a little further for me, and I know the very house where your aunt lives. Quite a coincidence. I'm not sure I haven't even been inside it, ages ago. Anyway, it sounds as if my train has finally arrived. Do come with me. It'll save you having to wait who knows how long.' She led him back along the platform.

The school kids were noisily pushing inside a still noisier train that had just chugged in. Hester took a few more steps that way, then saw that Gav had stopped following. She turned back until she was peering intently at him from rather too close. Her expression had become startlingly earnest again, full of something that he hadn't expected to see there and couldn't fathom.

'It's all a bit peculiar, I know. To say the least. But do let me give you a lift. Please. Fellow travellers.'

Caught off-guard, and used to enforced consent, he mumbled some kind of incoherent agreement.

'Good, wonderful!' she said, snapping back into the bright and unembarrassed mode he'd assumed was her natural state. 'The branch-line train doesn't leave for another few minutes. If you want to let anyone know . . .'

Gavin had completely forgotten promising Mum he'd leave a message from the station. He reddened, realising what he'd have to say.

'Oh yeah, good thought, thanks. Oh wait, is there a payphone or something? Mine's not charged.'

'I think there's one in the café.'

'Ah, thanks. I'll catch you up?'

The station café was empty of everyone but a couple of well-wrapped pensioners, morbidly stirring their tea. Gav stared at the phone. He paused for only a few seconds. That other train would be leaving soon. There was no time to worry about what he was doing.

The past few years of trying to bury his secret life had turned Gavin into a practised liar. By the time his father's voice had finished reciting its message, he knew what to say.

'Hi, Mum. I'm calling from the station . . . Got here fine. Auntie Gwen was a bit late, but she just came so, um, we're leaving now for her place. Ah, oh, by the way, it may be a couple of days before I can leave another message, my phone's run out and . . . I must have left the charger at home. Apparently Auntie Gwen knows a place I can charge it, but she won't be going there for a bit. Anyway, whatever, she said not to worry, OK, Mum? So I'm fine, hope you're having a good time. OK. Bye Mum.'

He ran out of the café, only just remembering his bag. Two minutes later he was squeezed in among the school kids as the train clattered and growled away from the town into the night.

Once or twice in the next half-hour Gavin wondered whether he was about to become the victim in the kind of story you read about in the newspapers. All the pieces were in place. He'd left a message for Mum telling her not to expect to hear from him. He'd gone off with a total stranger. She was, obviously, a nutter. He imagined some old snapshot of himself smiling out from the paper, beside an article detailing the mutilations he'd suffered before his body had been found abandoned in the woods. Nevertheless he kept following. He followed Hester off the train at a tiny station on a hillside above a town. He followed her into a boxy old car, barely listening to her apologies for the clutter and the smell – 'Oh dear, the mice must have made their way in while I was away' – and the encouraging monologue she kept up – 'It really isn't all that far as the crow flies, hardly any distance at all, but we have to wend our way round the river. Probably half an hour or so. You can't get much speed up in the lanes and even less when it's foggy. Who knows, we might run into your aunt coming the other way . . .' The only time he properly panicked was when the passenger door had clicked shut beside him in the station car park. His hands had balled into fists in his pockets and for a few moments he was convinced that this time he'd made a seriously stupid mistake. As she banged the gearstick into reverse, he was about to throw the door open and jump out, when a phrase she'd used popped into his head: *fellow travellers.*

By the end of the few seconds it took him to dismiss it as just another of her meaningless oddities, it was too late; they were out on the road and moving.

It was like being driven along a narrow trough at the bottom of the sea. High rough hedges closed in on both sides of the car and the headlights picked out nothing beyond the next winding of the road. Sometimes trees bent over them and the trough became a tunnel, a circle of white mist enclosed in a frame of skeletal branches. Occasionally they would pass a house stranded in the dark, the sight of its solitary windows only making Gav feel more like he was entering a labyrinthine wilderness. Hester, though, seemed sure that this tangle of sunken alleys was taking them somewhere: Pendurra. The way she was talking about it made it sound as if she was pleased to have an excuse to drive that way.

'. . . same family living there since who knows when. That's very unusual these days. The old estates, the grand houses with land around them, they're ruinously expensive, needless to say, and the land doesn't make money any more. No one knows how they've managed to keep it going. Though I gather he did something in the navy. It's not as if he's out and about drumming up business opportunities like some of them are. A sight of Tristram Uren these days is rarer than spotting one of those choughs.'

What? he thought, before remembering the illustration from her book.

'Of course, this being the country, there's gossip instead. Maybe folklore would be a better word for it. I have at least one near neighbour who's quite certain there are vaults of pirate gold under the house at Pendurra. In fact that's probably one of the more plausible rumours I've heard. Still, it's a curious old place. Rather lost in time, if you know what I mean. I'm sure your aunt's told you all about it? See, now I'm being nosy again. It must be something to do with coming home. I told you I was going native.'

She hadn't put any kind of question to him for a while, so he reacted slowly.

'What? Oh no, Aunt Gwen's not in touch much.' For an unpleasant moment he remembered the way his father liked to tell stories about her to embarrass his mother. 'I thought she just sort of helped look after the place.'

Without warning they were under a few scattered streetlights, and the hedges had given way to houses walling in the narrow road. Passing through the village, Gavin saw a cluster of masts.

'Here, we're turning round the end of the river now . . . Just have to wiggle along the other side for a few miles. Then you know as much as anyone else does. When your aunt first came to live here – what is it, ten, twelve years ago? – a few people got very overexcited. New and unusual happenings at Pendurra. Or at least something to talk about. It's all quietened down since then, as it tends to. Once it turned out she did shopping and grew petunias like the rest of us. Though that neighbour, the pirate gold one, still thinks she's a witch.'

'She is a witch,' Gav said. 'Or says she is. At least she said it to me once.'

'Oh, is she? Well, it's the trendy thing, I suppose. I ought to talk to her myself, perhaps she . . .' The sentence trailed off and left an uncomfortable pause. When Hester got herself going again, a few twists of the road later, she'd relapsed into merely pointing things out as they drove by. To Gavin, it was all just patches of dark, and anyway, he was remembering Auntie Gwen, how she solemnly explained to him as they walked in the park one weekend that she didn't believe in God but worshipped rowan trees and someone called the Mother. At the time – it had been during the last of her few visits to London, a number of years ago, before the world had turned against him – he'd been happy to listen. He liked the stories she told about animals and trees and the weather, and most of all he liked the feeling of sharing a secret with her. But he'd been confused by the way that whenever the two of them were alone together, she'd start asking him what he saw everywhere, bending down to him with an impossibly eager look in her eyes and whispering things about visible energies. (At first he'd thought she was saying 'vegetable energies' and it was to do with giving up meat like she had.) After she'd gone, his parents sat him down and explained that Auntie Gwen was weird, so he forgot about it. Then a bit later on they began telling him – *Oh come on Gav* – that he was weird too, and he wished he could talk to her, but she wasn't invited any more.

Now his father and mother were hundreds and hundreds of miles away and he was winding through the night towards her home. The hedges shrunk beside them, the road broadened enough to let two cars pass, and they drove up out of the thin fog. A field of brilliant stars spread overhead, smudged with cloud.

'Nearly there,' Hester was saying (as she had been for a good fifteen minutes), but Gavin didn't care. He didn't care that he was lost in the dark with a total stranger; he didn't care that Miss Grey had turned crazy and started screaming nonsense at him on trains. Unutterable joy was consuming him. It seemed to be flooding down from the sky, and each breath he took sucked more of it inside him. It was the feeling he knew from the end of his flying dreams, the moment just before you remember that you have to wake up, but it was as if this one time some kindly lord of the dream had told him the alarm would never go off.

'. . . and here we are!'

Gav blinked and looked around. He couldn't recall arriving. He'd missed the last few . . . seconds? Minutes? The car was pulled over by a tall hedge. The headlights showed a straight lane that sloped down ahead. At the fringes of their beam he saw a bare field to the right. To the left, two tall, flat-topped pine trees were shadowed against the faintly lesser dark of the sky. Beneath them, a pair of rough stone posts flanked a driveway leading off into wooded blackness. Beside the driveway, a little way beyond the gateposts, was a house.

Hester Lightfoot had cut off the engine and was getting out. Feeling slightly dizzy, Gavin followed.

A gusting wind blew about. There was nothing to hinder it. In all directions the land fell away gently. Gav thought he knew now what it had been like for the first man on the moon, his foot touching down on the rim of another world, suspended in empty space. He saw a word carved in the nearer gatepost: PENDURRA.

'Watch out – there's a cattle grid at the entrance. Tricky in the dark.' Hester felt her way over the bars without a backwards look. He had no choice but to keep following, until they were on the driveway, staring together at the house. With its cosy eaves and its little latticed windows, it could have modelled for a gingerbread cottage. Though every window was curtained, there were lights on inside, upstairs and down, and under the tiny pointed roof of a porch. Bare, twiggy stems climbed up over this shelter and along the guttering above.

'There's a car here,' Hester said, peering round the far side. 'And you can smell the woodsmoke. I'm afraid your train just slipped her mind. Or perhaps she got the wrong day. Shall we knock?' She stepped under the porch, banged on the door and called out, 'Hello? Ms Clifton? . . . This'll give her a jump. I doubt she gets too many knocks on the door all the way out here. Still, it's her fault for forgetting . . . Hello?' – more banging – 'Hello?' Gav went to fetch his bag from the car, suddenly shy about arriving like this, not wanting to witness Aunt Gwen's surprise and embarrassment.

But Hester was still standing under the porch light when he got back.

'I suppose we'd better try the door.' There was an iron latch below the keyhole. She lifted it and pushed. A crack of warm light appeared and brought with it a puff of air heavily scented with smoke.

'Hello?' she called again, more tentatively. 'Ms Clifton? It's your nephew. I've brought him from the station.' She opened the door wider.

Gav looked over her shoulder into a low-ceilinged room glimmering all over with spots and shards of firelight. If any of its numerous candles had been lit as well as the fire, it would have sparkled like a gem. It was decked out with coloured and translucent stones, strung on lines and hung along the tops of the walls, dangling from sconces. Each of them caught some reflection of the embers. On a grand-looking dining table of dark wood, pillars of scintillating glass held coloured candles, red and purple and cream. On the wall nearest the door there hung what looked like a circular stained-glass window in a frame. Beneath it was a shallow side table covered in burned-out tealights.

Hester's eyebrows had lifted slightly. 'Well, at least we can be confident it's the right house . . . Hello?' She leaned inside the door and called more loudly. 'Ms Clifton? Your nephew's here!'

The draught from the door stirred some of the trailing ornaments. Spots of light pricked over them. Nothing else moved.

'Oh dear. I'm much too British to go into someone else's house uninvited . . . Hello? . . . It doesn't look as if she's here, does it? But she can't have gone far. That must be her car outside, and the fire's lit . . .' She fiddled with her chunky necklace. 'Perhaps she had to go down to the main house for a moment. I wonder if we should check. I don't like to leave you here all alone.'

The words woke Gav from the half-trance he'd fallen into on the journey. Since waving goodbye to his mother, the afternoon had gathered a bizarre momentum of its own, carrying him along with it. Now, though, it had come to rest where he wanted to be. Time to take over.

'Oh, it's fine. Don't worry, I'll be totally fine now. Aunt Gwen'll be along in a minute. Fire's on and everything. I'll . . . I can just wait for her. No problem. Thanks.'

'Are you sure? You've never been here before, and I think you said there's no phone. I'd really be very happy to wait with you. God knows

I'm not busy, and that way if she doesn't come for a while I can drive you somewhere to—'

'No, really. Thanks. It's OK. And thanks for the ride, that was great, I can't believe she forgot to pick me up but then I sort of can believe it too if you see what I mean. I'll be OK now.' He could see the doubt in her face and began to feel desperate again. 'I can get myself unpacked while I wait, sort my stuff out.'

'Well, at least let me come in and make sure there's food. Or I could give you a ride down to the village. There's a shop there that stays open lateish, in case you needed anything. She'll probably be back by the time we return, and I'd certainly feel better—'

Very clearly, another woman's voice said, 'Let the boy go in.'

Hester stopped in the middle of her sentence, with her mouth open. There was no one else there. The voice had been close by, soft but rough, just like Miss Grey's. Gavin looked around for her before he could stop himself, forgetting that Hester was watching him. Then he noticed Hester gaping silently.

She stared back at him as if he'd sprouted an extra head.

'A-and,' she stammered, 'and better if there was someone here, but . . . but all right. If you're sure. All right, then. I'll . . . ah,' and she looked back towards the car in confusion. She turned to go, stopped and faced Gav again. 'What did you . . . ?'

'I didn't say anything. I thought . . .' He was seized by the urge to get inside and shut the door. Had Hester heard the voice? What else could have startled her like that? 'Thanks again. Thanks. Bye now.'

'Well.' She made a visible effort to recover her composure. 'Goodbye, then. Tell you what – I'll come back tomorrow, around this time, just to set my mind at rest.' He protested distractedly as he picked up his bag and stepped into the house, but she was leaving and he was about to shut Miss Grey out and that was all that mattered now. 'There, that's the second time I've broken my promise not to bother you any more.' He was just closing the door behind him when she called over the noise of the wind, 'And, Gavin? It was a great pleasure to meet you. Good night.'

'Thanks. Night,' he answered hurriedly, shutting the door.

Four

SILENCE.

No father, no mother. No screaming, no babble, no chatter. No one at all.

He began to hear what there was to be heard.

His own breath, still rapid after he'd been startled by the voice that was surely Miss Grey's. The wind in the branches outside, now comfortingly muffled. The steady hiss of the fire. He heard a car engine start, rise and fall – Hester must be turning round – and then rev up and quickly fade.

He eyed the door behind him warily, listening. He couldn't hear anything moving outside, but there was so much darkness around the house; he hadn't seen a single other light from its porch. *Let the boy go in.* Who else could Miss Grey have been speaking to? What was she doing out there? Pursuing him? How could someone else possibly have heard her?

The door had sliding bolts at the top and bottom. He pushed them across. In another room a tinny clock struck six. It made him check his own watch: still not working.

He dropped his bag on the stone floor and emptied his pockets on top of it: ticket, keys, wallet, phone. He dropped the watch too.

Further in the house, behind the wall where the round glass picture thing hung, he saw the bottom of a narrow staircase, carpeted in threadbare green. Opposite the foot of the stairs a heavy curtain hung across a doorway. The room he was in bent round the stairwell. It felt ridiculous to tiptoe, but he did anyway, passing in front of the glass circle; he now saw that its mosaic pieces portrayed a woman's face (high cheekbones and dreamy eyes) seen head-on, with wild hair flowing out behind, in a lurid array of colours. The Mother, maybe? The table beneath with the tealights did look a bit like a makeshift shrine. He looked around the corner. At the far end of the dining room an open doorway led to a kitchen. Branches of something that bore red-orange berries and slender, feathery leaves had been tacked up in bunches over the door.

There were a couple of dirty plates and saucepans by the sink, but no other sign of Auntie Gwen. Nor was she in any of the upstairs rooms, though an oddly intimate smell lingered in what was obviously her bedroom, in a way that made Gav a bit uncomfortable, as if he'd burst in on her in her pyjamas. The ceiling there sloped down almost to the floor, and an indecipherable jumble of stuff had been pushed into both corners. The only light in the room was a small lamp with a heavy red shade. He felt sure she wouldn't have left the light on if she'd gone far. There was a bathroom next door, the inhospitably chilly, unmodern kind, and at the end of the upstairs hallway another bedroom, which also had bunches of the orange-berried branches tied over the lintel. Pinned to the door itself was something he thought must be mistletoe. It looked like the stuff on Christmas-card pictures, though he'd never actually seen it before. The bedroom beyond was unlit, neat, odourless and anonymously orderly.

His room. She must have made an effort to leave a space cleared of her personality, somewhere his parents would approve of their only child occupying for a week.

Going back down, he hesitated before pushing through the drape at the bottom of the stairs. It turned out he needn't have.

He couldn't suppress a smile as he surveyed the benign chaos of his aunt's living room. Here was the real Auntie Gwen, the exact visual equivalent of what he remembered her conversation being like: a picture of enthusiastic untidy muddle. Over it all hung the scent of something woody and spicy, conjuring up her presence immediately, almost as if she were sitting in one of the chairs across by the fire. The same aroma used to arrive with her whenever she visited. Dad liked to make a show of sniffing the air when he got home from work and (as long as Mum was in earshot) mutter, 'Ah yes, that new fragrance, Imbecility by Dior,' or, 'Mmm, *eau de mented*.' She'd once shown Gavin how you dripped the drops of oil onto the little clay dish and then set it over the pot where the candle burned. She did it reverently, like she did most things, especially things involving candles. He looked around and spotted the pot on a huge heavy desk, surrounded by papers and scattered books. There were piles of books on the carpeted floor, books stuffed into odd pieces of dark and bulky furniture that were never intended to be shelves, books dropped in the corners of the chairs and resting, open, over the back of the long sofa that stood between him and the fireplace. Among the books were so many loose sheets of paper that it looked as if a couple more volumes had been systematically shredded and scattered like seed. Perhaps she hoped they'd take root in the mess and grow into new books. There was, he noted with a sinking heart, no TV.

A framed black-and-white photograph on the desk caught his eye, and after a moment's hesitation – the room was so obviously a repository of everything Auntie Gwen was thinking and doing, and its messiness so perfectly matched her own cheerful incoherence, that walking through it felt like snooping into her head – he picked it up.

It was a portrait, very faintly blurry, of an unconventionally beautiful woman with unblemished skin and a round mouth and hair that glistened. She was turning away from the camera, and her eyes were closed. It didn't look like a family picture, but it was the only one in sight. He put it back where it had stood, at the edge of the desk, under the room's single standing lamp.

Most of the desk was covered by an unfolded map, a proper detailed one at a scale that showed every twist of every track and each border of every field. It was so heavily marked with lines and circles and tiny pencil scribblings that Gav could barely make out the features it charted, but in the top corner he recognised the name of the station where Hester had left her car. Near the middle of the sheet was an area where many of the straight pencil lines converged on a number of small circles, and although any names had been obliterated under Auntie Gwen's graffiti, it was obvious that this was where he was. The pattern was like spokes on a wheel, leading into the centre: Pendurra. He examined the map for a while, trying to imagine the open sea out there in the night, the river with its narrow branchings fingering their way into valleys somewhere down beneath him.

The book lying face down and open on one corner of the map had a picture of Stonehenge on its cover and was called *Geomancy.* Stacked nearby, interleaved with torn yellow Post-its shelving out of them like fungi on the trunks of old trees, were *Mysteries of Stone Age Britain*, *The Ley-Hunter's Field Guide*, *Antiques of*— no, *Antiquities of Devon and Cornwall*, *The Track of the Wild Hunt* . . . Around and beneath the map, sheets of paper written over in Aunt Gwen's cuneiform handwriting spread chaotically. A few appeared to be diagrams with labels; some looked like lists with multiple crossings-out and insertions; most were chunks of written notes he didn't want to look at too closely. He had a strong feeling that visible energies would feature heavily in them.

Each time he stopped to look at anything, the silence became oppressively thick. The thought of Miss Grey wandering in the night outside, watching the house, was like a pair of eyes on his back. He made sure all the curtains were drawn tight.

The best way to keep busy while he waited, he decided, was to get himself something to eat. He went back to the kitchen and found a stocky fridge with a big blunt handle, which turned out to hold bowlfuls of what his father liked to call 'chicken feed': grainy, persistently brown salads. There was an open packet of biscuits on a counter by the sink, so he took a few of those instead and, spotting a carton of instant hot chocolate, lit a burner on the stove under a battered metal kettle. The clankings and clatterings in the kitchen dropped into the stillness of the house like pebbles in a pond, and were as quickly swallowed.

What did she want from him?

He meant to take his mug of hot chocolate back to the messy living room, sit down by the fire with any book he could find that didn't look too forbiddingly weird, and get comfortable. As soon as he passed the front door on his way back, he knew it wouldn't work.

He leaned an ear to the door, held his breath and listened. The only sounds outside were the bodiless sighs of a gusting wind.

He slid the bolts back, listened again, then pushed the door open a crack.

'Are you there?' he said. It came out as a whisper.

He swung the door wide and faced the dark.

'Miss Grey?' he said, louder.

The light under the porch was still on, and beyond that the curtained windows illuminated faint swatches of the grassy verge in front of the house, but all the rest was nothing. Hester had said the place where they'd got off the train was only a few miles away. If so, those miles had to be constructed of solid night. There was not even an inkling of the underglow that lit every night sky Gavin had ever seen, the electric afterimage of the city.

'Just go away,' he said. 'OK? I don't want to see you. I don't want to listen to you. This is my holiday. Leave me alone, all right?'

He nearly jumped out of his skin as a swift, small shadow darted out of the blackness towards his feet. A cat. Just a cat, speeding inside the house. He turned almost as fast, pulse racing, and bolted the door behind him.

The cat, a scruffy tortoiseshell, sized him up from under the table. He tried to laugh at himself for having been so startled by it. Actually, he should have expected it: he'd seen boxes of cat food in the kitchen cupboards. It looked like it was hungry now. It yowled at him, tail stiff, and followed him to the kitchen. He tipped some dry food into a bowl, but it only nosed at it and then chirruped again, twisting round his legs.

'Fine, then,' he said. 'Suit yourself. I'm eating.'

The company of another living thing was enough to diminish the eerie feeling that gathered in the silence of the house. Despite the various signs of Auntie Gwen's weirdness – the hanging crystals, the candles, the shrine, the mistletoe, the mess – Gav had to admit the firelight and the low ceilings and the mismatched, used-looking furniture made it cosy. He took his mug and a plate of biscuits and pushed back through the heavy green drape into the living room. He sat down in the chair nearest the fire. Half a second later the cat appeared, jumped into his lap and began kneading his legs.

Next to the arm of the chair was a box covered in a scarlet blanket, doing duty as a side table. This too was piled with Auntie Gwen's reading. He picked through the books, not very hopefully. *Wicca Almanac.* He thought he recognised that one; it must have come with her to London once. *The White Goddess. Moon Magic.* Et cetera. There was also a big, expensive-looking photo album. *Treasured Memories*, it said on the cover, embossed in gold. Slightly guiltily, Gav picked it up. He felt like Mum, poking around someone else's things, but he needed something to look at while he waited, and he was curious about what kind of photos Auntie Gwen kept. He couldn't think of anytime he'd seen her holding a camera.

But it wasn't a photo album; it was a scrapbook.

There were quite a few newspaper cuttings, some fading to sepia brittleness. There were photocopies of pages from books, and more bits of paper in her writing. She'd made notes on the pages of the album in many places. There were a few photos, all with a note written beneath them recording the date they were taken. There were a couple of postcards as well, carefully glued in. With a start, Gavin saw among the scraps a sheet in his own handwriting, in a scrawly version from years ago. It was a letter he'd sent her, just a couple of lines, with a bad scribbled drawing beneath them. He'd completely forgotten it. Why had she kept it, stuck in here with everything else?

D. A.G.
Thank you for the picture. That is not what she looks like at all. You have made her much too smooth. Here is my drawing of Miss Gray though I am not too good at drawing, I only got a 63 in art.
Love from Gavin

On the facing page was the picture Auntie Gwen had sent him. He remembered it now. Memory jogged, he glanced across at the framed photo on the desk. It was the same face. Auntie Gwen had more or less copied the photo. Her drawing showed the same head in the same pose, but with eyes open, the lips tighter, the cheekbones sharper, the whole face rendered more elfin and fantastical. She'd sent it to him as a present, with a note asking if it looked anything like Miss Grey. It was embarrassing to see his reply again, his childish handwriting, his fixation with marks, and beneath the message the even more comically childish pencil drawing representing the best Miss Grey he could do at the age of ten.

On the next page of the album another letter was stuck in. Above it Auntie Gwen had again pencilled the date, two weeks later than the previous letter.

D. A.G.
Thank you for the postcard. That is much more like Miss gray, though she looks a lot nicer. And she isnt made out of wood or her name would be Miss brown. I am much

too busy to write any more letters now. [That came straight from Dad. He chewed his lip in shame as he read it.] *How are you.*
Love from Gavin

And there it was, the postcard she'd sent, or at least another copy of the same picture, pasted in next to the letter. A picture of a wooden statue, a woman's head and raised hands, angular and grotesquely emaciated. It was supposed to be a bit like his own crude drawing; he could see that now. But it didn't actually look much like Miss Grey; he must only have said it did to stop Auntie Gwen sending him any more pictures. It occurred to him that maybe this had been the last postcard he'd had from her. Years ago – five years.

Under the postcard she had written, neatly, *Donatello, Maddalena.* The name, or names, didn't mean anything to him. He couldn't remember Auntie Gwen ever talking about anyone Italian.

Gavin began to flip through the album.

Then he wasn't flipping at all, but reading.

He read some of the pages over and over again.

He didn't look up until he was startled by the wheezing and chiming of the clock on the mantelpiece. Seven o'clock. He probably should have been wondering seriously about where his aunt had gone, but instead he was wondering what she'd been doing in this house all these years, whether there really was some point to all the mysteries she'd collected in this book.

He was also thinking about Hester Lightfoot.

The very last items in the scrapbook were two small clippings from newspapers. Over the first Auntie Gwen had written, *Oxford Mail, 18 November.* It read:

Professor Hester Lightfoot has resigned her position as fellow in anthropology at Magdalen College.

Professor Lightfoot became a controversial figure earlier this year when she admitted on a radio programme that she had cause to doubt her own mental health. Despite the support of colleagues and students, who maintained that her remarks had been taken out of context, there were calls for her to be suspended from teaching. The Mail *has now learned that she has resigned voluntarily. Neither Professor Lightfoot nor Magdalen*

College is making any comment, although sources at the college privately insist that it continues to support the professor and that the decision is entirely her own. Barry Squibb (19), a student of

And there the column ended. The second clipping was labelled, *Western Cornishman, 21 November*. This time the headline was included:

'NUTTY PROFESSOR' RESIGNS
Falmouth-born Hester Lightfoot, a professor at Oxford University, has resigned. Dubbed 'the Nutty Professor' after she made public reference to her mental-health problems, Lightfoot has surrendered her prestigious post before the end of the university term. No one so far has commented on the reasons for her decision. In a BBC programme broadcast in April, Lightfoot confessed that she sometimes 'heard voices' but claimed she was not delusional because she knew the voices were not real. She owns a house in Mawnan Smith, where villagers describe her as a regular visitor.

Beneath this article Auntie Gwen had written, *Hester Lightfoot, born Falmouth 29/11/62. Grandniece of John Nicholls. Authority on shamanism.* And John Nicholls had his own page, earlier in the album. Gav flipped back to check and found two photocopies of the same signature and a sheet of paper on which she'd transcribed some sentences from somewhere else: he'd been a local eccentric of some sort, back in the 1920s. Something about pagan rites and taking a vow of silence. *Never heard to utter a syllable*, it said.

The whole album was in the same vein. Almost all of it consisted of records of exotic or weird things connected, however distantly, to this part of the world. Some of them were legends Auntie Gwen had discovered in old books. There were summaries of theories about standing stones, and pictures of field patterns that, seen from high above, made the shapes of dragons. There were accounts of witchcraft trials, holy wells and saints' apparitions. Some were relatively recent stories, like the ones about the ghost of a small girl spotted in the woods at the edge of the river (accompanied by fuzzy magnified photos), or the man whose terminal cancer had been cured by a local priest, or UFO sightings out at sea. It all began to blend together into an indiscriminate fog, names and places that Gavin didn't know, many of them sharp with the sounds of a remote world:

Coverack, St Keverne, Manaccan. But then he was there too, and Hester. Whose birthday was tomorrow. Who told him she'd been kicked out of 'school'. Who'd apparently said something a bit like what he'd said to Mr Bushy.

Who'd heard the voice out in the dark; surely she had. Miss Grey's voice, telling him to go in.

He needed more light. His hands were shaking slightly as he took a thick log, scabbed with dry lichen, from the box beside the fireplace and dropped it onto the embers. He needed more food too, but suddenly the thought of pushing through the curtain to leave the room was more than he could face. He lowered himself back into the chair and pulled down a thick blanket that had been draped over its back. He would sit and wait for Auntie Gwen. He'd ignore the books, the papers, the treasured memories. He'd ignore his hunger. She couldn't be much longer.

Exhaustion caught up with him very quickly. He was asleep before the new log began to burn. He shifted when the cat decided to occupy the space between his curled-up legs and the arm of the chair, but didn't wake. He slept through the chiming of the clock and the rising of the wind. The rain didn't disturb him; it began gently, and as it grew steady and persistent, its thrumming on the windows blended smoothly with the popping of the fire.

What woke him was the cat abruptly leaping off his lap. For a few bewildered seconds he had no idea where he was. Then the clock struck twelve, and just as it finished there was a violent hammering at the door.

Five

A December day 1537

FROM THE HIGHEST window of the tallest house in the Jeruzalemstraat, the greatest magus in the world surveyed the city's steaming chimneys and stinking thoroughfares. All of it lay below the level of his eye, all but the church pinnacles and spires. They pointed up from the rabble and filth below, towards heaven.

The uppermost room of his house was his observatory. Ordinarily he would not have unlocked it during the day. Ordinarily he had no interest in examining the mundane panorama spread out beneath him. He came here on clear nights to watch the stars.

It was mid-morning, many hours before the sun would descend and unveil them, and with ominous swags of cloud piling in from the sea, it was unlikely the upper sky would be visible even then. No matter. By dark he expected to be abroad and on his way. This was not an ordinary day. He had ascended to the observatory only to take a last view of the city.

By dark he expected to have left other things behind him too. He gazed at the lofty white tower of the Vrouwekerk, symmetrical, harmonious, pure, a chorale in stone, and felt himself ascending with it, leaving the streets and canals and dwellings and people far beneath.

An uneasy thought intruded on his contemplations. Its burden was another farewell, one he very much wanted to avoid.

Best, then, to set to work, without delay.

He locked his observatory for the last time and went down through the house to the cellar. Glancing over his shoulder – since the autumn the suspicious reflex had become his unconscious habit whenever he entered his laboratory – he opened a room crowded with stoppered jars and chained volumes and caskets and boxes and dishes of magnificently bewildering variety.

Near the middle of the room was one large table, scratched and singed. In contrast to the racks and shelves around the walls, profuse with containers almost as rich and rare as the materials they stored, the table presented a scene of ascetic simplicity. A pentagram had been marked out on its surface in something that looked like chalk, though in no other way did it bear any resemblance to the humble substance of earth. At each of the diagram's five points was an unlit taper in a plain pewter stick. In its enclosed centre lay a hand mirror, its palm's width of coated glass reflecting the beams of the low ceiling. The table was otherwise bare.

The magus took a candle from the wall, peered once more up the stairs against imaginary intruders and then entered the laboratory, bolting the door behind him.

As always over these last three months his glance strayed first towards a wooden box with a silver clasp, sharing a shelf with a crowd of flasks and cases.

No visitor would have singled out this one box as being any more interesting than the scores of others spread around the magus's laboratory. It was far less rich and fine than the silver bowls with their lids of ebony, or the ivory caskets whose sides had been carved so that beasts seemed to chase each other around them, or the porcelain hexagons glazed in peacock colours with orient script. In fact, should the visitor have for some idle reason considered showing an interest in this box, they would have found that without realising it their attention had slipped elsewhere, for among the many, many enchantments the magus had used in its making was one that had the virtue of evading thought, of retiring unnoticed to the back of the mind. And should the visitor not be an honest visitor at all but a thief who had somehow learned of the existence of this particular box and what lay within it, and had strength of intention enough to overcome the enchantment and keep his mind steadily bent to the task of opening it (as, after a long pause, the magus was now doing), they would lift the clasp, look inside and see . . . nothing. For the pouch inside was warded not only from earth, air, water, fire, spirits, scrying and thought, but also from sight. Only a greater magus than Master John

Fiste (as from now on he had determined to call himself) would have been able to see by a light brighter and purer than the light of the eyes and so look past his wards, and Master John Fiste was the greatest magus in the world.

He withdrew a plain brown ring from the pouch, holding it thoughtfully between thumb and forefinger. Memories overwhelmed him.

For an instant an unexpected expression crossed his face. A painter might have borrowed it to portray a defeated emperor, one who had seen his whole kingdom lost.

He laid the ring on the table and crossed the room. Extracting a key from a pouch looped to his jerkin, he unlocked a long, low chest and drew out his staff, a length of wood almost as thick as his wrist, marked with sigils.

Thus armed, he knelt and prayed.

It was his custom to spend some minutes in devotion before he set to work. Ordinarily he offered thanks for the glimpses of the living universe that had been allowed him, praising the great Author by whose generative spirit the world was inhabited, sustained and moved. What was magic after all, he would remind himself at these times, but the commerce and the interchange between mankind and the rest of the living creation? It was a simple truth, though many thought it occult: the world was alive, a body filled with spirit like Adam himself. In ancient days those who understood this were acknowledged and revered as the holiest of men, prophets and hierophants. He gave thanks that he had been permitted to achieve such a station.

Though it hardly seemed like a blessing, in these fallen times. Now, those who called themselves pious looked askance at him. The magus pressed his lips tight as he knelt. He lived in a degraded age, a pygmy age. The new heresy preached that God's creation and everything in it was fallen and corrupt. Everywhere people flocked to its banner. Educated men weighed and measured the world around them like the new anatomists, who thought they could explain human life by slicing open corpses and prodding the empty flesh. The clerk of Frombork studied the gleaming volume of the heavens and determined that the Earth itself, the whole sphere of God's substantial creation, was a vast ball of dead rock spinning madly like a child's top, hurtling through oceans of emptiness. Amid this dark theatre where ignorance masqueraded as philosophy, the magus felt himself utterly alone, blowing on the last fading embers of knowledge in the hope that some future day the fire might blaze up again. He had students once, but they were gone. Mankind had turned its back on him.

Well, then. He was ready to turn his back on them.

His eyes opened and twitched towards the ring. The greatest gift in the history of the world had come into his possession (that was how he put it to himself, 'had come into his possession', while he meant to pray, though on this morning his heart and mouth were equally empty of devotion) and he would safeguard it and, through it, himself. For ever.

If he died, the gift and his art (which were, after all, one and the same) might be lost to the world. Mankind would forget that the universe was alive. No one would hear the echoes of the divine word that had spoken it into being. Adam's descendants would eat dust and ashes.

Therefore he had decided he would not die.

It was indeed not an ordinary day. He was on the verge of the greatest triumph of his life, a magic that had not been done since the world's long-departed golden age. He ought to have been exalted by wonder and reverent awe, but instead the thing he was trying not to remember, the farewell he so desired to avoid, nagged at his meditations, urging him to hurry, to seal the bargain and then be away, across the sea to England, where he could begin a new life.

He opened his eyes to check the ring again, as though it might have been removed while he prayed. It lay on the table still: a gift, a burden.

Prayer forgotten, he rose slowly to his feet.

He picked up his staff and, with a motion swift and imperious as a swordsman executing a salute, raised it high and traced a circle in the air. He spoke three words and then rapped the floor with its heel.

For a second the cellar room was flooded with a fiery light. It had no source, but seemed to stir with a restless motion of its own. Indistinct faces with lidless and pupilless eyes, smooth lips silently moving, flowed among it and then vanished, though strange reflections continued to flicker around the room: the curve of a silver bowl for a moment became a coppery cheek, the glass of a bottle caught the image of a stony gaze.

He gripped the staff tightly in his left hand. The feel of the familiar instrument of his authority went some way to refreshing his wavering confidence. The business was begun. Now he could show no weakness, no hesitation at all, or he might be lost for ever.

'Spirit!' he called, in a strong voice.

The answer was a faint, directionless whisper in the air and a red-orange gleam, as if the light of a smoky sunset had fallen into the windowless room.

'I require something of you. Remember your promise of service, as I come before you!'

He dared say no more. Always command, never entreat: it was the first rule, learned long ago, when he had begun to conjure with the inferior spirits. He steeled himself, remembering his mastery, and reached with his right hand for the ring.

It would only fit on the small finger. He eased it on, felt for its power and opened the passage wide.

Flame surrounded him. He stood in a livid column, licking and streaming upwards, thronged with faces. The fire swam with them, mask-like faces, empty, interchangeable, implacably dire. They dissolved and reappeared among tongues of orange and crimson too fast for the eye to catch. When the fire spoke, its voice was like a consort of many voices united, but all of them dry and thin and very far away, whispers of pages turning.

'Welcome, Magister. Are we paid at last?'

The magus reeled with surprise and sudden fear. He groped for an answer. Each instant of silence sounded like a weakness he could not admit.

'Your promise was to serve, willingly.' He held the staff tight, his hands sweating. 'I have not released you. I do not choose to release you now.'

'We serve.' There was something in its rustling chorus that always sounded like mockery. Its unexpected question had surely been meant to unsettle him. He steadied his resolve, growing angry.

'You will obey me now as you have before. You will not speak of payment. Nothing is owed.'

'Nothing, Magister.'

'Your bond is to serve, even until the last extremity. Is it not so?'

'It is so. Has the last come?'

'No.' The magus shuddered involuntarily. The ring seemed to burn with cold fire round his finger. 'No.'

'What do you require?'

Now, no hesitation. The decision was made. He raised the staff, feeling the phantom flames whirl about it, tethered.

'I require you,' he said, holding his voice steady, 'to safeguard a thing for me.'

'We have no power over things.'

'It is no corporeal thing.'

The voice emitted a long, hissing sigh.

'A spirit.'

'Yes,' the magus said. His throat was very dry.

'Of what station?'

'My own.'

There was an awful pause and then it sighed again. It was laughing at him.

'Do you dare mock me?'

'No. We welcome you. Only will it and you may dwell as we do. It is an easy matter.'

'Silence!' The insidious taunting revolted him. 'Silence! You dream that I would give you my soul unconstrained? There is a bargain, Spirit. I have made it ready and I will bind you to it.'

'A bargain.' The voice seemed to savour the word with a chilling luxury.

'It is here.' He clenched his jaw, breathed carefully. 'Before me.'

The angry sound began as a low hiss, the scrape of receding waves on a sandy beach. It gathered, rose, filling with airless breath, until it became the roar of a consuming fire. Gripping the staff firmly in both hands, the magus ignored it and began to speak. The words he spoke were in no language known to men living or dead. It was a tongue he had striven over decades to learn, each syllable and particle of it costing immense labour in the discovery, its rudiments pieced together from tiny scraps scattered in the darkest corners of the great library of the invisible world. It was never meant for human lips, and he sweated until his face appeared to be washed by a river of fire. The effort twisted his eyes closed. He felt resistance, protest, howling fury, but his will was stronger, and the authority embedded in his staff unbreakable. At his halting command the glow in the room began to gather, the impression of movement taking shape as a whirling orbit. It tightened around the tip of the staff until it was compacted into a blazing ball, as if he had thrust the wood like a spear into the lake of the heavens and lanced a comet.

The tip hovered over the table, above the polished silver mirror. Arms steady, he lowered the staff to the surface of the mirror.

He felt again for the power of the ring and commanded the spirit through the passage.

There was a soundless eruption of light. The magus threw up his hands to protect his eyes, dropping the staff to the floor. The moment it left his grip the air filled with fugitive whispers and strange cries, swiftly fading beyond the corners of the room. Streaks of fiery light followed them and vanished as quickly. He felt that he was caught in a shower of burning hailstones and cried out.

The room fell quiet.

Blinking to restore his sight, he saw the same five candles on the table, the same shadowed racks and shelves around the walls, the heavy door barred against thieves. Only one thing had changed.

The silk-smooth oval on the table, no bigger than the palm of his hand, was tinged with vaporous orange-red.

The magus stared at it, recovering his breath.

The mirror had, quite clearly, ceased to reflect the beams of the ceiling above. It had gained depths of its own. Somewhere down in them, a fire burned.

He fingered the ring. Triumph stirred in him. The ring had not betrayed him, then, despite her warning. The passage had opened at his will. He had been foolish to doubt himself. Was he not the greatest of the magi?

He averted his eyes carefully as he leaned over the table.

'Are you confined?' he demanded. 'Speak!'

The dry voice came as if from a coffin buried under the house. 'Why punish, Magister?'

'Answer. Are you confined?'

'We are.'

'Have you power to leave the place I have bound you?'

'We have not. Release us, Magister, to work your bidding.'

'You may not change your place until I release you?'

'We may not.'

His fingers closed around the mirror. To his flesh it felt like the same chill artefact of quicksilver and stannum and glass and magic it had been moments before. He lifted it into the palm of the hand that wore the ring and raised it.

'Then show yourself,' he said.

The mist cleared. He saw his own face, greying beard dark with sweat. The weariness of his expression shocked him. He had grown haggard.

His eyes burst into fire.

The mirror slipped out of his hand. Trembling, he fumbled after it. It eluded his unsteady hands and clinked down on the table. His fingers clutched at his face.

'As you wish,' said the voice.

No more than an illusion in the mirror. Of course not. He began to grow angry. Was he a child, to be terrified by a reflection? Was he a novice, to be shocked by a spirit's tricks?

He took up his staff. With the instrument of his authority over the fiery spirit in his hand, he reached once again for the mirror and raised it before his eyes as steadily as he could.

Within it his image gazed steadily back at him, the wall of his laboratory behind, apparatus glinting by candlelight; but the picture of him in the mirror had eyes that were circles of dancing flame, and its mouth curled with a joyless smile even as his own lips parted in revulsion.

The reflection of his mouth spoke to him. 'Do you see us?'

'Silence!'

His image raised a finger – his finger – to its lips and smiled again. The hand it lifted was the right. The magus saw that in the mirror it was not wearing the ring. Gripped by doubt, he glanced down and saw his treasure there on the small finger of his own right hand. It was his; it was not lost. She had spoken wrongly: it belonged to him. The mere sight of it restored some of his self-possession. It also reminded him not to lose time. It was unwise for him to wear the ring long.

He faced the infernal copy of himself as bravely as he could, reminding himself that he had seen worse.

'Hear the conditions I make,' he said, forcing authority into his voice. 'If you keep safe what I will give you, you will be freed. You will keep it until such time as another looks deep in this mirror. Then you will surrender it to them, and in that moment you also will be unconfined.'

The hideous parody of his face sneered. 'It is insufficient.'

It was fortunate for the magus – so he believed, at least – that he had expected this. He knew how the lower beings loved to kick against the pricks whenever they could, and he was prepared accordingly to bargain in return for the task he was imposing on it. If he had not already considered the means, he doubted he could have maintained the presence of mind to converse with the awful image facing him.

'Very well. Then I offer you flesh.'

The myriad voice sighed once more, a drawn-out, wordless, hungry groan.

'When you are free I will allow you substantial form. You will be my familiar. You will be more than spirit. Is this sufficient?'

There was a long pause. Then the reflected lips tightened in a deadly smile and whispered, 'It is.'

The smile made the yellow bile rise to his throat. He felt a powerful urge to be rid of the sight in the mirror. He laid it down quickly and fetched a small knife.

'Very well.' He had rehearsed these words, which, along with the act of putting aside the mirror, made it easier to speak calmly again. 'As I am man, made in God's image, my living soul belonging to myself alone and incorporate in this mortal body, so I will put into your keeping a part of myself, making that part spirit only as you are spirit.' He held the blade of the knife in one of the candles. The flame forked around it. 'When another looks deep into this mirror, you will surrender up that spirit to flesh again, and at that time you will also be free and may seek corporeal form.'

In the silence that followed he withdrew the blade, letting it cool.

'You may speak,' he said.

'By what power?' The voice was nowhere. The shadows in the corners of the room seemed to utter it.

He raised his right hand in front of his face. 'I hold the key that opens the passage between your world and mine.'

'It is not yours to hold.'

'Be silent!' the magus shouted. 'May your utterance be cursed! Go from—' He choked back his rage, horrified at how close he had come to finishing the sentence and so releasing the spirit from its service. He closed his eyes and let his heart subside. He could no more afford fury than fear. His decision was made, he reminded himself. There could be no contradiction.

Reining his passion tight, pushing the whispered words out of his thoughts, he put down the staff and held his hands above the mirror. He pressed the point of the knife against the skin of one finger, just below the nail, and pricked. A single drop of blood beaded out and fell on the surface of the glass. It spread like oil over water.

The voice made a long, wordless, whispering sound.

He picked up the mirror again. The glass was dry and smooth, and showed nothing but a cloudy red expanse, as if he were cradling a fragment of the dawn. He brought it close to his mouth.

Once again he felt for the power of the ring.

The

world around him sang with life. A dawn sky was scarlet, portending a terrible day. He was hurtling towards disaster. Its mists cleared suddenly and in the mirror a face that was nothing like his own returned his stare, eyelids peeled back with measureless, insane terror. It was an unknown face, a woman's face. It saw him as surely as he saw it. They saw each other's fates, the same fate, more dreadful than death

The magus had meant to breathe gently over the mirror, joining the air and water of his living spirit to the blood that was its earth and fire. But the vision dragged the air out of him. Instead of exhaling, he cried out. The glass fogged over and then blazed. An invisible wind howled through the ring, tossing him like a dead leaf, thundering in his ears. He heard the woman scream, with his own voice.

Then he crumpled to the floor.

The small mirror fell beside him, face up, blank with the dimness of the room.

Outside, dusk had come early. Fat storm clouds erased the day. Their load of sleet had begun to scour people out of the streets. While the greatest magus in the world lay in a dead faint, the storm grew fiercer. An angry demon was riding it, people muttered to themselves.

It was some hours before he at last emerged from his laboratory, the box with its immeasurably precious talismans tucked inside his travelling cloak. His servants knew better than to ask questions, even when they saw him as deathly pale as now. When, though, he called them before him, paid them all nine times what they had from him in a year and dismissed them, they went away telling each other – and, later, everyone else – that this night, surely, his final reckoning had fallen due.

Part II
Tuesday Morning

Six

THE HAMMERING AT the door wouldn't stop. Gavin clutched the arms of the chair, rigid with fright.

'Miss Grey?'

The bolts juddered. He'd been jolted awake and couldn't get hold of where he was or what was going on. Someone was outside. Someone wanted to get in.

He remembered thinking Miss Grey was out there, but he couldn't connect the thought with the relentless noise. Not the calm, withdrawn Miss Grey he knew, always so grave. Quiet as the grave.

There was a voice, faint, bleak. He could scarcely hear it at all over the rain and the hammering. It came from somewhere outside, beyond the curtained windows. It sounded like a cross between a person's voice and a keening animal, or merely the wind.

What if it was Auntie Gwen, coming home to find her own front door bolted? Could the rain and the night make even scatty, peaceable Auntie Gwen so frenzied that she'd batter and moan?

Could she have met something outside that had driven her to this?

All he had to do was get up and look.

When he saw things he didn't want to see, Gavin's habit was to stand still, put his head down and wait. As often as not they'd be gone by the time he counted to twenty. The green face would have gone back to being only an arrangement of shadows in the leaves; the stony-eyed crow twisting its neck to look down from the curtain rail would vanish into the pattern of the wallpaper.

He counted to fifty. By the time he finished his eyes were squeezed shut and his hands were over his ears, and still the banging went on.

The fire had faded to a pocketful of embers. He shivered as he pushed himself out of the armchair. His legs felt numb. He dropped to his knees, crawled across the carpet to the window and put his eye to the crack between the curtains.

There was a dead girl outside, trying to get in.

She was barefoot in the sheeting rain, thin and pale as paper, wearing something white and filthy and shroud-like which clung to her, sodden nearly to transparency. Her eyes were closed and her face was slack. Her legs were splattered with mud, as if she'd just dragged herself out of her hole in the ground. Rain bounced off her nose and lips and shoulders and streamed down her arms. One arm hung beside her like part of a carcass; the other was still beating at the door.

She moaned with her ghost of a voice, the same words over and over. 'Come back,' it sounded like. 'Come back, come back,' as if she'd been abandoned in her grave and was pleading with him to join her there.

Gavin curled up on the floor and started counting again. He tried to think of a big number to count to, but he couldn't. He was too terrified to think anything at all.

The banging stopped.

In its wake came a silence so absolute it made his ears sing. After as much of that as he could bear he uncurled himself and made himself look out again, knowing he'd never move from this spot on the floor until he was sure the zombie had gone.

She was not gone, but the arm that had been raised now dangled at her side, and the head – strewn with lank wet hair, a bony nose and chin poking out between them – had lowered itself. The cries stopped. She'd turned back into an upright corpse, motionless. The downpour rinsed mud from it.

She turned away from the house and shuffled off into the dark.

Gavin slumped to the floor.

The clock caught his eye: a few minutes past midnight. The witching hour. How had he let himself be lured here? No one lived here. It didn't feel like a house at all. It was a tiny island of light in a sea of ghastly dark. Waves lapped at its edges, threatening to swamp him. He sat as still as he could, listening for any movement, dreading the next sight, the next sound.

The clock was ticking on, which was a small reassurance, as he wouldn't have been surprised to see its hands whirl backwards or hear it strike thirteen. There was a scratchy rustle by the draped entrance and the cat nosed through the curtain into the room, looking at Gav as if disappointed that he should have found a corpse at the door at all out of the ordinary. He began to wonder whether it had actually happened, though he'd never learned what that meant, *actually happened.* It was a phrase his parents liked a lot.

But Hester Lightfoot had heard Miss Grey, out in front of the house. Or at least heard the same voice. It wasn't just him. She heard voices; the paper said so.

Perhaps she'd heard Miss Grey on the train as well. Hadn't she run out of the carriage suddenly, looking shocked and weepy?

When five cold and silent minutes had passed without anything happening except the cat treading carefully around the room looking for somewhere to sleep, he decided it was probably safe to move. He thought about getting the fire going. Light and warmth, and something to do. It looked ash-grey and cold, but when he knelt down to sweep the hearth clear he was surprised to feel warmth on his hands. Prodding with a shovel, he found embers. He dropped a sheet of old newspaper among them. A curl of smoke snaked up the chimney and then it was ablaze. Gav watched in astonishment. He'd expected a long struggle. They had a coal fire at home, and his father always insisted that no one else understood the mysteries of laying and lighting it.

The cat had occupied a basket in front of the fire and was curled up, tail over its nose. Its slow breathing, and the rising crackle of the fire, made the house much less creepy. Nevertheless he went on tiptoe across the room and held his ear to the green curtain for a long time before he dared go past it, and then the first thing he did in the dining room was drag a chair to the front door and wedge it under the handle. Then he went around the house switching on every light he could find.

He looked in Auntie Gwen's bedroom to see if she'd left a message or some other clue to where she'd gone. All he found was a wreck of clothes and spangly jewellery and towels and indeterminate wispy things. There was nothing odd about it, except in the way that everything about Auntie Gwen was odd.

He was beginning to feel the disorienting fuzziness that always went with being awake in the middle of the night. If he stopped moving he imagined he'd probably fall asleep on the spot, but he couldn't cope with the thought of what might happen if he closed his eyes. He went back downstairs to make himself tea. The kitchen window was uncovered – the only bare window in the house – and he felt horribly exposed in front of it, but he made himself put the kettle on. While it was heating up he got the fire going in the dining room, coaxing it back to life as surprisingly effortlessly as he'd managed with the other one. He lit all the candles beneath the glass hanging as well. If the luxuriantly soulful face that looked out from it was the household goddess, he thought he might as well tend her shrine. Maybe she'd help keep the zombies away and bring Auntie Gwen back.

Mug of tea clasped between his hands for warmth, he went back into the living room, surveying its chaos of paper and print. No doubt there were all sorts of clues about what she might be up to lying in plain sight, but there was no way of guessing where to start, and he shied away from the prospect of sifting through her scatterings the same way he'd always tried to steer her away from the topic of Miss Grey, or the naked girl in the pool in the park, or the crow in his bedroom, or everything else that used to get her so excited.

He checked the clock again. It was a very long time until dawn.

Putting his tea down on a pile of loose sheets and jottings, he settled back into the armchair. His eyelids felt heavy at once. To keep himself occupied, he picked up the scrapbook again. He went through it more thoughtfully.

He was leaning over the arm of the chair, having just picked up his mug, when he saw his name.

The base of the mug had left a circular tea stain on the piece of paper beneath. It was the back of an envelope, scribbled on like every other scrap. Gav hadn't been looking when he'd put down his tea, but now he saw that the ring had appeared round a single word, written in prominent capitals in Auntie Gwen's narrow handwriting. The word was caught perfectly, in the centre of the circle, underlined twice:

GAVIN

His first thought was that Auntie Gwen had left him a message. He hadn't noticed it before – the papers must have shifted around a bit when he put the mug down – but when he flipped the envelope over it turned out to be only some letter addressed to her, the address typed on the front: a PO box number in a place called Falmouth, a postcode. She'd jotted some kind of telegraphic list on the back. It must have been the nearest scrap of paper to hand.

The last thing she'd scribbled was his name. He frowned at the smaller notes above it:

Jess!!
chap girl?
(O.J.)
key chap Joshua Acres

well
Swanny's O?

Then a bigger space and, in overexcited capitals:

GAVIN

Jess? Joshua Acres? Not much more incomprehensible than any other bits of her writing he'd glanced at. And yet there was his name at the end, as if it was the conclusion to the rest.

He flipped the envelope over again to check the postmark. Posted from London, last Thursday. The letter must have just arrived. She'd jotted this down very recently.

He thought for a moment, then went and got her letter to his mother out of his bag, sitting by the fire to reread it.

It struck him that she'd practically begged Mum to send him down to stay with her. Something about the way she'd crammed the words onto the two sheets of paper. And how overexcited she'd sounded about seeing him again. Why? They hadn't spoken for years.

Where was she?

Miss Grey wanted him to be here. *Let the boy go in.* She'd found her voice. *Come*, she told him. And here he was, and someone else could hear her, and one of those things that couldn't *actually happen* had been right outside the door, making the house shake with its dead white fist.

He sat and stared at nothing. The heaviness washed over his eyes. The fire whispered to him quietly, and more quietly. He began dreaming even before he fell asleep.

Morning crept through the house like disenchantment. Gavin woke with a stiff neck and a groggy head. There were sounds in the house, ordinary domestic noises: a scraping plate, a cupboard door closing. Auntie Gwen must have got up before him. He rubbed his eyes, not quite recognising where he was. The room had changed its character completely by daylight, as strange rooms do. The dullness of a cloudy morning had got inside it. It looked tired, safe. Birds sang outside.

Something in the kitchen got knocked over. Auntie Gwen had always been clumsy. Dad had jokes about her magnetic hands that repelled everything. Gav wondered when she'd got back.

He stretched and got up.

'Auntie Gwen?'

The cat miaowed from another room.

There was no one in the kitchen. The cat had been nosing its bowl around on the floor. As he watched, it jumped to the countertop and tried to push open the handle of a cupboard, then sprang down again, leaning against his shins, demanding food. He found the right box in the cupboard and left the cat crunching and purring while he went upstairs.

'Auntie Gwen?'

He looked in every room, heart sinking as his memories of the night started to come back clearly and the brief comfort of the dawn drained away. The air of sudden abandonment in the house had been a bit creepy in the dark. Now it only made the place dreary.

She still wasn't home.

He opened all the curtains as he went, at last seeing the landscape the house sat in. It took a small effort of courage when he got to the living-room windows and thought of what he'd seen outside them in the night, but he opened those curtains too, looking out onto nothing more sinister than a patch of muddy lawn, the driveway, a simple iron fence beyond and then an empty field sloping down, just grass and the sky, with a faint concentration of cloudy brightness low and to the right suggesting that the sun might be rising. On the other side of the house, through the kitchen window, the view was blocked after a few feet by a tall hedge of something evergreen and glossy, shaded by taller trees behind. There was the edge of a clothesline, and under it one corner of a vegetable patch. Nearby sprawled a rosebush, in full flower, pink saucers defying the morning dullness. From the upstairs windows he could trace the passage of the driveway, starting at the gateposts where Hester had pulled up her car, past the front of the house, and then away to the left down the slope of a hill, where it disappeared into a brown and crooked wood.

He'd read about this kind of house. They built them at the entrance to fancy estates, like a guardhouse. Aunt Gwen was the estate's gatekeeper.

Or had been.

While Gav made himself toast and tea, he wondered what to do. He'd spent most of the last four years desperately wanting to be left alone. Now he'd got his wish. It wasn't exactly what he'd hoped for. He'd always imagined himself making Pot Noodles every couple of hours and otherwise alternating between computer games, reading and naps. Not once had it occurred to him that isolation would be so unsettling. He tried to picture himself staying and waiting for Auntie Gwen to show up. The hours chiming away, staring out of the windows, the unease gathering quietly at his back, growing. No. It would be awful.

So if he wasn't staying in, he'd have to go out.

The bathroom upstairs was too cold for anything beyond the most cursory splash, but he changed out of the clothes he'd slept in. He removed the chair wedged against the front door. It felt now like a stupid thing to have done, but still he had to go twice around all the windows to make sure there was no one or nothing anywhere near the house before he could slide the bolts back, and his heart was pounding as he opened the door.

He stepped out into a wide, quiet, chilly nowhere, crossed only by the neglected driveway. Somewhere in the middle distance there was the sound of a tractor chugging. It felt as if the farm machine must be on a different continent. Around to his left Auntie Gwen's car was pulled up on a patch of ground off the track. Out here it looked more like an incongruous piece of garden sculpture than a vehicle. Gav couldn't picture an engine shrinking the big green-grey world around him, collapsing its miles to scant minutes, carrying him back to towns and timetables. He was on his feet, and there were only two ways to go: right, out the gate into the lane, or left, down the driveway under the trees. Right would mean starting back the way he came, in the direction of the little station, and then the big one, and then home. Jamming his hands down in his trouser pockets, he turned left.

As soon as he stepped onto the driveway he heard a skitter of feet. Down in the shadows under the trees, someone had run round the curve of the drive out of sight. Someone small, smaller than Gav. He'd seen no more than a vanishing blur of dark clothes when he'd looked up. He was going to shout, but the stillness made him shy; he couldn't break it. The footsteps faded quickly.

He waited a short while, watching, then shrugged and followed on down the road. Experience had long since taught him to do his uncomfortable best to ignore things that came and went around him.

He walked into a wood. It smelled secret and autumnal, the musk of a thick layer of leaf mould sodden by the night's rain. There were still brown and withered leaves on the branches above, obscuring the day. In among the trees some tangly evergreen shrub had spread and grown over head height. The driveway curved and descended, shutting out the light behind. For the first stretch it was pitted and mossy; then the paving gave out and it became a pair of gravel tracks overgrown with grass. There was no sign of whoever had run down here a minute earlier, if anyone had. *Oh come on Gav.* The track he followed felt increasingly like it led nowhere at all, as though he was the first person to set foot on it for years and years.

The long curve soon brought him in sight of the lower end of the wood. When he saw the corner of a building, he stopped.

Ahead, the overgrown track ran out from the trees into a wide clearing, on the far side of which Gav could now see a garden border, and immediately behind that the wall of a very old house: sea-grey stone, punctured seemingly at random by narrow arched windows that looked as if they were barred against daylight, and a slate roof streaked by rain.

Pendurra.

It didn't look like it wanted him anywhere near it. He felt ridiculously out of place. The thought of explaining himself to whoever lived here was more alarming to Gavin than facing disembodied voices and dead girls and whatever else Auntie Gwen's home might throw his way. The point where adults got involved was, he'd finally confirmed (thanks to Mr Bushy), always the point where everything fell apart.

Still, he had to ask someone about Auntie Gwen.

As more of the house came into view, though, he wondered whether there'd even be anyone to ask. He came out from under the trees into a scene of profound desertion. The buildings ahead seemed as dormant as the garden in front of them, winter-stiff. The driveway ran through a wet lawn of ankle-high grass to the front of an ancient, sullen building; heavy gables, small mismatched casemented windows on upper floors, chimney-stacks jutting up like solitary reefs. It was nothing like a ruin, but even in a partial glimpse it gave the impression that whoever might once have lived there had long since covered all the furniture in dustsheets, locked the doors behind them and left the place to see out the decades on its own.

Woodland spread away on either side like arms opening wide to embrace the house; left, down the slope, which began to descend more steeply, and right, along the flank of the hill. In the broad space bordered on each side by the sweep of the trees was a garden of dry stems, bare branches, brown seed heads left as relics of the last summer, and patches of evergreen. It looked as big as a small park to Gav, while the house was a manor, almost a castle. Except that – like the garden – it felt out of season, its romance faded.

The front doors were dead ahead. They were dark wood banded with iron, and if they'd been taller they wouldn't have looked out of place barring the entrance to a prison. The prospect of approaching them suddenly seemed unthinkable: scrunching over the gravel beneath the blank windows, climbing the single step, knocking. He felt like a boy in a fairy tale. He'd taken a wrong turn in the forest and ended up at the gates of an enchanted palace no one was supposed to find.

Stuck for a moment, unable to turn back or go on, he was rescued by the sight of the door opening. A man was coming out, half backwards, waving goodbye to someone inside. Gav stifled the urge to bolt out of sight. Better to look like he knew where he was than to be spotted disappearing behind a bush. The man looked up at him in surprise, squinting slightly through little round glasses. Gav felt his face settling into its habitual rigidly indifferent mask, his reflex when being squinted at by strangers. He made an effort to look less hostile.

The man's appearance helped. Everything about him exuded unthreatening friendliness, from his unaffected smile as he approached to his stripy sweater and his scuffed corduroy trousers. He was shortish, a bit stocky, neither young nor old and had the kind of unremarkably pleasant face that you find hard to remember afterwards. His presence completely changed the character of the house and grounds. All at once it just looked like a big old place in the country. For the first time that day Gav thought that maybe Auntie Gwen would turn up in a minute, falling over herself with apologies at having forgotten to pick him up, and they'd have a week's holiday together just as he'd been expecting when he got on the train.

He was just beginning to wonder why this thought made him achingly, unbearably sad when the man hailed him.

'You must be Gavin, Gwen's nephew. Hello, welcome!'

'Uh, yeah. Hi.'

It was an unspeakable relief not to have to explain who he was. In fact, he apparently didn't have to explain anything. The man shook his hand and smiled as if meeting him here was the most natural thing in the world.

'It's good to meet you. Quite a place, isn't it? I wish I could say I live here, but I'm just on my way home. I only stopped in to see Mr Uren. I'm Owen. Friend of the family. I live just up in the village. I'm the priest, for my sins.'

'Nice to meet you.'

'They've been looking forward to your arrival.' He nodded back in the direction of the front doors. 'Were you on your way to the house? I can introduce you, if you like. Since you're here. A bit less intimidating that way. Not that there's actually anything to be intimidated by. What do you think?'

Gav couldn't see an obvious way to mention Auntie Gwen and found that he was utterly unprepared to say anything else.

'Tristram wouldn't mind you knocking on the door yourself – they're expecting you – but since we met . . . Gwen'll be along in a bit, anyway, won't she.' Gav couldn't tell whether this was a guess or whether Owen knew it for a fact, and the confusion threw him off still further. 'But why don't I show you in now? That way you won't have to feel like a trespasser if you want to go on exploring on your own. It's that kind of place, isn't it,' he finished, motioning around encouragingly.

'Um, yeah.' Gav felt himself being shepherded towards the grim doors, but had no idea how to stop.

Owen seemed determined to put him at his ease no matter how long he had to go on. 'Mr Uren can seem a bit distant when you first meet him. Like his house, I suppose. They're both very different from what you or I are used to. At least I assume you don't live anywhere like this? London, wasn't it? But you'll feel right at home with him very soon, I promise you. Anyway, I needn't tell you – your aunt's known the place almost as long as I have. And she tells a good story, doesn't she?' Gav opened his mouth and tried to take the chance to say something, but Owen misinterpreted his stall as shyness and kept moving, encouraging Gav to follow. They'd reached the front door; Owen pushed it open. 'In we go. Tristram?'

The first impression was a brown dimness, like the inside of a chest. As in Gwen's house, the smell of woodsmoke came at once, but here it seemed part of the walls, the floor; the air was saturated with it. It was mixed with something else Gav couldn't put a name to, except that it smelled *old*. Not musty or fetid, but old as if from another age: odours of stone and straw and cloth, materials and fabrics that time had outgrown. Or perhaps it was just the effect of what he could see, which was nothing like any house he had ever been inside before, except maybe some old historic place near his other aunt's, which they'd all gone to visit one Sunday after lunch, years ago, because his mother had wanted to. There was no everyday household stuff in sight. He faced a hallway that stretched back through the house, wood on all sides including the ceiling. There was no light except the illumination from a triple-arched window at the far end.

'Tristram? Your guest is here.'

The hall darkened even more as a tall, bent figure stepped in front of the window.

In silhouette, Tristram Uren looked like an emaciated wizard. He leaned on a walking stick, a strong jaw jutting from a shaggy head that braced itself against the stoop of his back and shoulders. His clothes didn't seem to fit very well. A jacket hung around him like a half-finished cloak. Gavin felt as if he'd been admitted into the presence of Merlin, just escaped from the tomb where the stories said he'd been trapped since Arthur's time.

'Ahh.' The voice was full of effort. 'Come in, come in.'

'We met outside,' Owen explained, raising his voice a bit. 'Gavin here must be an early riser. He was walking down on his own.'

'Up with the sun, like me. But not, I imagine, down with it.' He came slowly forward, switched his stick to his left hand and extended his right. 'Hello, Gavin.'

Even stooping, he was much the taller. Gav looked up into a face of outcrops and shadows: the bones broad and strong, hollows between them. He had the oldest eyes Gav had ever seen apart from Miss Grey's. Their light had gone out. His hair was bone-white, though there was plenty of it, reaching almost to his shoulders. Gav saw what Owen had meant, now. It was hard to imagine this man making conversation. The Merlin thought stayed in his head. Mr Uren did look as if he'd spent a very long time shut away by himself.

'Hi. Sorry – I hope you didn't mind me wandering around?'

'Not at all. You shall have the freedom of Pendurra, while you're here.' He turned and waved towards the window with his stick. 'Do come in. Come and see your domain.'

'Actually, I was just coming to tell you something.' He blurted it out to stop anyone taking him further inside and now found himself groping for words. 'I mean, I thought I ought to tell someone. Aunt Gwen, she's . . .' Missing? Vanished? Gone? 'She's not around. I haven't seen her yet.'

They both looked at him. Mr Uren's brow creased into a slow frown.

'Perhaps she didn't expect you up this early. She often walks down to the river in the mornings.' At first Gav didn't understand and only stared at his toes, wishing as usual that he hadn't spoken.

Owen chipped in to relieve an embarrassing silence: 'You might run into her if you go on down that way. It's a lovely walk. Through the oldest woods.'

'Or make yourself comfortable here,' Mr Uren added. 'There's bacon. Guinivere will follow soon.'

'Probably wondering where you got to,' Owen said.

The dimness hid Gav's embarrassed flush. Two people had now told him that Auntie Gwen was about to turn up. He felt stupid, as if he'd made some obvious mistake about what she was doing. 'No, I mean I haven't seen her at all yet. Not just today.' Had he gone to the wrong place? He'd had no control at all over his journey. He'd got caught up in it somehow, like a stowaway. The thought reminded him of the one fact he was sure of. 'She was going to meet me at the station but she never turned up.'

Now both men were looking puzzled: Mr Uren blank, Owen slightly concerned.

'But then how did you get here?' Owen asked.

Gav's mouth dried. There was no way he was going to tell them that he'd got a lift from a woman he'd met on the train, especially one nationally known as 'the Nutty Professor'.

'Taxi,' he mumbled. 'I waited ages, then got a taxi.'

Fortunately they didn't seem interested. 'And there was no one at the lodge?'

Just in time to prevent another idiotic silence, he remembered that those gatehouse places on the fancy estates were called lodges. 'No, the lights were on and everything, and the door was open. Unlocked, I mean. So I just went in.' He didn't know whether he sounded more like a criminal or a halfwit. There were things that had happened yesterday that he couldn't possibly tell anyone. *I don't want to hear it, Gavin, do you understand?*

'And no one was there?' Owen was asking all the questions. Tristram Uren might as well have turned to stone.

'Well, there was a fire lit and . . . So I thought, you know, with the taxi gone' – he felt a little tingle of relief at this plausible-sounding detail – 'I'd just go in and wait. But no. No one.'

'The car was there,' Owen said to Mr Uren. 'I saw it when I came past earlier. Did you happen to notice it when you arrived, Gavin? When was this?'

In his memory the clock chimed. 'About six. Yeah, it was – the car, I mean. I saw it. And everything looked, you know, like she was there. The lights and the fires, and everything was just lying around, like normal. I mean it looked normal. So I just thought . . . I'd wait.' Don't try and explain, he told himself furiously. Never try and explain. It only makes everything worse.

'And you haven't seen her since?'

'No.'

'Well, that's odd. I wish someone had known.' He and Mr Uren were looking at each other now, something unreadable passing between them. 'It must have been a lonely night for you. Not a proper welcome at all! How strange. Tristram?'

'I haven't seen Guinivere since yesterday afternoon.' He spoke slowly. 'Though I wasn't expecting to. She did tell Marina she was going to the station, I believe.'

'She sent that message for me yesterday,' Owen said. He rubbed his chin. 'Wanted to see me today. I'd wait for her if I could, but I need to be going. I got the message from Caleb. I gather she sent him up to the village to look for me.'

'Yesterday?'

'Yes. I was at the parish meeting. Poor chap had to go round the houses a bit. I'm not sure what Gwen thought she was doing sending him off like that. Maybe I should go and ask him about it.'

'If you would,' Tristram said. 'Gavin, I'm sorry. You must be hungry at the least, and worried too. Here we were assuming you'd already had your introduction to Pendurra. Please come in, sit down.' His manner had become very deliberately courteous, almost too deliberately, as if the courtesy was meant to conceal the fact that his attention was on something else.

Owen had put on his appealing smile again. 'Your aunt does have a bit of a reputation,' he said, 'if you don't mind me saying so. Easily distracted, let's put it that way. Though she was so looking forward to your arrival, I must say I'm surprised she managed to get distracted from that. It's all she's been talking about these last few days. Especially the last day or two. I thought she was going to explode with excitement. I must go. I'll find Caleb on my way out, shall I?'

'Thank you,' Mr Uren answered, over his shoulder. He was leading Gavin slowly down the hall, past pictures whose faces and figures were lost in the gloom, around unnecessary chairs jutting out from the walls like rocks in a shipping lane. 'I will take care of my guest.'

Owen nodded at Gav encouragingly. 'Then I'll see what else I can do. Gavin, good to meet you. I'm sure I'll see you again. I'm the local bad penny, I keep turning up. Don't worry about Gwen – she won't have gone far.' He headed back towards daylight. 'Tell Marina I'm sorry I missed her,' he called.

Mr Uren answered only with a wave of his stick. The door thunked shut.

'You were lucky to meet Reverend Jeffrey first,' Tristram said. He seemed to be choosing his words carefully. 'He's a . . . reassuring presence.'

No one would have said the same about Tristram Uren. Gav remembered a photo from Auntie Gwen's scrapbook. A formal portrait, black and white, in uniform, the picture of a dashing war hero. Its old-fashioned glamour had stuck in his mind. Not a trace of the confidence and energy of the handsome man in the old photo remained in Mr Uren now. He looked more akin to the inhabitants of the portraits hanging in the hallway, nameless faces captured looking hollow and remote and then forgotten, left to their inheritance of dust and soot. He addressed Gavin kindly, but still as if he was forcing himself to mind his manners.

'We can at least warm you up. There's a fire in the front room.'

Gav couldn't see what else to do or where else to go.

'Nice, thanks.'

'You managed all right last night, on your own?'

'Yeah, yeah, I was fine.' Well, apart from the corpse moaning and banging on the door outside. 'Aunt Gwen had everything set up.'

'That's something at least. She is an immensely capable woman.'

Gav was about to give a sarcastic snort when it struck him, first, that Mr Uren had meant the comment completely seriously, and second, that he had never in his life heard anyone say anything nice about Auntie Gwen before, let alone call her 'capable'. He was ashamed of his first reaction and took a moment to weigh his reply, so he could say what he was really thinking.

'She's great. Always been my favourite relative, by far.'

Mr Uren must have registered the sincerity in his tone. He stopped and looked round at Gavin again. It was a bit like watching a tree bend in a strong wind.

'She speaks very highly of you too, Gavin. You should have seen her when the letter from your mother arrived. I was almost offended to find out that she isn't exclusively devoted to us.'

This sounded like it ought to have been a joke, though nothing in Mr Uren's expression suggested that it was; it was a face drained of levity. Gavin must have looked uneasy, and Mr Uren misunderstood his discomfort.

'There's no need to be anxious,' he went on. 'If she's on the estate, my friend Caleb will find her, and if she isn't, Reverend Jeffrey will track her down, or start the right people looking. We're all used to her ways here, as she is to ours. Come and see some of what she wanted you to see, while we wait.'

The hall widened at the other side of the house, at the foot of an uneven but grand staircase. Following Mr Uren's gesture, a couple more steps brought Gav to the window and now at last he saw what the house saw.

Pendurra looked down across an open field and a long wood below to the mouth of a river and beyond it, glimpsed as a horizon of luminous grey laid over the green humps and folds, the sea.

Though he was a city child, Gavin wasn't totally unfamiliar with trees and grass and water. Even around his home he knew where to find them. He knew they meant space, quiet space, places to escape into, and so he'd already learned to like them. This, though, was something altogether different. It was as if the little secret havens of nettle and bramble, the patches of unbuilt or overgrown cityscape he'd known all his life, were seedpods, and here, now, they had burst open, their tentative promise of solitude blossoming into a whole world of stillness. There was a rhythm and a completeness to the landscape: a pattern of wild and tame, the patch fields and the pockets of woodland dipping and rising around the riverbanks, the river itself closed among them, almost out of sight but still threading the land and the ocean together. He barely took in the details of what he saw. He was feeling like he'd discovered the magic wardrobe in the spare room, the rusty gate in the untrodden back alley that opened into another world.

'A rather dreary morning, I'm afraid,' Mr Uren said quietly. He too was staring out towards the sea. 'I had hoped last night's rain would clear it all away.' He sighed and beckoned Gav towards an open door across the hall.

The room they entered looked slightly less like something you'd have to pay to go and see, although only slightly. It was recognisably a living room, one that people actually lived in. Though it was big and (like everything else Gavin had seen in the house) impressive in an old-fashioned way, it was also shabby with use and age, corners dusty, surfaces dull. It stretched along the back of the house, the side that looked down towards the sea. Three deep windows let in the daylight. On the opposite wall a fire burned in a stone hearth big enough for Gav to have comfortably sat inside. In between was an assortment of the kind of furniture he associated with those fancy antique shops that never had any people inside: big, ornate, mismatched, dull-coloured things that had been made, by hand, solidly enough to endure even when they started to look decrepit, as these did. Mr Uren invited Gavin to sit at a table in front of the middle window, where two people had obviously just finished eating. He left him there while he went out through a door by the fireplace, promising to come back with more food. Gav didn't much want to sit, or to eat, but to his surprise he wasn't starting to feel trapped. All he did was stare out of the window. Nothing was moving but the occasional seagull.

Mr Uren had barely returned, rather shakily carrying a brown teapot which gave off a smell that didn't seem much like tea, when he looked up from under his heavy brows, over Gav's shoulder.

'Ah, here we are at last!'

His face lit up. Actually lit up: the light was rekindled in his eyes, and a mass of shadow somehow disappeared in an instant from his expression.

'Here I am, Daddy,' said a voice behind Gav.

He turned.

The dead girl had just walked in.

Seven

THERE WAS NO mistaking her. Though her hair was dry and her eyes were open and her fingers were fiddling absently with the strings of her entirely unsinister pink pyjamas, he recognised her straight away, with such certainty that his heart gave a sickening leap of surprise at the sight of her come to life. He now saw that her beaky face was a softer echo of Tristram's, and though she didn't look older than twelve or thirteen, there was already a gawky, bony awkwardness about her that she'd also inherited from him, a slender child's version of his tall stoop. He was sure he could see traces of earth and grime on her finger and toenails. It was her. She had wailed and clattered outside his door at midnight and now here she was, looking at him with a brightly curious expression and a funny lopsided smile.

'You're Gavin,' she said.

Despite the pink pyjamas, the image of her as a walking corpse was taking a while to clear out of his head and he couldn't answer.

'Gwen says that because I'm like a daughter to her, that makes us sort of cousins.' She came and sat down next to him, picked up a crust of someone else's cold toast and began chewing, leaning into her father as he bent to kiss the top of her head. Abruptly her expression turned anxious. 'Should I have said that?' she asked, through a mouthful of food. 'You don't mind?'

'Sounds good to me,' Gav said, and was rewarded by a visible outbreak of relief on her face. Her features seemed to catch and magnify every expression, like a much younger child's. That was what had made her appear so lifeless in the night. Her face had been not just unmoving but entirely empty, switched off as thoroughly as it was now switched on.

'I haven't got a family, mostly,' she went on, licking a fingertip to dab at crumbs on the plate. Gav saw that Tristram, who had started back towards the kitchen, stiffened. 'Do you have lots of cousins already?'

'Er, no.' She appeared not to know what shyness was. This was an idea so extraordinary to Gav that he forgot to be surly himself. 'Not a single one, in fact.'

'Like me, then. Gwen said you mostly didn't have a family too, but—'

'Marina!'

She dropped her eyes to the plate.

'My daughter has a rather solitary life here, Gavin.' Once again, Tristram seemed to be picking his words very deliberately. 'Please excuse her manners. She's very young for her age.'

'No, it's OK.' He saw that she was chewing her lip. 'No offence at all. Anyway, you're right,' and as he spoke he realised it was true. He took defiant pride in saying it. 'I don't really. Not a proper one. So, yeah, cousins, I like that.' She brightened instantly, raising her thin eyebrows and wordlessly mouthing *sorry* to him. He tried to think of something harmless to say, but he had no practice at it. He'd spent the past couple of years learning to stop conversations, not start them.

Tristram let his hand rest on her shoulder and then frowned and peered downwards. 'You should wash your hands, treasure. Look at your nails.'

She did, spreading them all in front of her face. 'I already did. What's wrong with them?' Now Gav could see that her left hand – the one that had been battering Auntie Gwen's door – was bruised along the side. Tristram noticed it too: he took her hand in his and turned it gently in the light. His brow wrinkled again as he let it go, but he said nothing. Gav was quite relieved to see him shuffle back towards the kitchen, since Marina now reached down and pulled one of her feet up onto the table, looking at it quizzically.

'I did get pretty filthy, didn't I,' she said. Gav had to agree. Her toenails were even more stained than her fingers. The skin on the sole of her foot was like an adult's, hard and calloused. She stole a look over her shoulder and leaned closer to Gav, earnestly. 'I go wandering out of bed when I'm asleep sometimes, and when I wake up, I don't remember it. So they tell me.'

Gavin lowered his voice to a whisper. 'Hey, me too.'

Her eyes went huge. They were grey-blue, like the patches of clearer sky above the horizon.

'At least I used to,' he went on, 'when I was a kid, I mean, when I was younger. How old are you?'

'Gwen says I'm thirteen.'

He ignored the odd answer. 'Yeah, that's about how old I was when I sleepwalked. It's fine. Won't hurt you.'

She looked over her shoulder again to be sure her father was still in the other room and leaned even further forward; floppy blonde hair fell over her nose. 'My hand's sore. And I got unbelievably wet. That's why I'm late this morning. I've been trying to dry out my room before Gwen comes.'

Something began to sizzle in the next room.

'Did you ever go outside?' she asked. 'When it happened to you?'

'Yeah, I did.' Gav remembered with horrible vividness the plummeting of his heart when he woke to smudges on the sheets and the carpet of his bedroom, and his impotent efforts to hide them: remaking his bed as quietly as he could, dropping clothes on the floor to cover the stains. During one bad spell he'd got in the habit of sneaking a damp cloth into his room before he went to sleep, so he could scrub away any evidence in the morning. *Gavin, for God's sake, what are you doing in there?*

'I don't think I've ever gone out of the house before. I'm afraid to tell anyone.'

'You're telling me.'

'You're not a grown-up. Are you? How old are you?'

'Fifteen.'

'Is that grown up?'

She wasn't teasing. The seriousness was plain on her face.

'No, course not.' Her eyes dropped again and her mouth scrunched up. 'Well,' he added hurriedly, 'I mean, I'm still growing. Like, getting taller. But I'm not a kid, so . . .'

When people spoke to each other at school, it was all about trying to make each other laugh, and at the same time making sure you weren't the one being laughed at. Even with friends, when you wanted to be serious, you kept your guard up. Marina was already making him think of the time before his world had turned against him, when all you had to do was say what was happening, and that was fine.

'The grown-ups keep an eye on me,' she mumbled, not looking up. 'You don't have to, though, so it's different.'

'Yeah, that's right,' Gav said, though he didn't know what she meant. 'So Aunt Gwen's kind of like an extra parent here?'

'Ever since I was a baby, she says, and until I'm a woman. I wonder where she's got to.' An odd frown twitched over her face, as if she'd surprised herself by remembering something. Gav suddenly didn't want to be the person to tell her that Auntie Gwen was gone, but fortunately it didn't occur to Marina to ask him about it. She peered vaguely out of the window. 'Do you wish she'd looked after you instead?'

'What?' he said, and immediately wished he hadn't. Her eyes went anxious again.

'Gwen told me . . . or maybe I'm not supposed to say this.'

'No, no, it's fine. I know what you mean, actually. Actually, yes, I do. Wish she had. And' – he started blushing with the effort of saying it – 'you know, it's OK – you can ask anything you like. Most people don't bother.'

'Gwen said that too. She said I have hardly anyone to talk to, but at least they listen, but you have lots of people but they don't listen, which makes me better off.'

Gav was pretty sure he remembered what thirteen-year-olds were supposed to be like, and this wasn't it. But then, wasn't Mum always worrying that he wasn't acting like what she called a 'normal teenager'? Was this what it was like for adults when they met Gav? No, it couldn't be, because although Marina didn't make very much sense, he knew straight away that he liked her company, and adults didn't like his company. Not any more.

'Yeah, you probably are,' he answered. And all at once he could just say what he was thinking. It seemed simple, as natural as breathing, but he couldn't remember the last time he'd been able to reach into himself and pluck out the words as easily as picking berries from brambles. 'My mum and dad don't like me much, especially Dad. I'd have loved it if Aunt Gwen had been around. But then, she was happier here, you know?'

'She told you she liked looking after me better?'

'No. I mean, I just know. Actually, she never told me anything about—'

He was going to say 'you' but could see her face falling already. 'This place.'

'Really? Odd. What do you think, then? Do you like it?'

'It's . . . amazing. Living here, I can't imagine that.'

'Gwenny's always saying it's better than anywhere else.' She stared out of the window, into the grey distance. 'Though sometimes I think she just says it to make me not mind.'

Her father was coming back, a plate of bacon and fried bread tilting in his hand. She skipped quickly out of her chair and took the plate to the table, where she picked up a piece of bacon in her fingers before putting it back quickly with a muttered 'Whoops' and a nervous smile.

'Gavin has explained about Guinivere?' Tristram settled creakily into a chair. 'No? Well, sweetheart, it appears she may be a little late this morning.' He poured out some greeny-brown version of tea; it smelled suspiciously like grass. Gav was immediately much less hungry than he thought.

'Where's she gone?'

Tristram looked at Gavin; Gavin looked at his plate.

'No one seems to know yet. Ah, Caleb.'

Again Gav had to turn round to see who had come in.

Standing in the doorway was a man who looked at first sight like a cross between a gardener and a pirate. The gardener half had gnarled hands and wellies and muddy clothes and an obvious discomfort at finding himself inside the house. The pirate half was dark-eyed and dangerous-looking, with very long, very straggly black hair, and a general impression of belonging somewhere far away and lawless. He glanced at Gav and nodded awkwardly, without smiling.

'This is Guinivere's nephew, Gavin.'

'Hi.' Gav thought about standing up, twitched stupidly and stopped. Caleb did not look welcoming.

''lo.'

'Gavin, my friend Caleb, without whom we would all be lost. And speaking of lost . . .'

'She isn't here,' Caleb said. He had a strong West Country accent, which chimed perfectly with both halves, the gardener and the brigand.

'I thought not,' said Tristram. He obviously felt that Caleb had settled the question. 'Well, Gavin, your aunt must have been caught up in one of her outside interests. There's nothing to be concerned about. She'll be back later today, I'm certain. Perhaps she remembered too late that she was supposed to meet you and is looking for you in Truro.'

Oh God, no, Gavin thought. It hadn't occurred to him. What if she hadn't got Hester's message? What if she tried to call Mum and Dad?

'Do you know when she left, Caleb?' Tristram asked.

''fore dark yesterday.'

'Did you see her go?'

'No.' Caleb shook his head.

If Gav had been paying attention he might have found this exchange odd, but he wasn't. Sick to his stomach again, he was imagining his parents cutting their holiday short, getting a flight home. His father wouldn't say anything at all. He wouldn't need to; his silence would just make Mum feel worse, which would be all he'd want. When they found him and brought him home, he'd be able to enjoy weeks of twisting her guilt tighter anytime he felt like it.

'But she told you she wanted to see Reverend Jeffrey today?'

'Ah,' Caleb muttered, a curt affirmative. 'Asked me yesterday to find him an' let him know. Took a while to track him down.'

'She didn't say what she wanted to see him about?'

'No. Don't mind, though. Good walk.' Caleb was clearly edgy. His glance flickered around the room.

'And you told her when you got back?'

'Didn't see her. Still here, though.'

'Thank you,' Tristram said quietly. 'Then we must leave Reverend Jeffrey to sort it all out.'

'Alrigh'y.' Clearly relieved to be going, Caleb nodded. 'Morning, Marina.' He winked at her, piratically, an unexpected puncture in his surliness; she blew him back a kiss as he disappeared into the hallway.

Despite Mr Uren's reassurances, they all looked uneasy. Reassurance wouldn't have come naturally to him, anyway. Marina concentrated on eating; he watched her silently, oblivious to Gavin, who had the feeling that Tristram's dulled eyes were taking in nothing at all.

Marina looked up, holding her knife in mid-air. 'If Gwen's not coming till later, why don't I take Gavin out to the point?'

Tristram blinked. 'Why, yes, my sweet. Or wherever you wish, if he agrees. I had hoped you would. As long as you're careful.'

'Yes, of course.'

The knot in Gav's stomach loosened. Thinking about his parents had suddenly made him dread the coming day, as if a phone might ring somewhere in the house at any moment, summoning him back. The exchanges between Owen and Tristram and Caleb had made it worse. He couldn't help feeling there was something they weren't saying in front of him. He'd vaguely assumed Marina would go off to school, leaving him adrift in the dark old house. The prospect of getting outside – Gav had no idea where or what the 'point' was, but she'd said 'out' – made everything a little better. He certainly wasn't going to ask why she wasn't going to school. No one had put the same question to him; the least he could do was return the courtesy. Plus, whatever kind of place this was, he could tell – he could feel – that it wasn't meant for questions from outside. It held its secrets, as he held his. He understood what that was like.

'That'd be great,' he said.

'Good!' She hopped out of her chair, dropping her knife so that it clattered on the plate. 'Then let's—'

'Marina! Let Gavin finish, please.'

'No, it's OK,' Gav said quickly, taking a last bite and pushing back his chair. 'Thanks very much, but I've had plenty. I had some toast at . . .' and he realised he didn't want to say Auntie Gwen's name in case it made them solemn again '. . . at, um, earlier. Thanks anyway.'

Marina bounced on her tiptoes and spun behind her father's chair. 'I should get clothes, shouldn't I?'

'Yes, you should.'

She leaned round to kiss his cheek. 'Just a minute, then,' and she ran out. Gav heard her feet on the stairs.

She was back in the time it took Tristram to wave away Gavin's perfunctory offer to help tidy up breakfast and direct him to a bathroom. He'd somehow expected the kitchen and bathroom to be different from the rest of the house, like when you visited a cathedral or a castle and found a modern toilet block hiding inside stone walls and arched doors, next to a café where everything was plastic and stainless steel. But the kitchen was completely in keeping with the rest of what he'd seen, thick with smoky warmth and streaked on its rough white walls with soot. There was wood stacked against a wall between great antique stoves of blackened bricks; iron pans and kettles hung above. It looked more like a historical recreation of a kitchen than a place where anyone could actually cook food, and, alarmingly, the same kind of surprise met him in the bathroom, although after a period of embarrassing indecision Gav had found a handle that made something a bit like flushing happen. Better than anywhere else? Was that really what Auntie Gwen thought? It was a useful reminder that she was in fact crazy.

Marina was waiting at the foot of the stairs. Her father had vanished. Gav got the impression that he'd been transferred to someone else's care, and Mr Uren, released from his slow courtesy, was now free to ignore him. It wasn't a resentful feeling. The man had been polite enough, but Gav was much happier with him gone. What was it he'd said? *You shall have the freedom of Pendurra. While you're here*, but Gav was determined not to think about the end of his freedom, for as long as he could get away with it.

'All right?' Marina smiled. She'd tied most of her blonde hair back behind her head with a ribbon, but quite a few bits had been missed and were falling in random tufts around her ears and eyes. It made her look even younger, as did the brown jumper that was a size or two too big for her. She also appeared to be wearing slippers or moccasins; whatever they were, they were leathery and soft and didn't look right for going outside. Nevertheless she led him down the dim hallway to the door and, lifting an iron latch – the grey daylight briefly dazzled him – stepped out onto the gravel.

Crows drifted in and out of the fringes of the wood. Marina led him through a gap in a low stone wall and into an enclosed area of the garden where paths of unkempt grass ran between mostly barren flowerbeds. She chatted happily as they went, always halting to make sure he was right behind her; he felt like she'd trip over her own legs at any moment. He'd have liked to slow down and look around, or at least have a chance to take in the strangely antiquated scene in silence, but trying both to keep up and not to bump into her as she started and stopped used up most of his concentration, and whatever was left over he needed just to pretend to follow her enthusiastic chatter. She seemed to want to show him and tell him everything at once. She named each clump of green or brown and each tangle of sticks as they passed, with the manner of a museum guide introducing much-loved paintings. The botanical names meant nothing to him, though he quickly realised that everything in her world meant everything to her, so he did his best to nod and 'uh-huh' on cue. As far as he could see, the garden was just a rather sad mess of droopy green and dead brown. There were other things he wished she'd start explaining, but she seemed to get stuck on whatever was nearest. He didn't want to sound bored, though, so he made an effort to think of something he could contribute involving gardening. He remembered looking out of Auntie Gwen's kitchen window into her little garden plot and seeing that bush with its incongruously luxuriant pink flowers.

'Oh yeah. What about—'

'What?' she said, stopping abruptly on a narrow path; he nearly lost his balance pulling up short behind her.

'I just remembered. You know in the garden at Aunt Gwen's house? There's a really nice something I saw there. Some kind of rose maybe?'

'Yes! I know the one you mean. It is a rose. It's called Madeleine. It's got these outrageously pink flowers in summer. Pinker than pink.'

In the summer.

Of course.

She must have seen something in his face, because she stopped talking. They'd come to the far end of the walled garden, where an overgrown iron gate led out to a path between one side of the house and the edge of the wood.

What she saw in his face was not belated surprise at a rosebush blossoming on one of the shortest days of the year. No: the thing that stopped her short was the mingled fear and astonishment in his eyes as he realised he was about to tell her something; the unfamiliar effort of choosing to talk instead of keeping silent.

'Is everything all right?' Her oddly lopsided jaw had fallen half open.

'That rose, it's got flowers now. All over. I saw it this morning.'

She looked at him, head tilted.

'But it's winter,' she said, in a tone of voice Gav knew all too well. *But there's no one there, Gav. But that's impossible, Gav. Don't be stupid, Gavin.* He remembered again why he didn't tell people things.

'Oh yeah.' He looked up at the sky. 'So it is. Must have missed that somehow.'

'Roses don't flower in winter,' she said reasonably.

'They don't?'

'No.' Apparently she was as immune to irony as shyness. 'None of the bushes do. They need it to be warmer. They eat the sun, sort of.'

He watched her face, looking for veiled mockery, but she appeared to have been born without those veils. It was part of what made her look so much younger.

'Oh right,' he said.

'So it can't—'

'I'll show you.'

'What?'

Anywhere else, with anyone else, he'd have let it go. Forget it. My mistake. Clam up. Silently add it to the long list of small humiliations with which he recorded his days.

But Marina didn't seem to think he was stupid, or ridiculous, or lying. She just seemed mildly confused, as if she was in the middle of working out a not very complicated sum. To his surprise, he discovered that he wasn't afraid of what she might say.

It occurred to him that he couldn't remember the last time he'd felt that about any conversation with anyone.

'Come on,' he said. 'I'll show you. See for yourself.'

Her eyes twitched anxiously back to the house. 'But I said I'd take you to the point.'

'OK, we can do whatever afterwards. It's just up the drive.' It was an impossible thing, of course. He could only have missed realising it because he got so many other things wrong, all the time. Roses didn't flower like that in the last days of November. But he'd seen it, it was there, and he was suddenly sure that Marina was also different enough from everyone else he knew that she ought to see it too. 'It'll only take a minute. Yeah?'

'I'm not really supposed to go that way,' she mumbled.

'What? Why not?'

'It's not good for me.'

'What isn't?'

'Going, you know. By the gate.' The word 'gate' came out with a tiny clutch in the throat, as if she'd said 'graveyard' or 'quicksand'.

'You mean you never go to the lodge? Aunt Gwen's house?'

Her hands fidgeted. 'Yes, I've been there a few times, but I'm not supposed—'

'You did last night.'

'What?'

'Last night, when you were sleepwalking. I saw you.'

She stared wide-eyed. Her voice fell to a guilty whisper. 'Did you? Where?'

'Come on.' He started back towards the path and after a few moments she followed. 'I was in the room downstairs and I heard this banging on the door and I looked out of the window and it was you.'

'Me?'

'Look at your hand. No, the other one. See that bruise on the side?'

She turned her wrists as if wringing out an invisible towel, so he took the right one in his hand, feeling as he did so a strange blush that seemed to go down from his face into his chest rather than the other way around. Her hand was very small and very alive. He twisted it over gently and pointed out the mark.

'There. See? That's from banging the door. Aunt Gwen's.'

Then he was holding her hand up close to both their faces, the two of them leaning together, and she was looking up at him with her unnervingly defenceless expression, and nothing else was happening at all as the distended seconds passed by. He dropped her hand. The blush turned round and started going in the normal direction. He set off again, to conceal it.

She scurried beside him. 'What else did you see me do?'

'Not much. You stood there whacking the door for a while. Then it was like you gave up and sort of slunk off. You scared me shitless, actually.'

'You were frightened? Why?'

Once more he glanced at her sharply, trying to catch something that would expose her innocent-sounding question as a trick. Once again he found nothing.

'Well, OK, I had no idea who you were or anything, I just heard this banging in the middle of the night—'

'The middle of the night?'

'Yeah. Actually it was almost exactly midnight. And so I look out the window and there's someone I never set eyes on in my life, wearing like a sheet or something, and you're hammering and shouting at—'

'Shouting?'

Her voice had shrunk with sudden fear. For a confused moment he wondered if it would help if he stopped and held her hand again, but the moment passed, as such moments do.

'OK, not shouting really, just talking.'

'What did I say?'

'Not sure.' He tried not to think about the eerie moan. *Come back, come back.* 'I couldn't really tell.'

'I had a dream.' They were in under the trees. It couldn't have been an hour since Gavin had walked the other way down this same path, but already it felt as if that journey had taken him into a new country, a new world, like the night passage in Hester's car. 'I definitely did, but I can't remember it at all. Did you ever have that feeling when you went out in your sleep? Like something happened it was incredibly important to remember, but you couldn't?'

'Kind of the opposite, actually.' He could hardly believe he was saying it, putting into words something he would never have said aloud even to himself. 'Most of my dreams it's really really important to try and forget.'

He waited for her to ask what she meant, but for once she was quiet. Perhaps he'd finally said something in her language, something that didn't need translating.

'Anyway,' he went on, 'let me show you that rose, OK? I know you don't believe me about it, but it's there.'

'Hey! I never said I didn't believe you!'

'Yeah, well, I could tell. I've had a lot of practice.'

'Practice?'

'With people not believing me.'

'You have? OK, try me again.'

'What?'

'Try again. See if you can tell.'

'Um . . .'

'Tell me something and then tell me if I believe you or not. It's a test. A what-do-you-call-it? It's how you find things out. An expedient.'

'Experiment?'

'That's it! Go on, then.'

She appeared to be completely serious. He was going to tell her that it wasn't a game, that it was actually the whole story of his miserable life, but she was looking at him with such an air of earnest anticipation that he didn't have the heart.

'Er. OK. So. There's this rose in Aunt Gwen's garden and it's flowering. Now, today. Even though it's winter and everything. How's that?'

She was shaking her head. 'Useless. Do a new one.'

'Why? That's not unbelievable enough for you?'

'Just for fun. Otherwise it's boring.'

He felt a twist of anger. Boring? Fun? How could she have any idea what it was like for him?

'Right, then.' He stopped on the driveway. They were under the trees at the edge of the wood, the lodge beyond. His face felt hot and he spoke too fast. 'Try this one. There's a woman nobody except me can see. She's followed me around my whole life, but she doesn't actually exist. I was sitting on the train down here yesterday and she got on and shouted at me. How's that? Believe me?'

Something odd happened to Marina's face. Her hands went slowly to cover her open mouth, and her eyes opened wide. He braced himself for whatever she was about to say. *Oh come on Gav.* But he never found out what it was, because in the stunned silence that followed his confession the door of the lodge opened. The gardener-pirate Caleb emerged, looked down the track and saw them.

'Hoi!' He waved as if to shoo them back into the woods. Still tingling with the adrenaline fizz of having told Marina – told anyone – what he just had, Gavin stood his ground. Shut up, he hissed silently at himself. Stop letting all this stuff out. It'll only make it worse. But he was still wondering why doing it had felt almost like a relief when Caleb strode down to them.

'Hey.' He propped his hands on his hips. 'Where're you two off to?'

Marina looked at Gav. 'We were just going to look at something in Gwen's garden.'

'Whose idea was that, then?'

'Gavin's. He thought—'

'You can't go up by the gate.' He straddled the track like a sentry, barring their way. 'You know that.'

'We weren't going to. Just to the lodge.'

He glared at them as if he thought Gavin might have been trying to abduct her. 'Thought you were heading out the other way.'

'We're going to. Right after Gavin shows me something.'

Gav stared at his toes, cheeks burning again. Now Marina was making him sound like some kind of pervert.

'Nothing to see in there,' Caleb said, with a finality even she couldn't miss.

'Oh. All right.'

'Don't want you wandering around this morning, OK?'

This was how it always was with adults, Gav told himself bitterly. How could he have thought Pendurra would be any different? He'd hardly met this bloke and already it was obvious that Caleb thought he'd done something wrong.

'What do you mean? Why not?'

Caleb twisted the lanky hair behind his neck. His look kept straying over their shoulders, as if something might be lurking there. 'Jus' don't want you to. There's a good lass. All right?'

'But Daddy said—'

''s only for an hour or two. Couple of things I want to check on first. All right?'

'Is everything OK?'

'Course.' Even to Gavin, who'd only met Caleb that morning, this sounded totally unconvincing, but Marina apparently accepted it at once.

'Well,' she said meekly, 'OK.'

'Good lass. You could show your friend here round the house.'

'Actually Gavin's my cousin.'

'Cousin, then. Lots to see indoors.'

'But we can do that when it gets dark! I want to—'

'Jus' this morning. Promise?'

'OK, then.' She crossed her arms over her chest. 'Is something wrong?'

'Course not. 's only . . .' He stared down into the sombre mass of winter trees. 'Might be someone poking around. Jus' like to keep an eye on things.'

Gav remembered the small figure he'd glimpsed for a moment as he'd left the lodge that morning, but there was no way he was going to say anything. At least half of Caleb's surliness felt like it was directed at him, and his only defence was the old one: tight-lipped silence.

'Someone's come in?' Marina sounded disproportionately alarmed by the idea.

'Dunno. Let me worry about that, all right? Anyway, you promised now.' He cracked a grim smile and prodded her arm.

'But what about the garden? Gavin—'

'Doesn't matter,' Gav said. 'Come on.' He started back towards the house without waiting for her. What would be the point, anyway? he thought. Even if they went to see that rose, he knew it would be dry and dead. *You're imagining things. Oh come on Gav.* No need to go looking for humiliation when it seemed to be able to find him all by itself.

'Good lass,' Caleb said from behind him. 'You and your friend go enjoy yourselves. Inside, though.'

'Cousin,' Marina corrected.

'Cousin,' he echoed, but the tone said, *Stranger, outsider. Enemy*. Gav quickened his stride.

She trotted to catch up, her peculiar shoes swishing through the grass and damp leaves that cracked through the decayed driveway. 'Hey! Wait for me.'

'Sorry if I got us into trouble,' he said glumly, as she came alongside.

'We're not in trouble. Caleb said everything's fine.'

Gav looked back. The man had already disappeared from sight.

'He didn't seem too happy.'

'Oh, that's how Caleb always looks.'

'Yeah. Well, I don't think he likes me being here.'

'You? Don't be silly.'

'Oh yeah? Didn't exactly seem like he wanted to be friendly, did he? I've had warmer welcomes. Well, maybe I haven't, actually.'

She looked at him curiously for a few quickened strides, skipping to keep up.

'You're unhappy, aren't you,' she said matter-of-factly.

'Nah. This is how I always look.'

Again she missed his irony completely. 'No, it's not. You wanted to talk to me, back in the house. When you told me about sleepwalking. That was good. Now you're being growly, like Caleb.'

He stopped and faced her, about to snap something, anything that would shut her up and drive her away, make her leave him alone. She watched him, head tilted, quizzical. Something about her look held him back. After a few moments he realised what it was. She was examining him without contempt, or anxiety, or bewilderment. It struck him that he couldn't remember the last time he'd seen a look like that directed at him.

So he said, 'Sorry.'

'That's OK. Gwen told me most people don't understand you. She said it makes you sad.'

He snorted. 'She got that right.'

'She says the things that happen when you're young mark you on the outside. The same way you can make trees grow in weird shapes if you bend them when they're still soft. Like with Caleb, that's why he always looks like that. Gwen calls him Grumplestiltskin. Well, not to his face; that would be a bit harsh. She says it's because he ran away from home. No one was ever kind to him before Daddy and by then it was too late.'

'What about me then? Do I look pissed off?'

'Look what?'

'Pissed off.'

'What does that mean?'

Again, there wasn't the slightest sign that she was teasing.

'Um. Cross.'

'Oh. Sorry.' She stepped alarmingly close to examine his face. Her glassy eyes darted from side to side, full of restless life. 'No,' she said at last. 'You look . . . what's that word? Like glum, but a bit more serious.'

'Miserable?'

His humour was obviously too black for her to see. 'No, not that. Sort of in between. Morbose?'

'Morose?'

'That's it!'

'I look morose. Cool. Thanks.'

Now her face fell. 'Sorry.'

'Never mind. It's totally fair enough. My life is shit. I just never knew it was so obvious.'

'Shit?'

He could only stare. The tenor of the stare must have been obvious even to her.

'I didn't mean you don't look nice,' she mumbled apologetically, looking away.

'It's OK. Nice things don't happen to me.'

'Sorry.'

'Not your fault. I should have done what he did. Caleb. Run away from home. Ages ago.'

She looked sideways at him, shyly, hesitating to ask, but eventually her curiosity won out.

'So why didn't you?'

'Why didn't I run away?'

'Yes.'

He looked around at the snagging undergrowth on either side, the decrepit track running between. In the last couple of years he'd thought about it often enough. Seriously thought about it, not just indulging vengeful childish dreams. He'd lain in bed carefully planning it out. Every time he came to the same dead end in the plan. Stealing the money, OK; packing and leaving and buying a ticket, OK; and then going . . . where? That was the problem. The first few parts were wonderful to imagine – the triumphant ecstasy of escaping from his parents, cutting loose and leaving it all behind him – but then came the realisation that wherever he tried to go instead, he'd still be himself. There was no escape from that.

'I didn't have anywhere to go,' he said.

'You should have come here, like Caleb did.'

Easy for you to say, he was about to retort, but he could tell she'd meant it honestly. A shiver of wind stirred the last leaves overhead, and at the sound he gazed up and around, into the spaces full of calm shadow, the subtle unobtrusive browns of bark and litter and earth.

'You're right, you know. I should have.'

This won him a vivid smile.

'Well, now you're here, it's not a problem any more, is it? You can just stay.'

She said this the way she said almost everything else: as if it were obvious. Gav wondered for a moment whether it was worth trying to explain to her what the real world was like. It was plain to him by now that she was some kind of little rich girl with a silver spoon in her mouth and no idea how everyone else lived. Least of all him. Maybe, he thought, it would just be easier to say, 'Never mind,' and go back to the house and play hide-and-seek or whatever it was you did with kids who had a social age somewhere around eight.

Then it occurred to him that he wasn't the most reliable authority on how the real world worked either.

An odd feeling stirred in him with that thought. He looked at Marina, bright, untroubled, weirdly innocent. So innocent that she'd apparently just invited him to live with her, here, for ever.

The idea hung in front of him like a glimpse of paradise. Forbidden, out of reach, but almost unbearably beautiful.

He sighed. 'It doesn't work like that.'

'What doesn't?'

'I can't just . . . move.'

'There's loads of room in the house.'

'Yeah, I'm sure there is. That's not the point. You can't just . . . There's school and home and stuff.' Even the words felt like descending weights. 'I'm only here 'cos Mum and Dad had a holiday booked already and no one who could be around in the day so they needed somewhere to send me when I got— when I couldn't go to school for a bit. As soon as they're back I have to go home.'

'Do you really?'

'Course. Not everyone gets to live like this all the time.'

'I know that. But didn't you say they don't like you, your parents?'

'Yeah, I did.'

'So why go back there? Gwen likes you a lot. I do too, even though you look whatever it is. Morose.' She grinned an unexpectedly sly grin.

'Yeah, yeah, yeah. You'd be the same if you lived in my house.'

'Then don't. Stay here. We could talk. Gwen says you probably know what it's like for me better than anyone. You already did, about the sleep-walking, remember?'

Why can't I?

'Mum and Dad would never let me.'

'I don't get that. If they don't like you, why wouldn't they let you come and live here instead?'

Because that's not how things work. Because that's not how the real world works. Oh, come on, Marina.

He took a deep breath. What had got into him that he was suddenly sounding like Dad?

He made himself think seriously about her question. It wasn't as stupid as it sounded, really. It was all too obvious that he and his parents had been making each other miserable for a couple of years now. What was it, actually, that made them all keep going?

'It's 'cos they think they do,' he said at last. 'They don't actually like me, but they think they do. Or at least Mum thinks she does.' *Take care of yourself, Gav love. I love you!* 'Dad's stopped even trying to pretend.'

'So why don't they like you? I can tell you're nice.'

I don't know, he thought, with a surprising ache of misery. I really don't know. I don't know what I did wrong. It's not my fault. But of course he did know, really.

They were deep under the trees. He'd never been anywhere like this before in his life. It seemed untouched by time and the outside world. For all he knew it might have always been the same messy tangle of wet wood and silence since before people, before history. It was the forest where trees fell and there was no one to hear them. The real answer to her question burned on the tip of his tongue. He could grit his teeth and swallow it and go on being burned up inside, or he could spit it out.

'It's because I'm different,' he said.

She looked puzzled. 'Everyone's different, aren't they? That what Gwen always says.'

'Yeah, well, actually she's wrong.' His cheeks were burning. He'd never rehearsed this. He didn't know how to begin to say who he was, and it frustrated him that she couldn't even grasp the first principle. 'Everyone's the same. Everyone except me. Everyone else has one set of rules. I don't. I see things that aren't there.'

His heart was hammering and his mouth was dry as he said it. It was as far as he could go. He stared at her, waiting for a response: laughter, incomprehension. He couldn't believe what he was doing. Only eleven days ago he'd tried saying this in front of Mr Bushy. Eleven days ago. Friday lunch break. He'd sworn he'd never be so utterly stupid again.

What she said was, 'You too?'

Eight

Autumn 1537

TO EXPERIENCE THE moment that consummates a life's work: how many men are so blessed, in the ordinary run of things? But then the magus had always known he was very far from being an ordinary man.

For some thirty years, beginning when he was barely old enough to rub bristles on his chin, he had studied the unseen world, venturing among its secrets like a traveller in the ruins of an ancient city. In the halls where Moses and Pythagoras and the thrice-great Hermes once ruled, he took what light there was to find and made his way, passageway by dusty passageway. By patience and discipline he grew adept in his art. He learned the virtues of leaf, stone and star. He laboured at the forms of conjuration and compulsion that allowed him to converse with insubstantial beings. Over months and years of study he uncovered their names and taught himself the rudiments of the immortal language in which those names were pronounced. He bound spirits to serve him, and by their power loosened the warp and weft of time and space. His eyes strained through nights of study. His beard turned grey. He toiled for decades, until his name was famous throughout the palaces of Europe and he was as far beyond every other alchemist or magician or conjurer as the princes of those palaces were beyond the servants that swept their floors.

But all along he knew that his highest achievements were little more than fugitive glimpses of the true architecture and harmony of creation. Despite his fame, despite his lifetime's labour, he had done no more than creep like an uninvited guest around the humblest antechambers of the courts of wisdom, peering at fragments by rushlight – until the moment he first put on the ring.

That night, in his observatory, it was in one instant as if every door was unlocked, every casement opened, and the ruin made alive with light and pageantry and solemn music. He saw and heard the life all around him as it must have been in the infancy of the Earth, the golden age, when the breath of creation blew fresh everywhere, and men and spirits walked as neighbours beside each other. The ring's small circle was a vent through which that breath blew in on him. It was a crack in the wall that separated the mortal sphere from the realms of the undying. Through it he saw living spirits dance before him like figures in a gilded landscape, their music celestial harmony.

He tore the ring off the small finger of his right hand, his heart throbbing like the watchmen's drum.

His very first thought was: What have I won?

He tried to thank her the next time they met. Summer had ripened the fields ready for autumn to mow them down, and the evenings were becoming cool. They walked by the sea less often. She was as indifferent to the sharp offshore wind as to every other mundane concern, but he felt it keenly, down to his bones. Age was catching up with him. He could not suppress twinges of unruly resentment when he felt her hand in his, thinner and rougher than his own, and noticed that though she was all skin and bones, she never shivered beneath her plain cloak. At first he'd found her hardiness magnificent, a reminder of how miraculously different she was from everyday women, and loved her for it. But now, as the evenings darkened, it seemed to reflect badly on his own frailty.

His mortality.

Her silence had begun to grate on him too. When once he'd walked beside her in contented quiet, he now found that her paucity of words irritated him. It struck him as a kind of stubbornness. At the beginning of the year, when he'd first found her again, he'd thrown questions at her like a wild boy throwing stones at roosting birds. He'd been so perfectly entranced by the miracle that he'd somehow not minded how rarely she answered, how often she only turned her solemn look on him and said, 'I don't know, Johannes.'

As the year waned, he wondered how he of all people could have been content with such nothings for so long.

It was the same when he tried to thank her. His head was spinning with wonder, his heart brimmed with gratitude, and yet she seemed as unmoved by the gift she'd placed in his keeping as if the ring were no more than the modest hoop of wood it appeared to be.

They were in the rutted roads among fields south of the city, the ditches brown and stinking with a summer's worth of drowning weeds. She walked barefoot as always, the hem of her cloak soiled. It was harder by the week for him to see her for what he knew she was, no more an ordinary woman than he was an ordinary man. Still, he tried to remember whose love he had earned as he spoke. He was, after all, acknowledging a gift whose value could not be measured by the treasuries of all the kings and emperors of the world.

But despite his sincerity she only walked on, unsmiling. He felt rebuffed.

'I know now what the gift is worth.' His right hand clenched and unclenched. 'I wore it last night. Perhaps,' he went on, not entirely managing to quell the impatience in his voice, 'you did not fully understand it yourself when you presented it to me.'

At this she stopped, looked at him and gave him an answer at last. It was not one he had looked for.

'I made you no present, Johannes.' She took his hand. 'I gave you no gift. I offered you my burden and you accepted it. It is a heavy burden, heavier than you know.' Embarrassed, he looked away, to the long horizon. He felt her fingers tighten. 'If you cannot bear it, you must return it to me.'

At this he forced his face into a smile and said, 'For your sake, I would bear anything.' But for the very first time he knew he was dissembling before her.

The truth was that he treasured the ring for his own sake, not hers. Had he not devoted himself with unexampled constancy to seeking out the world's hidden truths? Was he not the greatest magus since the ancient days? Her ring, he understood, was his reward.

That evening, at the window of his observatory, watching the hunter heave his starry bulk above the eastern horizon, turning the ring between his fingers, he contemplated the worth of that prize.

He thought of the years he had sacrificed to earn his station. He thought of the strength he had lost in solitary study, the pleasures of life willingly foregone. He watched the stars in their fixed and highest sphere, far above time and decay and death. When he put on the ring, he could feel their sweet influence all around him, wasted on the uncaring city beneath. He was the only one who revered their crystalline glory. In a meagre study in Frombork the canon Copernik readied his hammer, preparing to smash the celestial spheres into nothing. The magus knew of his work. All educated men seemed to know it. All over Europe those who called themselves wise ranged themselves alongside the vandal, eager to slay the universe so they could pick over its broken pieces like so many watchmakers. And meanwhile the rabble shouted the name of the monk Luther, who preached that God was not to be found anywhere in His creation. His followers broke images and painted walls white so they could bring themselves as near as possible to the condition of blindness, and proclaimed their cause a holy crusade.

In such a world, was it not his duty to bear the gift of the living creation? And to go on bearing it, as she had? On and on?

For many years now he had worried about what would happen after his death. His own pupils had turned out as venial as common apprentices. Their interest in magic extended as far as transmuting base metal into gold and conjuring obedient spirits who promised buried treasure or maidens' hearts. He knew of no one to whom he could entrust his art.

Surely, then, this was the burden he willingly accepted: to defy time and decay and death, like the stars.

Immortality.

She had endured through inconceivable expanses of time with the ring on her finger. Why should not he?

He sought her out less often as autumn drew on. Each time he encountered her his heart would lurch. He hardly knew what to say to her any more, and she had never been afraid of silence. Sometimes they did no more than stand mutely together, hands clasped, reluctance in his face and the same abyssal darkness in hers. She never complained about his reticence. Reproach was not in her nature, any more than any other self-tormenting frailty. Still, where her gaze once exhilarated him, it now caused him discomfort. Those prophetic eyes seemed to look inside him.

One late afternoon he was returning from some business outside the city, riding slowly along a straight road under a greenish sky, when he saw her standing ahead, waiting for him. When she pushed back her hood, there was a look of strange disquiet in her face. It reminded him unexpectedly of the first time he had seen her – how beautiful she had been then, how marvellous. He dismounted and embraced her.

'Johannes.' Her coarse fingers traced the shape of his cheekbones beneath the skin. 'I have seen you drowned.'

He stiffened, then eased her hand away, smiling. 'No, *carissima.*'

'All that touches me suffers.' Her mouth was tense as if pulled tight by pain. 'A woman drowns but death escapes her. It was you I saw, Johannes.'

So this was what the surrender of her gift had left her, the magus thought sadly: a driveller. She seemed all of a sudden very frail and small. He stroked the tangled knots of her hair.

'Do not fear for me,' he said, as he would have reassured any fretful old woman.

A cart's wheels creaked on the road behind him. He looked over his shoulder and saw the plodding ox approaching, bringing another load of hay into the city. Its hooves rose and fell . . . and then rose but did not fall; the world around the magus and the woman went still, the green-tinted light suddenly luminous and clear like the heart of a gem. He turned back and saw that time had fallen away from her as well. Her face was the same, but now proud, fierce, full of fiery life, the face he had first fallen in love with: the face of a princess. Enraptured, he leaned to kiss her. She stopped him with a finger to his lips.

'You cannot bear what I have offered you,' she said.

It was in that exact instant that the magus determined to escape her.

He did not know it at the time, not consciously. All he knew was the rude shock those words gave, but that recoil was the seed that would grow over the next months into his hurried flight on the English vessel. His pride was wounded, and it stung. So suddenly and surprisingly and completely that it was like an emotion felt by another person, he felt a bitter determination to keep what he had won, to keep it for ever.

'You judged me wrongly, then?' he muttered.

'I do not judge, Johannes. You came to me and did not turn away. You heard me. For that I waited for you and for that I love you. Because of that I asked you to take my burden from me. But it is not lifted. It is still mine. I saw the woman in the water. I saw her drown and not die. Her fate was yours. A terrible fate. You must return what I gave you.'

Whatever the magus might have thought of the rest of her speech – and he had rarely heard her speak so many words at once – the final sentence drove every other consideration out of his head. He forgot who she was, her ill-fated name. He forgot what gift had been laid on her. He forgot the idyll of the spring and summer, when he had loved her with his whole soul. The only thought left to him was terror of losing the ring.

'I have accepted your burden, *carissima*,' he said soothingly, and was astonished at how false his own words sounded. But surely it was the truth, the noble truth? 'I have considered it and comprehended it.' No other man alive or dead these thousand years could have said the same; was that not so? 'I take it upon myself.'

'It will destroy you,' she said, and now he was equally astonished at how true those two words rang. *Te delebit*, a peal of fateful syllables, even though he knew she was exactly wrong: the ring was his guarantee against destruction. He had seen how. It would open his path to immortality.

'It has sustained you,' he retorted. And what was she after all but a woman, the weaker vessel? He was stronger as well as wiser.

'Do you envy that, Johannes? Do you envy what I endured?'

'No, certainly.' The lies had got hold of his tongue. Everything he said to her was the opposite of the truth, though he believed it.

'Then let me suffer again. Spare yourself. Return my gift.'

'It is not with me,' he said feebly, as if he was a boy caught thieving.

She clutched at his hand. 'You listen, but you do not hear.'

'Calm yourself.' He disentangled his fingers from hers and looked towards the city, hoping the lateness of the hour would rescue him. 'The gate will close. Let me consider this.'

'The gate will close,' she echoed. Her eyelids flickered and an unseasonal shiver ran through her. He doubted she had the city gate in mind. 'The gate will close. The gate will close.'

A straining creak came from behind him, and the splotch of the ox's hoof into muddy earth. He mounted and rode back to the city, leaving her whispering inaudibly to herself as the evening sky turned sickly yellow.

He sat awake all that night.

By morning he had determined to cross the sea, to England. It was an outpost remote enough not to be touched by the chaos and bloodshed the planets warned of. There were letters to be written and monies to be raised. He planned it all out while the stars turned, in feverish haste. Despite the sleepless night he began to work at his usual hour the next day, but now he locked and barred the door of his laboratory behind him. He put aside everything he had been studying before that morning, all the instruments of the baser alchemy. A new course consumed him. He unchained tomes he would once have hesitated even to touch, within whose bindings were the shunned and buried secrets of the pagan magicians. Ignorant of heaven, they had devoted themselves to the wisdom of Pythagoras and the Egyptians, who believed that souls might travel from body to body. He began to exhume the most ancient foundation of his art, the forgotten palaces of wisdom, whose only visible remains, like the wave-worn and barnacled spires of a sunken city making strange shapes above the ocean's surface, were the alchemists' fraudulent phantoms – the philosopher's stone, the elixir of youth, grotesque distortions of truths that had been lost since the time of Hermes Trismegistus.

Hermes had lived for nearly a thousand years, and so had Mahalalel and Methuselah the ancestors of Noah.

With the ring in his grasp, he dreamed of a magic that would preserve his soul from bodily death.

All the time he was haunted by the fear of losing it. The gift given in love had become a prize, a treasure, and like anyone else in possession of a treasure the magus became tormented by the need to guard it. It was his own; it belonged to him; it had to be shut away from thieves.

So he made the pouch and spent two weeks warding it, first from common sight and then, gradually, from all other harms and devices that he knew. The only thing he did not know how to protect it from was time: for, powerful as his wards were, they were nevertheless no more than sorceries, barely worth the name of art, and in themselves no more enduring than anything else made by men.

So he made the box to hold the pouch. He built it out of ash and alder, sovereign against fire and water, and then he made its clasp from silver, the moon's metal, receptive to charms.

Into the clasp he worked a spell of closure and endurance. It was a full day's labour. Even to call it a spell was demeaning. It was as far above the common magics inscribed on the bag as the magus himself was above a village witch. It drew down the virtue of Saturn, the most secret and lasting of all changeable things, whose station was proximate to eternity, whose meanings were hiddenness and permanence, and it laid that virtue upon the box. Not for ever: even the planets were ruled by time. But the measures of the spheres stretched inconceivably beyond the span of men, and it was only against men that the magus wished to guard his treasure. So he spoke into the clasp a potency measured by the circle of Saturn, and then he spoke it again, to double it. The spell was punishing to pronounce even once, but he could not stop. He had staked his life to his prize. He spoke the charm again, to double it once more, and then again, and then a fifth time. He reached the limit of his strength, but he had made a vault for his treasure that would endure for centuries.

Yet no wards could protect it from the thing he feared most, which was that she might raise an open palm to him again and take back what she had given. If his conscience had been clear, he would have understood the significance of this fear. She had told him plainly enough that the prize he planned to steal away to England did not truly belong to him, but he closed his ears and believed what he wanted to believe: an ordinary man, after all.

As autumn faded into winter, he rarely left the house, and never ventured outside the city. Two or three times he thought he saw her in the streets, as a man might think he sees his doppelgänger, and swerved away, forcing his protesting limbs into an undignified run. He set his servants to watch the door of the house day and night. In that manner, hiding from the truth, the greatest magus in the world prepared himself for his passage to immortality.

Nine

'I'VE NEVER TOLD anyone this before,' Marina said, her voice very small.

Gavin could only stare. He'd been ready for bafflement. He'd been ready to be dismissed, or ignored, or even laughed at. He wasn't even the slightest bit prepared for trust. He had no defence against it.

'It's only sometimes,' she went on. Her skinny hands twisted at the sleeves of her too-big jumper. 'Promise you won't tell anyone else.'

He blinked. 'Um . . .'

'I'm not supposed to let people see me. I have to be careful.' She hunched her shoulders. 'I know you think that's stupid, but I'm not supposed to. Anyway, she's never there for long, and I can't help it, unless I never went near the river at all and I couldn't give that up. I couldn't!'

She looked up at him so suddenly and passionately that he had to answer. 'No,' he said. 'Course not. But—'

'Promise you won't tell anyone? Not even Daddy. Please don't.'

His mouth worked without a sound for a while and then at last he managed to say, 'Tell him what?'

'You know. Like you said. The woman no one else sees. At least I don't think anyone else does. I asked Horace about it once. Carefully, obviously, not actually saying about her, I just asked whether there were people living in the river like that, and he said no, that was just stories.' The sentences tripped over each other in nervous haste. 'Anyway she always dives away if there's a boat coming.'

'Marina—'

'And I was reading this book once and there was a picture, so I showed it to Gwen and she said it was something the sailors used to imagine because they'd been away at sea so long. She said maybe once long ago there had been people like that but the world had changed. I think that's what she said. Or was that something else? I—'

'Marina, hang on.'

Her hand went to cover her mouth, a comically artless gesture.

'What?' she said.

Gav's head was buzzing. He felt that if he shook it and waited a moment longer, all the words she'd just spoken would turn out to have been hallucinations, and what she'd actually said would have been *Don't be stupid. Oh come on. That's impossible. You don't expect me to believe that do you?* But it wasn't a hallucination, and the reason he knew it wasn't was that he could see the back of her hand, the slight curve of her fingers, the funny twist of her open mouth behind it, and he'd never in all his life seen anything more completely real and true than those tiny details.

'What are you talking about?' he said.

She drew in a breath, opened her mouth, stood there for a second gaping like a fish, then closed it again.

'Come on,' she said. 'I'll show you. This way.'

And instead of carrying on towards the house, Marina stepped off the track into the woods on the downhill side. Her soft shoes sank into leaf mould up to her ankles, but she headed off round boughs and brambles as unhesitatingly as she'd walked on the driveway. The obstacles only made her gait a little gawkier than usual. 'Come on,' she repeated.

Gavin stepped gingerly into the carpeted mud. 'Wait. Weren't we going back to the house?'

'It's not too far.' Her voice came muffled by the damp woods. 'Anyway, Caleb said everything was all right.'

'What's not too far?'

'The lookout. Oh, of course, you don't know about it. It's a place where you can see through a gap in the trees to the river. It's just a couple of minutes. I sometimes see her there.'

'See who?'

'The woman you were talking about.'

'Miss Grey?' Gav said, half under his breath. He was completely confused now, his bearings lost as thoroughly as his steps in the trackless wood.

'What?'

Was it as simple as that? Had he suffered years of misery just because he'd been in the wrong place, talking to the wrong people all along? Was everything that was impossibly obvious to him just as obvious to this one strange girl? It was such an extraordinary thought that he didn't know what to do with it.

'Nothing,' he said. Then, 'Wait. Who's Horace?'

She spun round. 'How do you know Horace?'

'I don't. You said something . . . Just now, you said you asked Horace something.'

'Oh, did I? Sorry. He's my friend.' She almost made it sound like a job description, as if she'd said *He's my yoga teacher*. 'Come on, we should be quick. I did promise Caleb.'

'Marina?'

'Yes?'

'You know what I said, back there on the driveway? What I told you?'

'Yes?'

'Weren't you . . .' Surprised? Horrified? Embarrassed? 'You didn't think I was making it up?'

She turned back to him again, her face transformed by an enormous teasing smile.

'I thought you said you could tell when I didn't believe you.'

Before he could think of how to answer she was off again. 'There's a path just ahead,' she said, gesturing towards what appeared to be more tangled wet brown. 'After that it's not far.'

He jogged a few steps to catch up. Was she really taking him to see Miss Grey, the way Mum and Dad took him to visit the boring aunt in the country? They came to a narrow track, no more than a furrow in the rotting leaves. Off to their left was what appeared to be the edge of the wood. The snaking path continued downhill, the slope beginning to descend more steeply. Marina had begun chatting again, as if nothing they'd just said to each other was surprising, as if the secret that had haunted Gavin and shut him up in years of bitter silence was after all just as innocent and harmless as she was.

'There's a path for other people over that way. Along the edge of the wood. For walking. Hardly anyone ever uses it, but Caleb says you could get through the fence there if you really wanted to. This one only goes as far as the lookout, then the slope becomes too steep. It's all right for me to sit there, there's a footpath below but it's hidden. Hardly anyone's about at this time of year anyway. In the summer quite a few people go walking there, but then the leaves are out of course, no one can see. It's one of my favourite places. You see boats going past. Or just the tide going in and out, like breathing.'

He always seemed to be at least a few sentences behind her, no matter how hard he tried to keep up. 'What's wrong with people seeing you?'

'Oh, they're just not supposed to. Not you, though. Obviously. Come on, we ought to be quick. I think Caleb thought there might be other people around.'

'Other people?'

'From outside.'

'You mean like trespassers?'

'What?'

'People who aren't supposed to be here. You know, sneaking in.'

'Oh. Yes, that happens sometimes. You'll have to teach me all these words you know. What was that one for being cross? Pist?'

'Never mind. So Caleb's a bit paranoid about it, is he?'

'That's another one.'

'What? Oh. OK. I mean, he's always thinking there's people trying to break in?' Did they have to hide Marina away? Was that why her father had seemed so distant and Caleb so unfriendly? Because the girl was as haunted as he was and they had to protect her?

She frowned. 'No, I don't think so. But sometimes people do, by accident. From one of the paths. He has to go and steer them away.'

'Must be a bit difficult in a place this size.'

'What do you mean?'

'Well, you can't keep an eye on all of it at once. No wonder he's a bit para— A bit worried about it.'

It was a few steps before she said anything, as if she hadn't understood him. He concentrated on following, ducking among the glossy leaves of a stand of tall evergreen bushes.

'Oh!' She sounded like she'd just worked something out. 'No, he doesn't have to see everywhere.'

'What?'

'Caleb knows whenever anyone's here.'

''cept me!' said a boy, stepping out onto the path from an evergreen recess.

Gavin jumped so violently he lost his balance and lurched into the wet boughs.

Marina had all but sprung out of her shoes in surprise; now she whirled to face the newcomer, half breathless, half laughing. 'Horace!' she shouted.

'Bet you never saw me.'

'Of course we didn't!'

At the word 'we' the triumphant grin vanished from the boy's face. He flicked a suspicious look at Gavin, who was still busy righting himself, brushing his hands on his trousers and kicking clods of wet leaves from his shoes. Though the boy was small, Gav guessed he was not far off Marina's age, just a couple of years younger than himself. Unlike her (and unlike him) he'd grown into his body. Gav recognised his type from school: a neat, self-possessed, wiry kid. Give him a football and within minutes he'd have been impressing or embarrassing his elders. Noticing how deftly he slipped among the web of curving boughs, Gav thought of the slight figure he'd glimpsed running down the path into the woods as he left Auntie Gwen's house. It was obvious from his manner that he didn't want to be seen by anyone else. He had a dark cap pulled low over his forehead. He was an Asian kid – Gav thought maybe Chinese or Japanese. His eyes looked keen. When they met Gavin's, there was a mixture of curiosity and defiance in them, the boy's challenge to another, bigger boy.

'So who's this then?'

'Oh, say hi to Gavin. Gavin's my cousin. Well, close enough. He's visiting.'

'Saw you before, didn't I? Walking down from the lodge earlier on. Bet you'd no idea I was there neither.'

Gavin closed his eyes. It had only been half an hour since he'd felt himself stepping out of his shell, speaking to Marina, but the sudden intrusion of this kid was already making him want to crawl right back in again.

'No one ever sees you when you're sneaking around, Horace,' Marina said admiringly.

'Followed him all the way down to the house. Bet you never saw a thing.' Gav was pretty sure he had, for an instant, but it wasn't worth mentioning. 'Come to visit then?' It sounded like an accusation.

Marina answered instead. 'I just told you that. Anyway, what are *you* doing here this morning? Shouldn't you be in your school instead of following us around?'

'I weren't following!'

'You just said you followed me,' Gav put in.

'Yeah, well, that's different.' Horace glared at him before appealing to Marina. 'Never seen him before in my life, have I? I see some bloke I never heard of coming out of Miss Clifton's, walking down the drive, what am I supposed to do?'

'Gavin is Gwenny's nephew. That means his mother's her sister. He's allowed.'

'Nice to meet you,' Gav said, and this time he had the small satisfaction of seeing his sarcastic tone hitting its intended target, though Marina remained happily oblivious to the tension between the two boys.

'I wish you wouldn't jump out of the rhododendrons like that. You gave us a fright. What *are* you doing here today? Are you going to come exploring?'

'Just on my way out,' Horace muttered.

'You weren't going to stay? What's wrong? You don't look pleased to see me.'

The boy took off his cap and ran his fingers through his short hair. 'Course I am. Got to go, though.'

She pouted. 'Why? We were going down towards the lookout. Can't you come for a bit?'

'No. Not today, OK?'

'Oh all right then. How about at the weekend? Gavin will still be here then. We can explore together.'

'Yeah, maybe.' Horace looked about as pleased with the suggestion as Gav was. He jammed his cap back on.

'Good. So is today one of those holidays? Or are you being bad again?'

Horace blushed. 'Course not.' Now he was doing his best to pretend Gavin wasn't even there. 'Anyway, I got to go, innit.'

'You're acting very funny, Horace. What is it?'

The boy opened his mouth to dismiss the question, but stopped himself. He was, indeed, very fidgety; even Marina had noticed. He eyed Gavin, who thought it was pretty obvious what was wrong with the kid but certainly wasn't going to try and explain concepts like competitiveness and jealousy to Marina.

Nothing in Horace's look prepared him for the boy's question.

'You here with your mum then?'

'Huh?'

'Your mum. Miss Clifton's sister, yeah? She staying here too?'

'Er—' Gav began, just as Marina chimed in, 'No. Actually, Gavin's mother doesn't like him. It's because he's different. They sent him away on his own – was that it?' Gav had no idea how to shut her up. 'He told me earlier. That's why—'

Fortunately Horace rescued him. 'So there's no one else staying?'

'No. Horace? What's wrong?'

It wasn't just the grey light. The boy did look slightly pale.

'Nothing's wrong. Seen Miss Clifton this morning?'

Gav and Marina looked at each other. Her breeziness deserted her, all at once.

'Why?' he asked.

'Just wondering.'

Marina gave no sign of answering, so, 'She's gone off somewhere,' he said. 'No one's sure where.'

'Yeah, well, I know, don't I? Saw her down on the rocks just now.'

Gav's heart lurched. Marina was stung too. 'What? You can't have. Where?'

'Yeah, I did. Don't tell me what I saw. On them rocks by the cove. Where that ledge is, going out in the water.'

'When? Yesterday?'

'No, I told you! Don't you listen? Just this morning. Earlier on. I just come across, I tied the boat up, I was coming up the path by the shore and I saw her out there.'

'You can't have.'

Horace obviously didn't take contradiction well. 'Oh yeah? Why not?'

'Caleb said she's not here.'

This was the wrong thing to say. Horace threw his hands in the air, fists smacking against branches. 'Caleb! Bloody hell, what does he know about it?'

'Caleb knows whenever someone's here.'

'Don't be stupid! Doesn't know when I'm here, does he?'

'Of course he does, Horace.'

'Oh yeah? Well in that case why—'

Gav interrupted. 'Is that why you asked about my mum?' A faintly uneasy feeling was stirring in him. Horace and Marina stopped arguing. The antagonism slowly drained out of the kid's expression.

'Yeah,' he said. 'That's right.'

'I don't understand,' Marina said.

'You saw someone who might have been Aunt Gwen or might have been someone who looked a lot like her.'

'Yeah,' Horace said, suddenly grateful. 'See, that's what's weird. I was sure it was her . . .'

'It can't have been,' Marina put in.

Horace ignored her. '. . . but then she didn't look quite right, know what I mean? And she was . . .' The sentence trailed off. Horace looked back and forth between Marina and Gavin, unsure now which of them was his ally.

'She was what?' Gav prompted.

'It wasn't her!'

But Horace had made his choice. Something was weighing on him and he'd decided to confide in Gavin.

'I dunno. It was weird. She was like . . . bending over the river.' Horace mimed the action, crouching low and forwards, his hands waving strangely near his feet. 'Like she'd dropped something in the water and was looking for it, but in slow motion. And then . . . Yeah. Well.' Gav must have failed to look sufficiently impressed by whatever the kid wanted to tell him. Horace swept his cap off again and rubbed his head. 'Look, I got to get going.'

'Then what?'

'I know,' Marina said. 'You must have seen someone else who looks a bit like Gwen. Anyone can go along that bit by the shore. And whoever it was dropped something by accident and was looking for it, and that's what you saw.'

'You think I'm stupid or something?'

Marina flinched.

'You think I don't know what I'm looking at? I got perfect eyes, me. And I know everyone round here. And OK.' His temper was up. He straightened his shoulders belligerently, as if he was now coming out with something he hadn't meant to say but could no longer hold back. 'I know Miss Clifton's been acting weird recently. Yeah? Really weird. Bet you never noticed, did you? You never notice stuff like that.'

'Hey,' Gav said. Marina's head hung so low her chin looked like it might bruise her breastbone.

Horace now ignored him, talking fast and angrily. 'Saturday *and* Sunday she asked me to go see her. Bet you never realised, did you? You don't know everything goes on here. You nor Caleb. Something weird's going on with her, I'm telling you. You need to keep your eyes open like I do. I know lots more than anyone thinks. Lots more.'

'I know you do, Horace,' Marina mumbled from her chest.

Only seconds earlier Gav had been about to tell him to shut up and leave her alone, but now he was thinking of the empty house, the voice outside in the dark, the room littered with crackpot books and demented notes. The winter rose.

'What do you mean, something weird?'

'Dunno,' he began, sulky but superior. 'Hard to describe, innit.' He waited a moment to be sure he had their attention. 'But, OK, couple of days ago, Sunday. She said would I stop at the lodge before I went home. And when I did, she's, like, mental. Really mental. I mean, nice and everything, friendly, like usual, but she's so excited she can't hardly speak. Really wound up. I thought she was pretty freaky in the morning, but by the time I went up to say bye—'

'Wait,' Marina interrupted. 'In the morning?'

'Yeah. I stopped in at hers before I come and see you, and then on the way back as well in the afternoon.'

'You never told me you'd done that.'

'Yeah, well, you don't know everything I do, do you? And anyway, she's, like, all secretive. Kept smiling at me and going like this,' and he touched a finger to his lips. 'Weird. She wouldn't say why she wanted me to do all that stuff for her, but she—'

'What stuff?'

He looked at her exasperatedly. 'Let me finish, all right?'

Gav would have been happy to point out that Horace hadn't even started, at least not to any intelligible purpose, but he wanted to hear about Auntie Gwen.

'So look, on Saturday, the day before, yeah? She grabs me before I go home and says will I go check the post for her in Falmouth.'

'The post?'

'Yeah, she's got that mailbox there. Gave me the key and all. She said she's expecting a letter and it's really important. And she wants me to bring it when I come Sunday, the next day. She said that like fifteen times, like I'm some kind of moron. So anyway, she gives me the key to the box, yeah, and that evening I go and check for her and there's her letter. So I bring it over for her Sunday morning, like she asked.' Marina was nodding. 'I stop by there before I come down to see you, like I said. And when I give her the letter she . . .' He shrugged exaggeratedly as if lost for words. 'She looks at it like she's almost afraid to open it. Like it's a bomb. And then like I told you, OK, she says will I come by again in the afternoon before I go. So I did, and as soon as I open the door, she gives me this big hug and kiss and she's, like, totally off her head. Asking crazy questions. Over and over again. Mental.'

'Like what?' Marina said, when Horace's incoherent narrative showed no sign of resuming. Gav hadn't made much of an effort to keep up with whatever the boy was talking about, but he did find himself wondering about Auntie Gwen waiting to receive a letter. Which day was it Mum had got her letter, the letter he'd stolen and read on the train? Last Thursday? Would Mum have written back to tell her he was coming? Was he the thing she'd been so excited about?

'I dunno. It was just weird, OK? Like first she was asking about my mum. Like, was she going to that church meeting thing on Monday. All about it. She must have asked, like, five times. "What time is it? Is the priest always there? How long does it usually last?" How was I supposed to know all that stuff? But she's going on and on about it. On and on. "It's at lunchtime, isn't it?" Lunchtime, lunchtime, like that. Then she kept asking where we'd been, like she was my mum. "What were you doing all day? Where did you go?" Asking if we'd been to the chapel. Did your dad go with us? Or Caleb? "Are you sure? Are you sure?" It was like she was too off her head to listen.'

Marina evidently couldn't find anything in what Horace said to get worried about, though for his sake she tried her best to. 'Oh,' she ventured, after a pause. 'Yes, that does sound a bit odd.'

In all his life Gavin had never met a worse liar. Even that polite half-truth came out of her mouth blaring its insincerity.

'You don't get it.'

'No, Horace, I—'

'All right, then, forget it. Forget I spoke.'

'Horace—'

'Just forget it. I got to go anyway. Oh, and something else.' His face had darkened with sulky resentment. 'You won't believe this either. Someone was singing. Yeah, I know, I'm making it up. Well I'm not. I heard it.'

'Singing?'

Determined to have the last word, Horace was already ducking away. He moved amazingly deftly, barely stirring the glossy leaves. 'Yeah. Heard it in the woods near the chapel. Just now. Knew you wouldn't believe me.'

'Wait, Horace, I—'

'See you, then.'

'Horace!'

But the small figure was already hard to make out among the twisted shadows. They stared after him, Marina stricken, Gavin just happy to see the back of him.

'Don't forget the weekend!' Marina shouted after him. The boy bobbed away and vanished altogether in the undergrowth, heading for the edge of the woods.

'I think he decided to make an exit,' Gav said.

'A what?'

Gav suspected that Marina had no experience with displays of temper. In fact she didn't seem to have much experience of anything. She was the only person he'd ever met beside whom he felt positively worldly.

'He's upset. Wants to make it clear to us. So what was all that about?'

'I don't know.' She was still watching the direction he'd gone, as if she expected him to pop back out of the bushes any second. Gavin waited a while in silence in case she was right.

'But where's he from?' he asked, when he was sure the kid had gone. He couldn't get his head round the idea of an ordinary schoolboy popping up in these woods like that. 'I mean, where does he live?'

'Across the river somewhere.' She sounded distracted. 'Gwen says his mother's a kind of housekeeper for people there. She's from China, which is all the way on the other side of the world, past the sunrise.'

OK, Gav thought.

'So he just comes to . . .' He was going to say 'play', but the word didn't fit Pendurra. 'Um, visit sometimes?'

'Yes. He has his own boat. I've seen it. It doesn't have a name. I think that's wrong, but he won't listen to my suggestions.'

'So what was he on about? All that stuff about Aunt Gwen?'

'I'm not sure. He's not usually like that.'

'Like what?'

She was pinching her lip unhappily. 'He just ran off. Normally he likes talking to me. Gwenny didn't tell me anything about seeing him this weekend either.'

'Well, at least we know she's here now, right?'

'What? Where?'

'Well . . . wherever he said he saw her. By the river.'

'Oh. No, he can't have.'

'Because Caleb said she's not here.'

'Yes.'

Gav stared at her, but she gave no sign that there might be anything strange or surprising about what she'd just said.

'So even if someone else says they've actually seen her, he just knows.'

'Yes,' she said absently, looking around the woods.

'That's a bit hard to—' *Believe*, he was going to finish, but stopped himself. He'd had this conversation before, over and over again, when he was a bit younger than Marina. Except that he'd always been on the other side of it. The wrong side. So why was he trying to sound like his parents again?

'I think we should go back to the house,' she said.

'Huh? Why? What's wrong?'

'I don't know. Things aren't like they usually are this morning. I don't like it.'

'Shouldn't we go see if we can find Aunt Gwen?'

'We don't know where she is.'

'No, I mean check out whatever Horace saw. Wherever that is.'

'Oh.' She shook her head. 'Down by the cove past the chapel? No. I don't want to go that far. I promised Caleb.' She fingered her neck, exactly as if an invisible lead were attached to an invisible collar and she was checking whether it was tight.

'What's this chapel place?'

'It's a house all made out of stone. Just one room. It's off by itself in the woods, out towards the head. No one ever lived there, people used to use it to think about God. That's an imaginary person who some people think made the world. It's very old, nearly as old as the old parts of the house. Maybe we can go tomorrow.'

Gav just watched her worried expression until he'd confirmed to himself that she was again perfectly serious. 'You don't do much RS, do you?'

'What?'

'Never mind.'

Her head drooped. 'You know all about chapels already.'

'No, really, I just . . . Sorry. So, this place is on your land somewhere? Like private?'

'That's right. Along that way.' She pointed, though one direction looked exactly the same as another to Gav.

Something was nagging at Gav's memory, but he couldn't pin it down. 'So why was Horace talking about it like that? All that stuff about Aunt Gwen being excited?'

'I already told you, I don't understand. Come on, let's get going back.'

'No. Wait.' He was beginning to find Marina's nervousness a bit irritating. Or maybe it was that he really didn't want to end up back with the adults, stammering and looking at his feet. 'We ought to try and help figure out what Aunt Gwen's doing, right?'

'Let's just go and tell Caleb.'

Gav found himself wanting to postpone another conversation with Caleb for as long as possible. Perhaps this time he'd be blamed for making Marina break her promise to go back to the house. 'Look, how far is it to that chapel? That could have been her Horace heard, right? That singing. Maybe, I don't know, something's happened to her.' Maybe she's finally gone completely mad. *But how would you tell?* his father's voice sneered in his head. 'Couldn't we just go and check quickly?'

'You can't get down to that path from here. This way ends at the lookout.'

There was something about Auntie Gwen and a chapel, Gav thought. That was what was bugging him, at the back of his thoughts, somewhere. But how could he possibly have known anything about it? He tried to remember whether there'd been a mention in the scrapbook. 'So what's inside it? Is it just like a mini church?'

She frowned as if even talking about it made her unhappy. 'I don't know. It's always kept locked. It's too important to be left open.'

'What's important about it?'

'It just is. No one's supposed to go there. Someone tried once, a long time ago. Gwen told me the story. They were in terrible pain or something. There was someone else too, more recently. After that Daddy hid the key in the old office.'

Gav was reminded of the rumours Hester had mentioned. 'Is there treasure in there or something?'

'I don't know.'

'You've never been?'

'Not inside. Well, not since I was a baby, but that doesn't count. There's a kind of pool where they took me.'

'A pool? Water?'

'Yes, there's a hollow with a spring. They built the chapel where the spring comes out. That's the water that makes you well.' Makes *a* well? Gav thought. But Marina's voice was clear as birdsong; he knew what she'd said. 'We'll go and look this afternoon. If Daddy says it's all right. Come on.' She made to squeeze past him, back the way they'd come.

He sighed. 'Can't we at least go to the whatsit? Lookout. Hey, you were going to show me something.'

She pulled herself up short as if someone had yanked her invisible lead. 'Oh! I forgot.'

'Please? It's right here, isn't it?'

She ran her hands through her hair, raising damp tufts. 'All right, then. Just quickly.' But her mood had clouded over. Whatever confidence she'd been about to share with him seemed to have disappeared. Gav couldn't help catching some of her disquiet. The weird appearance of the boy with his mysterious apprehensions and nonsensical story had unsettled him, reminding him that Auntie Gwen was still missing. It had been a long time now, almost a whole day. Even she didn't forget things for that long, did she?

They went on in silence together, treading carefully as they traversed the slope. The land was slanting more sharply, right to left, and the track itself was little more than scars of mud. Looking up for an unwise moment to make sure he didn't lose sight of her ahead, Gav slipped and fell with a squeak of surprise into the wet leaf mould and earth.

'Gavin!' He stumbled as he tried to push himself up. By the time he was upright again he was almost coated in fragments of twigs and strips of sodden leaves.

She laughed, a smothered giggle that made her fold in on herself as if she were trying to disappear inside her oversized jumper. 'You look like a woodwose. I should draw a picture. Are you all right?'

He didn't think she'd really said he looked like a woodlouse, but he wasn't going to ask. He was so relieved to have lightened her mood again that he didn't much care either way. 'Fine. Just slipped.'

'Hold my hand,' she said. 'Just for this last bit.'

So he did. He blushed at being helped along by a girl two years younger than him and probably half his weight, or maybe for another reason, but she kept her eyes ahead as they negotiated a small upwards slope, and didn't see. There was an odd stab of disappointment when she let go of his hand as the track levelled out again. He wondered whether maybe she'd felt it too, because she stopped, and they stood a few moments, just the sound of their breath together under the winter branches. Only when he looked around did he realise that they'd reached the spot.

The 'lookout' was no more than a shoulder of bedrock sticking out from the roots and earth, a miniature cliff, its top barely wide enough for two small people to sit close together. A tiny stream dribbled down a cleft below it, and along the line of that cleft there was indeed a break in the mass of the trees, opening a narrow slice of the outside world to their view.

Gav had managed to forget how close that world was. Being under the trees was as good as being behind a wall. Pendurra had felt like a separate country. Now he was looking across a wide river, rippled and silvery and tarnished. It was more like an arm of the sea than the sluggish silty water that was what the word 'river' meant to him, the river he knew from home. The far bank was a slope of green, stunted trees by the water, a field above.

'You can see a lot more from the head,' she said, 'but out towards the sea. I like this view. It's like looking through a window. More happens here.'

There were mooring buoys in the river. The tide gently tugged at them. A cormorant perched on one, crooked wings open to dry. A breeze too slight to disturb the trees made patterns on the water like feathers.

'It's beautiful,' said Gav, more than half to himself.

There was no one to call him inside, no one to disturb him. He thought suddenly of Marina's naïve invitation: *You can just stay*. The idea of it welled up inside him with such terrible impossibility that his eyes misted. He sat down, wiping his cheek quickly on his sleeve.

'Are you all right?'

'Yeah.'

She squatted down beside him, surprisingly close. He turned his head away.

'I didn't mean to upset you,' she said.

To his utter surprise, he had to make a real effort to fight away another trickle of tears. He turned his shaky breath into a pretend gasp of sardonic laughter.

'You haven't,' he said. 'Trust me.'

'Gwen did say you were very unhappy underneath.'

He bit his lip and bowed his head. A gust of chill air stirred the trees above them into unsympathetic whispers.

'We should go back now,' she said, after a while.

'Marina?'

'Yes?'

'What I told you before? About being different?'

'Yes,' she said cautiously.

'I never told anyone else that either. That's the first time I've ever told the truth about myself.'

There was another long pause. When she answered at last, she sounded strangled with embarrassment.

'Remind me what it was again?'

Gav let out a slow breath, then shook his head. He couldn't stop himself chuckling bleakly as he pushed himself to his feet. 'Never mind.'

'No. Wait, sorry, I got in a muddle with Horace and everything. Sorry!' She stood up beside him. 'It was . . . That's right, that special woman you see. I do remember.'

'Doesn't matter. Let's go back.'

'Now I really have upset you. Please, I'm sorry.'

'Nah.' He looked around for the muddy track and began scrambling back without waiting for her. 'Some things you just can't really talk about.'

'No. You can. Or you and I can. I was going to show you, but I forgot that too.' He heard her slipping along behind, but he kept striding as best he could. Back to the adults, back to the real world, back to normal. She pursued him like the memory of everything he'd spent the past four years trying not to say. 'Sometimes when I go and sit there she comes out of the river and watches me. At least I think she's watching me. No, I'm sure she is. So I was hoping she'd come today and I could show you. Gavin!'

Was there any point even asking her what she was talking about? She was just weird, a weird girl who didn't know where China was and had never heard of swear words. Auntie Gwen was weird and had got herself lost somewhere. There was some weird Chinese kid wandering around in the woods. All just pointless, nothing to do with him, nothing to do with the nightmare he was locked in.

'Slow down a bit! Please don't be cross. I was listening, I swear. Maybe it's the same. I mean, the same woman. Gavin? We're like cousins, aren't we? So it could be the same. Sort of white, with greeny hair? Gavin, wait for me, please.'

Gav stopped and spun round.

'She's nothing to do with you. She's nothing to do with anyone else. She just follows me around.' Her jaw hung open and her eyes were round with shock; he might as well have been shouting and jabbing a finger at her like an angry teacher. 'She's not sort of white and she doesn't have greeny hair. She doesn't have anything or look like anything because she's not real. Get it? She's not real. She doesn't exist. She's nothing. She's just the curse of my fucking life, that's all she is. That's it.'

And now I'm shouting at Marina, he thought to himself, in the horrible silence that followed. The one person I've ever met who looked like she might have listened to me and I'm swearing at her. Nice one, Gav.

Marina swallowed and looked down.

'I don't think that's right,' she said.

What he would normally have done was turn round and march away. He didn't.

'You were telling the truth before,' she told his toes, in a barely audible mumble. 'But now you aren't.'

When she looked up again, he was the one who had to look aside.

'I'd better go first,' she said after a bit. She slipped round him. 'Come on,' she called over her shoulder, and led on through the wood, her stick-thin arms waving like antennae to balance herself, her leather slippers skidding on the wet ground.

He followed in silence. After a few minutes he'd decided he ought to say sorry again, but he didn't know how. He opened his mouth a few times to try it and failed each time. She didn't look back until the path returned them to the edge of the garden, its alleys of limp grass and its tumbledown borders, its stranded barren trees. The house loomed up behind it like an antique prison.

'You should probably get yourself tidied up a bit,' she said.

He looked down at his filthy clothes and hands.

'Yeah. Um, Marina . . .'

'What?'

He saw the words in his head and said them aloud, like a line from a play. 'Sorry I shouted at you.'

'That's OK. Horace does too, sometimes.'

'I didn't mean . . .'

But he couldn't say what he didn't mean, or did mean. That was his problem. He'd lost the power to say what he meant.

'Do you have some other clothes?'

'Yeah. Up at Aunt Gwen's house.'

'I'll wait for you here, then.'

'OK.' And to his shame he found he was glad of the excuse to jog away without another word.

Ten

HE HAD A quick look behind the lodge before he went in, to check the rosebush. Its flowers were still shockingly pink among the withered greens and browns. He traced them with a fingertip, feeling the night's rain lingering on the petals' impossible softness. He thought for a moment about plucking a bloom and taking it to show Marina, but what was he trying to prove? He'd had his chance to tell her about himself, about Miss Grey, to unburden himself, and he'd blown it.

His bag was right inside the door where he'd left it, which was a good thing: the silence of the house had become eerie and he had no wish to go further in. He dropped his damp clothes on the floor and changed as quickly as he could. The only other motion within came from the tealights he'd lit that morning. They were failing now. One sent up a sooty curl as he watched and guttered.

Marina was waiting for him in front of the old house. She examined him, arms folded. To his relief, she seemed to have cheered up. He'd noticed that his absence tended to have that effect on people.

'Now you look like a dressed-up woodwose. You know, you can tell that you and Gwenny are in the same family. Bits of your face are the same as hers.'

'She always used to say I take after my mum.' He remembered (a memory he'd forgotten he had, until that moment) Dad scowling at her once when she mentioned it. As if there were some competition over which of them Gav resembled more, and he'd lost. 'Her sister. Good thing too. Dad's side all look like hippos with freckles.'

'I know hippos. I've seen a picture.'

He decided that it was time to stop sneering at Marina's bizarre conversational habits the way his father would have. 'Good for you.'

'I'm more half and half. Gwen says my mother was the most beautiful creature she's ever seen.'

'Oh. That's, um—'

'Don't talk about it with Daddy around, though. Gwen says it hurts him too much to remember. OK?'

'No, right. So where is she now?'

'She died a long time ago.'

'Oh. Oh, I'm sorry.'

'I don't remember.' She sounded perfectly untroubled. 'I was just a baby.'

He looked around for a way to change the subject. 'So, how long has your dad lived here?'

She cocked her head. 'Always, I think. My mother did too, before she died.'

'Ah. You mean . . . your family's always owned all this?'

'I'm not sure. You could ask Daddy. He knows all about it. He's interested in history. I know he went away for a while. He was on a ship. He was in some kind of battle. They said he could come back and stay for ever.'

'That's great,' Gav said, a little bitterly despite himself. He couldn't help wondering what it would be like to be fond of one's parents.

'Gwen says he and Mummy were more in love than anyone. You know what that means? It's when—'

'Yeah,' he interrupted hurriedly. 'I know. So, um, what's a woodwose?'

'You don't know? It's a wild man who lives in the woods. Not near here. Other woods. I'll dig out a picture of that for you too. We've got one somewhere.' She bounced on her heels and scrunched over the gravel towards the rain-streaked front door.

The only child of a place like this ought to have been pale and silent, Gav thought, as he followed her inside. Flitting around like a ghost. Her mother dead, her father an aged recluse. But instead she'd come out as implausibly bright and shiny as the pink rose in the dead vegetable patch.

He wondered what she'd be like in a couple of years, whether the discrepancy between her world and everyone else's would catch up with her, as it had him, and crush the colour out of her and tarnish the shine.

He wondered when he'd see her again after this week, or if he ever would.

Her father was standing at the far end of the hallway. His back was to them. He was gazing out of the window Gav had looked through before, still leaning on his walking stick. You could easily imagine he'd been there since they'd left.

'Ah,' he said, turning stiffly. 'There you are.'

Gav hung back as Marina slid out of her weird shoes and trotted down the dim hall. The presence of another person instantly made him want to avoid having to make any sort of conversation.

'Where did you get to? Caleb said you were coming straight back.'

'I wanted to show Gavin the lookout. Sorry.'

'As long as you're here now.'

'What's wrong? Where's Caleb?'

'Wrong? Goodness me, nothing.' Her father touched her shoulder. Gav thought he didn't sound very convincing, but perhaps that was just his manner. 'Caleb has gone out for a while.'

'Where's he gone?'

'I'm not certain. Would you like anything to drink, Gavin?'

'Oh, um—'

'I would,' Marina announced.

She took him through to the kitchen. He looked around more thoughtfully this time, now that he felt less like an intruder. In almost every detail the room failed to correspond to any meaning of the word 'kitchen' he recognised. There was no fridge. There was no cooker. There were no right angles at all, no ambience of whiteness and stainless steel and order. There was no kettle or toaster. There were no spaces in which such things could have gone, or sockets to which they could have been attached. There weren't even any lights, he realised. In the high and vaulted ceiling, narrow iron-framed windows opened by arrangements of pulleys and dangling ropes. Their sooty panes grimed the already grey daylight. Marina ducked through an arched opening and returned with a bottle of some sort of juice. She'd pulled the sleeves of her sweater over her hands, as if the bottle were hot to the touch. She got a couple of glasses down from a shelf and twisted off the cap, still with muffled fingers.

They went back to the table where he'd sat before. The fire had been stoked into a big, raw, crackling thing, for heat rather than show. He thought he recognised the drink as elderflower juice, in some cloudy and bitter version, slightly unpleasant in the way expensive organic things always were. It wasn't hot, of course.

'Are you hungry?'

He was, but he remembered the peculiar stuff in the teapot and shook his head, promising himself handfuls of Auntie Gwen's biscuits later on.

'Daddy?'

Her father was still out in the hall, by the big window at the foot of the stairs. 'Yes, my love?'

'Have you found out when Gwenny's coming yet?'

'Not yet.'

'Oh.' An unhappy little sigh. Gav recognised the signs by now – the droop of her head, the wrinkle of her thin eyebrows – and tried to think of a way to change the subject, but Mr Uren continued, coming into the room.

'There's a good chance that Reverend Jeffrey will track her down soon.' The reassurance was directed at both of them. 'It sounds as if she was looking for him for some reason. That's probably where she went, up to the village. I'm sure something' – and he gestured vaguely with the hand that wasn't holding the stick – 'must have held her up.'

'I told you she wasn't here,' Marina murmured to Gav, leaning across the table.

'It hardly excuses her failure to meet your train, Gavin, but no doubt she'll tell the whole story when she arrives.'

'No problem,' Gav said. 'Least I got here.'

Mr Uren nodded pensively. 'Perhaps you should stay in the house until she comes. She'll be anxious to see you as soon as she arrives.'

Gav was sure her father had another reason for his suggestion, though he couldn't have said why. Maybe it was just that he'd spoken a little more firmly than usual. Marina, of course, didn't notice anything.

'Oh yes. Yes. I was going to show Gavin around later, but we should stay in, shouldn't we?'

'I think so.' He smiled half-heartedly. 'We'll find you some lunch in a while. I shall read quietly in my study and keep out of your way.' Gav cheered up at once. 'Come and get me if you need me.'

'All right, Daddy. Caleb thought we should stay indoors too.'

Something unreadable flickered over Mr Uren's expression, a deepening of the shadows of his face. 'He has a habit of caution, but . . . Never mind.' He picked up a book from the edge of the table. His hand was deeply wrinkled, an old man's hand. Much more like a grandfather than a father, Gav thought. He was certainly old enough.

'You don't mind staying here till Gwen comes, do you?' Marina asked him, as her father left the room through a door on the far side. 'I was going to show you around the house anyway.'

He found her simple certainty that Auntie Gwen was about to show up almost more peculiar than anything else about her, but he wasn't going to spoil her improved mood by mentioning it, so, 'No,' he said. 'Course not.' He wished he felt the same way. Some guardedness in Tristram Uren's manner had made him as certain as he could be that the old man wasn't telling them something. And it was obvious to Gav that he'd been waiting for them to get back. He kept thinking of the kid Horace and his weird story, his incomprehensible fidgety nervousness.

Singing?

But Marina was affected by none of this, and he was determined not to puncture her cheerfulness again. She wasn't worried, so why should he be? What was there to be worried about? He tried to make himself stop thinking about it.

It was surprisingly easy. As soon as Marina began conducting him behind the house's doors, along its crooked passages, up its stairs, it became impossible to wonder about anything else.

Gavin had unconsciously assumed that there was a real house hidden out of sight somewhere behind the historic façade. A private family home, where he'd see the fitted carpets, the electric sockets, the radiators, the TV. But the house grew darker and stranger and colder the further Marina led him into it. Its bones and joints kept appearing, the things he'd thought houses always kept out of sight. It was almost like the building was determined to prove to him that it concealed nothing. He saw great slabs of swelling wood embedded in the ceilings or branching from the eaves. He saw bare patches of grey stone anchoring places where walls met, and crosses and curves of iron studding those walls like giant rivets. The walls themselves were uneven, like landscapes – contours of stone behind whitewashed plaster. Except where the rooms had been panelled in dark wood, there were no smooth planes anywhere, no neat, flat, anonymous surfaces behind which all those things that made up a proper house could be hiding, the wires and pipes, the invisible water and heat and light. Everything was in plain sight, rough, used-looking and – most of all – nakedly ancient. Every door was a gate of wood. He could see the nails that held them together, each one a little different from the others. They creaked. He saw and heard the rings of metal that formed their hinges turning as she opened them. Each wall advertised its solidity; Gav kept reaching out his fingers to touch the stipples in the whitewash, the seams of the panelling, the knots in the wood, astonished at how explicit they all were. Even the glass in the windows was visible, full of minuscule waves and bubbles.

Above all the house was *old*, old with that sense of foreignness, forgottenness, that he'd caught as a smell the moment he'd stepped inside, old like the sounds of a dead language. It wasn't anything like a museum. Next to this, all the historic houses he could remember being dragged around were just like costume dramas on the telly. There was no pretence here, no masquerade. As Marina guided him through its dim passages and its mysteriously purposeless rooms, he felt like a visitor from another world. The idea that she actually lived here – that she sat in the strange-shaped chairs with the uneven legs, that she looked out of the distorting windows or warmed herself at the blackened fireplaces, that she kept things in the massive chests like sarcophagi – was simply inconceivable. But he knew better than to say so; he of all people knew better than that. He was never going to gape and blurt out *But there's no electricity! But there's no taps! But what do you do all day!* He followed, and listened, and tried his best to think of this impossible place as her home.

'Gwen says there probably isn't another house like it in the world.' Marina had stopped by the top of the stairs. A pair of keyhole-shaped windows looked out towards the headland and the sea. Adjacent was a niche in the wall that looked like it had once been a window too, but was now closed up and filled, like much of the house, with books. A lot of them were children's books with gaudy covers, looking startlingly unlikely in this setting.

'I'd say she's probably right.'

'What do you think? Do you like it?'

'It's . . .' He shrugged. 'Incredible. Must have stayed like this for hundreds of years.'

'Bits of it are older and bits are newer, actually. We haven't got to the oldest bit yet.'

'Yeah, but . . .' He chose his words carefully, remembering that a lot of what was obvious to him wasn't obvious to her. 'Even the new bits must be way older than most houses. Like Aunt Gwen's house. A lot of people would say that was quite old, but it's nothing compared to this.'

'Oh. Well, that's because people have been living here for longer. Come and see my room.'

There were clothes on the floor, and bits and pieces scattered everywhere else – scruffy-looking stuffed animals with a faintly tragic homemade air, scratchy clothes in muted colours, chess pieces, paper and pencils and playing cards and trading cards and kids' magazines. There was a rocking horse, its paint worn away in places to the bare wood. Apart from those things the room was as comprehensively unlike a teenage girl's room as Gavin could have imagined, not that he'd ever been in one. The bed, for a start, was a four-poster. It had heavy drapes of dark green. There was a large tub of stained metal – maybe copper – resting on a rug in one corner, a porcelain jug beside it, and a folding screen painted with crude flowers leaning against the wall nearby. Despite everything he'd seen so far, Gav refused for a long time to admit to himself that the tub really was a bath.

'I painted that myself,' she said. He realised she meant the screen, and made complimentary noises. 'Well, Gwen helped. We had to make the paints together and work out the mixes for the colours, but I did all the actual flowers.'

'They're lovely.'

'I might try the fireplace next.' Like almost every other room he'd seen, Marina's had a big fireplace with an iron grate and a heap of ash and a basket of scabby logs, obviously used every day. Well, how else would they keep the place warm? Its surround was of reddish wood carved into bunches of berries and leaves. 'I was going to do reds and browns for autumn. What do you think?'

'Erm. Nice.'

'Gwen and I draw a lot.' She gestured shyly at the paper on the floor.

Course you do, he thought. What else is there for you to do? Thirteen years living like it was still the Dark Ages. No wonder she was a bit different.

'Daddy's rooms are just next door but we shouldn't go in there without asking. I'll show you the best bit next. I saved it for last.'

Timbers in the floor popped softly as they passed. Centuries of traffic had worn the wood glossy, and where the daylight fell on it from deep-set windows it shone as if they were skimming through puddles of dark water. The passage turned an angle and up a couple of irregular steps, gained a higher ceiling and ended in a doorway of arched stone.

'You go first,' Marina said.

He pushed at the door rather nervously and stepped through onto the gallery of a high-vaulted hall flooded with chilly winter light. Huge beams of blackened oak spanned the ceiling at his eye level, still bearing the contours of the trees they'd been hewn from half a millennium ago. To his left was a whitewashed wall with three tall latticed windows that looked like they ought to be in a church. The gallery ran round the other three walls, a simple course of wood railed with thick posts and resting on the ends of beams that stuck out from the wall, except at the end where he and Marina had come in: here it was stone, carved in columns and arches.

'This is the oldest bit,' she said, unnecessarily.

Gavin had never seen a room like it. It was grand, but its grandeur was crude, almost primitive. He looked down over the balcony and saw a massive long table, high-backed chairs, a stone floor. Between pieces of furniture Gav had no names for, unexpected things leaned against the walls: a very old bicycle, a wooden ladder, a pair of brooms, an easel, a guitar.

'We don't play in here much in the winter. The big windows make it too cold.' Marina leaned over beside him, her arms propped on the pitted stone. 'But in the summer you can do all sorts of stuff. We got sheets once and made a longhouse under the table. Or we have races on top. This summer Gwen and I got enough paper to cover the whole of it and we invented our own world and drew a map. I might be able to find that. I could show you.'

'Sounds good.' He'd never seen a less likely setting for playing kids' games. And the prospect of hanging out with a thirteen-year-old girl who still wanted to play house wasn't exactly his idea of what to do with his unexpected week away from home, but he remembered his new determination to keep her happy. 'Oh, and you know what? This must be the best house ever for playing hide-and-seek.'

'Oh yes! I haven't done that for years. Gwen and I know everywhere now, but you could try and find me. That reminds me, I have to show you the hidden door.'

'I might have guessed there'd be one.'

She led him round the gallery. It was narrower on the long side of the room, only its low railing of wooden posts guarding the drop. Gav stuck tight to the wall. He almost bumped into her when she stopped abruptly, pointing across the room to the far side. 'See, if you look over there from here, you'd never— Oh!'

Where she was pointing, on the opposite side of the gallery from where they'd come in, the wall was hung with tapestries, though age and soot had obliterated all but vestiges of whatever scenes they'd once displayed. A break in the fabric appeared as a dark slit, and out of that slit poked the edge of a door.

'It's open,' said Marina, puzzled.

'Ah. Yeah, but I can see how usually it'd be hidden behind those things. Cool. Even now you can only just see it.'

'But someone must have gone through.'

'Well, yeah, presumably.'

'No one usually goes in there.'

'Where's it go?'

'I suppose it's fine to look,' she said, out loud but to herself. 'If it's open anyway.'

He followed her around, concentrating on not looking down. She stopped by the gap, pinching her lip. The door behind the tapestries was slightly ajar. A dry and dusty smell leaked out of it.

'So,' Gav said, wondering why Marina was now so uncertain, having been so excited about showing him everything else, 'what's in there that's so secret?'

'Nothing. It's not very interesting, just piles of old books and things. Not storybooks. Stuff nobody uses any more.'

'What's wrong?'

'It's just that Gwen and I were exploring in there once and Daddy came along and got a bit cross. He said it wasn't a good place to be poking around. Perhaps we should ask him before we look.'

'We're not going to poke around, are we?' He wasn't going to let meek Marina take over from happy Marina, not if he could help it. 'You're only showing me. Come on then.' He reached over her shoulder to push the tapestry back. It was much heavier than he'd expected. Half the weight was probably dust.

'Well, all right. It's only for a moment anyway. There isn't much to see.'

But there was.

Everywhere else she'd shown him, there really hadn't been much to see, in the literal sense. The house long predated the Age of Stuff; it was spare, rich only in emptiness. This room was piled with clutter. The door opened onto a rickety landing at the top of a small, steep flight of stairs, built into the room almost like a scaffold. They'd come in right under the ceiling. All around them, reaching down nearly to the floor, were tall cases like old-fashioned library shelves, and all the shelves were loaded with heavy leather-bound things too big to be called books. Ledgers, he thought, though he didn't know what it properly meant. Each one bore a label, a scrap of paper marked by antique handwriting in faded ink.

Every other room he'd seen had felt too big for what it contained, but this was the opposite. Though the ceiling was high enough to accommodate the staircase, and the outside wall wide enough for two tall windows, it was crammed, like an attic or a closet. The layer of dust was visible as a soft chalky fur. The windows were different too: sash windows, the only ones Gav had seen, and probably, he guessed, the only rectangles he'd seen either. The whole room was squarer, more organised even in its untidiness, a little more familiar. Clearly not as old as the rest of the house, despite dust and mouldering paper. It made him think of an old-fashioned bank, the kind prowled by sinister black-suited men with fob watches and whiskery sideburns. There were wooden desks with lots of drawers built into them, their brass handles speckled with tarnish. On the walls above the desks were big maps, printed, their palette faded pinks and greens and browns. On and around and between the desks was an extraordinary variety of boxes, everything from plain cardboard packing boxes to toolboxes and clunky ribbed suitcases and coloured gift boxes from shops whose names he was sure he'd not have recognised even if he wiped away enough dust to read them clearly. There were lots of framed pictures stacked on the floor, leaning face to face. This, at last, was what he expected an old house to look like: crowded and outdated and quietly desolate, full of unwanted things lapsing slowly into oblivion.

Marina sneezed.

'Bless you.'

'Thank you. It tickles my nose.'

'Hey, look.' He pointed at the stairs below them.

'What?'

'Someone went down the stairs. See? Look at the way the dust is scuffed.'

'Oh, you're right.'

'Where does that door go?' Gav pointed down across the room.

'That one? It comes out in the stables. Where there used to be horses. They were rebuilt at the same time as this room. Sort of stuck onto the side.'

'Well, it looks like whoever it was went out that way. See the bar?' A thick post of wood had been leaned up against the boxes. The brackets where it normally rested across the door were obvious.

'I see. It must have been Caleb. He lives in rooms at the top of the stables. He likes it better than being in the house.'

Gav wasn't surprised. 'Ah right. Can we go down?'

She sneezed again and wiped her nose on her sleeve. 'I suppose so. If you want to.'

'Just quickly.' Gav could make more sense of this room than anywhere else he'd been, abandoned though it was. He could guess what it had been before it became merely a place to forget things in. The ledgers must be records of some sort, and the maps looked like they might be charts of Pendurra. Perhaps the history of the house was stored here.

Marina stayed on the landing while he went down the stairs.

'What are you doing? We mustn't poke around, remember.'

'No poking. Got it. I just want to have a look at these maps. Is that OK?'

'All right.'

He squeezed round a stack of things like small shipping crates from the age of tea clippers. He was about to lean over the elaborate desk built into one side of the room to wipe the glass on one of the maps when a small gleam caught his eye. He bent down.

'Hey, Marina?'

'What?'

'I think Caleb opened one of these drawers.'

The brass of a handle shone out dully through finger-wide furrows in the dust. Someone had obviously lifted that handle, presumably the same person who'd made the prints on the stairs.

'Oh,' Marina said, without much interest, and sneezed again.

'Bless you.'

The racks of drawers filled most of the space under the desk. Like the ledgers, they were labelled: strips of paper inserted into neat metal slots, handwritten in a slanted curly script that made Gav think of top hats and horse-drawn carriages. A filing cabinet, from before there were filing cabinets. Records of parts of the estate maybe, judging by the labels. Their careful writing was still legible. *Higher Wood, South West Wood, Menakey Hide. Johnston's Acres. East Pasture. Guneal Acres.*

Squatting, Gavin went very still.

Beech Copse. Spring Acres.

The next one down, where the dust on the handle had been brushed away: *Joshua Acres.*

Joshua Acres.

Something clicked in his head. Then, one after another like dominoes, a whole array of things fell into place together.

'Gavin?'

He opened the drawer. There was nothing inside. He knew there wouldn't be, not now. He pushed it shut again and stood up.

'What is it?'

He felt as if he'd been walking around all morning with his eyes half closed, wilfully ignoring the worried looks around him, the things unsaid, the missing person.

'It wasn't Caleb,' he said.

'What?'

'Who came here. It wasn't Caleb. It was Auntie Gwen.'

'No,' she said, with a shake of her head. 'It can't have been.'

'This is the old office, isn't it?'

'What? Yes, it is.'

'Where you said your dad hid the key to the chapel. You said something about it. Someone tried to get into the chapel, so your dad hid the key. In here.'

'Yes. Do you mean—'

'Hang on.' He scrunched his eyes shut, trying to concentrate. 'When your dad found you and Aunt Gwen in here, and didn't like it. When was that?'

'I don't know. Less than a month. Not very long. Why?'

'OK. Did— Do you know where your dad put that key?'

'The key to the chapel?' She was beginning to sound nervy.

'Yeah.'

Auntie Gwen's senseless scribbled list, the one he'd seen his name on when he'd put his mug of tea down on it: *key chap Joshua Acres*. It was the thing that had been nagging at his memory all along, ever since Horace had stammered out his mishmash of a story. *Key chap*. Nothing to do with a person. The key to the chapel.

'I told you. In here.'

'Did Aunt Gwen know?'

'Know what?'

'That the key was in here?'

'I—' He saw her starting to panic.

'It's OK,' he said, feigning a calm he didn't feel. 'No big deal. I'm just wondering.'

'She did say something about it. I remember. When she and I came exploring in here, she said no wonder Daddy had hidden the chapel key here because it was such a good place, no one could ever find anything. She was joking about the mess.' She sniffed and wiped her nose. 'Is that why Daddy got angry? We weren't looking for anything, we just thought it would be a fun place to explore. I think we should leave now.'

'Yeah. In a sec.' He rubbed his forehead as if he could massage his thoughts into shape. 'Listen. Remember what your mate Horace said?

About Auntie Gwen being all wound up and asking about Horace's mum and some church meeting?'

'Horace isn't my mate,' she said, in a strange voice. 'He's my friend. I told you.'

Gav tried to keep his concentration. 'Yeah. Sorry. But that's what he said, isn't it? He said she asked him about whatever this meeting is. Over and over. For some reason.'

'Did he?'

'Yeah. Definitely. And wait. Just now, when you were talking to your dad. He said Auntie Gwen was looking for what's-his-name. Owen. Reverend Jeffrey.'

'That's right. That's how he knew where Gwen's got to.'

'No. That's not right.'

'But—'

'Let me get this straight. OK. So Owen said, this morning, that Aunt Gwen wanted to see him. You weren't downstairs yet, but trust me, he did. He said Caleb had brought him a message from her. Yeah? You heard that bit, remember? Caleb said she'd asked him to take a message to Owen. Said he'd had to wander all over looking for him.'

'I don't . . .'

'All right. This is it. Aunt Gwen knew Owen wasn't going to be at home.'

Marina looked blank.

'She knew. She asked Horace about it, remember? Loads of times. Whether this meeting was at lunchtime. I'm sure Horace said something about her asking whether he'd be there. Owen. So she knew Owen wouldn't be at home, but she asked Caleb to take him a message anyway. That's the point. When did he go yesterday?'

'Who?'

'Caleb. He went to find Reverend Jeffrey, yeah? When did he go?'

'I'm not sure.'

'Roughly. Morning? Afternoon?'

'Well . . . late in the morning, I suppose.'

'See? Lunchtime. And when did he get back?'

'I don't know. I don't know! I don't understand why you're asking me!'

'Marina, please. This is the last question, I promise. Then we'll go. We'll tell your dad what's happened.'

'What do you mean, happened?'

'Please. When did he get back? Do you know?'

'No. No. Well, he was away a little while. I helped Daddy with some pruning and he still wasn't back when we finished. Daddy was wondering why it was taking him so long.'

'Was he? Well, we know why.'

She just stared at him, leaning over the landing, mute dismay written all over her elfin face.

'Look. It was because Reverend Jeffrey wasn't at home, where Caleb would have expected to find him. He said so this morning, Owen did. He was at this meeting, the one Horace was talking about, the one Auntie Gwen kept asking him about. So Caleb had to spend ages looking for him. And Auntie Gwen knew. That's the point.' He thought he saw a glimmer of understanding in her eyes. 'She had a plan.'

Marina echoed him in a whisper, 'A plan?'

'She knew Caleb would be out for a while. That's why she sent him with the message. So he'd be gone for a bit. That's why.'

After a long pause Marina said, 'Why would she do that?'

Gav remembered that he'd promised not to ask her another question. It seemed like a good moment to keep a promise, so he thought carefully before answering. 'You told me Caleb knows when people are here.'

He remembered Tristram Uren asking, *Do you know when she left, Caleb?* Caleb's answer: *'fore dark yesterday . . . Did you see her go? . . . No.*

Marina nodded.

'Aunt Gwen wanted him to leave so she could go somewhere without him knowing about it. Somewhere around here. And once he was gone, she came in this room. Through that door up there. She came down the steps. We saw the scuffing in the dust. She got down here and she opened that drawer. She knew which one to open. She wrote down the name on the label, Joshua Acres. I know she did. I saw the piece of paper. It's up at her house. Somehow she found out that's where the key was.' *Key chap Joshua Acres.* 'Nothing's in there now. She took it and she went to the chapel, while Caleb was away. She must have planned it all out. Remember Horace said she was totally excited about something? She had an idea. She went there and then something happened.'

'Caleb said she's not here.'

'I know he did.' He tried not to shout at her, though her useless faith in Caleb was driving him mad. 'I know. So after she went there she left. Or maybe she didn't get there, maybe she took the key and then did something else with it. I don't know what happened, all right? But I do know she was supposed to meet my train. Yesterday evening, around half past four, she was supposed to be in Truro at the station. She didn't just forget. I never really believed that. And she didn't get there. So something must have happened in between. Between her sending Caleb off about lunchtime yesterday and coming right here and opening that drawer and taking the key and unbarring the door over there and going out, and the evening when it got dark and she was supposed to pick me up. She never even left to go to the station 'cos she'd have taken her car. It's got to be something at this chapel place.'

He'd tried his very best to keep talking as calmly and reasonably as he could, but even so she looked like she was about to cry. 'I don't . . .' she began.

'OK. It's OK. Let's just go tell your dad, all right? All I have to do is tell him that drawer's empty. He'll know if that's where he put the key. Yeah? That's all we have to do. Then he can sort it out and we'll find out what happened to Aunt Gwen. Everything'll be OK.'

'All right,' she said, plainly not reassured at all. 'Let's go.'

Now it was Gavin's turn to feel nervous. Having promised to do the talking, he wasn't at all sure how easy it would be to explain any of this to Mr Uren. Still, if it would make Marina feel better, he'd find a way.

But Mr Uren wasn't in his study.

The book he'd been reading was still there, open and face down on a table beside a deep armchair. The study was a corner room, much more cosily furnished than the rest of the house, almost like a normal if rustic living room, with a scattering of objects and pictures that for a change weren't centuries old.

Marina ran upstairs, calling. She came back in less than a minute.

'He's gone out. His coat's not hanging up.'

Gav felt guilty relief. He was increasingly sure that someone had done a thing they weren't supposed to. He had a feeling he was getting more and more involved in it without having the faintest idea what it was. His name had been at the bottom of that scribbled list, after all. Capital letters, double underlined. He wished he could remember the rest of it. The name Jess? It would be just like Auntie Gwen to have got some totally loopy idea and decided to involve him in it and spoil his week. The longer he could put off having to tell Mr Uren about it, the better.

'What should we do?'

Gav stared out towards the sea, thinking about his aunt. She might be a paid-up full-time weirdo, but at least he knew she'd have listened to him, without scorn, without anger. She didn't do scorn or anger. And he knew how eager she would be to tell him whatever it was he didn't understand about Pendurra and Marina and everything else.

'This chapel . . .'

'Yes?'

'Where is it exactly?'

'Down in the woods there.' She waved at the dark band of trees filling the view between the open field below the house and the sea.

'We should go look.'

'What? Now?'

'Yeah.' He made sure she was looking at him. 'I know that's where she went. I'm totally certain. Look, what if she had some kind of accident? Maybe, I don't know, she got stuck there somehow.'

'But Caleb said she isn't—'

'For God's sake, will you please stop saying that?' She shrivelled. 'All right. All right, sorry. I don't know, OK? But that's definitely where she went, definitely. I need to go see if she's OK, and you need to come with me to show me where it is.'

'We told Daddy we'd stay here,' she whispered.

'And he told us he was going to sit and read.'

He shouldn't have said that. The notion of being lied to by her father was obviously so apocalyptically distressing to her that it robbed her of speech altogether. 'Look,' he went on quickly, 'we're the only ones who know the key's missing. You told me yourself this chapel's supposed to be kept locked, yeah? And we're also the only ones who know that's where Aunt Gwen went. Your dad might not be back for hours. It'll get dark. I've got to go and at least check it out. If you want to stay here, I'll find it on my own.'

'This is horrible. I don't like it. This isn't how things usually are.'

'Yeah. Weird stuff tends to follow me around. Sorry.' He tried to smile.

'It does . . . it does make sense to make sure the chapel's locked.'

He seized on the hint of encouragement. 'Good point.'

'Maybe that's where Daddy went,' she said. He decided this would be a good time to start towards the hallway and the front door. She trailed along behind him like a reluctant puppy.

'Maybe.'

'But I'm not sure—'

'How far is it?'

'What? Oh . . . only a few minutes' walk.'

'See? So we'll check it out quickly and then we come right back. OK?'

She nodded unhappily. 'OK.'

He waited while she pulled on her mud-slicked shoes, then pushed open the burly door. Somehow it felt almost as murky outside the house as in.

'Round this side,' Marina said, stepping out, taking charge, wanting to get it over with quickly.

She set off through the garden again. At its far end, where it met the encircling woods, a morass of sticks had buried a wall, except where a gap under them revealed an iron gate. She wrestled it open as if it was made of lead and hurried out into the field of long grass that sloped away in front of the house. Gav followed her along its edge down a path of flattened blades marbled with fallen leaves. The tussocks beside it were still beaded with last night's rain, the air too chill to dry it and the sun nowhere to be seen. The slope of the field steepened as they left the house behind. Between them and the horizon white shapes wove among black: seagulls, flying higher than the crows, banking towards the sea.

Marina was subdued. She said nothing at all until they reached the bottom of the field, where a gap in the trees marked a track leading in under the canopy.

'This way.'

He hesitated before following her out of the light. There was no obvious reason to be frightened. He shoved his hands in his pockets and told himself not to be stupid. The strip of woodland they'd entered couldn't be all that wide. Looking out of the window at the bottom of the stairs, he'd seen open land beyond, and the river not far below. Yet from the inside it felt like stepping into a labyrinth of bark and moss and shadow.

Before long they reached a point where the path branched. There was a kind of bridge, just two planks of wood embedded in the mud. A trickle of water ran beneath it. One route followed the streamlet down to the left. 'The river's that way,' Marina told him, and his heart leaped at the prospect of getting out from the cover of the twisting rain-blackened branches, but she led on the other way.

They'd gone only a minute further when a noise like a pulse of wind passed over them. Instinctively, Gav looked up. The trees had not so much as shivered, but above them was a strange movement like the shadow of a small dark cloud blowing swiftly past.

'What was that?'

There was no sun to cast shadows. The clouds were unbroken pencil grey.

'What?'

'That noise.'

'Wasn't it just the wind?'

'There's no wind. I thought I saw . . .'

She followed his gaze up into the motionless crowns of the trees. 'A flock of birds?'

'Maybe, but . . . big.'

'The rooks sometimes fly together.'

He shrugged, trying very hard to ignore the inexplicable tightness clutching his back and shoulders and guts. He'd have suggested they turn round and go home except for the prospect of trying to explain to Marina why he'd changed his mind. 'Never mind. We nearly there?'

'Yes, very nearly. Just up the path a little. Wait.'

'What?'

She raised a hand and stood very still, so he did the same, holding his breath.

Then he heard it too.

It was muffled and faraway. It was the kind of oddly sourceless sound you might hear from a very high window in a quiet street, the sash open just a couple of inches and a radio on in the room inside, or someone practising an instrument. Except that in this case the instrument was a crystal harp, or the radio was tuned to the melody of the spheres.

'Listen!' Marina whispered.

Or it was a sound blown through an invisible window from another world, the land of lost enchantment. The voice that sang was untouched by earth, like a star fallen in among the trees, calling to its impossibly remote kin.

Marina's eyes were shining. 'Just like Horace said! Come on!'

But now, finally, Gavin knew something was happening that was not like anything he had known before. The odd atmosphere in the house, Auntie Gwen's absence, Marina and her peculiar conversation – all these things were strange to him the way everything was strange to him. Being with her had made him accept them. This was her world. If she wasn't worried about it, why should he be? But now, rooted to the spot by his sudden dread, watching her hurry on up the path, he saw, all at once, that her innocence was fragile and terrible. She feared nothing because she'd never had anything to fear. She knew nothing because she'd never discovered how ignorant she was.

Something was wrong.

He wasn't imagining it. An impossible shadow had flown over the wood, and now there was distant singing under the branches, inhumanly beautiful.

It begins.

Come.

'Marina!'

She stopped for a second, twenty paces ahead, diminutive under the great contorted trees. 'Isn't it lovely? Come on!'

'Marina, wait!' He stumbled after her, but her vacillation was dispelled. She was the eager child again, excited about showing him her world, which she understood no better than he did. She pointed ahead.

'There it is, you can see it now. Hurry up!'

'Marina, hang on.'

He'd crested a small rise and the trickling stream had come back into sight. Footway and waterway clambered a short distance together, ascending to a hollow scooped out of the hillside. She was already making her way lightly up the steeper slope.

'Wait!'

'It's just up here,' she called, without turning round. He scrambled after her until he could see ahead.

Some thorny-looking growth overwhelmed the bank of earth at the back of the hollow. Half buried in the vegetation, overhung by the same rough-barked knotty trees that dominated the woods, was a roundish building of worn stone with a pitched roof. There were smaller trees screening it in front, dark straggly evergreens. It looked old, lost, silent, secreted away in woods that had grown and fallen and regrown many times in its history, a relic of some pious impulse that had been dead for centuries. Meant to stay undisturbed, like a tomb. The track led nowhere else; the tangled undergrowth beyond was impassable.

Marina had got ahead and wouldn't wait for him. 'Come and look! It sounded like it came from here somewhere.'

Her peculiar shoes slipped and slid on leaves and earth wet from the night's downpour, but she was quick, so that when Gav saw something night-dark and cruel-faced and impossible uncurl itself from behind the stone parapet above the chapel door and flit down out of sight, he knew he'd left it too late to stop her. He stumbled forward, trying to shout a warning, but horror had stopped his throat. She was concentrating on keeping her footing and hadn't looked up, or back, and he was desperately clumsy on the muddy track. There was a rush of sudden noise all above them: a flight of crows shaking loose from the branches, croaking all together as they sped up towards the light. 'What?' he heard her say, and she turned back for a moment to see him righting himself, but before he could even catch his breath, 'Oh look!' she called excitedly. 'The door's open!'

She had reached the clump of trees in front of the building.

'Stop,' he heard himself yell. 'Don't—'

Too late. She was no longer listening. She was peering round the open door into the chapel.

All the excitement drained out of her in an instant.

Gav saw her mouth one small word, swallowed by the hiss of the woods: 'Gwenny?'

She had taken three hesitant steps forward by the time Gavin scrambled and panted his way to where she stood. Without thinking, he grabbed her hand to pull her away. As he did so, his eyes strayed inside the door and he too froze.

It was the light that stopped him. It rippled and burned dim, like a sunset seen through water. The rest of the interior was night-black. The unearthly radiance glowed around a pool set in the floor, turning the water to dusky fire.

Silhouetted against that light, a thin woman knelt beside the pool. She was a black outline. The dark concealed her.

Two things only caught the gleam and shone. Beside the pool, close to where the woman's hand knuckled on the stone floor, the metal clasp of a small box was glinting, and looped onto a slender silver chain, hanging down from her neck as she crouched forward, something small and darkly glossy reflected tiny star-specks into Gav's unblinking eyes.

His mind had gone blank. The earth under him and the air around him, the damp woods and the winter sky, none of it had any hold on him any more. The singing had stopped.

An invisible voice spoke, a whispering chorus of dead leaves. The molten glow stirred with the words.

Flesh, Master. Recall your promise.

The woman spoke in a voice horribly like and horribly unlike a voice Gavin remembered. Each word was a hard pebble in her mouth.

'Who are these?'

'Gwenny?' Marina whimpered.

Children of the house. The other voice was nowhere. It rustled from the chapel's stones like speaking dust. *The girl, a changeling. The boy, an orphan, and ward of her you seek.*

The shadow of the woman's head lifted. 'Then bring them in.'

Gav found his will again. He tugged on Marina's shoulders and turned to run. There was a confused terror of sudden whirling green in front of his face, coming at him from everywhere. Marina screamed. He was buffeted and scratched. He flung his hands up, closing his eyes, and something crashed into his midriff and sent him sprawling back though the doorway. Marina had fallen behind him. He tripped over her and struck his head, hard, on the stone inside, falling into darkness.

Eleven

Summer 1537

CARISSIMA, 'DEAREST', WAS what the magus called her. The name he had first known her by was an ill-fated one. Other names had been given by those who once venerated her, but that was long, long ago, and in his eyes they no more properly belonged to her than the beggar's rags she wore.

'*Carissima*, the world is changing.'

She answered, 'Change is the law of things, Johannes.'

It was the fall of a summer night. All around was a flat horizon, calm water on one side, on the other the marshes and the wet plain beyond them, pocked with stumpy windmills. He and she walked along a ridge formed of sand and the stiff dune-grass. Though traces of the day hung around its edges, the sky was more brilliant than anyone alive in Gavin's day could imagine. There was no moon, and Earth shed little light of its own in the year 1537, so apart from some skeins of cloud there was nothing to dim the stars. He looked up at their silent multitude.

'This is a new kind of change. It touches even the fixed sphere.'

She gazed upwards also, but said nothing.

'Perhaps it touches even you.'

She put her hand in his. It felt like parchment, dry and yielding. He opened her palm but read nothing there. She rarely spoke at all unless he broke the silence first, and sometimes not even then. He'd become used to the idea that he had to earn words from her.

'The world has grown indifferent to you and I.'

The Latin they spoke to each other composed their conversations to this courtly, formal manner. Johannes could never imagine addressing her in his native speech, though for all he knew every tongue in Christendom was known to her. It would be like a priest saying the Mass in the language of a Saxon peasant, addressing the Author of all things as if He were a market butcher. And yet such things were done now, he reminded himself.

He stroked her open hand with a fingertip. 'You are forgotten, shunned as a beggar by all save me, and I grow old, *carissima*, I grow old. What will you do when I am gone?'

This time she answered at once. 'I will grieve for you and long for you, my lord.'

Domine, my lord, master. She never spoke anything but the truth. The wonder of it almost drowned him.

'I would spare you that grief if I could,' he murmured, holding her close.

'Would you truly, Johannes?'

The question surprised him. He met her look deep and unreadable as the sea. 'Yes,' he answered, full of reckless love. 'I would. I would do anything for your sake.'

She leaned her head on his arm. 'You will regret what you do.'

'Never,' he assured her.

'Never is a long time.'

'I know my heart.'

She smiled sadly, or came as close as a face not made for smiling could. 'No one knows that.'

'Do you doubt me?' He was a little hurt, but it was no use expecting her to mollify him. He might as well look for sympathy from the sea along whose edge they walked.

'You have said yourself that the world is changing,' was all she answered, as she returned her gaze to the sea.

'Not my heart. Not I. I still know what I have always known. But for other men, yes. Inconstancy grips the world. Even the wise no longer pay heed to my knowledge. And where the learned lead the unlearned will follow. I fear there will be no one to come after me.'

He would have said more, but she pressed weathered fingers against his lips. 'That is twice you have spoken of your death,' she said.

'Kiss me, then.'

The stars became pinpricks of hard light, and the hiss and thump of the sea was muffled. They still stood on the dune, but now wrapped in a space that was not there or then, or anywhere or anywhen. As their lips parted, he saw her as he had first seen her, the gaunt solemnity of her face now rich with beauty. There was not a king between the utter west and the farthest east who would not have risked his throne for the chance to hear this woman call him 'my lord', *domine.* Giddy with bliss, he forgot his worries and drew her down to the cool sand.

But though her warning went out of his head, the change he felt and saw in the world was not so easily ignored.

Its first manifestation had been the indifference he began to meet with out of doors, an indifference sometimes bordering on disdain. When he had been an honoured doctor under the protection of the counts Palatine, petitioners had doffed their caps at his door throughout the year, and riders had brought letters from the greatest princes of Europe. Now no one came. If letters arrived, they were answers to his own prior supplications, and he dreaded reading them, because the refusals they contained were offered with something akin to contempt. Even his own patrons were unwilling to meet him publicly. His art had always been feared by the ignorant, and often treated with suspicion even by the educated and the noble, but never in the annals of magic had he read of it being ignored, let alone mocked. There were those now who openly compared it with the tricks of strollers and mountebanks, as if the living spirits of the universe, in all their myriad gradations, were no more than puppets or painted cards.

He did not expect the common herd to distinguish his art from the puerile dabbling of the malicious or ignorant nobodies who called themselves magicians. But when he saw that even studious men no longer had any use for the wisdom he had spent his life pursuing, it was a different matter. It was not because they thought his art unholy, or even dangerous. It was – he only grasped this slowly – because they thought it irrelevant.

Antique. Dead.

That mankind was the pinnacle of earthly creation the magus did not of course dispute, but these new philosophers made man the measure of all things. It was as if nothing existed at all except as it appeared to his eye and was subject to his hand. All the subtler presences of the world, invisible and intangible, had no meaning for them at all. To their way of thinking, magic was not a sin, not a thing to be feared, or even doubted. It was merely unnecessary.

Insidious as these opinions were, he might have dismissed them as simply another case of the usual folly of the world, were it not for the details that were circulating about Copernik's work.

The deranged theories of this one obscure canon in his faraway town at the mouth of the Vistula possessed the magus with a diseased fascination. He could not ignore them. The more he acquainted himself with them, the more he saw in Copernik's single annihilating idea an epitome of the whole cancerous philosophy of the age.

He knew, needless to say, that Copernik was wrong. He knew it the same way he knew that spring followed winter, that water flowed downwards. For decades he had been perfectly familiar with the several virtues of the fixed and the wandering stars. Seated in his observatory on a clear night, he could read their motions as easily as others might read a handbill, and while he worked in his laboratory, he mapped the auspicious or baleful influences they shed as they circled the mortal sphere. And yet! And yet he could not deny that Copernik's dreadful system corresponded in every particular to every motion that the mere eye observed. It dogged him like a recurring nightmare, that vision of the universe reduced to timbers and nails in a shipwright's barn, a thousand disassembled dead fragments of the beautiful vessel whose parts they were. Everywhere around him honest men, men whose diligence and intelligence he acknowledged, shared the same vision. Their universe was a place not of creation but of manufacture, as if God were only a cunning architect, and wisdom consisted in deciphering the ingenious procedures by which His world had been mortared together. In the long light evenings, when noise from the streets carried inside the house, a reminder of how the indifferent city pursued its business outside his doors, he sometimes found himself looking at the codex open on his table and seeing only an inert heap of brittle vellum that would fray into dust after he was gone, the wisdom of ages decayed to inky rubbish.

As midsummer passed, he tried to tell her more explicitly of his doubts and fears. The more he spoke of it, the more an unfamiliar melancholy began to take hold in his thoughts, as if he was no longer sure of what he knew to be true. She listened patiently, as always, but he began to feel he was throwing his words away.

One day he asked her to be silent and listen until he had finished speaking, and then he told her all he knew of Copernik's hypothesis. She listened as she always did, solemnly and without looking away; he sometimes felt that she never blinked.

When he had finished, a sick dizziness came over him, as if he were trying to balance on Copernik's spinning top. He knew the order of creation, sphere within sphere, the Earth at its still centre, and yet in his thoughts he could see the system of Copernik laid out like the mechanism of a giant clock, each part perfectly fitted, flawless. His understanding had split in two. He had no hold on himself: each half stared across an abyss at the other.

'But which is true?' he cried out, welling up with childish tears. 'Which is true? Why will you not tell me the truth?'

She held his head between her hands. Her expression was mute grief, as if there was something she wanted to say but could not: a pitying look. It was the first time he had seen weakness in her face.

'Is that what you want?' she asked, when he was quieter. 'To know the truth?'

When he thought back on that question the next day he was ashamed. It pained him to remember begging her, who called him *domine*, to settle the disputes of the clerks as if she were Holy Paul in Rome. There was a lingering humiliation in having been comforted by those knuckly hands.

For the first time in a number of months he turned to work as a distraction and a relief. It occurred to him how far he had neglected his studies since the spring, and he found a guilty pleasure in returning his attention indoors, where she did not come. When they did meet again, he was careful not to refer to the subject that had troubled him.

It was some weeks later, and he had assumed his aberration was forgotten, when – most uncharacteristically, and out of nowhere – she put the same question to him again: 'Johannes, can you bear to know the truth?'

It was a startlingly unpleasant surprise. They were walking, peacefully until that moment, by a musty riverbank on a warm afternoon. The magus's mood soured at once.

'I am *magister*,' he answered loftily, after a pause. 'A teacher. It is not for my own sake that I dedicated my life to knowledge. If I do not seek truth, who will? I cannot let the whole world suffocate in ignorance.'

'The end you fear,' she said, 'is coming.' She was quivering slightly despite the summer heat.

He looked at her in astonishment. Who was she to speak to him of fear? Unwanted, accompanied by a prickle of shame, the memory of having cried in her arms like a boy with night-terror came to him again.

'I am not afraid,' he said.

'My gift is going from me.' She seemed not to have heard him. Her voice sounded strained, as if she were ill, or unbearably tired. She stumbled in the lank grass and would have fallen if the magus had not caught her shoulders. 'Johannes.'

'*Carissima*.' He was amazed by how frail she felt. Her head bowed against his chest and a deep shudder ran through her, so violent that the magus instinctively looked up to see whether a sea wind was stirring the tops of the alders, or a cloud had blown across the sun.

'I have carried this burden so long. For so long. I am tired.'

Puzzled, he smiled an uncertain smile. 'Then let me give you ease.'

'You alone did not turn away from me,' she whispered. 'You stayed to hear.'

He had never known her in this mood before. Usually so self-possessed, she seemed – he scarcely believed it – afraid. It softened him. His pride could not support the idea of receiving comfort from her, but now it was his turn to give it instead his truculence melted away.

'I love you,' he told her, for (though he did not know it) the last time.

'You are still free to choose.' Her eyes seemed to search inside his, pursuing some certainty that slipped away like an otter in the riverbank. 'Men and women are always free. Will you take my burden from me, Johannes? Can you bear the truth?'

He looked down at her, speechless.

'It is a terrible thing to give,' she went on. The afternoon glowed around them and the sluggish water passed by, thick with drowned pollen, insects crowding above it like flakes of dust in low sunlight. The day seemed altogether ordinary and yet the magus was beginning to suspect that something extraordinary was about to happen, that he was about to find out why she had come to him, across the ages, a living miracle. 'I have tried not to speak of it. I have tried, Johannes. Words sting me and I stop my mouth. But I knew as soon as you came to me. I knew, though I fear for you.'

He held her shoulders gently, coaxing. He was sure the answer to all the questions she had shied away from was near the surface now, coming up into the light. 'What is it that you knew?'

She hooked her hands over his arms. 'All that time I have known. All that time I have waited for you. Waited, waited. A long road, Johannes.' She was unburdening herself of words as if they were stones round her neck. His heart beat hard as he stood ready to catch her.

'I am here now. Let me comfort you.'

'Is this what you truly wish? To bear the burden? To know truth?'

He could hardly believe what he was hearing and yet the meaning of it rushed up towards him, into the clear open air. Her burden. The truth. It was the very meaning of her ill-fated name: it was proverbial.

Prophecy.

He watched in mounting wonder as she unfolded her hands from his arms and clasped them together.

There was a ring she always wore. He had barely noticed it before, even when their fingers were knotted together in passion. It was merely a pauper's ring. Plain, oak-brown, unadorned. A beggar's ornament. Now she was slipping it from the index finger of her left hand.

He laughed a brief laugh of baffled delight. 'Do you mean to wed me, then, *carissima*?'

She stared at the ring with intense concentration and ignored his jest.

'Once I broke a pledge.' Her voice was barely audible, buried under the weight of ages. 'This was my punishment. To carry the pledge with me always, and to know it broken.'

The magus was used to riddling speech. It was the stock in trade of insubstantial beings. Lacking flesh and lacking freedom, they did not have the capacity to lie and so would often resort to evasions and obfuscations. He had never expected to hear anything of the sort from her mouth, however. He wondered whether she was distracted or feverish, though not once had he imagined she could suffer ordinary afflictions.

She took his left hand and opened it, palm up.

'I saw this, long ago.' She lowered the ring into his palm. 'The last punishment. Offering my burden to him I love. My gift.' She withdrew her fingers. The ring lay in his open hand, warm and smooth.

Her gift, the magus thought. His head felt as sluggish as the summer river, but through the confusion and surprise a swell of deep excitement was gathering. He knew what her gift was. Everyone did, everyone who could read. *To know the truth.* And he knew how long she had carried it. *Always.*

Unendingly, beyond time. Deathless.

He closed his hand over the ring.

Part III
Tuesday Evening

Twelve

THEY WERE RUSHING through a tunnel. The noise of it filled his head, and she was there, in the dark. Except now for some reason he wasn't frightened, and the tunnel wasn't coming to an end. Miss Grey looked steadily at him from somewhere that wasn't next to him and wasn't far away . . . There was a lot of pain, he noticed. The whistling dark began to rub away at everything. It seemed like she and he and the train were all about to dissolve into black sound, and then she said his name. She said it wrong, like she always did: instead of the 'v', which made your lips sneer for a moment, there was a liquid run of vowels in the middle, her mouth forming a little circle, a kiss.

There wasn't a train after all. Only her, speaking in the dark.

'Are you afraid?' he heard her say. 'Don't be afraid. You have come home.'

She couldn't make the pain go away, but nevertheless he was reassured.

'The door is opening,' she said.

'Welcome,' she said, and smiled. Her eyes looked different, less distracted. Oh, I know, he thought, it's because she's seeing right inside me. But where was he? He couldn't work it out.

'Come,' she said. Then after a pause she repeated it, more sharply. Her look hardened. Then a third time, now definitely not an invitation but a command: 'Come!'

I can't tell where I am, Gav thought. How can I go anywhere? He recognised this nightmare now. It was the one where everything got heavy, your muscles stopped working, you had to will each separate movement of your limbs but you could never get them to add up together. You couldn't make yourself go.

'Come!' she cried a fourth time, as if something terrible would happen if he didn't. The rushing got louder; the end of the tunnel was coming fast. Everything was swept away.

He saw his hand in front of his face. He recognised it. I know it, he thought, like the back of my hand. He tried twitching it and saw the fingers flex. He made them touch his forehead, where it hurt. The press of fingertips against his skull scooped out little hollows in the pain. He was lying somewhere hard, cold and almost entirely dark. Something was wrong outside, but he couldn't remember what, or what he thought he remembered couldn't be right. Under his cheek and palms was stone. A stone floor. On the floor there had been, kneeling—

He pushed his head up and looked around wildly. The ache flared up and out; he scrunched up his eyes and gasped. Going back to unconsciousness seemed like the best idea, but the opportunity had passed. All around his throbbing skull and his scratched arms and his bruised ribs and his dry mouth there was something else pressing on him, a tingling, insistent sense of being under threat.

He'd seen . . . He'd heard—

Terror seized him, made him pull his knees under him until he was crouching, panting, staring into the impenetrable darkness. A moment later the convulsion took its toll. He tumbled onto his knees and clutched his head and moaned.

An invisible voice croaked, 'Drink.'

He cringed backwards, thumping into hard wood behind him. There was a patch of faint light smeared across the stone and he pressed himself onto it. 'Who's there?'

'Drink. Water. Take off the ache.'

There was something wrong with the voice, horribly wrong. The mouth that made it sounded bone, not flesh. Though the shadows hid it, it was close.

'Who's there?' He twisted round wildly, looking for any disturbance in the dark. A second later and he was squeezing his head in his hands and keening with pain.

The voice said something like a caw followed by a choke. Then, 'Drink. Here.'

A gentle *plip* came from nearby and suddenly Gav could see water. Little ripples were moving across it, raised edges glimmering. He realised he was desperately thirsty. The water was close, and the dark voice seemed further away. His mouth begged to drink. Slumping onto the cold floor, he pulled himself forward, inching along until he came to a lip of stone, worn smooth. He dipped his fingers down.

'Drink.'

In the darkness he had the odd sensation that he was putting his hand into the earth. He cupped some water in his hand, splashed a few drops onto his tongue.

Then immediately his eyes were wide open, though seeing nothing. The taste in his mouth was not just chill water, but something else, a memory he knew but couldn't put a name to, something he'd forgotten for a long time. It was so vivid it drove everything else out of his head, the agony and the fright, and so forceful that it was a few heartbeats before he even noticed they were gone.

He lifted his head and looked around. He could hear outside sounds, a muted gusting wind, and also an inside sound, that special kind of audible silence that belongs to old, undisturbed places. A line of dim daylight trickled through a finger's-width gap beneath a closed door behind.

He scooped another handful of water to his mouth, feeling it wash away the last of the pain.

'Feel better.'

For a few tenuous heartbeats he'd hoped the water had washed the voice away too. It croaked from the utter darkness, flat, harsh, passionless, much too close. Gavin backed away on his hands and knees towards the strip of light under the door. The shooting stars had gone from his vision. He was looking into sheer black, like the mouth of a stone well opening in front of him.

Someone lived at the bottom of it.

Something.

'W-who . . . ?' he stammered. 'Wh-what—'

It moved.

Swathes of dark resolved themselves into volumes of shadow. A man-sized blot was gathering. Its shape was badly wrong. It made a dry scraping sound as it came closer. Limbs swayed. A curved black thing touched the floor. There was a little glister there, an opacity hard and smooth enough to shine.

Like a claw.

Gav threw himself at the door. His hands thudded into it and scrabbled around, banged on it, fumbled for a handle.

'Locked,' croaked the voice.

'Let me out.' He found a heavy metal latch and rattled it frantically. Echoes rang around him. The door did not budge. His fingers pressed into the crack beneath, reaching for the outside. 'Help! Let me out!'

'Can't. Locked.' The grim voice was closer. It came from a body that seemed to swallow light. 'No help.'

'Stop!'

'OK.'

'Don't— Get back!'

'OK OK.' The shape slid back into unbroken shadow.

'What . . . what . . .' Gavin's palms squeezed against the underside of the door. His fingers curled and clung to the wood. 'Where . . .' Each question crumbled away before he knew what he has saying. 'Where . . . Who . . .' He knew where he was. The wind outside brought it back to him, that and the thick wood blocking his escape. The stone chapel, abandoned in overgrown woods. With a surge of dread he remembered how he'd stood at its doorway, looking in, and seen something too appalling to think. He thudded his head against the door to try and expel the memory. The molten light had fled and he was sealed inside, with . . . with . . .

Absolute darkness. He couldn't bear it, couldn't bear the silence it concealed.

'Are you there?' It came out as a strangled squeak.

'Yes yes.'

'Who are you?'

The cawing noise again.

'What?'

'*Corbo.*'

'Wh-what are you doing?'

'Watch. Talk.' A grating monotone.

'I want to get out.' His eyes scrunched shut. Tears were leaking out of them.

'Can't.'

'I want to go home.'

'Can't.'

'I want to get out. Let me out. Get me out. Get me . . .' His voice rose to a horrible shrieking whine before he ran out of air and his mouth gagged vacantly. The panic emptied into despair. Knees pulled up, head bowed between them, he curled tight against the door and the unforgiving stone. His shoulders shook weakly for a while. Tiny moans squeezed out of him and vanished into the silence.

In a little while everything was still.

'Can't,' the voice reminded him, after a long pause.

'Just shut up,' Gav whispered.

'OK OK.'

He raised his head and wiped his nose on his sleeve.

He'd been stuck in a lift once, a few years ago. Him and a babysitter. They'd been in there quite a while, in the dark, some sort of power cut. The babysitter got her phone out and used it for light. They'd sat together playing games on its tiny screen, sharing the little rectangle of phosphorescence, just the two of them. Eventually there had been lots of banging and shouting and thumping, and then the point of a crowbar appearing between the doors, prising them open, letting in blinding light and a crowd of busy, anxious faces asking busy, anxious questions.

For the next couple of months whenever the babysitter took him out he'd insisted on going in as many lifts as possible, but they never got stuck again.

Outside a seagull shrieked. The air seeping through the crack under the door was as cold as its cry.

'Are you there?' Gavin said, when his breath was steady again.

'Yes yes.'

He swallowed. 'Who are you?'

'Told you. Corbo.'

'Who's that? What's going on? Why am I locked in here?' He bit his lip to stop the rising panic taking over again, and hugged his knees tighter.

'One, two, three.'

'What?'

'Who, what, why. One, two, three. Hard answers. Too much.'

'What . . . ?' As he tried to steer his way between bafflement and the horrible buzzing drone of fear, it occurred to him, out of nowhere, that this was a conversation. He was not understanding, the way he normally failed to understand. It was a straw of familiarity to clutch to. His old friend ignorance.

'Are you . . . are you shut in here too?'

'Yes yes.'

He swallowed, wiped his dry lips. 'Why?'

'Told you. Watch.'

'Watching what?'

'You. What else? Water, stone. Not going away, *wraaaaaa*.' The last sound was a long guttural rattle, like a caw.

'Who . . . who . . .' He took a deep breath. 'I mean what. What are . . .'

The answers had been coming so swiftly that the silence dangling from his suspended question was horribly unnerving.

'. . . you?' he finished. 'What are you?'

There was a clacking sound and another wordless gurgle, *kkrrrrr*. Gav pushed himself tighter against the door, terrified that it might be moving again. 'No. Don't—'

'Hard one,' it interrupted. 'You try. See for yourself.'

'Wh-what?'

'What are you? You try. Not so easy, *caaaarkk*.'

He tried. 'I-I'm,' he stammered. 'I'm . . .'

I'm locked in the dark with an invisible beast. I'm lost. I'm alone. I'm special. I'm cursed.

'I'm frightened,' he said. 'I'm so frightened. I'm cold. I'm scared.'

'Bad time.'

Despite himself he choked a bitter laugh. 'You could say that.'

'Get worse.'

The cold crawled up from the stone he sat on, into his spine.

'What's happening?' he whispered.

'Not much. Talk. Bored.'

He stared hopelessly at the virgin dark, trying not to imagine whatever it was that stood there watching him and yet unable to prevent an image appearing on the black screen. The glimpse of a clawed and withered toe, the grim croaking voice, the clacking of a hard beak. A monstrous bird.

'No, I mean . . .'

When he was six or seven, there'd been a couple of weeks when he kept being woken up by a crow in his bedroom. He never forgot it. He only had to think about those nights for a moment and at once he was reliving the fear, the thrashing of his arms in the dark to keep the wing-beats away from his head, knocking over his bedside light, groping around frantically on the floor for the switch and, when he'd found it, crouching rigid in the corner, staring at the blunt black head swivelling and tilting as it eyed him from its perch on the curtain rail. And when Mum rushed in, the thumps and bangs and yells having panicked her too, the head bobbed about to watch her, until eventually she said, 'There's nothing there,' and once she said it, it turned out she was right: the bird was gone. His mistake. Even though he couldn't stop making it, until one night Dad came in instead.

'I mean . . .'

When he was two – Auntie Gwen had told him the story – they'd all gone on holiday to the beach, the three of them and her. There were crows roosting above the cottage they'd stayed in, and he'd cried every time he heard them call. Every time, Auntie Gwen said, day and night. At first they'd thought he was ill with some invisible and terrible affliction, and put him in the car, where he stopped crying, and took him to the hospital, where there was nothing to cry about and nothing for any doctor to find wrong with him, but as soon as he was back at the little house under the tall pines, he began to scream again. So after two days of their week's holiday they had come home (except for Gwen, who thought she might as well stay, and then fell in love with the area and ended up never coming back at all).

'Not here. Not in here. I mean . . .'

Gwenny? The woman he'd seen, here, the thin silhouette, the right shape and size. And then something had spoken, and after that a chaos of terror and motion and falling.

'What's happening with . . . with my aunt? And Marina? Where are they?'

'Aunt. Marina.'

It took him a while to understand. Oddly, being forced to puzzle out the toneless replies worked as a barrier against the creep of mindless fear. It gave his thoughts something to get a grip on.

'My . . . The person I saw. Here. And Marina. The girl who came with me.'

'*Caaaarkkk*, aunt. Sad boy.'

He waited, but it said no more. The silence was as suffocating as the dark. A question, he told himself. Ask a question.

'Where . . . where is she? Where are they?'

'Gone. Out.'

'Out? Where? Why?'

'House. Waiting.'

'The house? They went to the house?'

'Yes yes.'

'They . . . Waiting? For what?'

'Witch.'

'What do you mean, which?'

'What I said. Listen. Stupid boy.' There was scratching, hideously loud in the locked chamber.

'No, sorry. Don't— Please. Don't come closer.'

'OK OK.'

Sorry? He was apologising to this thing? This monster in the dark, this skeletal voice, which he was now sure belonged to the gargoyle blur of bent wings he had glimpsed on the roof of the chapel, descending like the image of death itself as Marina clambered innocently towards the door? His thoughts scattered again. How long had he been unconscious? The patch of light that crept in under the door and spread over the stones, the patch where he sat, was shrinking. His hands clasped each other. He felt the small scratches all over them.

'Why am I here?'

'You came. Followed girl.'

'I mean inside, locked inside.' The memory was suddenly appallingly fresh. 'Something hit me. It was pushing me, something rough. Knocked me over.'

'*Aaaaaark*, Holly.'

'What?'

'Holly.'

'Like in the tree?' No answer. 'A holly tree?'

'Yes yes.'

'Trees can't . . .'

'Crows can't talk, *caaark*,' and it coughed out its chuckle again.

'What . . . you mean . . .' But Gav couldn't put this into words. If he tried to say the thought aloud, everything would crumble into madness. Uncontrollable fear waited for him, lapping around his heels. Something else, he thought desperately. Ask something else.

'Marina,' he said. There was a confused memory: her scream, a protracted instant of fear, falling. 'Is she OK?'

'No no.'

'What?'

'No no.'

'What . . . Is she hurt?'

'Inside.'

'Inside what?'

'Hurt inside. Grief, *krrwwww*. Misery.'

In the silence Gavin listened to his breath, fast and shallow, as if it was about to run out.

'Misery?'

'Echo. I say you say. Stupid boy. Bored.'

He tightened his fists and squeezed his eyes shut. He wondered if there was no voice at all. Of course there wasn't; there couldn't be. *Oh come on Gav.* It was all inside him, the darkness inside mocking him. He'd brought it with him here. He'd infected Marina with it.

'Let me out,' he whispered.

'Can't. Told you. Listen.'

'When? When can I get out?'

'Come back. Open door.'

'What? You mean when they come back?'

'Who.'

'Marina and, and my . . . And the person. Who was here.' Gav felt his voice faltering again. Whatever it was that was so wrong, at the centre of it was the shape silhouetted against that unearthly light.

'Her. Yes.'

'So when? When are they coming?'

The voice cawed very softly. '*Caaaaark.* Can't say.'

'Why not? What are they doing?'

For the first time there was a hesitation before the answer came, and he heard a brief shuffle in the dark. 'Told you. Went up. Waiting. Took half-girl.'

'The what? Marina?'

'Yes yes.'

'And they left me here?'

'Yes yes.'

'Why?'

'Bait.'

'What?'

'Bait.'

'Bait? Like in . . .' He struggled for something to make sense of, anything, before the gathering cold and dark dissolved him completely. 'Bait? For what?'

'Witch.'

'Which what?'

'*Kkrrraaaa*, witch. Old witch. Old mad witch. Old old old.'

He dared not fall silent. If he stopped talking there'd be nothing left at all; he'd fall without stopping. It was more like a tomb than a chapel. Silence and blackness and deathly cold. 'A . . . a witch? Bait for a witch? Me?'

'Yes yes.'

'But . . . what's . . . What have I got to do with it?'

'Everything, *kkrrwwww*. Stupid boy.'

His voice withered to a whisper again. 'I don't understand.'

'Learn fast. Bad time.'

'Help me.' It was scarcely louder than a breath. He felt the tears pushing up again.

'Can't.'

Of course not. He was alone, finally utterly alone. The thing in the dark wasn't real. He should know better. Except that he didn't know anything at all.

'Who am I?'

'Sad boy. Stupid boy. Names, *aaaarrkk*. Lots more.'

But this time he had meant the question only for himself. It was the thing he didn't know, the hole in the middle of him. He'd never known it was there, the hole, until Mum and Dad and everyone had starting telling him about it. Even then he hadn't asked himself the question. Not until now, when everything else had gone.

He didn't really hear the reply from the dark, because as soon as the question was whispered aloud he remembered another answer, spoken by another voice, a voice like dead leaves.

The girl, a changeling. The boy, an orphan, and ward of her you seek.

He sat unmoving, eyes wide open.

After a long, long time he said, 'Corbo?'

'Yes yes.'

'What's a ward?'

'Ward. *Wrrkk*. Belonging thing.'

But he hadn't really needed to ask. He read a lot, he always had. It was a way of surviving as an only child in an unhappy home. Mr Bushy had noticed it and steered him towards some Victorian novels, library books with fusty slow-starting stories that he was always just about to give up on when they suddenly got interesting and he ended up needing to know what would happen and spending weeks reading to the finish. One of them had featured a ward. It stuck with him: the idea of a child who didn't really belong to their parents, who was just surviving until the time when their inheritance would come and the people they'd thought of as their mother and father would be revealed to have no connection with them at all, no power over them.

Orphan.

Here, in the dark, was his wish coming true?

Ward of her you seek.

He mouthed her name to himself soundlessly, afraid that saying it aloud might break the spell: *Miss Grey*.

Old mad witch. Miss Grey, who wasn't real, so they said, except to him. Miss Grey, whose worn and patient face was unchanging, ageless. Miss Grey, who had shocked him by suddenly raving aloud.

'Corbo?'

'Yes yes.'

'This witch,' he said slowly. 'You mean . . . she'll come here . . . because of me?'

'Could do.'

'And then what?'

'Gets killed.'

He froze.

'What?'

'Gets killed.'

His heart and mouth turned to stone together.

For the first time since inviting him to drink from the pool, the thing spoke unprompted. 'Told you. Bad time.'

'Corbo.' The strangled grip had closed round his throat again, the dread. 'Let me out.'

'Can't.'

He rattled the door behind him again. 'Please. Let me out. Please.'

'Can't. Locked.'

'Who—' He shoved himself against the door, but its ancient timbers were far tougher than him. 'Why—' The wind picked up again outside, out in the open, moaning more fiercely. 'Who wants to kill—'

'Names. Can't say.'

'But why?' He was crouching on his feet, tight against the door, fingers roaming for the lock. 'Why would anyone—'

'Told you. Bad time. Bad beginning. Your sort, *ccraaak*. Too much wanting. Do this, do that. Do without suffer. Take without give. Same old same old.'

The answer went over his head like birdsong. He found a patch of rough metal. He plucked uselessly at it. 'There must be . . .' He was completely blind; he couldn't even figure out the shape of the door. 'There's got to be—'

An abrupt commotion of rustling and scraping made him sink to his knees in terror.

'Man coming,' croaked the voice, much nearer. 'No talk.'

'No. Don't—'

The blackness took shape. A mass of it came towards him; atop it, something glinted like a fragment of polished slate. Everything happened at once. There was a lull in the wind, and he heard footsteps outside, moving through the wood. At the same time something locked round his wrists: a fierce grip that pressed and curled like fingers but had no warmth or softness. The grasp jerked him upwards. He saw a thin and strangely bent black arm, and, before he was dragged out of the sanctuary of feeble light, a gleaming round eye, and he smelled breath that reeked of sour meat and earth. The arm was appallingly strong. It pulled him away from the door as if he was made of paper.

'No talk,' the voice grated, right by his ear. He was dragged deep into the shadow to one side of the door. He would have collapsed had its grip not stayed clamped on his arm. 'No talk. No sound.' With paralysing horror he felt a touch on his neck, some beaked and bony part of its face nudging his bare skin.

Heavy steps trod through the sodden leaves towards the door and stopped. There came a rattle – a key in a lock – and a heavy creak. The door was opening.

The sound and smell of the twilit wood rushed in. Through blurry eyes Gavin saw a dark oblong swing towards him, silhouetted by a chilly pallor that was more welcome to him at that moment than any sunrise. The thing had dragged him behind the door so that it blocked his view as it opened. He couldn't see the man at the entrance, breathing hard as if he'd been running. An old man's breath, shaky.

The last dusk light fell into the chapel through the door and for the first time Gavin saw something of where he was. Two squat columns flanked the pool, which was a hexagon of darkness in the middle of the space, a hole opening into nothing. There was no altar, no furniture, nothing more than a couple of smudgy rectangles against the back wall which must once have been pictures, now decayed almost to invisibility.

On the far side of the pool from the door, just where Gav had seen it before, a small old-looking box lay on the bare stone, its hinged top open. Behind it was a scrap of glinting fractured metal, a small mirror, its surface shivered with cracks. They were the only things to see. Gav could almost feel the man's eyes falling on them.

'Ah, God,' the man said, in a broken whisper.

The outside air blew in and drifted against Gav's cheek, exquisitely precious. His heart sank in despair as he heard the man shift, turn round.

Barely daring to breathe, he fixed his eyes on the edge of the door as if the force of his gaze alone could hold it still.

The door began to swing closed. Gavin couldn't help himself. He twitched forward, terrified of losing the light again. At once the hideous grasp tightened. His gasp was drowned out by the scrape of the hinges. The latch clanked shut.

The steps started up again and faded. Now that he could do nothing but listen, he was sure he recognised their unhappy cadence, and the catch of grief in the voice. It was Tristram Uren who had made his way here, seen whatever it was he needed to see, and was now limping away.

The pressure against his neck eased and then the grip released him. He crumpled down onto stone.

'Gone,' said the voice, above him.

Gav crouched on hands and knees, shivering.

'Didn't lock,' it added.

He looked up. His eyes hadn't yet readjusted to take in the tiny sliver of fading twilight under the door; he couldn't see a thing. It was true, though. He'd surely heard the noise of the key turning in the lock before Tristram had opened it. He hadn't heard it again afterwards.

After a careful pause he said, 'Corbo?'

'Yes yes.'

'Can I go?'

'*Aaaaark.* Not locked.'

'Will you . . . will you stop me if I try and leave?'

Again he was unnerved by the long pause before it answered. He had a strange feeling that it was struggling with its reply.

'No no,' it said at last.

He crawled a few inches towards the door. The thing did not move behind him. He went on until his groping hand felt wood. Very slowly, he stood up and found the latch.

'Um,' he said, 'do you . . . ?'

Silence.

'Do you want to come out too?'

'*Wraaaaa.*' A rough-edged, passionless groan. 'Want, yes. Go, no. Take your chance.'

He inched the door open. Sweet wild windblown air poured over him, and he saw the crowns of trees tossing against a sky whose last blue had almost surrendered to black.

'Um,' he said, unsure where to look, 'Corbo. Thanks.'

'Suffer for it,' the voice croaked. Already it sounded small. The tumult of the wood overrode it.

'I'm sorry,' Gav said.

'Go. Learn fast. Worse next time.'

He stepped out into the open and began to run.

Thirteen

IT WAS ALL he could do to keep his footing. The path was barely visible. He ran full pelt through slippery stony three-quarter darkness, gasping aloud each time a twig plucked at his legs or arms. Behind the screen of trees to his right, slow-moving water turned the dusk into a sinister velvet glimmer. He couldn't believe how dense and alive the dark was. He fought back the urge to call for help. Anything might come, anything: the croaking clawed thing, the other thing he wouldn't let himself think about, or not until he'd got himself away, far away.

Try knowing better than that, he told himself savagely. Just try!

He sprinted faster. He tripped more than once, tumbling into the mulch of muddy leaves, scrabbling up again. The scrapes on his hands stung against clammy earth. He looked over his shoulder: nothing but whispering black. He blundered on. He tried to remember the way he'd come with Marina but nothing looked the same, it was all just deep shadow, and anyway that was in another world, a lifetime ago.

A slit of lesser darkness appeared ahead. At the sight of that break in the trees he forced himself to go faster, afraid it might vanish.

Quite suddenly he was out of the wood, a purple-black sky opening above him. He ran into the field. Above, the outline of the ancient house squatted against the horizon like a stone beast. Firelight sputtered behind the lower windows. For a moment he thought he saw someone moving in a corner room. He raised his head, slid on the wet matted grass and fell heavily. The evening damp clung to him as he scrambled to his feet again. Legs and lungs began to burn; stopping had made them worse.

Go, he told himself. Go go go. Get away, get out. He tried to make himself think. It was impossible. His pulse thudded in his ears like a galley drum. It sounded like words, like the Corbo thing's hideous pronouncement, *Bad time, bad time, bad time.* His feet thumped the same rhythm against the ground.

At the top of the field the iron gate leading through the overgrown wall was still open, though he could barely make out where it was. He had to slow down to find the spot, and when he put out his hand to push the bars of the gate, it was as if the metal was the beast's claw, pressing on his skin again.

He stopped in the darkness under the tangle of dry stems, hands on his knees, breath heaving. For the first time he thought about where he was going. The front door of the house wasn't far away. Should he warn them? Could he find Marina again, make sure she was OK?

What could he say?

What if they knew?

Was this what no one had told him about Pendurra? That it was haunted, that it was cursed even more horrifyingly than he was?

At the groaning sound of a heavy door opening he froze, holding his breath. The front door.

From where he crouched he saw light spill onto the gravel in front of the house. A vivid, slick red-orange light, quivering with sinister motion. Someone was there, coming out. He heard a step.

Something.

He bolted. He dodged and ducked through the garden, veering away from the clumps of darkness as they loomed up over him, following avenues of shadow close to the edge of the trees. When he reached the mouth of the decrepit driveway, he risked a quick glance back over his shoulder.

The light outside the house was gathered into an eerie floating ball like phosphorescence in pitch-black water. It hovered at the head of a stick, and the stick was held in a person's hand, and the person, invisible behind the evil light, was coming towards him.

He put his head down, gritted his teeth against the burning protests in his legs and sprinted into the dark. He hadn't seen who it was. He hadn't wanted to. Now he only wanted to get out. Run up the drive, through the gates, out into the road, the real world, out out out. Anywhere else.

The driveway was completely invisible under the trees. He followed it without knowing how. He couldn't slow down no matter how blinded he was. When another light winked suddenly through the cage of branches ahead, he yelped in terror, but an instant later he identified it as electric light, harsh and bright. The light in Auntie Gwen's porch.

Someone stood there.

He almost fell again. Trapped, he thought, and for a terrible second he saw himself back in the stone tomb, the door slamming shut behind him. Then the person under the porch light moved. Perhaps she'd heard his steps under the trees. She turned and peered down towards him. He recognised the silhouette, and at the same moment he remembered her promise, which at the time had been the last thing he wanted to hear: *Tell you what – I'll come back tomorrow, around this time, just to set my mind at rest.*

He ran on. She stepped away from the porch as he came, staring curiously into the darkness from which he fled.

'Is that . . . ?'

He twisted round to look back down the driveway. Through the screen of old trees he glimpsed the light that was never firelight, bobbing its way slowly up the path.

Hester Lightfoot only gaped at him, astonishment all over her face.

'Get me out of here,' Gav said. 'Please. Now.'

On the other side of the river, Horace Jia slouched at the back of a bus and tried to cheer himself up with the thought that his day probably couldn't get any worse.

He'd been late to school, of course. Really late. The kind of late where they'd probably ring Mum. He had his excuse ready – Horace prided himself on being prepared for things – and anyway as long as he kept coming nearly top in everything he knew Mum wouldn't freak out about a thing like that, but he could do without a lecture, especially today. And he'd have to stand there and take it, or she might really flip out and take away the key to the boat. And then he wouldn't be able to cross the river any more.

Not that he cared. (He slouched deeper, pressing his cheek to the vibrating window. Dark out already.) What do I care? he told himself furiously. Who cares about Marina anyway? She never listens to me. Thought I was lying. Thought I didn't know what I saw. Did she think he didn't have other people to hang out with? Maybe he'd forget about going over there. For ever. Leave her with her doddery old dad and mental Miss Clifton and that freaky Caleb bloke who looked like he never washed. See how she likes that. Maybe then she'd wish she'd been a bit nicer to him.

Maybe he'd even tell.

Tell.

The thing that mattered most to Horace Jia was that he had a secret. Having a secret was wonderful. Nothing could take it away. No one else owned it; no one else could touch it. It was there when he went to bed, there when he woke up, there whenever he wanted to think about it, a little warm golden nugget in the back of his mind. Sometimes it tingled as if it was a part of his body. Sometimes he thought he could make it tingle there just by thinking. Close his eyes and bring it close and send a shiver down his own spine.

But sometimes it wanted to burst out. *Hey, guess what. You know that weird old house across the river, the one no one knows anything about? I sneak in there all the time. Yeah, I do, I swear. And there's this girl who lives there, and I'm her best friend, and she's really . . . really . . .*

He clamped his arms tighter across his chest. No way he could tell anyone. Even if it was the best secret in the world. If anyone else ever knew that he sometimes clambered over the wall from the footpath and ran up through the old woods and hung out with Marina, they'd stop him. It was probably illegal or something, even though Miss Clifton always told him no one minded as long as he kept quiet about it. Plus he always told Mum he was going to meet up with friends or go exploring on his own. If she found out he'd been lying about it for a whole year now, that'd be it. No more boat. No more freedom.

So what? he told himself again. Who cares? He tried to think about other friends he could go and see, friends he could do normal stuff with – PlayStation and football – but when he imagined things like that, his secret went heavy and bright like gold inside him and made the rest of the world shadowy and too small, as if he'd switched the lights on during a movie.

Marina'd spoiled it. Going off exploring with that other kid in tow. Her and crazy Miss Clifton going mental at the weekend. They'd ruined it for him. Ruined his life.

The bus reached his village. He clumped off and marched home, keeping his head down. With any luck, he thought, Mum wouldn't be back yet.

But it wasn't his lucky day. He saw lights on behind the curtains as he came down the lane. Worse, there was another car pulled up tight against the garden hedge, right in front. A visitor.

Horace's heart sank even lower. Mum had this thing about visitors and food. Anyone who set foot in the house couldn't leave until they'd been offered everything from biscuits to cake to half that evening's tea. And then there was the chatting, chatting, God, all that stupid gossip about people nobody cared about. What was there to gossip about? Everyone did the same stupid crap every day. The only thing that ever changed was that old people got sicker. *Is she any better? . . . Oh, I'm sorry to hear that.* He couldn't face it. Not this evening, not after the morning he'd had.

'Horace? Is that you?'

Who else would be opening the door, Father Christmas? 'Hi, Mum.'

'Come and say hello.' He smelled tea and a whiff of ginger cake, but no actual cooking yet. She and the guest were in the sitting room at the back, out of sight. 'Did you put your shoes neatly?'

Yes, he had. He aimed a phantom kick at them. 'Yes.'

'Did you have a good day at school?'

Sounded like they hadn't rung her, at least. Unless she was just being polite while someone else was in the house. Too embarrassed to tell him off in public. Horace hung his bag on its peg by the front door, put his coat beside it. 'Yeah, fine.'

'You remember Reverend Jeffrey, don't you?'

He froze with his arms still up by the peg, heart pounding. The day that hadn't been able to get any worse wobbled, tipped and plunged down into total disaster.

Mum still hadn't seen him yet. For a few crazy seconds he thought about legging it back outside. *Sorry, Mum, just remembered I left something on the bus!* Hide in the neighbour's garden till he saw the car leave. But what good would that do? Avoiding the bloke wouldn't help. If he'd told her, he'd told her. Even running away wouldn't help that.

He shoved his hands down in his pockets. His right fist tightened round his keychain. He felt the little key, sticky with sweat. The key that opened the padlock that sealed the tin compartment in the stern of the boat where the tiny outboard lay stored. The key that meant while she was off cleaning rich people's houses all day long at the weekend or in the holidays he could go where he liked. The key to his secret.

'Horace? What are you doing? Come in. Don't be rude.'

He shuffled miserably into the back room. Mum was in the high-backed chair she always took because she thought it was the uncomfortable one. Owen Jeffrey – one of the four people in the world who had the power to give away Horace's secret – had been forced into the horrible puffy fraying armchair that cut your circulation off at your knees and made your back feel like it was being bent in two, otherwise known as the 'good' chair.

It faced the door. As Mum craned round to inspect him, Horace met the priest's eye.

Owen winked.

'Say hello, Horace. What's wrong with you?'

'Hello.'

'Here, you can cut another slice of cake, and get yourself a plate. What happened to your hands? They're disgusting!'

The bloke couldn't have told her. No way she'd be fussing the same as usual if he'd told her. She'd have been in shock. And what else was that wink all about? Braced for the worst, Horace didn't know what to do with himself.

'Go to the kitchen, please. I don't know how you get yourself so dirty.'

'Hello, Horace,' the priest said.

So what was he doing here? Had he just been waiting for Horace to get home, so he could make him admit everything in person? But he didn't look like he was about to tell anyone off.

'I only stopped in with a quick question,' Owen said, stretching his back uncomfortably. 'I'll be on my way soon.'

'Are you sure you won't have some dumplings? I have the water boiling. They only take a few—'

'No, thank you, Mrs Jia.'

From the kitchen, Horace listened to the familiar argument. He ran the water ice-cold before washing his hands. They felt clammy.

'I have to get back for evensong,' Owen was explaining as Horace returned to the sitting room.

'But that is not for another hour! That's better, Horace. Cut a slice for Reverend Jeffrey, please.'

'Honestly, no. I'm quite all right.' He leaned forward a little to catch Horace's eye and repeated, 'Everything's quite all right.'

'What is this? When did you become such a rude boy?' Now Mum was doing her thing where she made a joke of him – another reason he hated it when there were guests around – but he was so relieved to discover that the priest obviously hadn't told Mum anything about his visits to Pendurra, he almost laughed along himself.

'You're standing there like a sheep. Doesn't he look just like a sheep?'

'Sorry, Mum. Slice of cake?'

'Really, no.'

'Go on, Horace.'

Owen roused himself from the chair's swampy upholstery as best he could. 'Please. You've been very kind, but I'm fine. You'll try Professor Lightfoot again later and ask her to call me as soon as possible if you find her in?'

'Yes, yes, of course. She ought to be home. I know I saw the lights on opposite earlier. I can't guess where she has gone. But I'm going tomorrow to help her. And I will try again tonight. Maybe Horace saw something?'

'Saw what?'

'Next door. As you came by just now.'

'Mrs Pascoe?'

'No. Didn't you hear? The professor. Mrs Lightfoot.'

'That's not next door, it's across.'

'Horace!'

'Sorry. What about her?'

'Did you see if she was at home?'

'Thought she's never here. It's her holiday place, isn't it?'

'I stopped by,' Owen put in, explaining, 'to ask if your mother happened to have bumped into Professor Lightfoot. I'm trying to get hold of her.'

'Nah.' Horace definitely didn't want to say anything that might delay Owen's departure. 'Didn't see anything.'

'She arrived yesterday!' Mum threw her hands in the air, as if Horace's ignorance of the pointless comings and goings of mad old ladies was personally embarrassing to her. 'I told you! I don't think you listen. I think too much computer games. It rots your brain.'

'We don't have any computer games, Mum,' Horace said darkly.

'But you always go and play with your friends.' She turned to Owen, catching him easing himself out into the hall. 'All day long they play these games. It isn't good, is it?'

'I'm sure God doesn't mind. And besides' – he directed a peculiar smile at Horace – 'I have a feeling Horace is good at finding more interesting things to do with his time.'

Horace went red. His secret throbbed at the back of his skull like a bruise, but Mum didn't notice anything. She was too busy chasing the priest down the hall.

'At least take a slice of cake with you.'

'Well, all right, then.'

'Oh good! Horace!'

'I'll get it,' he called, and ducked into the kitchen.

'Wash your hands again first!'

They felt like they were on fire. The bloke wanted Horace to know it was OK, he wasn't going to tell her. That was obvious. But how come? Grown-ups ganged up on kids; that was the whole point of their existence. He heard them talking by the front door while he got out a napkin and folded it round a slice of the ginger cake. No matter how big he made the slice, he knew Mum would send him back for a bigger one. He knew the whole routine; he'd done it a million times. But just this one time he was spectacularly relieved that everything was the same as usual.

'What is this? Don't be so mean to a guest. That is half a slice. Go.'

'It's perfect.' Owen took it from Horace, then shook hands. 'Thank you. Nice to meet you again.' He opened the door and squinted across the street towards Hester Lightfoot's house. 'Doesn't seem like anyone's home, but I might as well knock one more time just in case. Do please—'

'Yes, of course. I will keep trying.'

'Great. Thanks so much.' Though Owen was already in the lane, Mum didn't want to shut the door. When something was going on, she couldn't bear the idea of not being involved.

'Don't stand there in the door. You let all the cold air in.'

She was actually the one holding it open, but Horace stopped himself pointing that out. He always had to bite back his retorts. He hoarded them for later, for his own room, where they'd all come out at last, his long bedtime monologue of fractured, whispered resentment.

'So you didn't see anything in her house just now?' his mother asked, stepping back inside with evident reluctance.

Guess what, Mum. Some of us don't spend our lives wondering what the neighbours are doing. Some of us really don't give a shit. 'No. I just came home.'

'Her car still isn't there.' Mum lifted the net curtain over the square window beside the front door. He thought of it as her spyhole. 'It's a strange time to be driving. It's so dark.'

'That's 'cos it's night.'

'What?'

'Nothing.'

'Don't mumble like that.'

'Sorry.'

She turned back to the view across the lane. 'Did you know Professor Lightfoot was a friend of Miss Clifton?'

Fortunately Horace had turned back towards the stairs, so his mother couldn't have seen the surprise on his face.

'What?'

'I think we have to go to the doctor to look at your ears. I said, did you know Professor Lightfoot knew Miss Clifton? Miss Clifton is that strange woman who comes to church sometimes. The one—'

'Yeah, I know. What's she got to do with— Why would I know anything about that?' He tried to sound as bored as Mum's conversation usually made him, as bored as he dared.

But she was still watching the house opposite hopefully, and for once didn't reprove him. 'Reverend Jeffrey was looking for Miss Clifton. He went to the train station in Truro. She was going to pick someone up there, he said. Something like that. But he said there was a message for her there from Professor Lightfoot.'

'Why's he looking for Miss Clifton?'

'I don't know. It's not my business. You don't ask why someone does something. What would you think if I was always asking you why you do this, why you do that?'

Under normal circumstances Horace would have been thinking a lot of things, all of which would only have been whispered aloud upstairs in the solitude of his room, after lights out, but this time he was busy answering his own question in his head. Because something weird happened to her. Because I saw her acting really strange down by the river and everyone else thinks she's disappeared completely. And Marina wouldn't believe me. Told me I didn't know what I was talking about.

'She's a very strange woman. I don't like to know about her. All that Old Age business.'

'It's called New Age, Mum.'

'Reverend Jeffrey ought to talk to her about it. God will not like it. Whatever you call it.'

Uh-oh, Horace thought, here comes God. Mostly he liked it that Mum was so into church and everything – it gave her lots of other people to fuss over and boss around and force to eat her food – but sometimes the subject started her off on one of her lectures. Miss Clifton might be a total psycho, and look like a grown-up pretending to be a mosher, but at least she never lectured you.

I know her a lot better than you do, he thought, and the slow burn of his secret lit up and spread through him, sunshine on a stone. Loads better than you think I do. You have absolutely no idea how much I know about Miss Clifton.

So where had she gone? What was the priest doing looking for her all the way over here on the wrong side of the river?

He closed his eyes involuntarily and saw again the strangely dishevelled figure bending over the water, trailing hooked fingers through its surface as if hunting raw fish. All wrong somehow.

He shook the memory out of his head. Who cares? he thought. His secret was still safe. He still had the key to the boat. Everything'll be all right tomorrow, he told himself. Tomorrow'll be a better day.

* * *

'Well. All right.'

Hester was a shadow in the driver's seat, her face ghostly in the glow of the dashboard. Gavin slumped in the seat next to her and stared out at the road's contortions. Engine-warmed air washed over them.

'So,' Hester began again. She snuck a glance across at him, perhaps checking that he was awake.

After a while she sighed. 'The thing is, I know just what it's like. When you're being pestered to talk and all you want to do is be quiet. Truly I do.' She glanced across again. 'Can I at least ask if you're OK?'

'I'll survive,' Gav said.

He wondered whether even that much was true.

Now that he was watching the world go by, sealed behind glass, smelling car smells and listening to car noises, passing isolated houses and villages – bright windows through which he glimpsed scenes from an ordinary night, a man feeding a baby in a high chair, the spectral blue radiance of a television on a white wall – he couldn't get hold of the day he'd just lived through. It was as phantasmal as the TV images, and as quickly lost from view behind him. There couldn't be any such ancient houses. There were no such girls who'd never heard swear words and didn't know where China was, no such clawed feet scraping stone. He'd imagined it all. He was imagining things. *You're imagining things, Gav.* Except this time, at last, at long last, he knew he wasn't.

'Where are we going?'

'You know,' she said, in the same mild conversational tone he remembered from the train, as though as far as she was concerned ferrying a haunted teenager back and forth along twisting country lanes at night was as ordinary as driving to work, 'I hadn't thought about it yet. Wherever you like. Should I take you back to the station?'

'The station?'

'I can put you on a train. If you want to go straight home.'

'God no. Not that.'

She gave him a long curious look before turning back to the road. 'My house, then. To start with. If that's all right with you?'

He couldn't answer. He couldn't think of anywhere else. He couldn't think of anywhere at all, the bright windows, the rooms with TVs and fathers and children. She manoeuvred the car round a twisting descent and over a brief bridge barely wider than it was. The road was a black stream, down which their little white bubble floated.

'So,' she said eventually, much as Mr Bushy used to do when no one in the class could answer the question he'd put before them and he gave up and tried a new one. 'Did your aunt turn up in the end?'

Gav winced. Of all the things he didn't want to think about, that was the worst.

'I don't think so.'

Her eyebrows lifted slightly. 'You don't think so?'

'Sorry. I don't want to talk about it.'

'As I say,' she said quietly, 'I entirely understand.'

He leaned back and closed his eyes. Usually whenever anyone said *I understand* to him, it meant the exact opposite. It was what Mum said when she actually wanted to say *I don't believe you.* But this time it didn't matter who believed him or not. The things he'd seen and heard loomed in the darkness behind, impossible, unforgettable.

He shivered violently. Hester made a solicitous noise and twisted a dial on the dashboard. The petrol-flavoured air turned warmer.

'I should never have left you on your own,' she said. 'I'm so sorry.'

He hugged his hands under his arms to stop them trembling. 'Not your fault.'

'I don't know what possessed me to do a thing like that.'

'I do,' Gav said.

The car twitched. Stubble in the hedge clattered against Gav's window like claws. Hester pulled the wheel straight again, her hands suddenly tight.

'Careful,' Gav added.

'What did you say?'

Why had he said it? Why hadn't he just kept his mouth shut like usual?

Because, he realised, she really did understand. He thought of the newspaper clippings in Auntie Gwen's weird scrapbook. Hester Lightfoot, the Nutty Professor.

'I know.' He kept his eyes on the ghostly white circle ahead, the dark skimming past. 'What made you do it. So it's OK. It's not your fault.'

'I'm sorry,' Hester said, after a short silence. 'I'm afraid I don't follow.'

Perhaps it was all because of talking to Marina. She'd unlocked the part of him that had stayed silent about these things for the past four years, and now he couldn't close it again. Or perhaps it was because he couldn't any longer see the difference between saying it and not saying it, not after what had just happened to him. With a twist of pain he wondered where Marina was now. If she was anywhere.

'"Let the boy go in,"' Gavin said.

He was pitched forward hard as the car twisted crazily in the narrow lane. Hester braced her arms against the steering wheel as if she was about to tear it loose.

'*What?*' she said, all mildness gone. 'You heard that?'

He braced himself in the seat. 'Watch it.'

'Say it again.' Her fingers flexed convulsively on the wheel. 'Say the words again. Please, Gavin.'

'"Let the boy go in."'

She went so quiet he was afraid he'd turned her to stone. The car drifted worryingly.

'Um.' Gav stole a look across and saw her staring straight ahead as if seeing some other nightscape altogether. 'Mind the . . .' The word 'hedge' was lost in the abrupt scrape of twigs against the door. Hester jerked her head round as if she'd just woken up.

'God, sorry.' She got the car back under control. They drove up to a benighted village of dark houses and mournfully solitary streetlights. 'I'm all right. Sorry about that.'

'Not your fault,' he said. 'None of it is.'

'None of it?' she echoed him distantly, as if she couldn't believe what she was hearing.

Everyone had always told Gav it was his fault. *Stop being stupid, Gavin. You're just making it up.* But it wasn't, and he hadn't been. He'd been right all along, and so had she.

'You're not crazy,' he said. 'You never were.'

She raised one hand to her mouth and whispered something inaudible into it.

'The voices,' Gav added. He was worried she'd go into a trance if he didn't make her say something. 'And all that. It's not your fault.'

She turned to look at him. It was too dark to see her expression.

'May I ask,' she said, 'how you know all this?'

'There was a thing in the paper. Sorry about your job.'

A brief and unhappy laugh. 'That's not really the part I was asking about, but thank you.'

'I got kicked out 'cos they thought I was mad too. Well, suspended. But I'm not. You aren't either.'

They both kept their eyes ahead, on the shallow pool of light and the dark beyond.

'You know that for sure, do you?' she said eventually.

'One of them's real, at least.'

'One of . . . ?'

'Your voices.'

She turned again and looked at him for so long he was sure she'd drive off the road.

'There's only one,' she said at last. 'There's only ever been one.' She sounded steady, but Gav thought he could hear the depths of pain below the calm surface. 'But you see, "I hear voices" sounded so much better than "I hear a voice." Much easier to say. It's almost a joke, isn't it? "I hear voices." Whereas in the singular it suddenly sounds so very . . . intimate. Not just hallucinations everywhere like, oh, you know, like mad people have. One particular conversation instead. With just you as its victim, and your tormentor almost like someone in the family.'

Gavin became acutely aware of the distance between them, though it was only half the width of a car.

'Sorry,' he muttered.

'Oh,' she sighed. 'No. It's all right now, anyway.'

They watched the road slide under them in silence.

'Actually,' she went on after a while, 'I've always known I was sane.' They'd come to a stretch of road Gav thought he recognised from the previous evening. It ran through a tall open wood, silhouettes of trees around them like pillars in a church. 'I always knew it wasn't actually a' – her fingers made quotation marks in the air – 'voice in my head. That's what I tried to say, when it all became too much and I felt I had to say something. I've always felt . . . whole. In myself. I've always known she was . . .' Hester sighed. 'Someone else. Some other person or being or ghost or what have you who for some reason, or maybe for no reason at all, attached herself to me. I know, it sounds properly insane, doesn't it?'

'Not to me,' Gav said. 'So that was her before as well?'

'Before?'

'On the train.'

Both her hands jerked up from the wheel. Gav lunged to grab it, terrified, as the car veered wildly to the edge of the road. One set of tyres ran into soft earth on the verge, sending them bumping and skidding sideways, thrashing wet undergrowth. He shoved the wheel over and managed to keep the car clinging to tarmac as it ground to a halt.

Hester clutched his arm with both hands.

'Tell me,' she said, hoarse, frantic. She appeared not to have noticed nearly killing them both. 'Tell me why this happened to me.' Her grip was beginning to hurt. 'Please tell me why. Please.'

The car had stalled. The only sound was her breath, racing.

He tried to tug his arm away, unsuccessfully. 'Um. I think we're on the wrong side of the road.'

For a few seconds he thought she hadn't even heard him. Then her grip unclenched.

'My God,' she whispered.

'I think' – he withdrew his arm carefully and put as much calm in his tone as he could muster – 'maybe it would be better if you just got home.'

She gazed at him as if he'd suggested going to Mars.

'I can drive if you like,' he added, which wasn't strictly true, but he'd watched other people do it and always thought he could probably work out the motions. Plus he doubted he'd be any more of a danger to their lives than she was.

'What? No. Sorry.' She rubbed her hands on her legs, pulling herself together. 'I can manage. Yes. Home.' She started up again and eased the car back onto the road. Gav kept himself ready to lunge for the wheel again.

'How much further is it?'

'Is what? Not far.' She expelled a shaky breath. 'It's all right. Honestly. Look, this is the head of the river now.'

Another village had appeared at the end of the wood. Gav saw signposts with names unknown to him, bright for a moment in the headlights and then lost. He watched Hester out of the corner of his eye. She held herself straight and tight, forcing herself to concentrate.

Miss Grey's other victim. Never in a million years would he have guessed there was anyone else in the world who shared anything like his torment, let alone that it would be someone like this, an ordinary middle-aged woman.

When she at last broke the silence, it was as if she'd been sharing his thoughts.

'You really heard all that, then.' Gav thought it was safer to say nothing, though she seemed to have recovered herself. 'Oh, don't worry,' she added, catching his eye. 'I won't run us off the road again, I promise. It's just . . .' He watched her shake her head slowly. 'An extraordinary thing. All that shouting on the train, in the tunnel. You heard it all too?'

'Yeah.' No swerving yet, but he thought he made out a wet gleam in her eyes. 'Yeah, I did.'

'So . . . have you always . . . ?'

She couldn't bring herself to say it aloud, but he saw what she was asking.

'Actually,' he said, 'that was the first time.'

'The first?'

He stared into the dark, remembering Miss Grey. 'I've never heard her shout like that before. Never heard her say anything really.'

He only realised what he'd said when the car began to slow down.

'You mean . . .' Hester began, and an edge had come back into her voice.

Gav cleared his throat. 'Actually, would you mind pulling over for a sec?'

'What?'

'Just for a sec.'

'Promise you're not going to jump out and run away?' She appeared to be serious.

'Promise,' he said.

'Because I couldn't stand that.' There was a spot where the lane widened; she nudged the car against the hedge. 'I couldn't bear to come so close to the answer and then never know.'

'I don't have any answers.' They came to a stop, idling in the empty road.

'Right.' She pulled up the handbrake. 'Safe as houses. Now you can tell me about it.'

'About what?'

She took a careful breath. 'You said you'd never heard her speak before, which means . . .'

He waited.

'How long?' she asked, finally.

'All my life.'

She clasped her hands tight and wiped at her eyes with the knuckles. Gav looked away, embarrassed.

'So, she was . . .' The tremble in her voice sounded desperately like hope. 'She was there, on the train. My voice was . . . actually . . .'

'Told you you're not crazy,' he said, and then he had to pretend to study the tangled shadows in the hedge for a while, as though he hadn't noticed the tears.

'Oh, look at me,' she said at last. 'Pull yourself together, Hester. I'm sorry. I'll stop in a minute.'

'Don't worry about it.'

She found a tissue in some compartment and blew her nose loudly. 'There. Oh goodness. I'm all right now. You did the right thing asking me to pull over.'

'Maybe we should change the subject.'

She laughed. 'Let's get going at least.' Very deliberately, she released the brake. 'There. See? I'm all right. I can't quite stop crying, but I'm all right. It's not far, anyway.'

'Sorry,' Gav said again.

'Oh, Gavin.' He couldn't remember ever having heard his name spoken with more heartfelt emphasis. 'Please don't keep apologising. Later on I'll try and explain what you've done for me today.' She shook her head again in wonder. 'I'm only crying because I'm so happy. Yesterday would have been enough, but this is—'

'Yesterday?'

'Being released. I thought that was all the miracle I needed. Well, it was, actually.' She wiped her cheek with her sleeve. 'But now to find out that all along . . .'

Memories began to stir uneasily in him.

'Released?'

This night you go free.

'You don't know?'

'Know what?' Of course he didn't. She thought he knew about Miss Grey, but he didn't. He didn't understand at all.

'I'm sorry – I somehow assumed you'd know.' She glanced at him and, seeing the blank face, explained. 'She's gone.'

'Gone?' Gav whispered.

Old mad witch.

Gets killed.

'It was just,' Hester peered at the dashboard clock, 'just this time yesterday. Right after I dropped you off. I was driving just like this, along these lanes, and . . . I knew. Perhaps I won't try and explain what it was like, but anyway, I knew. I knew it was over. She's left me at last. My voice. Our voice, I should call her, shouldn't I? Our voice. She's gone.'

Fourteen

Late winter and spring 1537

FIRST LOVE CAME to the magus late, but when it arrived, its effects were the same as they always have been, for everyone, young and old. He thought of nothing else. He shut himself in his house and could do nothing. He sat among his books, his heart broken. Yet however much he railed at the servant spirit, it would not return him to her again.

'Take me back.'

'We will not, Magister.' The dry voice floated around him like smoke.

'"Will not"? I command you. I require obedience!'

'We may not lead you into harm.'

'What harm can there be? Take me back! Or I will . . .'

But for once his threat was empty, and he knew it. The spirit ruled by his staff was his agent in the insubstantial realms. He could direct it – had directed it – to afflict other dwellers in those realms, compelling them to his will, but in doing so he had surrendered a portion of his power over it. He could not make it punish itself.

One of the first laws he had learned, at the very beginning of his arcane studies, was that there was always a cost. Everything gained from the spirits was paid for with something lost, no matter how subtle the equation.

It would have been fortunate for the magus had he borne that lesson in mind, later, but soonest learned, soonest forgotten. He had become used to authority. Growing in power over the years, mastery became his habit, and the bonds on which it rested no longer occupied his attention. Which made it all the more bitter when he now found himself unable to compel the spirit to his most urgent desire.

'Great harm, Magister.'

'There cannot be!'

'We speak only truth. Forget her. She is a cursed thing.'

'Forget!' The magus ground his teeth in despair. It might as well have asked him to forget to breathe.

'It is the gift of your kind. To forget.'

'Silence!' Even the suggestion of being taunted by such a thing was beyond endurance. 'Silence! Answer only as I bid you!'

The ruddy glow haunting the laboratory, embers in an invisible bonfire, seemed to waver and retreat.

'You conducted me there once.' Silence. 'Can you deny it?'

'No, Magister.'

'Then do so again!'

'You would not return.'

'So be it!' In the frenzy of his longing, he felt he would rather be a ghost at her side for ever than a living man separated from her by vast oceans of time. 'So be it! Let me go and never return!'

'We may not do you harm.'

And it was true. Years before, when he had won the fiery spirit to his service, surprised by its willingness, he had guarded against the dangers attending all transactions of the sort by binding it to do him no injury. Now his own word was turned against him, and his own word was immovable. He raged and wheedled, even – to his later horror and humiliation – begged. Entreaties were as useless as commands. He could not return. There was no way back to her.

What, then, had she meant by her whisper *You will see me again*?

Legend named her a prophetess. Nothing more of her had survived to the magus's own time. There were obscure and contradictory fragments of stories, useless to him, but he and everyone else knew that her name was a byword for the gift of prophecy. He could only pray, with childish fervour, that the legend was true, that those five whispered words were indeed prophetic and their promise would come to pass. But as the dark days and weeks passed, pelting his house with February's freezing rain, he lost hope and sank into torpid misery. However much he tried to warm himself with the memory of her promise, he no longer believed it. He began to doubt whether she'd even spoken the words.

So another truth she told him was buried. Her legend spoke of that too.

The god loved her, it said. *The bright god, the destroyer, god of the lyre and the laurel and the long road.*

She accepted his gift, which was prophecy.

Then – so the legend ran – *she changed her tune and spurned him. But he did not withdraw the gift. His revenge was crueller: he twisted it against itself.*

Her mouth would still speak hidden truth, but the truth would always be left hidden: secret, powerless. Never used, never understood. No one would listen. She would prophesy and no one would believe her.

In that broken exchange rested all the magic in the world. But

the magus was habituated to power, as we have said, and this is a mystery he would never grasp.

He spent his sleepless nights combing the codices of his library and his patrons', seeking any remnant of her story, searching for any clue that might open a door back to that time so unthinkably long past, that dry hill and many-gated citadel whose very name was now a legend. He neglected his observatory and laboratory equally. His heart was no longer in the work. Letters arriving at his house stayed unsealed.

He formed twenty different schemes to force the spirit to do as he wished. These were the only times when his listlessness gave way to frantic exertion. All the efforts were equally useless. The spirit, meanwhile, offered to bewitch other women and swore they would make him forget her. It was mockery, and he knew it. Worse, he knew he deserved it. It had been just such an unworthy impulse – the urge to set eyes on the most beautiful woman in the world – which had caused the spirit to open the door through time, and so lost him his heart.

'Why did you not deny me then?' It was folly to throw recriminations at a thing possessed of neither a conscience nor a soul, but sometimes his furious grief got the better of him. 'You deny me so obdurately now. Why did you agree so readily when I gave you that first command?'

'We serve your will, Magister.'

'You do not.' He rubbed his bloodshot eyes. 'You serve only your own malice. You glory in my despair.'

'Unjust, Magister.'

'Unjust? Was it justice to obey what was only a whim of mine and now to deny me when my soul hangs in the balance?'

'We safeguard your soul.' There was a sibilant relish in the dry echoes of its voice that would have made an ordinary man quail.

'You wish me broken so you may go free. Is it not so? You hope to see me crushed by misery.'

'We wish you preserved.'

'Be gone,' he muttered dully, and the phantom light fled from the room.

The bell of the Vrouwekerk rang the days in and out, and gradually the furious clamour of his despair subsided, settling into a low constant ache. For want of anything better to do he resumed his work. The sun regained some of its warmth, tempting him out of doors again, and then, when the packed snows thinned, out of the city.

The day came without any warning at all.

It was early in March, a cold afternoon already going dull, and he was riding in a copse looking for early shoots of the blue squill, when he saw a vagrant woman crouched beside the remains of a fire. He dismounted and picked his way to her through the muddy snow at the edge of the track, thinking to ask her if she knew where to find what he sought, and to start her fire for her. She lifted her ragged head and watched him as he came. When he was close, she rose to her feet. He was surprised to see her move so easily and stand so straight; his surprise was trebled when she spoke his name. All he saw was a beggar, coarse cloak hanging off her like a scarecrow's, a thin face worn ageless by weather, facing him as fearlessly as the proudest *mevrouw* in the city. The first thing he thought was that she might be a witch. She was bold; her strength seemed unnatural; she had recognised him. His grip was tightening on his staff when at last he met her black eyes directly and saw how they shone.

The vagrant spoke in Latin.

She said, 'I promised you would see me again.'

His staff dropped out of his hand, spattering slush, and a moment later he fell to his knees and shouted a great cry of thanks for the purest moment of joy that his days had ever gifted him.

When his mouth was capable of speech again, he said, 'Are you a phantom? Is this a blessed vision?'

Her answer was to reach out and touch his face. The hand was rough but full of tenderness, old and young together. He felt the living heat of her, as ordinary and yet as entirely miraculous as the small warmth of the March sun.

'How?' he stammered. He was afloat in an ocean of speechless wonder. He could barely open his mouth without drinking in so much of it that he feared he might die of joy.

'You came to me once,' she said quietly, 'and did not turn away. Because of that I have waited for you.'

He seized her hand in his and pressed his lips to it. Her skin closed his mouth against the rising flood of words: questions, exclamations, cries of sheer delight, all pressed upwards from his heart, so thick they threatened to choke him. They dissolved against the simple sensation of her body against his, tangible as the snow and the earth. In the face of a miracle, all questions were mere air.

She refused to mount behind him, so he walked as well, leading the horse over the frozen ruts. That became the way they always met, that spring and summer. He would find her at the fringes of the rougher land, wood or marsh or sea, and they would walk together and talk or be silent as the mood was. She was shy of people, though the travellers and drovers and peasants outside the city walls never gave her a second glance. To every eye except his she was no more than what he had momentarily taken her for – a vagrant or a common woman, coarsely clothed, no more worthy of notice than a mule – but to him she was a miracle made flesh. Sometimes when they spoke, she told him of places and people that were as strange and marvellous to him as the fantasies of high romance, though in truth any words would have been precious to him so long as they came from her. Sometimes he wished for no more than to stand and hold her small hands in his. Her appearances and disappearances, her silences, the unfathomable air that clung to her, none of that troubled him at all next to his certainty that his prayers had been answered and his love rewarded. And sometimes when they were together it was as though the air thickened around them and the passage of time itself lost its hold, and then she was not only a beggar woman but a princess as well, the woman he had first seen that impossibly distant night, and then the magus forgot everything: his questions, himself, the whole world.

Still, the questions could not be held back for ever.

'How can it be that you are here? The world itself has grown ancient since we met.'

'It is a long road.'

'And you have trodden it all that time? Yourself?'

She looked down at her hands. 'I could not do otherwise.'

'It is beyond believing.'

'I know,' she whispered.

The land was in its drunken riot of life. Young green clothed the meadows and woods like an exhalation. The magus would have suspected himself of being bewitched with happiness had it not been for the enduring distance between him and her, a remoteness nothing could bridge. The shadow of centuries was palpable on her. The thought of everything she must have seen and endured defeated his imagination utterly, and yet every time he looked into those profound eyes it seemed all too plain.

'And you did not forget me?'

'No. I do not forget.'

'You are not a woman, then.' He pushed back her hood. A woman's face looked back at him, ordinary enough except for its peculiar solemn beauty and its subdued strength. 'You are a goddess fallen to Earth, sent to bless me.'

'I am not blessed, Johannes.'

'Then tell me. Tell me how you crossed such a span of time.'

'The burden I bear,' she said, 'is endless.'

'What burden, *carissima*?'

She shook her head and folded her fingers around his. 'It brought you to me once. Now it has brought me to you.' And that was as much of an answer as she would give.

In her presence, it was enough for him. He asked nothing more from the world. For months he had longed for that, and only that, and when he thought back on his longing the tide of joy flooded so high it erased every other thought as a wave wipes footprints from the sand.

But when he was alone again he meditated on what she said. His love and longing went still and a small, strange curiosity peeped up beside them like the tiny flower of a garden weed.

It brought you to me once. What was it that had brought him to her? His art, surely – his unworthy whim, so eagerly acceded to by the companion spirit. So what was it, then, that had brought her to him?

That was the mystery, beyond conception, beyond credence. Did she mean to say it was his art that had again performed the miracle? Had he summoned her across time without knowing it, by his great mastery and by the sheer force of his love?

The magus was all too ready to believe it of himself.

After all, he began to think, the more he contemplated this marvel, was not his art the image of her fate?

Legend called her the prophetess whom no one would believe. Was that not indeed his fate also? When one considered it? Was he not also the master of holy wisdom scorned by the world?

'You spoke once of your burden,' he reminded her, some weeks later. His giddy bliss had tempered itself and he had begun spending more and more of his solitary hours thinking, wondering.

'Once was enough.'

He reached his arm across her shoulders. 'Is it not lifted now we are together?'

'Lightened, yes.' She leaned against him.

'But not lifted?'

She looked at him without a word.

'I share it with you,' he went on, feeling peculiarly nervous, as if he were asking her for something he could not be sure of having earned. 'I have not suffered all that you have suffered, but some part of it belongs to me also.'

His mouth and his heart teemed with wonder and gratitude, but underneath all that, unspoken even in his private thoughts, was a deep conviction that Providence had blessed her at last with him, that he had come to save her.

This was his old habit of mastery, under the new guise of love. She was a cursed being – somewhere he had heard that; he could no longer recall exactly where – but it had no weight with him. His wisdom and love together would break the curse. And then she would belong to him always and – the dream stole quietly into the furthest recesses of his heart as spring came on – he would become as she was. A human creature still, shaped in the very image of God. A human creature, but one who was as endless as life itself.

Immortal.

So his temptation began, though he never knew it. For all his wisdom, he was not wise enough to know his own desires. Not then, nor that autumn, his love fading with the year as first love does; least of all long, long afterwards, when he decided – as if unwillingly; as if the seed of the decision had not been present all along, planted beside his love – that in order for him to inherit her immortal gift, she would have to die.

Fifteen

HESTER POINTED AT a signpost as they turned off the main road. 'My village.'

A few minutes later lights appeared. First, the garish luminescence of a garage, looking as if it had been sliced out of a suburban high street and dropped in the middle of nowhere, then a post office, a row of unlikely shops, a thatched pub at a crossroads. The pub was the only building that looked alive. They turned into a narrow street of bungalows and boxy concrete cottages, squatting behind front gardens, nudging close together as if seeking comfort against the dark spaces behind. Under the last street-lamp, Hester inched the car through an open gate onto a patch of gravel.

'Let's make some tea first,' was all she said.

From the outside the house was sad and shabby. When she reached under a bush to pull out the door key, Gavin found himself expecting a bare light bulb and the smell of stale carpet.

Nothing could possibly have prepared him for what he saw when she clicked on the light.

His immediate impression was that he'd stepped onstage. A fantastic crowd of motionless faces greeted him, all appearing at once like an expectant audience. The walls of the room Hester shepherded him into were hung with masks.

There must have been thirty of them. They leered and scowled and smiled and stared, impassive or threatening or serene, terrifying in their sinister silence. They were fantastically various. Some jumped out of the wall at Gav with a jolt of disturbing familiarity. The bright red sharp-cheeked one with the demonic grin and gaudy brows came from those Japanese plays whose name he couldn't remember. There were elongated wooden faces with protruding lips that were like things he'd seen in a lesson about West Africa. An eerily smooth, creamy-white, glistening and blank-eyed one made him think of Venice and torchlight and disturbing carnival. But he couldn't look at any of them for long. If his eyes stopped moving, he was instantly overwhelmed by the hallucinatory conviction that other faces were inspecting him behind his back. If it hadn't been for the reassuring mess below them, Gav thought he'd need to run from the room, but beneath chest height the place was cosily shambolic, all overstuffed bookshelves and harmless clutter. There were two mismatched fraying sofas with a low table between them. The table had obviously come from somewhere very far away, its incisions and curlicues and smoky grey wood unmistakably tropical. He felt like he'd walked into a mad explorer's trophy room. No wonder the slatted blinds over the window were folded tight shut.

'They are a bit much, aren't they,' Hester said, from behind him. 'Come into the kitchen. It's more bearable there.'

He followed to the back of the house with relief. The most the kitchen had in common with the front room was a pleasantly unkempt feeling: slightly too many things, not quite enough places to put them away. A wide unshuttered picture window, its corners fuzzy with condensation, looked onto mere darkness. The other walls were mercifully bare apart from a clock and a framed poster. Hester bobbed down and switched on a little electric fireplace, then set about the kettle and the cupboards, ferrying packets of food to a dining table of the kind of varnished wood that looks and feels like plastic. She kept up a reassuring commentary. 'Right. Bread. Ham. Oh look, here's that flowery biscuit tin; we could use it as a centrepiece. There. Hold on, that's the kettle, I'll do that first. Extra warmth . . .'

It was as if they'd silently agreed to suspend whatever they'd begun to share in the car. Household rituals had temporarily banished it.

'Help yourself, please,' she said, once the table was full, and he did, though not as eagerly as he'd thought he would. He just let her talk.

She spoke about living with the voice at her ear, but she almost made a joke of it, and before he knew it he was drawn into sharing stories. He told her how he'd plucked up courage to see Mr Bushy the Friday before last, and the Sunday morning someone had rung from school to tell his parents they thought he was in a state of 'nervous exhaustion' and needed some time off and perhaps we could schedule a discussion about whether this is the ideal environment to meet his needs? The whole tangle of shame and bitterness he felt as he repeated the tale was dissolved by the way she laughed at it and then told him her own version of much the same experience. She even made him laugh himself with her impression of the person who'd lectured her about the importance of preserving the confidence of hmm hmm hmm, and surely she'd be better off without hmm hmm, and please be assured of the continuing ahem ahem, and then asked her to resign.

'So I moved my stuff down here over the autumn.' She dunked a biscuit in her mug. 'Well, not all of it. This house isn't nearly big enough to accommodate just the books, let alone the rest. My parents bought it as a holiday home. I've been coming here for years. It seems like the right place to retreat to. I can't do without the books, so they'll have to live in boxes for a while. They're all upstairs, along with the things I couldn't be bothered to unpack. Everything I left behind can just be sold. It's funny the things you decide are indispensable.' He thought she was staring absently at the wall, but then she nodded towards the framed picture. 'Like that. It was the very first thing I put up.'

It was a poster from a museum, advertising an exhibition. Most of it was taken up by a reproduction of a painting. Now that Gavin looked at it properly, he recognised something about it, though he couldn't say what: maybe he'd seen the style before. Something Old Mastery. It showed two heads: a bearded man, deeply wrinkled, and, leaning over his right shoulder from behind, whispering in his ear, a young and almost painfully beautiful face, heavy-lidded, either a long-haired boy or a girl with strong bones and thick eyebrows. The old man looked as if some profound and astonishing train of thought had just been set in motion by whatever the beautiful boy or girl murmured in his ear. The youth's expression was so radiant with gentle solemnity that Gav felt slightly embarrassed to be staring at it, like squirming at the slushy bits of a film.

'Ah,' he said.

The young boy/girl laid a hand on the old man's shoulder, or maybe it wasn't quite touching: delicate, sweetly intimate. Hester gazed at the two of them, her expression suddenly pained.

'I think perhaps the only time I might have truly lost my reason was once when I went to see that painting. It's in Paris, in the Louvre. I went on Eurostar. A sort of pilgrimage.' She picked up her mug and held it in mid-air, as if she'd forgotten about taking a sip of tea halfway through the motion. 'They had to escort me out of the gallery. When it closed, I should say. I wasn't hysterical or raving or anything dramatic like that. At least I assume I wasn't; I don't really remember. Anyway, it was embarrassing enough as it was. Apparently I couldn't stop looking at it, all day long. I couldn't move.'

'Oh,' he said. 'Yeah, I see what you mean.'

'It was the very first thing I brought down. I put it in the back of the car and hung it up before anything else came in the house.' She took her sip. 'Sort of like my patron saint. He's St Matthew. The gospeller. His symbol's an angel; that's the angel whispering in his ear.'

Gavin got the point at last and suddenly thought he understood where Hester had displaced all the rage and horror that were missing so conspicuously from her manner. 'What about that lot in there?'

'Hmm? Oh, my masks, you mean. Yes, you're quite right, it's the same idea. The concealed face, I suppose you could say. Though of course I tell myself I collect them just because I like them. And to be fair, some of them are objects of professional interest to me. Ex-professional interest, I should say, now that I find myself forcibly retired.'

Gav remembered the newspaper article. 'They're shaman masks?'

She raised an eyebrow at him.

'Sorry,' he said. 'It was all in the paper.'

She sighed. 'That's all right. It's an odd feeling, being other people's business. I even had someone from the local rag phone this morning, wanting an interview. You can just imagine that, can't you. The Nutty Professor in her own words. The phone kept going after that, in the end I had to unplug it.' She nodded towards an ugly wall-mounted object of cream-brown plastic, the cord beneath it trailing loose. 'Thank God this place is antique enough still to have the kind you can unplug. Anyway. Yes, more or less. There's no such thing as a shaman mask per se, but four or five of my menagerie are totemic objects of one sort or another, or modern interpretations of such objects. Used for communicating with the spirit world, essentially. Like opening a channel. Not that you want a tutorial on the subject. A couple are rather rare and valuable. Not exactly museum quality, but still the real thing.'

She dabbed at crumbs on her plate with a fingertip.

'I thought,' Hester said after a while, eyes on her plate, 'I'd want to ask you what her face is like. Speaking of faces. I thought I'd want to know. But it turns out I don't. I really don't.'

And there it was, out in the open again.

He heard the effort in her voice. He glimpsed again how she must have struggled to stay sane.

'It's almost as if I'm afraid that talking about her might bring her back. Like a bad omen.'

'I think you'll be OK,' Gav said, not meeting her eyes.

'Oh, do you?'

He wished he hadn't spoken, but now she was watching him intently. 'Yeah. Something's . . .'

'Don't talk about it if you'd rather not. We don't have to. Believe me, I know how difficult it is.'

I don't want to hear about this, Gav. Don't be ridiculous, Gav. Mention that name again, Gavin, and I swear I'll make you wish you hadn't. No. Not any more. He wasn't going to try and pretend Miss Grey didn't exist, not ever again.

How could she be gone?

He gripped his hands together under the table and tried to keep his voice casual. 'No, it's OK. I just mean . . . something's changed. With her. I'm pretty sure you don't have to worry.'

After a pause she said, 'May I ask what?'

'What?'

'What changed.'

Gav rubbed his eyes. 'Well, OK. On the train. She's never been like that before.'

Hester leaned towards him, disconcertingly curious. 'And you said this has been all your life?'

'Yeah. Long as I can remember. She's always been there.' Don't start crying, he told himself. 'Know what's stupid?'

'Nothing, I suspect, but go on.'

'It was only, like, three years ago that I figured out that . . . that she . . . That I was . . .'

She waited patiently while he battled the humiliation of tears.

'That she's not real,' he finished, and gulped at his tea.

'That isn't stupid,' she said.

'It felt pretty bloody stupid.'

'I was thirty-three.'

He looked at her, wiping his nose.

'Thirty-three years old. Nearly thirty-four. It was an autumn day in 1996. October the sixteenth. I could hardly forget the date, could I?'

A shiver went through him, but only on the inside. Absorbed in her memories, she saw nothing of it. 'I'd lived a good part of an adult life. A normal, rather privileged, on the whole unusually happy life. I was down here for a weekend. I was walking along a path by the river, over on the other side. As I began one step' – she mimed walking with two fingers, lifting one forward – 'my life was much the same as anyone else's. Anyone who's more or less secure, at least. And when I put my foot down . . .' The finger tapped on the table. Hester stared at it, an unfathomable look on her face. 'It wasn't.'

But all Gavin was thinking about was the date: 16 October 1996.

His birthday. The day he was born.

'I wasn't a child. I thought I knew the difference between reality and delusion. I did. I do know the difference. But in all these fifteen years I've never been able to persuade myself which of the two she is.'

It's my fault, he was thinking. It's all to do with me. The thing in the chapel had said so. The thing that couldn't really have happened, the thing he'd run away from, the thing he didn't want to remember.

What have I got to do with it?

Everything. Stupid boy.

He'd brought Miss Grey into the world with him, like some insane living shadow.

'Did she frighten you?' Gav took a moment to realise she'd directed the question at him. 'When you were younger?'

'No.' The memories opened up suddenly beneath him, misty landscapes of vanished happiness. 'Never. Not until a couple of days ago, when she started screaming like that.'

'Is she . . . ?'

'What?'

Hester got up and began clearing the table. 'I'm sorry, Gavin. I know I shouldn't keep trying to talk about this. I'm going to shunt you off to bed soon, anyway. You look absolutely shattered.'

'Bad day, yeah.'

Get worse.

'I'm sure. But it's so hard not to keep on asking. For me it's like you've arrived in my house to cure me of fifteen years of accumulated suffering. Every word I can exchange with you undoes a little bit of it. Do you see?'

Embarrassed again, he nodded.

'What I was going to ask was, is she . . . is she like a . . .' She opened her arms helplessly. 'Oh, I don't know. Is she anything like . . . a normal person? A woman?'

Miss Grey, who'd always been there. 'Yeah. Well, no, not normal. Not at all. But not . . .'

Hester laughed mirthlessly as he trailed off. 'Language isn't a very good tool for describing the indescribable, is it? A lot of what we used to call "primitive" cultures are much better at this sort of thing than us.'

But now it was Gavin's turn to be deep in memories.

'She was my friend,' he said quietly, staring at the tablecloth.

Hester came and sat down opposite, without a word.

'Mum and Dad never understood.' He'd never imagined himself telling anyone this. It was like a dream, like someone else speaking. But then he'd never imagined himself missing her either, and yet there was no other explanation for the swelling misery inside him. Miss Grey, gone? 'Dad used to get so angry every time I said anything about her. He tried everything. He made this rule that every time I said her name he'd go up to my room and take a pound out of my piggybank. If there wasn't any money in it I had to go straight out and wash the car or mow the lawn or whatever. To earn the pound. So he could take it away. That's how he used to do it. He'd take the pound coin out of his pocket and give it to me and make me put it in the piggybank and then he'd take it right out again while I watched. Didn't matter what time of day. Even if it was bedtime. He sent me out to do the car in the middle of winter once. In my pyjamas with a bucket and sponge. Mum . . .

Anyway. Miss Grey was there, at the end of the street. Just seeing her made it OK.'

Hester reached across the table and patted his clenched hand.

'Miss Grey?'

He blinked. 'Just a name I made up. Stupid, I know.'

'You kept a name for her?' Hester asked, very gently.

'Are you really sure she's gone?' he said, biting his lip.

Her fingers closed over his. 'Oh, Gavin, I'm sorry. I do know she isn't looking over my shoulder any more. I can just feel it. But I don't know anything about your situation at all. Please don't think I have anything to tell you about your friend. All right? Gavin?'

He nodded tightly.

'I found you an hour or two ago running like the devil was at your heels. I left you by yourself in an empty house, just because she told me to and I was too cowardly and too tired to refuse. That's all I know. I don't know the first thing about you or your life or what she wants with you. So please don't—'

'What d'you mean, wants with me?'

Hester let go of his hand.

'You mean when she said to leave me at Aunt— at the house?'

'Not just that.'

My oldest friend, he thought. My only friend. Until now. Until today, when at last he needed her, when he'd finally discovered that he could stop trying to know better, that Mum and Dad were wrong, that Mr Bushy was wrong, everyone else was wrong, everyone but her. She'd tried to tell him something. She'd found her voice. And now she'd left him.

Had she given up on him? Had he driven her away?

'Look. I've known her a long time. If "known" is the right word. As long as you, probably. How old are you, may I ask?'

'Fifteen.'

'Just as long, then. Fifteen years, a month and, let's see, thirteen days. And in all that time I've never known her do anything like this. Do anything at all, in fact. I mean, I've never seen a discernible motive. I've never known her act like a rational agent.'

She waited for him to speak, but he couldn't. She sighed, then got up and began clearing up again, stacking plates in the sink. 'She told me to take that train, Gavin. She . . . Truth be told, it was one of the worst outbursts I've ever known. I'd only gone back to Oxford to turn in keys and finish up a couple of things. But I was planning to stay an extra day or two. You know, there were people I wanted to say goodbye to. That sort of thing. Dinner invitations. I'm supposed to be at one of them even as we speak, in fact. But on Sunday night . . .' She heaved a deep breath. 'Well. Why don't we just say that I didn't get very much sleep and that I was on my way to the station at the crack of dawn. It only . . . stopped when I left the college. And then when I arrived at Reading to change trains, it started up again. I had to go and lock myself in a stall in the ladies'. It was very clear to me which train I had to wait for. Very, very clear. It was very clear which carriage I had to sit in. Which seat.'

'Miss Grey told you to sit opposite me?'

Hester nodded. 'Not in so many words. Believe me, nothing was ever that straightforward. But yes. In the seat, that is. Nothing was said about you. I thought you were just another passenger. I had no idea you were . . .'

Ward of her you seek.

What did Miss Grey want from him? What did it have to do with Marina, the house, the beast in the dark?

'You see,' Hester began, as if the silent interval hadn't happened, 'I would never have expected the things she said to have any particular point to them. This is the thing that worries me. Over all those years I've never known . . . her . . . do anything like that. I'm not . . .' She hesitated. 'I'm not sure how good a thing it is for her to have an interest in you. Do you see?'

'She's always been there for me,' Gav said, but he was thinking, Until now. Corbo's voice came back to him, its curt flat rasp: *Gets killed.* Was she dead? Was Miss Grey dead?

He shivered violently.

'Yes, I know. Forgive me.' Hester had misunderstood his spasm. 'I understand your story isn't the same as mine. But you haven't told me anything about what's happened to you.' There wasn't the least hint of accusation in her tone; she was simply stating the case. 'I took you to Pendurra, and then she left me, and then today, there, whatever happened to you happened. No' – she raised a hand – 'no, I'm not asking you to tell me. I'm just explaining why . . . Well, forgive me for saying it, but why I'm worried about you.'

'I don't know what happened to me today.' She was about to interrupt him; he cut her off. 'It's true: I don't know. Something weird's going on. They're all mixed up in it.'

'All who?'

'Aunt Gwen and the Urens and—'

'Tristram Uren?'

'Mr Uren and Marina I mean, yeah.'

'Marina?'

'His daughter.'

He'd surprised her – not just surprised, but shocked her.

'Daughter? Tristram Uren has a daughter?'

'Yeah. I met her.'

'Good God. How old is she?'

'Said she was thirteen.'

'Thirteen!'

Hester looked completely dumbstruck. Apparently Marina's existence was as astonishing to her as Miss Grey's.

'Yeah.'

'You're certain this girl you met is his daughter?'

'Yeah, the whole "daddy" business sort of gave it away.'

'Yes, I'm sorry. Of course. Sorry. But how incredible. No one has ever mentioned her.' Her fingertips drummed on the counter. 'It's different in London, you see, but down here everyone talks about everything. I've heard all the rumours about a wife and so forth, but no one so much as hinted at a child. Where can she have been all these years?'

'I don't think she gets out much.'

Hester studied him with her thoughtful eyes. 'Well, well,' she said.

But he was thinking about Marina too. The one person who might know what he was talking about and he'd ignored her, dismissed her the way people had always dismissed him. I should be there, he thought. Something really bad's happening. Miss Grey sent me there and I just ran away.

'I should go back.'

'No.' Hester put down the plate she was drying with a decisive *thunk*, making Gav look up in surprise. 'No. Gavin. Look. I haven't the slightest idea what you saw or did today, but I can see the state of your clothes and your face, and I can see how tired you are. You need time, and strength. Trust me. I know a little bit of what this is like. I may know better than anyone. We shouldn't even talk about it any longer. I know, it's my fault. I have a thousand things I want to ask you. But they can all wait. Any idiot can see that you need some peace and a night's sleep.'

When she said the word *sleep* it was like casting a spell. The idea of lying down somewhere, not having to talk, not having to think, made him almost weep with longing. Did he seriously think he was going back out into the dark, back towards the chapel and what he thought he'd seen there?

She tried to offer him the one bedroom upstairs, but when he saw the spare room – a space not much longer than he was, squeezed under the eaves and stacked to the ceiling with packing boxes – he absolutely refused. So he helped her shift boxes around until they found one with all the blankets and cushions, and together they piled them up until they'd made something like a fabric nest between cardboard cliffs. By the time that was done, Gav could barely hold himself upright.

'I'm afraid there's no light for you,' Hester said. The room had a window, but the boxes completely blocked it.

''s fine.'

'You'll be all right, then?'

'Yeah.' Truth be told, he was glad of the barrier between him and the night. 'Thanks to you,' he added.

She grinned. 'I'd say, "You're welcome," but that wouldn't be the half of it. I have a suspicion you've saved my life, actually. I'd never have admitted this to myself before yesterday, but I'm not sure how much longer I was going to be able to carry on.'

Gav looked away.

'I didn't do anything,' he said.

'Oh, but you did. You did. You just don't know what it was yet.'

It sounded a bit like a joke, but her voice was all simple assurance.

'Gavin?'

'Yeah?'

'I don't hate your friend. I never hated her. I'm only glad she's gone because I'm old. I'm worn out. I'd rather have the easy life. I want to be like everyone else again.'

He couldn't think of anything to say at all.

'You're different.' He felt her eyes on him and suddenly realised what made her look clever. It was that you could tell she hadn't made her mind up about things before she looked at them. What was that thing Mr Bushy always said? She didn't *judge*; she *appraised.* (Sleepily he remembered the instruction from so many English lessons: *I don't care whether you think it's good or bad, Stokes. I want you to tell me how it works!*) Her eyes took things in, generously. Like she'd taken him in.

'You don't have to be afraid of it, Gavin. It's a marvellous thing. Don't be afraid to find out.'

Learn fast.

'Good night then,' she finished, closing the door behind her.

'Night.'

Horace had been sitting at the desk under the window in his tiny room, moodily pondering nothing in particular, when he saw the car pull up at the professor's house opposite.

He'd been about to shout something. Mum was in bed – *Up early tomorrow. I have to go to Mrs Ambell and Mrs Standish in Falmouth and then come back in the afternoon to help the professor. I have breakfast all ready for you. Make sure you brush your teeth this time* – but she'd still asked him to keep an eye out in case he saw the mad old bat come home.

And then he thought, Why should I tell her?

He knew exactly what would happen if he did. Mum would get out of bed, in her slippers. She'd come into his room and peer out through the net curtain to make sure the car was actually there, as if she couldn't trust him to identify a car on his own. And then she'd go across the street and invite the nutter in. For a chat. And food. And he'd already told her he'd nearly finished his homework so he wouldn't be able to get out of going down and being polite unless he came up with another excuse, really quickly.

Except he didn't need to think of an excuse. All he had to do was not tell her the old headcase had come home.

What did it possibly matter anyway? He shouldn't encourage Mum.

Why should she care what the neighbours were doing? No. Forget it. He glanced at his wall clock. Mum wouldn't get out of bed now.

He watched idly as the professor got herself out of her car. He couldn't remember the last time he'd seen her. Everyone knew about her, though. The village idiot.

Looks like she's got a visitor too.

Someone was getting out of the passenger side. Not another old person, surprisingly. Seeing anyone who wasn't nearly dead was a major surprise in this craphole village. Some kid.

Kid?

Horace stood up from his desk as the boy straightened beside the car. Light from the streetlamp in the lane fell through the bushes of the cramped front garden, picking out the visitor's face.

Horace felt his secret turn to lead inside him.

After a few numb seconds he reached under the lampshade and turned off his desk light. Carefully, so Mum wouldn't hear anything, he sat on the desk and pressed his nose to the glass, just in time to see the two of them, the woman and the boy, go into the house opposite. As they opened the front door they were caught in a box of brightness, made unmistakable. Just for a second or two, but long enough.

Horace sat in his room with his light turned off for a long time, and when he finally went to bed, it was hours before he managed to sleep.

Sixteen

EVENSONG COMPLETE, AND the usual handful of attendees sent back off into the night with sufficient good wishes, Owen decided to drive up to the lodge to see if Gwen had found her way home yet.

He knew he ought to have walked, really. The cold was no worse than any other overcast winter night, and he'd have warmed up anyway going up the hill to the crossroads. It wasn't all that far. But it was very dark, the kind of dark that presses around the edges of a torch's beam. Some of the villagers would be out walking their dogs in it, perfectly undisturbed, but even after all his years of living in the parish he'd never become used to being outside on his own in that kind of pitch black.

So, rather guiltily, he took the car.

He was swinging right at the crossroads on top of the ridge when a swathe of the impenetrable night above detached itself with a sound like the sky gasping and flew in front of the windshield. Owen cried out and swerved the wheel away. With a terrible crumpling noise and a bruising jolt his car ran into a hedge, throwing him against the seatbelt, crushing the breath out of him and filling his eyes with a chaos of shooting stars. His head spun.

Silence fell around him apart from a small hiss, steam leaking from the wrecked engine.

After a while he shoved the door open groggily. He couldn't quite remember what had made him do something so stupid. His skull throbbed. He ran his hands over his legs. They felt shaky but intact. Cold air gusted around him.

He staggered out. One headlight was bust, but the other still shone, embedded in the hedge, making strange shadows. He had no other light. He cursed himself for his carelessness. Leaning in the door, he tried the ignition a few times, but though it scraped and rattled, the engine wouldn't catch.

He patted his pockets with one hand, steadying himself against the car with the other. No phone. He'd left it at home. Half a mile away at most, but that half-mile was as black as the seabed. He opened the boot and felt around for a torch, but he knew there wasn't one there. Carrying a light in the back of the car was something else he'd never learned to do, even after two decades of country life.

The lodge at Pendurra was only a couple of hundred yards eastwards along the lane. He didn't like to bother Gwen at this time of the evening. She might not even be there, he reminded himself, though in the woozy aftermath of the crash he found himself wondering why he thought that was so. But borrowing one of her endless candles would help light his way home.

The darkness reminded him of something. He looked up, nervously.

It must have just been a big bird, he thought. It must have flown down against the windscreen somehow. Gave me a fright. Ridiculous.

He set off towards Pendurra.

He went slowly. His shoulder hurt more than he realised. Each step seemed to jog it. After a little while the lane made a gentle bend, and the faint illumination from the car vanished from the tarmac in front of him. Without it there was nothing in any direction but a few distant spots of light from houses beyond the high fields.

He was busy persuading himself to start walking the last thirty yards when he heard steps, and a small, flickering, bobbing light appeared ahead. From out of the gate of Pendurra someone came into the road, holding a lantern in which a single fat candle burned. The lantern was shaded so that it shone only ahead, towards him.

'One comes, master,' said a rich warm voice.

The lantern wobbled, its chain clinking. Then it swung sideways and for an instant its dim light flowed across something beside it. Something huge, something that should not have had the power of motion. Something that should not have had anything resembling a face.

Owen dropped to his knees in the road.

'Jesus Christ,' he said.

The lantern settled again. Now everything was shadow behind it, dark, like the dark that had plunged towards the car and made him crash. Not a big bird.

The silence was broken by another voice, a woman's, but cracked, harsh, tight. It said, 'He takes me for his saviour.'

The arm that held the lantern raised it higher to cast its light further along the road.

'Is this a holy man?' the same person said.

'I cannot tell,' murmured the first voice, the beautiful one, invisible behind the lantern.

'You!' A grotesque bark. 'Do you have power of speech? Do you understand me?'

Owen pushed himself unsteadily to his feet. The only thing he was aware of was fear. He'd never known what the word really meant before. It washed all over him in one merciless flood, driving everything else out.

'Beware, master,' hummed the invisible voice.

'Jesus,' said Owen, without knowing he'd spoken. His feet were backing away, tiny trembling steps. 'Jesus.'

'He welcomes me.'

'It may be, master.'

'You.' The lantern twitched. 'Do you welcome me?'

Owen stopped. The fear roared in his ears.

'An imbecile,' the harsh woman's voice said, after a moment. 'Drive him away. Guard this gate afterwards. Let no one enter.'

There was another noise, abrupt and loud, a hollow thrashing in the air. Owen flinched away from it, raising his hands. The light vanished. Something scratched on the road ahead.

The darkness spoke to him, a third voice.

'Go.'

His legs wouldn't move. Nothing moved.

'Go,' it said again, toneless. 'Now. Back.'

The darkness rattled on the road again. As if it had feet. As if the feet were coming closer.

Owen screamed. The shout pierced his terror. He staggered backwards. The dark cried out in reply, a horrible squawking cry. In the instant before he turned and ran Owen thought he saw it moving, spreading, a misshapen black mass opening arms to enfold the world. Still screaming, he fled.

Gav woke in absolute darkness with no idea where he was.

He panicked. He knew he wasn't at home in his own bed. He couldn't remember why not. He'd woken instantaneously, with no memory of having slept. Time and the world had fallen away and left nothing at all.

He flailed his arms wildly. He was tangled in something. His hands struck cardboard boxes. For a split second he felt nothing but invisible walls around his head, as if the darkness itself were solid and closing in. He was enwombed in it, or buried alive. Then the heartbeat passed and he remembered what the cardboard boxes were. In that same moment a sound came, the first sign of a world outside.

A bell struck.

It struck again. A morose church bell.

And again. The clang, its dissonant decay, then another. Time came back to him, measured by the tolling.

Midnight.

Gav lay still. Stupid to have freaked out like that, he told himself. He remembered bedding down in Hester's spare room now. The blankets had got twisted around him.

Someone had said not to be frightened. *Don't be afraid. You have come home.* Who was that? Must have been Hester. He was in her home. But he felt like it hadn't been her. Hadn't it been someone right here, beside him in the dark?

He must have dreamed it.

He was possessed by a sudden and overwhelming conviction that he'd forgotten something. It was that feeling of having left something behind by mistake. He needed to go back and get it, then everything would be OK. If only he could remember what it was.

As his breathing slowed he began hearing another sound, very quiet, somewhere in the house. Disentangling himself from the invisible blankets, he propped himself up on his elbows to listen.

Must be Hester snoring, he thought, a funny humming snore. But it didn't quite have the rhythm of human breath. Maybe something downstairs like a dishwasher running overnight. Downstairs was where it seemed to be. Hester didn't have a dishwasher, though, and the sound wasn't steady enough to be anything mechanical.

He decided to ignore it and roll over and go back to sleep.

He noticed then that he was very awake. Completely alert, as if he'd slept for hours, though it was only midnight.

The feeling of something forgotten was prodding him insistently. It was just on the edge of his thoughts. He hunted after it. Maybe it was because he'd rolled up at Hester's house without his wallet or his keys or any of the stuff that he normally patted his pockets to check for whenever he went out.

Strangely, as soon as he had that thought it was answered by the complete certainty that he didn't need them. He didn't need his wallet. He didn't need his keys. He'd never – the thought made him dizzy, as if the floor had vanished under him – need either of them or anything like them (phone, train ticket, his watch, toothbrush, change of clothes) ever again.

How could that be?

The faint noise seemed to be moving downstairs. It sounded almost like someone poking around on the ground floor, muttering and humming to themselves.

Gav sat up, feeling around him for the piles of boxes. Hadn't Hester mentioned that some of her masks were valuable? Could there be a burglar down there?

He got to his knees and groped in the dark. He couldn't remember the shape of the room at all, only that it was tiny. His head knocked against a box, making something rattle.

He remembered scrabbling for light against the inside of a closed door, a wooden door. That must have been a dream. The memory was so vivid he could taste the panic again in his throat, but he couldn't ever have been locked in a place like that. With a thing like that. *Oh come on Gav.*

He crouched, squeezing his head between his hands.

Don't be afraid, someone had told him. Hester, or someone else, or maybe both of them. But he was. He was terrified. He felt as if he was on the brink of some huge dark drop. He couldn't understand why he was so sure that it no longer mattered about his wallet and his keys and his watch and his life and the world. That was supposed to be the stuff you couldn't do without. He was only fifteen. What else was there? Just this darkness? Nothing at all?

He inched forward and his probing fingers found a door instead of cardboard. He pushed.

A nocturnal glow appeared. The world came back into position. He saw the top of the stairs, and another doorway adjacent: Hester's room. The glow came creeping up from a nightlight she'd left on in the kitchen.

There was definitely someone down there, making odd quiet rustles and murmurs.

'Hello?'

Nothing. He'd barely called out loud enough to hear his own voice. Stupid if it was a burglar, he told himself. He should shout or bang the floor, frighten them off. Or wake Hester up. Call the police.

But it didn't sound like a burglar. It didn't sound like a body moving around. It was more like a whispered conversation in a weird language, with snatches of muffled singing. Did Hester sleepwalk?

'Hello?'

He stood up and took a couple of deliberately heavy steps along the hallway so whoever was below would know someone was awake in the house. The faint noises continued untroubled, no change at all.

He put his ear to Hester's door. Slow, heavy breath. She was asleep in there. He thought about waking her up, but it was the middle of the night and he felt stupid. All that had happened was that he'd had some weird dream (hadn't he?) and couldn't get to sleep, and now he was scared in the dark like a child. Stupid. Now that he thought about it, he realised what must have happened. She must have gone back downstairs after he went to sleep and listened to the radio, then forgotten to turn it all the way off. Perfectly straightforward explanation. The noise sounded like a mix of static and fragments of music and talking from a remote station, not quite tuned in.

Might as well go down and switch it off, he thought. (The thought resonated weirdly in his head like a suggestion from outside, *switch it off switch it off switch it off switch it off . . .*)

In the kitchen the dim frosty nightlight picked out glossy passages in the poster. The old man and the whispering angel at his shoulder looked as if they were painted out of moonbeams. The weird radio noise was coming from the front room. Gav had reached round the door and was feeling for a light switch when he remembered this was the room where the masks were.

He pulled his hand away. Far better not to see them at all. He prodded the door open a little wider and leaned his head in nervously, looking for the telltale light of a radio.

There wasn't one.

Of course there wasn't. There weren't things like that any more. He'd gone over the brink and left them behind.

There were only voices in the darkness.

Invisible, inhuman voices.

The voices called or whistled or sang from far away, very far. It was as though he'd stepped in through the broken door of an abandoned palace, and from rooms deep within or high above, from cells at the top of the loftiest and remotest towers, the cries of stranded survivors drifted down to him, in languages no one but they had ever understood.

One jab at the light switch, he told himself, and he could turn it back into Hester's front room. He imagined the light flaring up, blinding him for a couple of seconds, and then as he blinked and shielded his eyes the space would come back as he remembered it, a bit crowded and messy, the horrible ranks of faces staring from the walls.

He didn't hit the switch.

He listened.

He thought perhaps there were five or six different voices. It was impossible to be sure.

He did, however, know for sure where they were coming from.

He pushed the door from the kitchen wide open, letting more of the nightlight's glow into the room.

The faces around the walls were drained of colour, reduced to eerie lumps of darkness. The fact that he couldn't see their eyes made all the difference. He could feel them watching him anyway, but it wasn't quite as bad. He could concentrate on their voices instead.

The sounds floated distinctly around him like currents of air. The masks were muttering or chanting or whispering to themselves, or perhaps to someone else, another presence he couldn't see.

Edging behind one sofa, the row of shadow shapes arrayed on the wall in front of him, he reached his hands out, carefully.

Creepy to look at, the masks were wonderful to touch. His fingers felt lines and volumes, the textures of different materials, curves made by mould or knife, precise or rough. *Sculpture's a tactile medium*, their art teacher was always saying. Some of the masks were intricate and elaborate. Others seemed to be constructed out of just a few shapes, coherent like stones. Without him really thinking about it, his fingers felt their way along the row, wondering where the voices came from, looking for a match between shape and sound.

He knew instantly when he found it. It was like an electric shock in his hands. The voice flowed up through them and into him, inside him, filling him.

It knew him.

He jerked his hands away.

The mask he'd touched was a big wooden one, jutting out from the wall as if the bow of a model boat had crashed into Hester's house. He was still close to the kitchen door, so a smudge of ghostly light fell across it, picking out its crude strong lines, the blunt ovals of its eyes.

. . . four or five of my menagerie are totemic objects of one sort or another. Not exactly museum quality, but the real thing.

The weird chorus drifted around him. One particular voice definitely seemed closer now, as though a mouth had turned to him directly. Deep, rich, hollow, heard as if through water.

Don't be afraid, said another voice, behind him, in the back of his thoughts.

Gav extended his hand again and rested it on the long wooden head.

The voice sang

hunger, solitude, freedom. It sang the blue light above and the black deep below, the salt currents channelling between clefts of rock to coasts and shallows where forests of mossy hemlock reached over the water's edge, gathering rain. It hymned fat meat at the surface and swells of food scattering below. Blood and sustenance. It sang its name, a word there had never been an alphabet for

ma'chinu'ch

Gav pulled his hands back, reeling, the world spinning around him. The song went on, following its ancient course, but now it was outside him, as if by removing his fingers he'd closed a door on it. It had turned back into mere sound. The language, the meaning, was gone.

He breathed deeply, tempted for a moment to sink back into that ocean of joyful hunger. He heard the senseless syllables whispering distantly, *ma'chinu'ch, ma'chinu'ch.* Where, he wondered, were the other voices? He edged along the wall towards the shuttered window, touching very gingerly, ready to jump his fingers away.

Part of him wanted to go back to bed. The sensible thing to do, it said, would be to close all the doors, go back upstairs, bury his head under the blankets and wait until he got to sleep, no matter how long it took, leaving the inscrutable presences to carry on their mumblings undisturbed. It might be hours. Wait until dawn, if he had to.

Another part listened to the otherworldly sounds and told him not to be afraid.

His fingers found a snout of rough wood and twitched again, and his heart jumped. Another voice found him, coming alive, a chthonic mutter tinged with a ferocity that made him pull his hand away almost at once. With that momentary touch something that prowled and pursued had turned to face him. Gav breathed hard, his fingertips still tingling. He peered towards the mask, trying to make out its features in the near-dark. It was the last in the row, furthest from the dim light coming through the kitchen door, and all he could see was the rough shape: a triangular shadow with a thrusting muzzle, slightly open. Parted jaws. Its guttural tuneless chant separated itself from the blended whispers and seemed to circle him.

Ducking closer, his left hand nudged the slatted blind at the window. It wobbled, exposing a crack of cold white from the streetlight in the road outside.

Gav felt around for the cord of the blind. Should have thought of that before, he told himself, relieved beyond any obvious reason. His idea was to open the slats of the blind just a tiny bit, letting in as much of the outside light as he needed to see the mask while leaving the rest of the room safely obscure. He'd close them again before he went back to bed. Hester obviously didn't want anyone looking in on her.

He found the cord and tugged carefully. The slats swivelled apart. He peered out, looking for the single lamp-post in the lane.

There beneath it, as still as if she had taken root in the road, her shadowed face raised towards him, was Miss Grey.

Part IV
Night

Seventeen

A January night 1537, and another night

WITHIN THE STILL water in the silver bowl, a room appeared. A painted, firelit room, squat columns vanishing up through smoke to an unseen roof. The hiss and spit of the fire and the sound of a chanting voice came very distantly and obscurely, like noises underwater. As the scene grew clearer and a group of white-and-scarlet robed figures became visible between the columns, the magus caught his breath. Bending over the bowl, reflected firelight shone in his eyes.

'They assemble for a rite,' said an invisible voice, a susurrus of dead leaves. The greatest magus in the world stared into the bowl, transfixed.

'Is that truly Ilium?'

'We show you what you bid us show, Magister. Obedient always.'

The robed figures moved blurrily, like actors in a dream. He saw their barbarous faces. Narrow, strong-jawed, dark in the oily firelight.

'Shall we conduct you there? Then you may sate your eyes on the woman as you please.'

His breath caught in his chest. The most beautiful woman in the world, that was what he had commanded the spirit to show him. An idle thought, a whim. He had never imagined it would throw the doors of time open so wide. A mere trick of clairvoyance, and it had led him to this: the brink of legend. Helen. Helen of Troy.

But then, he reflected, it was testimony to the immensity of his power of command. He was almost ashamed of how unworthy the original impulse had been, how easily and lightly he could make marvels possible.

'That is the royal household?'

'We know nothing of men, Magister. We do your bidding merely.'

'Then show me the woman.' His eyes hadn't wavered from the obscure scene, not for an instant.

'We must approach.'

'You will conduct me back?'

'As you wish.'

'It is a great distance,' he said. 'Far greater than any we have spanned before.'

'Do you doubt us?'

'No.'

'Do you fear for yourself?'

'I?' He shook his head. 'What have I to fear?'

'There are old powers, Magister. Beware them.'

He laughed shortly, still without looking up. 'You waste your warnings on me, spirit. I conjure with powers little less than angels. Conduct me now.'

'That is your command?' The voice with its hundred dry echoes seemed to swell with subtle triumph, but the magus, heart pounding, did not notice.

'Yes. I desire it. Now.'

The blurred shadows at the edges of the water's surface rippled and spilled out. The firelight burned brighter, tinged with coppery green; at the same moment the magus was overwhelmed by a rich, astringent savour of Asiatic smoke. It swamped him as the shadows did. He felt himself floating in them, dizzy, light enough to be spun on the currents of scented air. When he came to rest, he was there, in the room where the priest wailed and poured oil into the fire while the king and his family attended. Although his mortal body had not moved from his laboratory in the cellars of his house, the ghost of that body turned its head towards the gathering of men and women.

'In the second rank, Magister,' whispered the possessor of the dry voice, who now appeared as a phantom of flickering burning light in the shape of a naked and sexless human.

But the magus did not need to be told. As soon as his bodiless gaze had fallen on the slender-necked girl standing just behind the queen, he had known her. Her exquisite head was tilted demurely down in honour of the goddess, whose crude bronze image glowed dully from its sooty niche. But there was an assurance in her sly eyes and her settled, faintly smiling lips, which showed all too clearly how well she knew her own unrivalled beauty, and foretold how she would continue to exult in her loveliness even when it had brought years of misery to all the rest of those standing with her in the shrine that night, even when it had brought destruction to the shrine itself, and fiery ruin to the city that housed it. Helen. Her name, after all, meant *torch.*

'Fix your eyes on her. Feed them.' The magus scarcely heard his companion's urgings. Dissolved in wonder, he scanned the smoky room, the rough faces, names destined to live for incalculable centuries, outlasting nations and empires, outlasting even the stone of their own tombs.

'There is peril for you elsewhere,' the burning spirit warned, a sly whisper. The magus gave it no more attention than one ghost gives another.

'Deadly peril,' it added. On its blank face, under the lidless and pupilless eyes, a strange smile spread. The magus never saw it. His attention had been distracted by a pair of eyes pointed, unexpectedly, in his direction. They were a little further back from the group, at its edge. They were not roving idly, or watching the goddess dutifully, as all the others were.

They were fixed on him.

He returned the look.

The phantom of naked silent flame whispered a single word:

'Lost.'

Its serpentine hiss went unnoticed. The eyes belonged to a woman who was staring at the corner where the two ghosts were. Horror spread over her face.

There was a dreadful scream. The room surged with sound and motion, men's barbarous voices raised in anger. Amid the commotion the magus studied the one who had seen him and saw him still, judging by the unmistakable focus of her fear. A young woman, with a hunted expression and dark hair that was as disordered as all the others' was oiled and fine. Shrinking backwards, she raised an arm, pointed directly at him and screamed again above the clamour, in a powerful voice rich with dreadful conviction, and went on screaming until someone struck her mouth. She went spinning to the floor. Dark blood smeared over the back of her hand. Tangled hair fell like a half-closed curtain in front of her eyes; she clutched at it. Her jaw shook as if resisting the torture of speech. The tormentor was too strong: her back arched, the sinews of her neck sprung tight as a viol's strings.

'Johannes Faust!' she cried. 'Johannes Faust!'

Bloodless and bodiless as he was, the magus felt lightning pulse through him. A fury erupted in the room. The woman cringed against the floor, covering her head. A man seized her by the wrists and dragged her up on her feet, shouting. Another man, an old man in the front rank, spread his hands, gesturing for peace.

'My name,' the magus said hoarsely. 'She knows me.'

'Return now, Magister.'

'Who is the one that knows me?'

'Magister, do not delay.'

'Answer me!' The men were pulling her out of the room. He made to pursue and felt the spirit's recalcitrance holding him back like a ghostly anchor.

'Release me!' She was already disappearing into the exterior shadows.

'Heed us, Magister.'

'You disobey? You have no freedom to do other than as I command you!'

The empty face bowed, the trace of a ghastly smile on its glimmering lips.

'I must question her.' The rite was reassembling. The family and their attendants returned their attention to the droning celebrant by the fire, the crude idol in the wall.

'She is cursed, Magister.'

'Who is she? By what name is she known?'

The voice lingered over the sibilance, as if the word were the hiss of a dying fire:

Cassandra.

Its answer held the magus like a spell.

'Did you not know her, Magister, as she knew you?' Its voice writhed among the chanting. Lost in a rapture he had forgotten he could feel, stretched out on the first stirrings of a peculiar bittersweet longing, the magus heard it only as the sound of cloth sliding over a stone floor.

'Cassandra,' he echoed.

'She who broke her pledge, who scorned her gift. Now it scorns her. She betrayed the bond between mortals and spirits, Magister. Now she carries the betrayal with her. Beware her.'

The last words broke through the magus's fog of wonder. 'What?' He frowned. 'What riddling is this?'

'Her curse is called magic, Magister.'

The magus began to grow angry. She was gone who knew where. He was losing time.

'I must speak with her. Show me where she is.'

'I cannot.'

'What? Do you dare offer disobedience?'

'No disobedience. I am bound to ward you. Her curse is heavy.'

'Curse?' the magus scoffed. 'Do you imagine I am ignorant of it? Is it not proverbial? A trick of speech, no more.'

'You are ignorant,' the spirit whispered, an answer that might have been calculated to enrage him.

'You think I do not know what every pedant knows? Of course I know her legend.' An argument between ghosts, chittering like mice in the roof. 'To know the truth always, but never to be believed. Is it not so? She prophesied the fall of this city' – he waved his spectral arm, gesturing contemptuously at the doomed family – 'but they scorned her. You call that a curse? The truth is not a curse, Spirit. Not for such as I.'

'Maybe, Magister.'

'She called me by name!' He gazed towards the dusty tiles where she had crouched. 'She is a prophetess. I will speak with her. If you refuse to conduct me, then leave me.'

'God-ridden,' the shimmering face answered, leaning towards him. For a moment he seemed to hear burning in its speech, the sound of destruction. 'God-broken. She holds the open door in her hand and suffers for it.'

The magus would hear no more. By nature he could never tolerate the suggestion of a threat. Already a private hunger was gripping him, excluding all doubt. This was not the first time he had performed the extraordinarily difficult magic of clairvoyance, but never before had he felt anything like the shock of recognition and sympathy that had come when the fabled prophetess cried his name. He had arrived at the border of revelations and mysteries that had been lost for millennia. A whim, a foolish whim had opened the path to this vanished age of heroes, men and women who battled and bartered with spirits as familiarly as quarrelling neighbours. He could not turn his back on it.

Most of all, he could not turn his back on her. Cassandra! Who saw what no one else could see and was despised for it. And to have now become one of her visions, himself! – no wonder, really, that he forgot Helen and, for the first time, found himself falling in love.

The spirit protested as long as he permitted it to speak, so he silenced it and then banished it. He could not let cowardice hold him back. He would find another guide to return him to his true body, when the time came.

Then, a spectre among the towers of Troy, he made himself go out into the night and look for her.

He could, perhaps, have drifted through the many-gated city that night like the ghost of twenty centuries of songs and stories, watching the flesh-and-blood men and women whose short and barbaric lives were destined to be rendered undying by almost as many poets as there were years. From the top of one wall he looked westwards across the plain and saw the ominous light of watch-fires. There, he supposed, slept men whom time would remember as all but gods themselves. But nothing in all this world of bronze and fire and brutality was worth anything at all next to the one woman they despised.

He searched fruitlessly. There was no order to the buildings that he could discern and, once inside, no arrangement of rooms he could recognise. After what was a long time measured by the turning sky of that place and age, he found himself once again in the painted hall where he had begun. The fire was out. Beetles and rats stirred in the shadows.

She was there, waiting for him. She greeted his ghost by name.

They spoke for a long time, the prophetess and the phantom, in a language that would have sounded like raving to anyone in the city. They spoke like equals. In his thirty-odd years of studying the breadth of creation, celestial and sublunary, the magus had always known each being he conversed with to be either lesser or (rarely) greater than himself, and accordingly had always listened humbly or interrogated imperiously. That night, for the first time, he simply heard and answered.

When the high window-slits began to hint at dawn, she told him he had to leave.

'I must see you again,' he said. She knelt near the fire-pit, hands clasped around herself. Even though he was free of his flesh, he longed to touch her. She was as beautiful as wisdom. 'Tell me,' he begged, 'how and when I can find you.'

'I cannot, but I know you will.'

He felt joy surge in his thoughts just as if his heart had leaped under bone. 'I will return as soon as I have the power. The next night.'

'You will not.'

'I will. I swear it.'

'No.' She crouched lower, quivering slightly like a dying flame. 'But you will see me again.'

He remembered the trickle of blood from her mouth. 'How can I leave you here?' his tongueless voice said. 'I know as you do what will happen, in this very room.'

She looked at the statue of the goddess, then back at him.

'Then you know what will happen, whether you wish it or not.'

'I would use all my power to spare you that, if I could.' He could not bear the thought: the screams of terror as the city burned, the bronze armour hot with blood and the light of the flames, an enemy emptying ten years of fury onto her. This was why he had sworn never to love. Love enmeshed you in the horrors of a fallen world.

'There is no such power. Yet because you hear me and wish me kindness, you will see me again.'

'Then tell me how! Teach me the art by which I can return!'

'You will not return.'

In the east, above the mountains, a rich desert blue was spreading skywards. The magus knew he must go, but at that moment he would have surrendered his soul to stay a phantom at her side for ever.

'Where, then? Tell me only where and I will work without cease or rest until I have found the way that leads me back to you.'

'I cannot say. Yet you came to me and did not turn away and so you will see me again, even if I wait a thousand winters.'

'A thousand winters?' he whispered.

'And more. Twice a thousand. And more. The road-god leads me a long road. Now go. You must.'

It was true, though he fought against it. 'But when?' he cried, as the heavens opened wide to welcome the unseen sun and he began to slip away. 'When?' She blew on his ghost and the breath lifted him up like a feathered seed, and then there he was, lying on the floor of his laboratory late on a January night in the year 1537, his staff on the floor beside him and his face wet with tears.

Eighteen

IT TOOK GAV a very long time to make up his mind to go outside.

For a year and more he'd dreaded the sight of Miss Grey. Since he'd got to grips with the awful discovery that she wasn't real, he'd wished for nothing more than never to see her again.

She stood unmoving, her shapeless cloak gathered around her, looking at the window from which he looked at her. The unkempt curtains of her hair hid her face. Even so, Gav could tell she was watching him, as he'd so often seen her watching, waiting. The alien murmurs floated around him all the while.

He remembered how he used to talk to her, back in the time before he'd understood that she wasn't supposed to be there. It had never seemed to matter that she didn't answer.

He'd never be that child again. That particular happiness was dead and buried. There was no unlearning what he'd learned so painfully from Mum and Dad and Mr Bushy and everyone else. Yet his heart had betrayed him, leaping with joy when he'd seen her, just the way it always used to.

He tiptoed to the front door and opened it as quietly as he could. He was afraid she might have vanished in the interval, but as the night air poured in, he saw her there still, waiting. Hester had hung his coat by the door. He slipped it on.

A wintry desertion lay over the road. The houses with their meagre front gardens petered out to his left into unlit barrens of fields and empty roads. Everything seemed frozen. You couldn't imagine dawn coming, windows lighting up, people getting into cars and driving away.

Something about Miss Grey was different.

Her stillness had changed. Gav couldn't have said how. Maybe it was just that she was standing under the lamp, interrupting its pool of bleached light like a rock jutting from the sea. He was more used to seeing her at the edge of things.

He remembered a word she'd said to him: *Come.*

It occurred to him that he had a choice. He could, if he wanted, go back inside, shut the blind and head up to his makeshift bed. That was the sort of thing he'd been doing recently when she showed up. She was easy enough to ignore when he set his heart on it, or at least she had been until she'd started climbing in trains and shouting in his ear. Still, he could close the door on her if he liked. Shut her out like a vagrant. It was in his power.

But if he didn't do that, if he went out into the road to join her, he'd be doing what she'd told him to do. *Come.* He'd be giving in.

He looked around. It was past midnight. His parents weren't even in the country. He was in a village he couldn't name, hundreds of miles from home, standing on the doorstep of a house full of singing masks that belonged to a woman he barely knew, a woman who'd rescued him from a place where he'd been locked up in the dark with a monster.

It was fairly obviously time to stop trying to know better than Miss Grey.

Even that name felt stupid for her now. A childish joke. No name felt right, he thought, as he wriggled around Hester's car into the silent road. She looked like she was beyond names.

'Gawain,' she said.

Confused, he stopped in the lane. He hadn't expected her to talk. She never talked. She wasn't the kind of person who spoke in that kind of voice, a normal talking voice.

The sound of her speech was peaceful and certain as old stone.

'You left a door open behind you,' she said.

He turned round dumbly, saw Hester's front door half open, then turned back.

'Take off your shoes.'

He was in the middle of the road, ten paces from her. Another indeterminate pause and then she stepped towards him, her cloak rustling over the tarmac. Small bare feet poked from under it. He saw the tight set of her mouth, the familiar gaunt, faraway face, the unfathomable eyes. The worn white light and the perfect darkness all around drained her of any colour. When she was close enough to touch, she pushed back the cloak and knelt down by his feet.

She undid his shoes. Velcro crackled.

She lifted each foot in turn and slid the shoe off. Then, one after the other, she held his feet up and pulled off the socks. Her fingers were deft, unhurried, their touch slightly warm. She put the shoes and socks aside, carefully, laid her hands gently on his two feet and held them for a moment, as if confirming they were bare. As she leaned back to sit on her heels, she looked up at his face. The tumble of hair over her cheeks fell open.

'Don't put them on again. Let the earth hold you up.'

He might have nodded, or whispered 'OK,' or neither. He was too entirely lost to know. Time itself seemed to fall into the darkness of her gaze and be held motionless there. His heartbeat sounded like a distant echo in his ears.

'I . . .' he began. It seemed like he ought to say something. 'I . . . um . . .' He looked up and down the street. No one and nothing moved. His own stammering words sounded absurdly small, lost in the night. What was he even doing trying to talk to this . . . this thing? This phantom, this mistake? She rose to her feet again.

There was a difference in her eyes too. They were less like a wild bird's. A person was looking back at him.

'I thought you were . . .'

She waited. Her stillness was inhuman.

'Gone,' he finished.

'I am gone,' she said, in that voice dark with age. 'Through the door you left open walks my end.'

He stared, mouth half open.

'Will you take my burden from me, afterwards?'

In the desert of his thoughts he stumbled across a fragment of something the Corbo beast had said. *Old mad witch.* She seemed so calm, but she was just the same as on the train after all. A malfunctioning mouth.

To his astonishment she slipped her hands out from her cloak and closed them over his. They were dry, knuckly. She took a step closer, raising their hands between them, fingers knotted.

'Gawain,' she said. He was amazed at the warmth of her. She was so small and frayed he thought she'd be as insubstantial as cobwebs. She had never touched him before, except in dreams. 'You are free to choose. We all are, though the road-goad watches the road. Will you take my burden from me?'

He couldn't look at her, couldn't look away from her. He was coming unmoored. 'What did you call me?'

'The name your mother gave you.'

It was the way she always said it, in his dreams, but he'd never heard it aloud before, clear in the cold air. Every word she said made him feel like he was hearing language for the first time.

'I don't understand,' he said.

Her fingers tightened over his. 'Nor I,' she said. 'Will you take it and let me go free?'

His answer came to his tongue unexpectedly, a complete surprise, although as soon as he said it, he knew it was true. 'I don't want you to go.'

She turned her head to the side and lay it on his chest, next to where their hands were intertwined. All he could now see of her face was her nose sticking out of the tangle of hair. He felt her head rise and sink with his breathing.

'What do you mean,' he said, 'your end?'

'Who can answer that?' Her head nestled against him. 'It is the mark I cannot see beyond. I've lived so long, Gawain. So long.'

Old old old.

'What's happening?' The question dropped of its own accord from the block of his bewilderment, a fragment calving from a glacier.

'This,' she said. 'And then the next. And so it goes on, next and next and next, all down the endless road. You'll see.'

'See what?' All he seemed to be able to do was echo her.

'Everything,' she answered. She looked up. 'That is the burden. Will you bear it?'

Because her face was so close, the face he knew better than any other in the world, and also because he remembered at that exact instant that it was the face he loved better than any other in the world, the fact that she'd asked him a question four times finally sunk in, and so he answered it.

'OK,' he said. 'All right. Yes.'

A silent change rippled through her. Her eyes closed, her lips opened slightly to release a breath – he saw all these details with perfect clarity; he remembered every tiny motion, even years later – and, as if the warmth of sunrise had just fallen on her, she gave a barely perceptible shiver of relief.

'Um . . .' he began, as she leaned her head on his chest again. Now he was afraid she was going to go to sleep. He pictured himself stuck there till morning. People would come out of their houses and find him standing there in the middle of the street with no shoes on, propping up an old mad sleeping non-existent witch. 'What burden?'

'It will come to you today.' Her eyes didn't open. He watched the lines at the corners of her mouth, etched in the harsh lamplight. A catch came into her voice, as if talking was suddenly uncomfortable. 'You will bear it on your back. You will not know it. You will lose it. Lost in whiteness. You must go and find it. You must go, Gawain. Across sea and land, on the other side of the night, where an ocean girl tends it. An ocean girl tends it. An ocean girl.'

When she'd gone quiet long enough for him to be sure she was finished, he said, 'What are you talking about?'

'The truth.' She swayed back, disentangling her fingers from his. He noticed that his bare feet were incredibly cold.

'What truth?' Hazily it occurred to him that he'd probably never spoken a stupider sentence in his life, which was saying something.

'There will be fire and blood.' She shivered. Her hands vanished inside her cloak, clutching it to her tightly. 'Truth hurts. It's a heavy burden, Gawain. One took it from me before and could not bear it. The world will find it a bitter weight.'

His head was spinning. He wanted to go back indoors, get warm, go to sleep. He couldn't believe this was happening.

'What do I do?' It was all he could think of to say. For years he'd imagined her as his guide and guardian. 'What am I supposed to do?'

She stared quietly back at him for a while and then answered. 'Will you kiss me goodbye?'

'Goodbye?' His mouth shaped the word without a sound.

She stepped close to him and turned up her face.

It was like kissing moss. She smelled of dry earth. Breath from her nose tickled his cheek.

'That is the last true kiss you will receive,' she said, as she dropped back onto her heels.

'When—' he began, but he couldn't get hold of what he thought he'd wanted to say. While their lips had touched, he'd closed his eyes, and in the momentary darkness he had felt, distinctly, the motion of the whole earth around him, and the inconceivable ancientness beneath his feet and above his head, between which life flickered and flowed as gaudy and slippery and thin as an iridescent film of oil on the surface of the ocean.

'And my last also,' she murmured peacefully. 'My death comes.'

A red light flared behind him, throwing stark shadows across the road. With a gut-wrenching shock Gav realised they were standing in the middle of it and were about to be run over. He was still so stupefied by her kiss that the coming car registered painfully slowly, as if he had to construct the thought of being about to die piece by piece. The light grew intensely bright. He spun round, throwing his hands up, turning in useless slow motion. He wondered why the car was making no noise. He wondered why he couldn't accelerate his chilled limbs to push Miss Grey out of the way or jump before he got crushed.

Then he stood facing dumbly down the lane, all those thoughts skidding away as crazily as they'd arrived.

There was no car. Headlights were white anyway, not orange-red; he remembered that now. The light had faded almost to nothing. He couldn't see what had caused it. There was nothing there. All that remained was a hazy shimmer in the air like the evanescent tongues of flame around the charred wood of a dying fire. The glow was concentrated around Hester's front garden. For all he could see it had fallen from the sky and was now dissolving into her house. It dimmed, a miniature sunset, and was gone.

Gav turned back to Miss Grey, half expecting to see her prone and crumpled in the road. She regarded him as solemnly as before.

'I think,' he began. He stuck his hands in his pockets, looked up at the now empty sky and then down at his toes. 'I really think . . . you should tell me what's going on.'

'A door is open,' she said. 'For a long time it was closed. It shut me out.'

'No,' he said, before she could go on. 'No, listen. What's going on here, now? I need to know.'

A thud came from somewhere behind him, inside Hester's house, but Gav couldn't take his eyes off Miss Grey. Though she was standing still, she seemed to stagger. The cords in her neck tightened. Her eyelids fluttered.

'A woman sleeps,' she said. 'Other women sleep. Men sleep. Children sleep.' Her eyes closed tight as if something had hurt her. 'A woman who is no woman sits awake. She sits by the light of a fire that is no fire and dreams of salvation for the world. A death that is no death waits for her in the water.' Gav wanted to interrupt, but the mad monologue was gathering speed like a tumbling boulder. 'A boy sleeps. The water waits for him. He will bear my burden. *O o kakka.*' Flickers of pain creased her face. '*Iew iew.* In the branches the feasters dream their feast. Gawain. Gawain. A boy stands in the road. The road is dark before him and behind.' A dreadful stain of panic spread through her voice. 'A long road. A long road!' Gav stepped towards her, suddenly and absurdly worried that she was going to wake the neighbours. '*Otototoi!* A boy stands at the beginning of a long road. It will scratch and tear his feet. It will flay his back. It will hold him up. Let the earth hold him up. Behind him my end comes out an open door.' She was shaking like wheat in the wind, hugging herself. 'At last. At last. Destroyer. The final arrow is loosed. The empty quiver. My death. My death! My death! My—'

He reached out and grabbed her shoulders. The babbling and shivering stopped at once, as though he'd silenced a struck bell. She drew in a long, gasping, wordless breath, coming up for air. She opened her eyes.

In the sudden silence something rustled among the bushes of Hester's garden behind, some night animal.

She relaxed.

They looked at each other, Miss Grey and her ward.

'There it is,' she said, with a kind of smile.

'What?'

'My death.'

Light erupted behind him. As he spun round he heard a deep and unspeakably malevolent growl and saw a spray of cold fire. The sky filled with screeching shadows as roosting crows took sudden flight. Gav's knees gave way, terror dropped him to the ground, and as the billow of flame faded he saw in the road outside Hester's house the lean face of a huge black dog, crouching keenly, its fanged mouth dripping burning gobbets. In its breath was the undersong of the hunting mask, *Kill kill kill.* He stumbled to his feet. Miss Grey stood just as she had, perfectly unmoving. He looked to her frantically for help and knew that she was no help at all. She'd never been any help. The beast padded toward them, a brutish rumble coming from behind its clenched jaws. Liquid flame puddled on the asphalt behind it. Gav edged away. The dog swung its massive black head and fixed its eyes on him. They were burning too, smouldering with feral malice. His legs trembled; the air turned to ice in his lungs; it was all he could do not to collapse in a heap.

The horrific gaze released him, turning deliberately away.

It fixed on Miss Grey.

The black dog twisted back its head and howled. Fire spurted again from its throat. Gav threw his hands up to his face. It came slowly forward, towards her.

She looked pathetically tiny. She stood before it as if paralysed, as if already dead.

'No,' Gav whispered.

Its claws raked against the road. The head lowered, fanged mouth parting, trickling oily flame as it approached her. Still Miss Grey did not move.

'No,' he said, louder. 'No.'

A ripple ran over its black flanks. Its muscles bunched. It halted. Its head swivelled round to him. There were still runnels of fire in its mouth, red-gold saliva. Oh shit, Gav thought, that was stupid, suicidally stupid, but it was done. He met its gaze. I'm going to die now, he decided. The realisation seemed more weird than tragic. Let's get it over with.

The dog appeared to swallow uncomfortably. Its mouth opened, its tongue stiffened, and it spat out a strange, hollow bark.

Gav was so amazed at not yet being ripped to shreds that he became reckless with terror. 'No,' he repeated. 'Stop. Clear off.'

The quiver ran through it again. It shook its head as if in pain, and its tail dropped between its legs. Gav stood straighter. His knees wobbled ridiculously, as if he was a toddler, but he hadn't collapsed, he hadn't fallen, he wasn't dead. He took a deep breath and made himself speak clearly and firmly, the way you were supposed to talk to dogs. 'Get out of it.' Insane bravado made him shout louder. 'Piss off. Go on.'

It twisted round and ran away into the dark.

He stared after it. He couldn't feel his hands or feet or his heartbeat. Trickles of sweat turned icy on the back of his neck.

'That was well done, Gawain,' Miss Grey said.

Breathing hard, his fists slowly unclenching, he swivelled round to her. There might have been the faintest of smiles on her shadowed face.

'I . . .'

'Don't forget me,' she whispered. She touched her fingers to her lips. 'No one else will remember. You only.'

'I . . . What?' he said. 'No. Never.'

'You were always a kind child. It was you I loved. Goodbye.'

'Hey.' But she was suddenly swift. Her cloak floated out without a sound, she stepped out of the pool of light, and the shadows began rubbing away at her as she walked down the lane towards the dark. 'No. Wait.' Gav was too astonished to react. Hadn't he just driven away her death? He'd saved her. Now she wouldn't have to leave him after all. No goodbyes. They could go back to how it was when he was little and she was his best and only friend. He'd never wish her away again, never.

'Wait!' The darkness welcomed her amazingly quickly, as it had swallowed the hideous dog. He darted down the lane after her, but already he couldn't even see she was there, though he knew she must be. He'd always known she had to be there. Even when home was at its worst and he was shut in his bedroom crying face down into his pillow so no one would hear him, he'd known deep down that she was out there somewhere.

'Wait!' He ran out of the puddle of light and couldn't see a thing. He blundered on in the dark and smacked into an invisible parked car, stubbing his naked toe hard on some lump of metal. He fell into the road, clutching his feet, screeching in pain.

'Stop!' he shouted desperately, when his breath came back. 'Please!'

A light came on in an upstairs window.

'Please.' He stared out of the village, into the black. Nothing.

'Don't leave me alone,' he said, barely louder than a breath.

The creak and slide of a window opening.

'What the hell's going on out there?' shouted a man's voice.

Gav hunched into a ball on the road, hugging his knees, gazing after her.

'If I hear anything else, I'm calling the police! Do you understand? People are trying to sleep!' The window banged shut crossly. A few moments later the light flicked off.

'Please come back,' he said, to the darkness.

When he'd been a little kid, he used to think she came as soon as he wanted her. If he was feeling particularly lonely or sad, or Mum and Dad were being particularly mean or unfair, it always seemed like she'd be there before long, looking up at his window with that face that was never cross, maybe pointing out something that would cheer him up: a cloud shaped like a dragon, a tiny winged brown boy perched on the garden fence. Part of the misery of growing up had been realising he couldn't make her come and go any more than he could make it rain. She wouldn't answer his call. She never came when he begged. He'd said all the words he would ever be able to say to her. He was shivering in a country lane in the middle of the night. That was all.

He looked back towards the streetlamp. The road was empty but for his shoes, sitting like wreckage in the glare. He stared at them for a long, long time. He kept thinking he was going to cry, but he didn't. He felt hollow. A great many memories passed by in the darkness, things he'd tried not to think about for years because he'd been doing his best to forget Miss Grey.

The church bell struck, one dismal stroke. It sounded like a single word: *Come.*

'Goodbye,' he whispered, and touched his lips. They told him his fingers were freezing. His feet were freezing too.

You're on your own now, he thought to himself. It's all up to you, Gav. Gawain.

It was something she'd left him with.

He tried saying it aloud, not much more than a whisper. 'Gawain.' He muttered it a few more times, to get into the habit. I'm someone else now, he thought. Gavin's finished. He's the one Mum and Dad used to say things to, all the stuff he now knew was rubbish. *You're too old to make up this nonsense now, Gavin.*

'Gawain.' It made him feel older, and more serious. A courtly name, and an old-fashioned one. It settled around him like a ceremonial garment. He straightened his back.

It was all he had to begin with. Still, it struck him as the right sort of beginning, now that he thought about it. It was like being knighted. Arise, Sir Gawain. Your destiny awaits, whatever it is. Go forth and . . .

What?

What would he do, now he was on his own?

He sat cross-legged on the tarmac, his toes tucked under his thighs, and thought, slowly and carefully, about everything that had happened to him since Miss Grey had found her terrible voice on the train. He didn't try to believe it, or not believe. He made very sure not to try that trick Gavin had learned of putting his head down and letting it pass, clamping the impervious mask on his face and waiting for it all to go away.

Then he thought, just as slowly and just as carefully, about everything she'd said to him. This time he didn't let himself dismiss it as nonsense, the way Gavin would have. There was no more Gavin. Gavin was finished.

He sat quietly, letting the words echo around inside. *My burden . . . You must go and find it . . . An ocean girl tends it. An ocean girl.* The words were all of Miss Grey he had left, so he held them close.

A cold while passed. He began to think he understood what Gawain had to do, who he had to find.

A dog barked, banishing the echoes. He jumped to his feet at once, scanning the night, heart drumming. He heard it again, somewhere off beyond the village, perhaps closer this time.

After a few seconds' hesitation he trotted back to the streetlamp. He couldn't help glancing over his shoulder every few steps. Nothing stirred. He picked up his shoes and socks, and made his way back into Hester's house. There were no voices inside now. The room was so quiet he could hear Hester's peaceful breathing through the ceiling.

He clicked the door shut, felt for the bolt in the dark and locked it.

But he knew Miss Grey had been talking about a different door. There'd be no closing that one behind him, not for him. Not for anyone.

Nineteen

THE DEAD OF a winter night, before the dawn of another world.

Dressed all in black, a woman who was no woman leaned on a staff thicker than her wrist and looked out through a screen of stunted blackthorn towards the sea. She shuddered in the cold.

Behind her stood a thing like a misshapen shadow.

In the distance, around the curving bay, a hazy glow lit up the underside of heavy clouds. A lighthouse speared its intermittent brilliance across the water. There were other, smaller lights around a wide harbour mouth, navigation markers winking red and green and white. The woman surveyed this view silently.

When she eventually spoke, her voice grated strangely in her own mouth.

'The stars have fallen.'

The edges of the shadow ruffled, as if it too were shivering.

'These are the latter days,' she continued, after a silence. It was not clear to whom she spoke, if anyone. Her gaze remained fixed across the bay.

'Are the towns burning?' she asked. 'I see no smoke.'

'No fire.' It was the shadow that answered, in a voice even harsher than hers.

'Then perhaps the mouth of hell gapes beneath the clouds there. Perhaps the harvest has begun.'

'Bad time,' the shadow agreed.

'Is this truly England?'

'Yes yes.'

She twitched and shrugged in her clothes as if they didn't fit properly. 'The twilight was dismal. Perhaps the sun and moon have also fallen.'

'Dawn coming. Long way off.'

'This is a dying world.' The shadow might as well not have corrected her for all the attention she paid it. 'Or already dead. Its woods and fields are barren.'

Across the river valley a light winked out. An upstairs light in a house, perhaps, or a bulb failing at someone's front steps.

'Did you see that, puka?'

'No no.'

'Even the stars expire where they fall. Their virtue is long gone. I feel it. They are scattered here cold and silent.'

'Not stars,' muttered the shadow, but the woman must have thought it was agreeing with her, if she was listening to it at all. She addressed it as one might address a dog.

'I was dead too.' Her voice sunk to a rasping whisper. 'I died and returned.'

There was no answer to this. The woman stared out at the black water, remembering. Her free hand rose absently to her chest, where something small and smooth and round hung like a pendant from a silver chain round her neck. Her fingers closed around it.

'I bear the seed of the world's life.'

Up here on the higher ground of the headland there was always wind, even on a night as still as this. The shadow shifted, seeming to fold inwards, huddling down for warmth. Its motion made a rustling noise, pulling the woman out of her reverie.

She spoke over her shoulder. 'The pilgrim at the gate. Do you remember him?'

'Can't forget.'

'He knelt and greeted me in our saviour's name.'

'Made him go. Ran off.'

'Perhaps I would have done better to hear him out. Perhaps . . .'

Silence returned. The woman stood, rapt by her unfinished thought, until the cold broke through her dreams and she shivered so violently she had to clutch the staff with both hands. For the first time she turned round, away from the wide view northeastwards.

'Does the dryad still watch the gate?'

'Yes yes.'

'Good.' Prodding around in the grass, she found the path that led back down towards the woods and the house. 'Follow.'

The shadow moved silently behind her as she shambled clumsily along the path.

'What of the old man?'

'What.'

'Is he in the house still?'

'Sleeping.'

'You are certain?'

'Last I saw.'

'Good. I would prefer not to have to silence him as I silenced the changeling girl.'

'Poor girl.'

For the first time the woman's voice gained an edge. 'What are these people to you, puka? I am your master. No one else.'

The shadow evidently had no answer.

'The girl knew nothing of who she was. The old man knows nothing either. Let him sleep until he can be useful.'

'Long sleep.'

She stopped and turned to face it, though it was nothing more than an outline of absolute darkness against the velvet black of the night.

'This is a fallen world. If I am to restore it, I must not be hindered. Not by children and old men and their weeping and senseless questions.'

'Big if.'

'Least of all by you, puka.' She had ignored its muttered rejoinder entirely. 'Never think that I cannot punish you. Never think that.'

'Bad enough.'

The resentful answer might as well not have been spoken. 'You will not let the old man leave the house.'

'Sleeping.'

She raised her voice. 'You will not let him leave.'

No answer was expected, and none given.

'No one must leave and no one must enter. None but the witch, if she comes.'

'Not far.'

She leaned forward towards the blackness. 'Let us hope so, for your sake. Let us hope your disobedience is quickly undone.'

'Door opened,' it protested. 'Man came.'

'Do not answer me. I have little patience with your kind, puka. I gave you the substance you crave and you repaid me with disobedience.'

'No no. Never said—'

'Silence!'

The shadow shrank in a little.

'Tomorrow,' she went on, when she was sure it was listening, 'you will search for the boy who escaped you. You will not be free to eat until he is found.'

'Might be far.'

'You will not be free,' she repeated slowly, 'until he is found.'

The shadow's only answer was a wordless groan, *wrrraaaaa.*

'For ever, if need be. I will not be disobeyed. Least of all by such as you.'

No answer.

'Acknowledge it.'

'Yes yes.'

'Well, then. I have sent my servant spirit to look for the boy, but it is no more than spirit. Your obedience will be required tomorrow. Prove it to me then.'

'Yes yes.'

She resumed her laborious struggle along the dark rough path. The manner of her walk – crouched, leaning heavily on the staff, sliding her feet beneath her – gave the impression that she didn't trust her legs to keep her upright. 'You are certain no one else has entered?'

'Yes yes.'

'What of the man who came to the well? Whom the dryad struck?'

'Hairy man.'

'Yes. He has not returned?'

'Ran off. Last I saw. Can't say now.'

'Once I am within, watch the woods. If the old man wakes while I rest, see that he does not leave the house. Let no one enter.'

'Cold,' it muttered. 'Dark.'

She raised her voice. 'Do you understand?'

'Yes yes.'

'I must not be obstructed. There may be dangers here.'

They went on in silence. The gorse and thorns grew thicker beside the path as they descended.

'I must not be,' she whispered. 'The world needs me, in its death throes.' One hand strayed to her chest again, where the small thing hanging on the silver chain bounced against the front of her padded jacket. 'For this I overcame death.'

The shadow had fallen a few steps behind. 'Bad time,' it croaked softly. 'Poor girl.' A gust of wind rattled the spiked branches above and the words went unheard.

Part V
Wednesday Morning

Twenty

HORACE WAS ALREADY awake when his mother came upstairs. He felt like he'd hardly slept at all. He rolled over and closed his eyes, waited for her to come and sit at the end of his bed.

'Time to wake up, small boy.'

He feigned bleariness. 'Is it?'

'It's seven o'clock. I have to go early. Everything is ready for you downstairs.'

'Thanks, Mum.'

'Do you have anything special today?'

His secret was glowing so hot it made his cheeks burn. He rubbed his face. 'Just a normal day.'

She patted his legs under the duvet. 'All right. Work hard. Don't be late.'

'I'll try.'

'I might still be with Professor Lightfoot when you get home. You can just come and knock on the door.'

'OK.'

'She must have come back late. The car is there. I put a note through her door.'

'Right.'

'You have everything you need?'

He didn't mean to, but he snuck a quick glance at his keychain on his desk. That was all he needed. Even if what he was going to do today meant that she took the key away in the evening and never gave it back, he had to have it until then.

'Yeah,' he said.

He was amazed she couldn't actually see his secret flaring inside him. Maybe I could pretend to be ill, he thought suddenly. When she finds out I didn't turn up to school today. I could say I felt ill on the bus. Mum liked it when people were ill, it gave her a chance to fuss even more than usual and make weird drinks. All he'd have to do was get back before she did. Then he could say he'd come home and been in bed all morning.

'Mum? What are you doing today again?'

She stood up, sighing. 'Mrs Standish and then Mrs Ambell. They are both outside Falmouth. I have to take two buses.'

'Right, but aren't you coming back here?'

'Yes, I told you.'

He tried to sound casual. 'So what sort of time?'

'I told Professor Lightfoot about two o'clock. It depends if Mrs Ambell will drive me. Why are you asking these questions? You don't usually ask these things.'

'Just wondering.'

She looked as if she was going to ask him something else, but then Horace's desk clock caught her eye. 'I should hurry. The bus might come early. These drivers always go too fast.' She kissed him quickly on the top of his head. 'Have a good day.'

'Yeah, I will.'

'It's going to be a nice day.'

'Great. Bye Mum.'

He sat on the edge of the bed, listening to her making her usual over-complicated preparations for leaving the house. Finally he heard the door swing open.

'Bye, Horace!'

'Bye,' he called.

'Don't be late!'

'I won't.'

'Bye!'

The door clicked shut and the house went quiet. He heard her walking away, up the lane.

His hands were tingling and his breath felt short. It was like the feeling he got sometimes before an important game for the school. Not nervousness. He didn't have anything to be nervous about. He left that to the other kids. No, Horace knew he was going to be the hero.

But he'd never been this kind of hero before.

Anyone could be a hero in football. Well, anyone as good as him, not that there was anyone as good as him. But this was different. This was like an adventure story. The kid who's actually a secret agent.

He was going to save Marina from the spy.

He went over to the window and moved aside enough of the net curtain to get a good view of the house opposite. The car was still there. He couldn't see any signs of life inside, but then Professor Lightfoot always kept her blinds tight shut even when she was home. Everyone knew she was completely mad.

So what was that kid who'd pretended to be Marina's cousin doing there?

Horace had lain awake hours after his bedtime trying to come up with a theory. Nothing had made much sense, except for one feeling he was sure of: the kid was some sort of impostor. Horace told himself he'd known that all along. Right from the start there was something dodgy about him. He could tell as soon as he'd seen the kid come out of Miss Clifton's house, looking shifty. And then the kid had got himself in with Marina and made it so she didn't listen to Horace any more. And now it turned out he was involved with the mad old cow opposite. They must be planning something, the two of them.

He'd had some ideas in the night about what it was, but now that daylight was coming – cold clear blue spreading upwards, drowning the last few stars – they all seemed a bit unlikely. Never mind, he thought. He was going to find out the truth.

He got dressed quickly, settled down at his desk, and watched, and waited.

Low sunlight poured in through the picture window in the kitchen.

'They're promising us a whole day of this,' Hester said. 'According to the forecast.'

Gav fiddled absently with a breadknife. He wasn't at all hungry.

'Sure you slept OK up there?'

It wasn't the events of the night that felt like a dream to him. It was all this: the kitchen table and its plastic tablecloth, wooden butter dish, white plates, a packet of cereal, the humming fridge, the crumbs on the counter, the arc of condensation in one corner of the window, the phone with its cord dangling loose. He sat among them like a visitor from another planet. He thought he could still smell the night in his clothes.

'Gavin?'

'Gawain,' he corrected, automatically.

'Sorry?'

He made an effort. 'Nothing. Slept fine, thanks.'

Hester studied him thoughtfully. 'You do know you can stay, don't you? As long as you like. I should make that clear right away. Whatever else you have to worry about, don't worry about that.'

He half smiled. 'Thanks,' he said. 'Means a lot.'

But he couldn't.

He couldn't stay. He could tell just by looking around that he didn't belong here, with the cereal, the loaf of bread, the phone, all of that. He had somewhere to go, somewhere where everything was different. He had someone to find. *An ocean girl.*

'I think I'll go for a walk later.' Hester was happy to be the one making conversation. 'Shame to waste a day like this.'

'Mmm.'

'My first day of freedom.'

It took a while for that to sink in. When it did, he looked up at her.

'A new dawn.' She gestured at the rich sunlight. 'It could hardly be a better day, could it?'

'Oh,' he said, thinking of his goodbye kiss. 'Yeah.'

Hester came and sat down at the table opposite him. 'I'm aware that this isn't a very helpful question,' she said, 'but. Are you all right?'

'I don't know.'

She wrinkled her brows, making her look even more professorial than usual, then shrugged. 'Fair enough. Sure you aren't hungry? You know, you're like the anti-teenager. Up before nine and not wanting anything to eat.'

The anti-teenager. The anti-person. He knew exactly who he wasn't. Why hadn't he asked Miss Grey who he was, when he'd had the chance?

There were so many things he should have said to her. A lifetime's worth, all now wasted.

'She's gone,' he said.

Hester didn't try asking what he meant. She just watched him with sympathetic attention and then patted his hand.

'I'm sorry.'

''s OK. I think . . .' He wouldn't have tried to say what he thought, but Hester's steady look drew it out of him. 'I think it was time.'

'Ah.'

In the silence the fridge buzzed.

'So will you go home now?' Hester asked.

Gav couldn't help a snort of laughter. 'God, no.'

She waited a while, then tapped the table as if a decision had been reached and pushed back her chair. 'Good. Then why don't I run you over to Pendurra and we can pick up your stuff? You had a bag, didn't you. When you're ready. And after that we can just . . . take it from there. All right?'

Back to Pendurra, yes. He'd lain awake a long time after going back up to his nest among the cardboard boxes, wondering whether he had the courage to return. In the daylight, with butter-yellow sunshine drenching everything around him, the idea seemed a lot less daunting.

You must go and find it . . . Across sea and land, on the other side of the night, where an ocean girl tends it. Pendurra was across the river. A new morning had come. And the name 'Marina' had to mean something like 'of the sea', didn't it?

So, yes, back there. But not to pick up his stuff, his bag with the wallet and the keys. He was finished with all of that. He'd gone past them. Now he had to go past the other things, voices in the dark and silhouettes in sickly firelight and black mouths breathing fire, until he found Marina.

'Yeah,' he said. 'That'd be great. Thanks.'

He helped her tidy away the breakfast he hadn't touched, listening while she chatted, infinitely grateful that she never seemed to expect anything more from him than the occasional 'Mmm'. When she went back upstairs to the bathroom, he looked in through the other door. The front room was shady, the shutters still tightly closed the way he'd left them before going back to bed. Light from the kitchen fell in along the near wall, picking out the ridges and protrusions of the masks, sending dramatic shadows into their recesses. He saw the long blunt wooden one, the great saucer of its eye, the carved line that made its mouth, the crude strong curves like breaking waves. It was hard to guess what beast it represented, but when he closed his eyes he remembered traces of its song and felt he knew it, a wild surging water thing, though he still couldn't name it. He reached for the light switch to get a better look.

Nothing happened. He clicked the switch a few times, up and down, up and down. Nothing.

'All ready?' Hester came down the stairs and saw him in the doorway. 'Ah. You don't want to go in there unaccompanied? I can't say I blame you. Here, I'll go first. They're used to me, they won't bite if I'm there.' She bustled past him, flicking the switch he'd tried a moment before. The lights came on at once. 'There we are. Now, if you just look down and run for the door, you'll hardly— Oh!'

Surprised by the genuine alarm in her voice, he followed her look.

At the end of the row of masks on the near wall, right beside the window, there was a conspicuous gap. A nail angled down over a scab of flaked plaster, and there was a dusty outline on the paint.

Gav felt suddenly queasy.

'Well,' Hester said, 'that's strange.' She crossed the room and peered at the floor.

'What?' Gav said, although he knew what.

'It looks like I have an escapee.' She didn't look amused at all. She felt around the sofa, pushing it back.

'Missing one?'

'Yes. The black dog. One of the more unique ones. "More unique", sorry, what a ghastly solecism. It's a Finno-Baltic totemic object. Rather valuable, actually.'

'The black dog,' he echoed, now feeling cold as well as nauseous.

'Am I just not seeing it? This is ridiculous. It can't have fallen far. It's a wooden mask. Looks rather like a bad-tempered wolf. It can't just have vanished.'

'Um . . .' he said. 'What do you mean, totemic?'

She paused her search to glance sharply at him, still holding the pot plant she'd been looking behind.

'Well, it's a rather technical issue. We can't be sure, of course, but it certainly had the kind of function that we'd call ritual, or religious. It's not just an image of a dog, put it that way. Not like a statue. It's to do with maintaining a relationship with the spirit world.' She put the plant down. 'Opening a door. The mask is a sort of vehicle for a spirit. Or a dwelling place. Or a mouth.'

A mouth dripping fire. A mouth snarling with fury.

'Do you know something about this, Gavin?'

'Gawain.'

'Sorry?'

He focused on her, avoiding the hideous memory. 'Nothing.'

'You don't know what happened to it, by any chance?'

He only shook his head.

She raised her eyebrows wryly. 'But . . . ?'

'I . . . ah. You may not be getting it back.'

She looked at him for a long time before shrugging mildly. 'That would be a pity,' was all she said.

It became suddenly clear to Gav how patient she was being with him. She was, quite obviously, waiting for him to shed his tongue-tied surliness and let her into his confidence as gracefully as she'd admitted him to hers. The problem was there was nothing he could tell her. He had no language for it. *Your mask came alive in the night and breathed fire and attacked my imaginary friend, but I drove it away and it ran off into the dark and now I don't know where it is.* With a stab of awful grief he remembered how Miss Grey always kept silent (except in his dreams, the sweet unbearable dreams). And then when she spoke he'd thought it was only raving. He felt the truth boiling up inside his closed mouth. If he parted his lips, out it would come; he'd be telling Hester everything. She'd never believe it or understand it. Not even her. Not even if she wanted to. No one could.

'It's all right,' she said, seeing the distress in his face. 'Don't worry about it. Later. OK? We'll talk about it later.'

'Sorry,' he said feebly.

'Come on.' She took his arm firmly. 'Let's go for a little drive.'

Back there, he thought, as he followed her into the car. I'm going back. I'll be standing there again, in a few minutes. He'd have to figure out some way of getting rid of Hester once he arrived. Then he'd have to figure out . . . everything else. Find Marina. *You must.*

But the car wouldn't start.

The two of them looked at each other.

'Any gift for this sort of thing?' she asked drily, turning the key again. There was no response at all, not a cough, not a click. He shook his head, wondering exactly what gift he had. The gift for breaking things, maybe.

Hester sighed. 'Oh well, I'm going to have to get this dealt with. Sorry. It's hard to get by in the country without a functioning automobile. Someone'll have to come and take a look at it.' Thinking of the light switch, Gav imagined how that conversation might go. He was going to have to get away soon. 'There's a garage in town. They're usually quite good about sending someone along. I've had problems with this old banger before. Probably something obvious.' It was obvious enough to Gav, but he wasn't going to tell her so. 'I'll go and give them a quick ring.'

Unsure what else to do with himself, he traipsed back into the house after her. She looked up the number, prodded buttons, looked at the receiver, shook it and turned a disbelieving look on Gav.

'Not working.'

He pointed at the dangling cord.

'Oh. Oh God, what an idiot. Forgive me.'

''s fine,' he said, as she knelt down to reconnect the phone to the wall socket beneath.

'Fiddly thing . . . There we go.' It clicked in. No more than two seconds later, as she was getting back to her feet, the phone rang.

Hester let it ring ten times, fifteen, then shrugged at Gav and picked it up. 'Hello?'

Her eyes closed wearily as she listened. 'Yes, it is. Yes . . . No, I'm afraid I wouldn't. I'm sorry . . . No, I have no comment at all. Excuse me.' The receiver was still quacking as she replaced it.

'Someone from the local paper again.' She knelt down again. 'That'll teach me.' She pulled the cord back out from the wall. 'There. I've always hated this machine anyway. Just more disembodied voices in my ear, isn't it? When you think about it. The last thing I need. I'll walk up to the garage, it's only ten minutes.'

Gav's heart leaped. Ten minutes there, ten back, a few more to talk to someone. She'd be gone more than long enough. He didn't need any time to get himself ready.

'You'll be all right for a bit?' She was already pulling on a fleecy coat. 'Of course you will, you're not a child. Can I get you anything while I'm out? I'll be passing the shop.'

'Nah, I don't need anything. Thanks.'

'By the way, I wouldn't answer the door if anyone comes. It seems unlikely this early in the morning, but just in case. That chap from the paper sounded alarmingly keen on getting his interview, and I've already had a note through my door this morning asking me to call the local priest. I imagine he's concerned about my welfare. Such is the price of fame.'

He smiled uncertainly. 'OK.'

'Though I don't have a spare key . . . Look, I'll just leave the door unlocked. In case you want some fresh air or something. I won't be long anyway.'

'I'll be fine.'

'Just make yourself at home,' she said as she went out.

'Don't worry.' He wasn't sure when, or even if, he'd see her again, so he added, 'Bye.'

She grinned her wise and rueful grin, and closed the door behind her.

There was a travel clock in one of the bookshelves. Ten past nine. He let the second hand sweep a full circle before he moved at all. Then he knelt on the sofa and began sorting quickly through a stack of maps he'd noticed at one end of the shelves. He found the right one, an old and much-used copy worn badly at the folds, and opened it out.

It was the same one Auntie Gwen had on her desk, though of course Hester's copy wasn't overwritten with lines and circles and spidery annotations. He remembered where on the map those lines had converged. There was the name, printed in the Gothic-looking script that meant, *Historic building. Pendurra.* It looked so innocent there: tiny crooked pink rectangles for the house, wedges of green for the woods, the blue streamlets doodling through them. Pendurra. Just another place. It took him a little longer to work out where Hester's house was, but eventually he spotted the name of a village and remembered it from the sign on the road.

Lines and letters on a map. On paper it looked no different from any other patch of the country, except perhaps for the visible pressure of the sea, carving the coast into knuckles and hollows, thrusting long, branching estuaries inland like cracks in old concrete.

Hester's village was on the wrong side of one of those cracks, the big one. Of course it was. She'd driven him round the river twice, there and back. But no more than a couple of miles west of where he was, a dotted line slanted across the blue tendril. A ferry.

Across sea and land.

He checked the clock again. Five minutes gone already. If he spent much longer sitting and thinking about it he might miss his chance. He couldn't let Hester try to go with him. He couldn't get her involved in whatever was waiting for him. He belonged away from people. His place was with the deep woods, the croaking voice in the chapel, the house overlooked by time. The girl no one else even knew existed. He had to vanish like Marina, like Miss Grey.

He should never have run away. It was Gavin who'd fled. Gavin, who still wanted to be like everyone else; Gavin, who thought he ought to know better. *Oh come on Gav.*

Gawain folded the map and stuck it in the back pocket of his trousers.

He was about to head out when he noticed a pad of paper and a biro on a side table. It occurred to him that he could probably do a bit better than one mumbled 'Bye'.

On the pad he wrote:

Have to go. I don't know when I'll be back. Thanks for everything and don't worry about me. Enjoy your walk.

He put the pad down in front of the door, stared at it, then picked it up again and without knowing why added:

Stay warm.

He walked out of the village fast, head down, the low sun sending a long shadow before him.

*   *   *

The first time Horace saw them come out of the house, he jumped up from his desk so abruptly the chair fell backwards behind him and clanged appallingly loudly against the radiator. He threw himself to his bedroom floor, convinced he'd given himself away, before finally gathering the courage to worm his way back to the edge of the window. He heard the slam of car doors. They're leaving, he thought! They must be going back there! He knew he could reach Pendurra faster. It was a good twenty minutes to drive round. He could beat that, if he ran down to the beach where he kept the boat and then ran up through the woods on the other side.

But then the two of them got out of the car, looked at it moronically for a bit and went back inside the house.

Confused, the only thing Horace could think of was to keep watching. He'd almost missed them coming out. You had to be patient to be a secret agent, he told himself. Heightened senses. Ready to swing into action at any moment.

When he saw the Nutty Professor come out on her own and head up the road, and realised the kid must be alone in the house, his pulse went wild. This was the chance, he told himself. Get a closer look.

He kept forgetting things. He raced downstairs to get his shoes on, then raced back up to collect his keys. Then at the front door he noticed he'd put his school uniform on, out of habit. The blazer had bright yellow lines on it. He hurried back up the stairs to his room to collect his dark coat and his cap, then down again, already convinced that even those few seconds away from the windows were too many. Then he stopped with his hand on the latch, suddenly realising he didn't have a plan.

At that moment he heard the kid come out.

And then he hardly knew what he was doing at all, because this was it, this was the moment, this was when he had to be the hero, and there was no time to think about it. He waited for what he thought was just long enough, then let himself out, pulled his cap down and followed.

Gawain walked fast out of the village, westward, the sun at his back. He crossed the street a couple of times to avoid people, or places where there might be people: shopfronts, a bus-stop, a house with an open door. He didn't slow down until he'd left the houses behind and come out between hedges and placid trees, their every leaf alchemised into gold by dew and the rising glory behind. Every minute or two a car would come past and he'd squeeze tight to the hedge, automatically. His thoughts were far away.

He stopped at a junction in the road to check the map, leaning against the signpost where a steep lane came up from the left. Through the alley it carved in the hedges he saw a green ridge in the distance. The water between it and him was invisible, hidden in its valley, though the map showed it wide as a bay. In any direction but the way he was heading, the sun stung his eyes. He stuck the map back in a pocket and set off again.

The road led him on westwards a few minutes before forking into two narrowing lanes. He turned left and soon found himself descending through a green tunnel of overhanging trees, mercifully empty of any traffic at all. Holiday houses, glum in their winter exile, appeared beside the road. Where the descent flattened, he walked round a tight curve between whitewashed walls and came out suddenly by the river.

The river!

The water glinted almost at his feet. All around it the land folded tightly downwards, as if hiding it under a fringe of black rock and hanging woods. He'd arrived among a cluster of buildings strung along its bank, overlooking a strip of beach. It was as much a finger of the sea as a river, though upstream, to his right, it seemed ready to narrow and quieten just where the far side of the little cove he was in cut it off from view. To his left, the near side of the cove ended in low cliffs that hid the sea. Straight across from him was a postcard-quaint village gathered around the mouth of a creek. There were boats moored between, most covered in tarpaulins, as if hibernating. From among the buildings behind came occasional voices, the noise of windows opening. Morning sounds.

Further downstream on the opposite bank, the broad Pendurra woods curved round and closed off the view. They didn't look so deep or dark. He could see the edge of them, and the top. Just a patch of green, like on the map, with normal stuff around it, roads and farms and fields.

Was he really going to go back there and try to understand whatever secret it hid, try to make sense of everything he had seen and heard? Him?

All he had to go on was what Miss Grey had given him – a name, and a few words, a senseless promise – and the memory of turning Marina's hands in his. He'd find her, somehow. He'd trust Miss Grey, like he should have all along. Things had only turned bad when he'd started trying to know better than her.

He looked at his feet with a twinge of guilt.

Nothing incomprehensible about that instruction. *Don't put them on again. Let the earth hold you up.* Mad, maybe, but not incomprehensible.

He'd put his shoes and socks on that morning, up in Hester's tiny spare room, because . . . For no particular reason. Because that was what you did in the morning, what normally happened. You put your shoes on.

A small floating jetty stuck out from the edge of the beach, its landward end mounted on wheels so it could follow the tide up and down. That had to be where the ferry went from, Gav thought, though there was no boat tied up to it. All the vessels on the moorings clogging this patch of the river were silent and unmanned. The only activity was on the shore beyond him. Someone at the far end of the beach had unloaded a small inflatable from the back of a Land Rover and was hauling it down to the water.

Gawain sat on the edge of the road, took off his shoes and stuffed his socks inside them. He dug his toes into the sand. He thought it a bit unlikely that Miss Grey would only have wanted him to go barefoot once he got to a beach, but it was a start, he told himself. Got to start somewhere.

Carrying his shoes, he wandered over to the jetty. He felt conspicuous, although the only other person in sight was the man with the inflatable. He was climbing into it. His bulk made it look bathtub-sized and about as seaworthy. It lolled and wallowed as he fitted a pair of plastic oars and pushed out into the shallows.

The slats of the jetty felt icy under Gav's bare feet. He resisted the urge to put his shoes back on. One thing at a time, he told himself; one thing at a time. The next thing was to get across this river. There was a small sign lashed to the end of the floating dock, looking like it might be displaying a timetable. Of course, he thought as he walked out to investigate, I don't have any money. I don't have anything. But what else was he going to do? Turn back? Put his shoes on, go up the hill again, along the lane to Hester's house, apologise for sneaking out, ask her to take him to the station and buy him a ticket so he could go back home and be Gavin and spend the rest of his life pretending none of this ever happened?

The sign was indeed a ferry timetable, as he'd hoped, but that was as far as his hopes were met.

Seasonal service, it read. *May to September.*

So much for his first step.

He looked across the river, feeling as useless as he ever had. A faint mistiness was creeping into the day, the light whitening and thinning. Hester had mentioned something about how long a journey it was if you went round by road. Miles. There was all day to walk, but the idea of returning to Pendurra at twilight or in darkness was almost as bad as the thought of going home. He crossed his arms on the rail of the jetty and bent down, closing his eyes, banging his head on his knuckles in frustration.

When he opened them again, he saw something moving in the water.

His first thought was that it must be a seal, right here by the dock. That thought lasted less than a few heartbeats.

The submerged shadow grew beneath him and rose. The head that broke the surface was sleek and wide-eyed and mournful as a seal's, but it belonged to no animal.

A human face looked up at him from the water.

Or it was what a human face would be if it had hardened to marble and then eroded for centuries under the ebb and flow of the tides. Hair like a thick fringe of pale green river-weeds floated around it. Pearlescent eyes, blinking slowly, fixed on him. It rose a little higher, the drifting fronds making long, lazy curls on the water's surface. Its pallid mouth opened and made a bubbling whisper Gawain could scarcely hear. The air seemed full of noise, though it was no more than the cries of gulls and the intermittent sounds of the village behind, someone shouting to someone else, a car starting further up the hill; but enough to drown out the voice from below. He knelt down and hung his head over the edge of the jetty, close to the alabaster face.

'Hey!' Someone was shouting, closer behind him.

The mother-of-pearl eyes fixed on him. The pallid mouth worked slowly, fish-like, releasing a bubble of air. He thought he heard words, faint as the pop of the bubble.

'. . . find my child . . .'

Twenty-one

Four hundred and seventy-four years

As the magus had unwittingly foretold, the prophetess was forgotten. The ring she bore, the open passage between mankind and the rest of the living universe, lay sunk in the rocky shallows where Master John Fiste (formerly Doctor Johann Faust) had drowned, sealed up for centuries in its cocoon of enchantments. As well as the greatest magus in the world, he was also – for centuries – the last. His name became a byword for the end of magic.

Its vestiges withered and rotted, or were gathered up and destroyed, weeds in the garden of knowledge. The subtle presences of the world, those things that could not be measured or counted or reasoned, were forgotten too. Some guessed, perhaps, that something had gone out of the world, but subtle absences are not easily felt, and forgotten things often disappear as if they had never existed at all.

Wise and brilliant people had no reason to worry themselves over a loss. Their world was filling with new things. They charted them, recorded them, named them, drew them, catalogued them, studied them, calculated their motions, pondered their rights and wrongs, bought and sold and bequeathed them, assembling a new world the way printers' men plucked the type from their boxes and turned the fragments of metal into great volumes of authority and permanence. What the new age wanted were tools: hard, persistent things that did what you wanted them to do without getting in the way. Magic had never been a good tool. What use was a power that set its own conditions? What good was a knowledge that kept itself secret and shied away from plain words?

Who wanted a voice like ancient Cassandra's, always right but never heeded?

So, her gift was forgotten. Her curse was complete. The truth she had carried since the beginning of history was no longer even true. She faded from the world, becoming a ghost, a trace, like a carved and painted idol eroded by wind and sand until it looks no different from the rest of the desert rubble.

The last place she might have been seen was on the banks of the shaded estuary near where the magus's ship had foundered. There were legends that told of a ragged woman walking there alone, as if in mourning. People said she appeared and vanished like a vision. It was a time of bitter doubt, and faith just as bitter. The king's men had ridden down only that year to drive out the monks, and the truth seemed as open to question as the land. Many claimed that the apparition was a saint: the Magdalene, they swore, full of grief.

In tribute to those legends, some decades later, a shrine was built in the woods. The lord of the land at the time followed the old faith and was eager to remember that a saint had appeared in his demesne in his grandfather's time; but not too eager. There were burnings and executions in the cities, after all. So the chapel was a modest sanctuary of wood and stone, far from the roads. A pool was made to catch the water from a spring, and the walls were raised round it. The water, they said, was blessed by the saint's hand. It saved the lord and his family from the plague when it came up the river, but this too was a secret best kept within the shade of the old trees. Everyone agreed that the age of miracles had passed. It was unwise to attract attention. The lords remembered that their family had been granted the estates only because the monks with their old devotions had fallen foul of the king. They had no wish to lose them again.

A habit of secrecy, a close-mouthed character, seemed to pass down through them, inherited from one to the next along with the woods and pastures. The river was a busy thoroughfare in those days, unrecognisable from the wind-ruffled strip of silence Gawain contemplated from the ferry dock. On any day it was cluttered with masts as if another spindly wood were trying to take root there, and all along its inland banks there were wharves and quays with tracks leading up the valley side, noisy with hooves and straining wheels. But where the south shore angled out towards the sea, under the windows of the house at Pendurra, the comings and goings always stopped short. Yellow-flowering gorse and stunted blackthorn covered the higher land, impassable. Where the valley folded the lower slopes away from the salt wind, the greenwood grew dark and thick.

The family divided, married, spread, dwindled, left, returned, until the now antiquated house that faced out towards the sea was separated from the rest of their possessions and left to one of their remotest and humblest branches, along with the wild corner of land it overlooked, while the life and vigour of the estate moved to the finer mansion upriver. A civil war convulsed the country, the county and the family, the old connections were entirely severed at last, and the house and its woods were all but forgotten.

The kingdom grew rich. The whole continent grew rich. Its currencies were the laws of matter and motion and circulation. It was an empire of things. Manufacture made them; commerce exchanged them. Theories were written to govern their movements, from the greatest of them to the smallest, planets to pennies. When those laws reached their limits, telescopes and microscopes discovered still greater and still smaller things. But no one ever found the box with its silver clasp, carried by the currents until it lay wedged in a drowned fissure of rock beneath the low cliffs at the mouth of the river, holding inside it the forgotten magic of ages now condemned as barbarous, superstitious and fearful.

The magic, however, could not entirely forget itself. The powers that the drowned magus had commanded, and that thousands and thousands of far lesser charmers and blessers and shamans had dimly invoked, could not simply die. Their shadows haunted the place where the ring lay. They were drawn around its tomb like mourners, or pilgrims, or simply (since neither grief nor reverence had any meaning for them) like iron shavings to a magnet. The water that trickled from the spring in the Pendurra woods was the only fresh water in the whole empire of reason and commerce that was not just water, but something else too, something Johann Faust would have understood as the meaning or the virtue of a spring: something cleansing and life-giving. The house that stood there was not just an artefact of materials pinned and mortared together, but something else too: a haven, a mark of dwelling and permanence.

Anything that grew on this unvisited and backward slope of land grew among the echo of magic and might be touched by it; anything that left the place lost it. The house was empty sometimes and changed hands more than once. Living in the half-presence of these old, abandoned influences was by no means a blessing, and the older they became, the harder it was. What had first been mystery became superstition, then silliness and then something literally unthinkable and impossible. Nevertheless the house at Pendurra never decayed, the spring never failed, the orchard planted in the lee of the woods flourished even when it was untended, the beds of oysters spread where the river met the sea, the crows and gulls never robbed seed from the long field that was cleared on the higher slope.

The place sustained itself, but, by the same token, it kept itself apart. Because it needed nothing from outside its gates, it had almost as little to do with the wide world beyond as did the prophetess's ring in its long concealment. The swifter the world became, the more Pendurra lagged behind. The mines that burrowed all over this furthest corner of England never touched the rocks on which the house stood. Less than a mile from its door, bulky wharves received taller and faster ships, and they floated downriver with their cargoes of tin or gravel or slate right under the shores where, according to legends that no one now read, the Magdalene had walked, but they had no reason to stop. Inland, beam engines rocked on every hilltop. Water and fire made steam, and steam drove Europe faster. Whole nations hitched themselves to its power and rode it forward, into the age of speed. But the faint powers that shrouded Pendurra were embedded in rhythms that could not hasten or change, the rhythm of what came to be called 'nature' because it was no longer the same as the world. It was where no one lived. It was an imaginary country.

Nothing rapid, nothing accelerated, could take hold at Pendurra for long. No one bothered any more to try and change the house and keep it up to date. It was like 'nature': you recognised it by its retrograde, nostalgic changelessness. Sons and daughters of the estate saw how the engines pumped wealth and brilliance into the hands of those who drove them, and left to join the rush, leaving the house and its lands in the care of whoever was willing to live in the modest lodge they erected for the purpose at the gates. Increasingly often, the whitewashed or wood-panelled rooms of the old house were empty. But even if an owner returned after years, or decades, there were no beetles in the wood, no cracks in the glass, no bats in the chimneys or moths in the tapestries. The caretakers smiled and took the credit and waited patiently for the sons and daughters to leave again, as they always did before long.

Except for Rufus Uren.

Rufus was born half the world away, third son of a tea planter in the Himalayan foothills. He grew up with only the vaguest notion that his mother was heir to some minuscule unprofitable backwater of an estate in some odd corner of the old country he had never seen but mysteriously owed his loyalty to. Other people dealt with that sort of thing, deferential business-like employees whose whole reason for existence was to keep complicated distractions out of sight. If there was no money to be made from it, best to turn it over to those people and forget it. Or sell it, someone once suggested: but there was some difficulty, apparently, something about the house being unmodernised and inconvenient. And besides, it was a piece of Mother England they could call their own, which was a fine thing, surely?

Then Mother England called in her loyalties, and Rufus Uren and his brothers sailed to join the war against the Kaiser. The brothers were dead within weeks. Rufus did not die, but when the end of the slaughter came, he might as well have. He'd left most of his reason and all of his will to live in the trenches when he arrived back in England, shell-shocked, aimless, ruined at the age of twenty-three. His parents hadn't survived the massacre of their sons. The deferential people took over. They talked discreetly to other deferential people, made enquiries. Rufus Uren was found and told he was now the owner of Pendurra. A telegram was sent to the caretakers, advising that Captain Uren should be met at the station, since his mental capacities had suffered as a consequence of service and he was prone to distractedness. With that, the employees in their tactful suits discharged their duties and withdrew.

The utter silence of Pendurra reached inside Rufus, touching the last interested fragments of his thoughts. He shut himself up inside it. The caretaker couple who had been living in the lodge with their daughter were happy to look after him. So few young men had come back, after all. They became fond of the convalescent: he was almost young enough to be their son.

Their daughter became fond of him also. As she grew into adulthood, she spent more time with him than anyone else did, bringing him his meals, reading to him, finding him when one of his walking fits took hold and he was still out of doors when darkness fell. Her parents didn't see that she had become too fond. They were horrified when she became pregnant, but there was nothing to be done about it except keep quiet and hope for the best. Although the boy Tristram was born healthy, his mother suffered so badly that she never recovered.

Her dwindling strength seemed to rouse Rufus. Perhaps having people to care for – the woman and the baby – gave him the strength of defiance. Death had turned back into an enemy he could face and fight. When he was certain he was going to lose this battle, he insisted on marrying the dying woman and acknowledging his son. So Tristram Uren became the heir, and his grandparents were named his guardians. After his father died – grief-struck, Rufus outlived his wife less than three years – they brought him up to love the place as they did.

Tristram never lost the attachment. His grandparents sent him away for the education they thought proper, but he hurried back whenever he could. He learned how the world worked, and what his place in it was, and so understood while still at school that his home was somewhere not quite real, a relic of a way of life that wasn't supposed to exist any more. This made it more essential to him, because it reminded him of the parents he had barely known. He thought of himself as the progeny of ghosts.

When he was finished with school he joined the navy. His friends all drifted towards the city or the university towns, warrens of brick stranded in green plains. The navy at least kept him by the cliffs and, at first, not more than a hundred miles from the house whose mysteries preoccupied him more and more. Or so it was for a few years, but then, inevitably, it took him far away, off to deserts where (much to his surprise) his ship was called into action, messy and utterly inglorious, and where (to his still greater surprise) he showed exceptional skill and courage.

He was on the other side of the globe when his grandmother died, and by the time he arrived in England again his grandfather was dead too: another broken heart. He came back to the estate one windy autumn morning to find it abandoned. Yet as he opened the doors and windows, he knew by some strange instinct that it wasn't empty.

With the thanks and assurances of a grateful nation, he resigned his commission and stayed. Though barely thirty years old, he withdrew inside the house and its grounds, unable (and unwilling) to loosen his entanglement in their secrecy and silence.

Like the last ward of a massive lock falling into place, Saturn neared the completion of its sixteenth orbit since the magus wove its influence into his spell. The enchantment began to thaw, its frozen architecture softening as if under a breath of summer air. The prophetess knew it, or it knew her, and a whisper of her existence slipped back into the world. Others felt it too, though they had no idea what it was they were feeling, since in the course of five hundred years the gift they had been born with had ceased to have any meaning or use at all. One was Hester Lightfoot, a clever scholar with a scientific mind that was not the slightest good to her when she caught the echo of the prophetess's whispers one day and could not shake them off. Another was a teenage runaway in the streets of Bristol who, for no reason that he could articulate to himself, lied and stole his way to the place that was pulling him with a force as certain as gravity and, when he got there, hid in its woods until Tristram found him, recognised the compulsion that had driven him and took him in. There were many others who could only ignore what they obscurely felt, helpless in the presence of something they had no language for.

Other kinds of things stirred also. Beings that for centuries had not been *there*, as the empire of reason understood it, began, gradually, to overlap again with the world. Like a reflection in a window, appearing when the light outside dims, they shifted towards presence.

The world began to move at the speed of light. Time and distance all but vanished inside the microscopic blur of circuitry, ethereal flickers and pulses and waves of information. Tristram and his property and its phantoms sat among it, archaic and inert as rock.

There were no apocalyptic portents when the magus's spell finally broke. Saturn crossed the sky and one day – an October day in the year 1996, no more obviously remarkable a day than any other – the box was no longer concealed and protected as it had been. Anyone might have found it, or no one. Its wood began to rot in the salt water. It might have decayed. The bag inside might have been caught by a surge of the tide and carried out to sea to decompose. The mirror in its velvet sheath and the ring (neither of which could rot) might have each been lost for another half millennium, or for ever.

The person who did find them was the runaway refugee, Caleb, who still had no idea why he had been born the way he was, but had at least learned that Pendurra was the only place he could exist, not least because he felt everything that happened in and on this one small patch of land as if it was part of his own body. He noticed the narrow crack in the cliffs out towards the headland the way you or I might notice an itch. Eventually he gave up trying to forget it, took the dinghy from the cove and rowed out along the rocks until he had come as close as a boat could bring him to the place where the itch appeared to be. When the tide was unusually low he found he could get even closer, scrambling over kelp-matted and barnacled stone. There was a tight cave, three-quarters flooded. He only went in because he knew something was there. He only found it when his waterlogged shoe scraped against something that was softer than rock. He had to plunge down into the absolute blackness of the water before his hands could touch it too. He dug sand away from the tiny silted hollow where the box lay wedged, holding his breath for as long as he could each time, finally prising it out between raw and bloodied fingers.

That night he worked the silver clasp loose and opened the box. There was the strangely marked leather pouch still nestling in its padding of wool, and inside it two things: a palm-sized oval of metal in a velvet sheath, and a plain smooth ring. The metal made him feel deeply uneasy, so much so that he would not take it out of the velvet. The ring made him feel sad. And that was all there was to them, as far as he was concerned.

The itch, though, had gone.

He showed them to Tristram the next day. The two of them stood there, looking at the velvet and the ring and at each other.

Caleb's only ambition in life was for nothing to change. He remembered the misery of being anywhere but where he was, the wrenching, permanent ache of his childhood. All he cared about was that he never suffer it again. That was the full extent of his interest in Pendurra.

As for Tristram, he wondered whether Caleb had uncovered the clue to the ghostliness he felt shadowing his whole life, the mystery he'd inherited with the house. But now that it was lying in front of him, he too was thinking that maybe it was better for secrets to stay undisturbed. A velvet mirror-case and a ring, what did that tell him? Nothing at all. They put them back in the pouch, closed the box over them and left it at that.

Caleb slept easily. The feeling that had been nagging at him was gone; all was well again. Tristram, however, could not sleep.

In the middle of the night he went down through the house and studied the box by the light of a nearly full moon. He thought of his dead parents and grandparents. There was no one to ask, and there would be no one to come after him. He was in his sixties, a recluse. The imperturbable silence of the house stretched back and forward in time. There was just this one moment when perhaps it might speak.

He put on the ring. It would only fit on the little finger of his left hand.

The first thing that happened was that he saw that the sheathed mirror was alive. Something dwelled in it, something that did not belong; it was out of place and wanted to leave. This unsettled Tristram so much that he had to put it back in the pouch and shut the box over it. Then he saw that everything else was alive too. The box was alive. It was wood, no, two woods, sharing wood's graceful strength but otherwise with different personalities, one more pliable and patient, the other stubborn, loyal; and it was also silver, which was cunning and secretive and teasing. The table he sat at was alive, and the floor his feet rested on. (He stood up, putting a hand down to steady himself.) The house was alive. It wasn't just a thing; it had a presence. The moonlight was exquisitely alive, like a rain of bittersweet music flooding in around his feet. Everything was still as it had been, the shabby old room and the shadows and the dust, but everything was also itself, brimming with being: like the difference between a beloved face asleep and awake.

Every night after that, when he was sure Caleb was asleep, Tristram went downstairs and put the ring on his finger and walked for as long as he dared, often nearly until dawn. For those hours it was as if he walked inside a symphony. Tristram had found his ghosts. Sometimes he was sure he felt them in the air nearby, just behind him, ready to be glimpsed if only he could turn his head quickly enough. Sometimes he was so sure of it that he thought he saw a face, a solemn, age-worn woman's face shrouded by curtains of dark hair. Or perhaps that was just the face he imagined when he held the ring itself up to his eyes. It was alive too, of course, alive with unfathomable vertiginous ancientness and a kind of hollow patience, a grief that had worn itself out.

When the moon had waned almost to nothing, he walked down one night to the edge of the river. He reached the cove and was standing on the little crooked stretch of sand when someone came out of the water.

For all those hundreds of years there had been no such thing as mermaids. *Mythical creatures*, the encyclopaedias said. This was how the world was divided since the last and greatest magus had drowned: facts on one side, legends on the other. In the vicinity of the prophetess's ring, though, the line was fraying. The sea-creature had seen Tristram when he'd first wandered near the shoreline, wearing on his finger the passage between her world and his. She had fallen in love with him at once, and when he saw her step up out of the water, gleaming as if made of moonlight, how could he not be utterly enchanted, as spellbound as any man who saw a mermaid was fated to be?

He gave her the ring as a wedding band. It kept her human, or as close to human as she could come, though she couldn't go far from the water for long, and she could not pass out of the gates of Pendurra at all: in the world beyond there was no such thing as she was. Tristram didn't mind. As far as he was concerned she might as well have descended from heaven. He loved her blissfully, passionately. He no longer felt like a hermit sealed in a haunted house. Pendurra became their home: his, Swanny's (so he called her), Caleb's and then, two summers on, Marina's. The baby should not have been possible, but there she was, growing month by month, with a whole future lying in wait. There were things that needed doing and preparing for, everyday things Tristram had not had to think about for many years. So he talked to the friend who knew him best and whom (apart from Caleb) he trusted most, and Owen Jeffrey looked around, and that was how Guinivere Clifton came to be invited to live in the lodge and join the strange family.

Five hundred years earlier any village grandfather anywhere in all Europe could have told them it wouldn't last. You didn't need to be as wise as the magus to know that human creatures and those other kinds of beings could never pretend they were the same. The tales of their unhappy conjunctions were part of the folk-knowledge of every household where stories had ever been listened to. But in the last decade of the twentieth century there was no one to tell Tristram what was coming. By then it had become a rule that fairy stories always had happy endings. It was part of what made them not true. That was the kind of fantasy Tristram thought he had entered, as if the ring was a magic wishing ring that had granted his desires, and no questions asked.

But the ring was still a burden as well as a gift. Swanny sickened, gradually, not so much in body as in spirit. She loved her spouse and her daughter with a fierce devotion, but she could not continue year by year to pass as something she was not. That was another simple rule known to the ages before magic was forgotten. The ones who crossed too easily from one nature to the other were vampires or were-beasts or the like, monstrosities who no longer had their own life at all and lived by eating others'. Swanny began to disappear to the sea for hours, and then for days. She couldn't say why, but Tristram didn't need to ask.

Marina did, though. By now she was a child just turned two and they could all see that she wanted her mother like any other child. Worse, they had to answer her crying and pleading when Swanny was gone.

Tristram and Swanny stayed awake together from one dusk to the next dawn, and by morning they had admitted to each other what needed to be done. It broke him irreparably. They could only hope, together, that Marina would recover, but they knew it must happen before she was old enough to remember the day that eventually had to come.

The last thing Swanny did before going back to the sea for ever was to take off the ring and put it in Tristram's hand. He shut his eyes tight so he wouldn't have to see her leave. Then he couldn't bear to open them and look at the empty space where she had been, so he sat, howling in grief, the smooth cool circle crushed tight in his fist.

It was still there when Guinivere finally came into the room and gently eased him to his feet. She saw the way he held it unthinkingly, like a life-line. By the next morning, though, it was gone. Unable to endure the sight of it, needing to blame something for taking away his happily-ever-after, he had gone out secretly in the night one last time, the ring once more alongside the sheathed mirror in the box with its silver clasp, and locked them all together in the shrine that had been built centuries before in honour of the ring's bearer.

This time, however, it was not lost. The prophetess's gift had returned to the world, albeit marred and unrecognised. Through it she knew herself again, despite her half a thousand oblivious years. She knew something else too. The world was about to change again, the most cataclysmic change of all: she felt it coming. As if waking from a coma, it would have to face everything it had forgotten.

There was only one thing left to wait for, and she felt that coming as well. Her burden could not be bequeathed to this new world until it was first put in her hands again. And that could only happen when he who had taken the ring from her came back, at long last, to return it.

Twenty-two

'HEY! HEY, HELP her out!'

Gawain barely registered the yell from the beach. He bent down to the woman in the water, not sure if he'd heard the whisper or imagined it. It was almost impossible to distinguish the sounds her mouth made from the scratching of tiny wavelets at the edge of the river. The eyes blinked, transforming the face for a moment into a beautiful ivory mask. Inexplicably, he had the feeling he knew it from somewhere.

'. . . her to the water . . .' His blood thrummed in his ears.

'What?' he said.

From behind, from another world, someone shouted, 'For God's sake, don't just . . . Hey!'

'. . . oar lock,' came the whisper, perhaps. 'I saw her.'

At the edge of his vision something was approaching. He ignored it. He couldn't have lifted his eyes from the face in the water if his life had depended on it. He crouched right down onto his hands and knees.

'. . . where my wedding and . . . I saw . . .'

'Out the way!'

Eyelids closed slowly and the face sank down, gathering its trailing fringe, sucking it under. The jetty shook and clanked as footsteps ran up behind Gav. 'For God's sake,' a woman was saying, 'let me . . .' The steps came beside him and stopped as the voice trailed away.

There was nothing below, not even a shadow.

'What the bloody hell?' The accent belonged well north of where they were. Gawain got to his feet, still holding his shoes in his hands, and saw a flustered woman with a harried face, panting hard, staring back and forth between him and the river, her expression in the middle of changing from frantic urgency to angry confusion. 'Did she drown? Did she go under? What's wrong with you?' She dropped uncomfortably to her belly and stuck a hand down into the water.

'No one drowned,' Gav said.

'There was a girl in the water, I saw it! What happened? Where's she gone?'

'There wasn't a girl.'

'I saw you bend down!' She was shouting quite loudly now. The man who'd pushed off in the inflatable, and was now transferring himself into one of the moored dinghies, stared at them across the harbour. 'Why didn't you help her? What the hell were you thinking?'

'Nothing's there,' he said, remembering the words you were supposed to use from all the times his father had said them to him. 'See for yourself.'

The woman stopped splashing her arms around in the water. Gawain held out a hand. After a long pause she took it and hauled herself to her feet. 'Then who . . . ?' She scanned the shallows and shook her head before rounding on him again. 'Then what were you doing? I saw you talking. I saw a face.'

He only shrugged.

The woman's agitated expression changed to an odd kind of fear and Gawain had an abrupt premonition. He was going to have to get used to seeing that face.

'She can't have just . . .'

Gawain ignored her. Something else was stirring, some other memory. Something about a white face and green hair.

'Oh, never mind,' the woman muttered crossly, and stalked back down the jetty.

Now the dinghy was heading his way, the man in its stern sculling forwards. He caught Gawain watching him and stared back, too intently, from between a peaked cap and a heavy beard. Suddenly feeling surrounded, Gawain turned to escape. As he looked around, his gaze ran across the ranks of bare trees on the opposite shore, mute ancient guardians gathered around the hidden house, and he stopped as still as if he'd turned into one of them.

He remembered where he had seen the face in the water before.

The woods, the house. The lodge above them. And in the lodge a room littered with Auntie Gwen's jumble, and in the room (he closed his eyes) a single black-and-white photograph. And in the photo a smooth, round-mouthed, almost luminous face: the same face – gentler and warmer, but in its perfect symmetry and its sculpted clarity definitely the same – that had just emerged from the water to plead with him.

A white woman with green hair.

'Hoping for the ferry?'

He'd blanked out completely. He hadn't even noticed the dinghy nudge against the jetty. The bearded man stood up in it, fingers on the tiller, eyeing the mooring cleats.

'What? No. No, I . . .'

He felt rooted to the spot. All his instincts told him to get away, from people, from questions, from disbelieving and disapproving faces. One barely audible whisper held him in place: *Find my child . . .*

Something Auntie Gwen had known.

'Noticed you checking the sign. Don't run in the winter. Out of season. Place is a bloody zoo in the summer though. Need a ride?'

The man looped a rope round a cleat and eased his boat tight to the dock. A dirty white sail lay folded in the bottom of the hull. Gawain saw the name painted on the stern, straddling the rudder: *Nymph.*

'Hop in if you do. Wind's come up a bit, should be able to sail. Only take a couple of minutes.'

The sailor's eyebrows were as dense as his beard, and the peak of his cap was pulled right down over them, so all Gawain could see of his face were unfriendly eyes that gave nothing away.

'That's . . . um.' The breeze seemed to have words in it, faraway but urgent: . . . *her to the water* . . .

'Long walk otherwise. That or wait till spring.' The man nodded towards a perch in the bow.

He'd come here to try and cross the river. Why was he even hesitating? 'OK. Thanks, then.' Gav lowered himself in clumsily, still holding his shoes, and sat with his back to the mast, knees cramped tight. The man pushed off with an oar and began unfolding the sail, causing a lot of alarming wobbling. They floated surprisingly quickly away from the dock, the surface of the river close.

And under the surface, out of sight, the white woman with her snaking green hair. The secret Marina had wanted to tell him. *I've never told anyone this before.* He'd been so tightly wound up in his own misery he'd barely listened at all. Now he couldn't remember what she'd said. He'd shut her out, the way everyone had shut him out, but she'd told the truth.

'Seen a woman in the water, did you?' the man asked, as casually as if making a remark about the weather.

The rustling and grunting and wobbling carried on behind him, and now he could feel the wind tugging at the boat. Tiny curling waves appeared under his feet. Trapped in the bow, Gav gripped the gunwales, closed his eyes and cursed himself.

'Don't like to talk about it, eh?' The man hauled on a rope, pulling the sail jerkily up the mast. It flapped around like a huge dying fish. Gav gave silent thanks for the racket it made, sparing him from having to say anything at all.

'I can understand that.' The boat twitched and leaned like a living thing as the man pulled something tight and settled in the stern. They slid between the dormant boats on either side.

'Often think I should have done the same. Should have kept my bloody trap shut. I'd still be out here every day, though.'

This sunk in slowly. When Gawain at last understood, or thought he understood, he couldn't help twisting round to stare at the man. The sailor gazed levelly ahead, hand on the tiller, as if his passenger wasn't there at all.

'Fifteen years I been looking,' he said. 'Maybe today's the day. Might see her again now you're here.'

Horace stopped at the forking of the roads.

He'd let the other kid get too far ahead. Stupid! Now he couldn't be sure which way his quarry had gone.

But then – he took off his cap and fidgeted with his hair – what difference did it make, when you thought about it?

He grinned. All that mattered was him getting to Pendurra first. And that was going to be cake. He'd have got there first even if the old nutter's car had been working, but now the kid was on foot he had all day. All he had to do was go down to his boat, cross over, find Marina and tell her everything he'd seen. She probably wouldn't believe him, but he'd make her. *Go on then*, he'd tell her, *show me where he is. Your 'cousin'. Bet you won't be able to find him anywhere here. And when he finally shows up and won't tell you what he's been doing, say the name 'Professor Lightfoot' to him and watch his face. Professor Lightfoot. And when he asks how you found him out tell him it's 'cos Horace saw through him. Horace knew he was bad news. Horace found out what was going on and came to warn you. Should have listened to me all along, shouldn't you? Know better next time, won't you?*

He strolled down the overhung lane towards the river, rehearsing this conversation over and over again in his head, imagining what Marina would say. *I'm so sorry, Horace. You were right all along. I'm so glad you came to warn me, Horace. You saved the day.*

He heard a raised voice from somewhere down by the pub. He didn't particularly want to run into anyone. If he was going to come up with some brilliant excuse later on, he didn't want Mum finding out he'd been down here by the river. He ducked into the lane that led to the car park above the pub. From there he was high enough above the roofs of the holiday cottages to check out most of the beach. It looked safely deserted. The only thing moving was freaky Mr Frye's boat. *Nymph*. What a gay name for a boat. Course he's there, Horace thought, with a small inward sneer. Mr Freak. Goes out every day 'cos he's crazy. Thinks he saw a mermaid once and keeps trying to catch it or something. Mental. He'd heard Mum talking about it.

Hang on. Someone sitting in the bow?

Horace shaded his eyes against the reflected brilliance of the water and peered. The small dinghy with its dirty white sail veered round, moving into open water beyond the moorings. The sail swung abeam, blocking his view of the front of the boat again.

No. Couldn't be.

Could it?

He tried to tell himself he must have imagined it. It had only been for a second. Hard to see anything anyway, with the sun like that.

But now, as he skidded back down the wet grass and hurried out into the lane again, the awful logic of it loomed clearer and clearer. The professor was a headcase and she had something to do with it. Miss Clifton was basically OK, but definitely off the deep end, and she had something to do with it. And now that psycho Mr Frye.

A conspiracy. A conspiracy of freaks.

He ran down to where the lane opened out to the river. The boat was more than halfway across already. It was stern-on to him and he still couldn't get a look at anything in front of the mast. There was a funny light in the sky too, an odd haze, as if someone had thrown the thinnest of veils over the morning.

The dinghy eased towards the opposite shore, heading for the ferry landing. It swung round to nestle against the stone steps. Now Horace could see that there really was a person squashed into the bows. The person stood up and climbed ashore. For a second or two, as he turned to say something to the man in the boat, his profile was clear to Horace's keen eyes even at that distance.

Horace grabbed his bunch of keys from his pocket and sprinted across the beach.

Out of the corner of his eye Gav noticed a small dark figure running along the opposite shore, but he was too busy trying to figure out what to say to the man in the boat to give it any thought.

'Well,' he tried. 'Thanks again.' Not *Yes, she was really there.* Not *No, you didn't imagine it.* Not *I know what it's been like for you.* How did you even start to say things like that?

The bearded man swivelled himself forwards and made some adjustment to the sail. The wind was stiffening.

'Nympholepsy,' he said, as he fiddled around in the dinghy. He sounded out the syllables one by one.

'Er . . . sorry?'

'Nympholepsy. Word I heard a few years back. Judge told me that was my problem.' The man looked up. 'Know what it means?'

Gawain shook his head.

'Dictionary definition: "A state of rapture, supposedly inspired in men by nymphs. Hence, a frenzy of emotion inspired by something unattainable." I had to look it up. Dictionary don't say if it's curable.' The current gradually pulled the boat away from the steps where Gawain stood. 'Cost me my wife and kids, pretty much everything except *Nymph* here.' He patted the gunwale in front of him. 'Think I'll ever see her again?'

He wants my help, Gav realised, finally. If I tell him yes, he'll probably sail away happy. Gav could see all of this in an instant, written on the man's obdurate look.

'I don't think so,' he said.

The sailor turned away, blinking.

'I'm sorry,' Gawain said, to his back. Then, louder, as the sail filled and the dinghy leaned away, 'Thanks!'

He didn't want to see a grown man crying, so he started quickly up the steps. What was he supposed to say to everyone? *Hello, did you know there are fire-breathing dogs in the lanes and mermaids in the seas, but don't ask me how or why or what we're supposed to do about it, now have a nice day?*

But Marina spoke his language. Gawain hurried through the village, his eyes on the wooded slopes above. It couldn't be that far to the ridge at the top, where the gate was. He saw a road curving uphill, but he didn't want to take a route anyone else might be using if he could help it.

Just as he had that thought, someone came out of a tiny house right beside him. He looked down quickly to avoid any eye contact and saw that he wasn't wearing his shoes.

Stupidly, he stared at his empty hands. He recalled tucking his shoes down in the bottom of the dinghy. He'd never picked them up again. How could he not have noticed? His feet were streaked with earth.

'Good morning!'

He glanced up in confusion towards the elderly woman at her front door and saw her eyes travel down to his feet and up again. That look began to spread over her face. 'Ah . . . chillier than they said it would be, isn't it?'

'A storm's coming,' he answered, and walked away. He had no idea what made him say it. Until the words had come out of his mouth he hadn't known it was so.

But the morning was indeed darkening, and as he hurried between the motley windows and eaves he heard the valley behind the village beginning to hum to the music of a cold wind. He put his head down and trotted on. His bare feet seemed not to feel the pebbles of the road. He found a sign for a footpath leading straight up the valley behind the village, into the trees. The path was concrete at first, but as the houses shrank to tiny terraced cottages and then gave out altogether, it became packed mud, kneaded with old bootprints. Branches closed above it. He watched his feet as he walked. He knew he ought to be wondering how he was walking on the rough roots and loose stones without his shoes on, but there was no one to answer that question either.

He walked on, the old track beckoning him ahead like a bent arm, in among a faded tapestry of ferns and bark and the brittle rust of fallen leaves. He came to a junction marked by a wooden post. It seemed like a good excuse to sit on a flat stone and check the map, though the real reason he stopped was that as the light dimmed and the trees turned restless, he was suddenly in less of a hurry to get where he knew he had to go.

The map showed the footpath leading up through the wood towards a crossroads at the top of the ridge. The entrance to Pendurra was just a little east of where the roads met. Maybe a mile away, a mile and a half. He'd be there soon, very soon, and then . . .

A crackling in the undergrowth made him look up.

Something like a big animal was moving through the brambles and ferns. Gawain's heart ballooned against his ribs. He'd thought he was completely alone. The shambling thing was the size of a bear.

He stood up, tipping the map off his knees into the mud.

It pushed its way through the trees until it showed itself to be a man, crouched and shaggy, matted with leaves, coated in earth. Gav picked up a length of fallen branch. His hands wouldn't hold steady. Something Marina had said jumped from nowhere into his head. The thing that wasn't called a woodlouse. *It's a wild man who lives in the woods.*

The wild man saw he was there, straightened and stopped.

It was Caleb. He must have spent the night in a hole in the earth, but it was still just about identifiably him. His stare was like an animal's; there was barely a trace of the human left on him, his straggling hair thick with the litter of the winter ground and all the rest of him lathered with mud. Gav gripped the length of wood more tightly.

Caleb twitched, then came on towards the path. Now there was an unmistakable hostility in his approach. Gav glanced back down the way he'd come, but he couldn't make himself start running, not back to the village where people might be. He tried telling himself there couldn't be anything to be frightened of. It wasn't very convincing.

The man looked unhinged. He crashed through the screen of branches and came out onto the path, his hands still thrusting aside imaginary obstacles.

'You,' he said.

Gawain lowered the stick, but not all the way.

'What . . .' Caleb began, limping a couple of steps down the path towards him. 'What . . .'

Gawain tried to say something. Not a sound came out.

'What . . . you . . . done?' Abruptly Caleb broke into a run and lunged at him, swatting the branch aside. Gav tried to duck away, but Caleb got hands to his jacket and heaved him close. His hair and beard stank like fur. 'What you done? Eh?' Gav wriggled his hands onto the man's arms but couldn't push him away. 'What you done?' Caleb let him go with an angry shove.

'I haven't—' he began, but Caleb leaned over him and roared, the pitch of his voice more grief than anger.

'Was all right till you came! Now look!' He gestured furiously at nothing.

'Caleb?'

'Why don't you . . . jus' . . .' His mouth worked silently, then clamped shut, and he dug his hands deep into his filthy hair.

'Caleb,' Gav said carefully, in the abrupt silence. 'What's happened?' But the man only swayed from side to side, grimacing. Gav straightened slowly. The earth felt cool and heavy under him, woven through with its web of dormant roots, studded with old rock. 'What's going on?'

Caleb twisted away. Gav saw that his clothes were scratched all over, as if he'd dragged himself through a bramble patch. What he'd thought was a shambling crouch was actually an injury; Caleb was holding an arm against his ribs, wincing as he turned.

'All gone mad,' he whispered.

'Are you OK?'

'We was all right before you came. Now what'll happen?' Caleb banged his fists against his knees. 'Now what?'

'Caleb?' But the man was deaf to him now. Gawain could have just stepped round him and gone on his way, leaving him crouched and whining.

Instead he said, 'I'm going back there.'

Caleb's head whipped up. The wild eyes were now full of fear.

'You can't.'

'I have to.'

'Don' make it worse!'

'Worse? Worse than what? Caleb?' The man was shaking his head and backing away. 'Is Marina OK? Tell me what happened.' Fragments of bark and leaf dropped from the shaggy head. Gawain wouldn't have been surprised to see a vine grow out of Caleb's mouth, like one of those carved heads in old churches.

'It's all come back,' he said. His eyes darted around the wood. 'Everywhere. Ah. Hurts to cough.'

'What happened to you?'

'You did!' Knots of caked hair fell over his eyes as he glared up again. 'You happened! And then everything come alive! All in the—'

And then he was holding completely still, listening.

'What?' Gav said, suddenly far more nervous. Caleb had frozen as if someone or something had appeared on the path right in front of them, but Gav couldn't hear anything beyond the trees' bleak whistle. 'Caleb? What?'

'One of them,' Caleb muttered, and peered up.

'One of . . . ?'

'Coming,' Caleb said.

Gawain's mouth went very dry. He looked around, panic rising.

'Looking for you,' Caleb added hoarsely, and his eyes peeled wide.

Now Gawain's heart was juddering so hard he could scarcely breathe. Caleb backed away from him, down the path.

'Caleb, listen.' The man was shaking his head manically. 'Where's Marina? Caleb! Is Marina OK?'

Caleb's only answer was to spin round with a gasp of smothered pain and run limping towards the village.

'Wait!' There was sweat on Gav's hands, already turning icy. A hollow sound rushed overhead, deeper than the wind's hissing malediction. He looked up instinctively and caught a blur of shadow in the corner of his eye, blanking the trees; when he turned to follow it, it was gone. He reached down for the branch he'd dropped, trying to force some of the wood's firmness into his hands.

Above the trees the shadow reappeared, moving, so dark it sucked the weakening light out of the day. It grew. It was no shadow; it was solid, a mass of blackness, spreading as it descended. He curled his toes into the mud to stop himself bolting, trying to remember how he'd stood up to the hideous dog. This is what I've got to do now, he tried to remind himself. *You must.* This is what I've got to get past to find her.

The trees above cracked and shivered as the black thing plunged through the branches.

Twenty-three

UNLIKE MORE OR less everyone else in what had for hundreds of years until that day been able to think of itself as the rational modern world, Gawain had not grown up with the instinctive sense that there was an absolute difference between possible and impossible things. He'd been baffled and astonished often enough by the previous forty-eight hours, but he'd never had to confront something whose mere existence he couldn't accept. So when he looked up the path and saw by the full light of day the thing that alit there, he didn't pass out or lose his grip. He was witlessly terrified, the terror of the cracking ship or the crumbling bridge, but the fear was pure, there was no madness in it, and his utter determination not to flee held long enough for him to survive the first unspeakable moments and so recognise what he was looking at.

Its squat blunt head jerked from side to side. It opened a sharp black thing, part mouth, part beak.

'Hairy man gone,' it croaked.

Gawain clutched the branch, squeezing the blood out of his fingers. The beast stood on the path ten paces ahead of him.

The aspect of it that was not manlike was, as he'd guessed in the dark of the chapel, all raven or crow. It watched him with eyes like polished stones set in a black head. It stood like a man, but stiff, awkwardly upright, balanced on legs that narrowed to leathery sticks and ended in gruesome talons, four claws splayed over the earth. Gawain saw the spindly arms that had lifted him as easily as if he were a baby, and the finger-claws that had gripped him. The arms flexed and bent at strange angles, making a mass of blackness behind them shiver and compress.

'You go too,' it added. The head twisted again, each unblinking eye taking its turn to stare at him. 'Go back.'

Out here in the open air, the voice sounded brittle. It worked its throat uncomfortably to make the words come out, the beak stabbing at air.

He licked his lips and swallowed. No stammering now.

'No,' he said.

'Danger. Go back.'

'Hello, Corbo.' He couldn't look into its eyes. Their stony brilliance was too predatory. He didn't like to look at the cruel beak. He tried to fix his gaze on its broad chest.

'Hello hello.'

'Have you come to stop me?' He wondered about fending off those talons with the branch he'd dropped. It seemed unlikely.

'Avert.'

'What?'

'Avert.' The neck twisted back. 'Warn,' it said, with effort. 'Bad ahead.'

Gawain swallowed again. 'I . . .' He heaved a deep breath. 'I can't go back.'

'Turn about.' Corbo demonstrated, hopping and spinning a full circle. To keep its balance, it spread its arms slightly, the wing-feathers opening behind them. 'Go down.'

'No, I mean . . . I have to go on.'

'Says who.'

'I do. I just have to.' *You must.* He wasn't sure what he was saying. If he'd stopped to think about the fact that he was having some kind of conversation with this thing, his head would have spun into irreversible disarray. He concentrated on the feel of the ground beneath his feet.

'Bad ahead.'

'Where?'

'Not where. Who. Danger ahead.'

'Danger? What? How close?'

'Soon.'

'What . . . what kind of danger?'

'Bad kind.'

'I mean . . . what is it? What's wrong? What's going to happen?'

'Can't say.'

'Why not?'

'Can't say.'

'Well, OK, then.' A monster in my path, he thought. This is who I am now: Gawain, battling monsters. 'Then I can't go back. I have to go on.'

'Did before.'

'What?'

'Did before. Ran. Ran away, *aaaaark*. Ran ran ran.'

Gawain flushed. He felt himself being mocked, though Corbo had left every word as flat and toneless as ever.

'That was yesterday,' he muttered.

It watched, remorselessly inexpressive. It wouldn't fill anything in for him. There were no unspoken exchanges with a thing like this. A question, Gav thought. Come up with a question. It always answers me.

'Why are you helping me?'

'No use. Don't listen.'

'OK, but why? Yesterday, in the chapel. You let me go, I know you did. You could have stopped me. Right?'

'Paid for it.'

'And you said you wanted to leave too.'

Nothing.

'Right?' he prompted.

'You heard.'

'Who's doing this, Corbo?'

'Can't say.'

'Why not?'

'Ask ask ask, *kkraaa*.' Its beak-mouth squirmed and snapped. 'Waste time. Go.'

'Won't you . . .' Gawain swallowed. 'Won't you get in trouble?'

Corbo shook out its arms abruptly. A ridge of feathers ruffled open on each side, shivering with a noise like rattled twigs. Gawain flinched as the thing swayed, suddenly lighter on its feet, its head stretching up and then swinging down.

'Bad enough now. No worse. Stuck like this, *caaark*. Feather and filth. Day and night. Hot, cold. Hungry, *wraaaak*. Hungry.'

The feathered arms unfurled fully, a huge black curtain, and beat the air in agitation as if trying to shake themselves loose. Gav threw up his hands and was saying, 'No, don't, sorry—' but his voice was lost in the rush of noise. Its clawed feet scratched at the earth. It thrust its neck towards him.

'Go. Last chance.'

Stupidly, Gawain could only think of the woman in the village. I can't go back there, he thought. I haven't got any shoes on. Someone might see me. 'I can't!' he yelled back. It twitched; he almost thought he'd surprised it. 'I can't go back,' he went on, desperate. 'OK? Or how will I ever find out? I can't just . . . run away.'

The hard bright eyes stared back.

'And, um, I don't think you can stop me.'

'*Wwrrrkkk*,' it said softly, wings settling.

'I'm right, aren't I?'

'Yes yes.'

'Why, Corbo?'

It fidgeted before answering. Was he imagining it or did it suddenly look shifty? 'Soon learn.'

'Will I?'

'Likely.'

'OK, because, um, I want to know. I need to find out who I am.'

'Told you. Stupid boy.'

'Yeah, but apart from that.'

'*Aaarrk*.' It hopped from foot to foot. It made two gargling sounds that sounded like they were meant to be syllables but made no sense to him, unless maybe it was trying to say, 'Gawain,' while swallowing a frog. 'White Hawk,' it carried on. 'Go on then. Up to you. Say you come. Have to. Have to tell.'

Up to me? he thought. Corbo backed a little up the path. Suddenly it looked ungainly, bedraggled, defeated.

'I'll help you,' he said. 'If I can.'

'Too late. Holly came.'

'What? Who?'

'*Caaaark*, listen. Stupid boy.'

'Who . . . Is Holly the one who—'

It shivered its folded wings and interrupted. 'Soon see. Snow coming. Get inside. Forward, back, up to you. Go. Man there.'

A muted flash lit up the trees. Gawain spun round.

There was someone on the path behind, a middle-aged man, an ordinary man. Under a blue woolly hat, his face was white as paper. He held out the phone he'd just used to take a picture. Corbo's wings filled the woods with a sound like a waterfall and it clattered through the branches above, vanishing behind the canopy.

Gawain and the man stared at each other.

Without moving his jaw, the man said, 'What the hell was that?'

It had never occurred to Gawain that someone else might be there. This never happened. He had his two lives and they never overlapped. No one shared both with him, not even Auntie Gwen, who'd probably wished she could. That was how it worked. People were like his parents: they didn't want to know. Looking into this man's face, Gawain saw something he'd never seen before: the wreck of his two worlds colliding.

One of them, he saw, would sink.

'It's called Corbo,' he said. The man didn't blink, but his eyes slowly turned towards the obscured sky. 'You probably shouldn't go this way.'

The man just stood where he was, as if the power of motion had abandoned him, which at least made it easy for Gawain to start up the hill again, in the other direction. He pulled his jacket more tightly around him as a chill swept through the wood. Swinging the branch beside him like a staff, he had the feeling he was tracing a fault line over the earth and behind him a crack was widening, the world crumbling into it in his wake.

The river was increasingly choppy. Guts churning, Horace smacked the hull of his boat into each wave. I'm not far behind, he told himself. Only a couple of minutes. I'll catch up. No way some city kid's going to get there before I do. He wiped his nose with his sleeve and twisted the throttle on the outboard until the boat juddered and bucked as it skimmed the whitecaps. There was a speed limit on the river but so what. He didn't care. Spurts of bitterly cold spray leaped up from under the bows. He saw freaky old Mr Frye's boat heading out towards the open sea. Mr Freak. Hope he sinks.

There was nowhere to leave his boat at the ferry steps, so he steered into the harbour. There were a couple of old farts up on the road, staring disapprovingly as he came in too fast, his wake setting the buoys lurching.

So what. Let them stare. Everyone stared at him. The Chinese kid. OK, you two, here's something to watch.

He aimed the bow straight at the shingly foreshore where the stream opened out into the harbour. Just when it looked as if he was going to ram his boat onto the stones, he threw the motor into reverse. The grating screech of the engine filled the village and out of the corner of his eye Horace noted with satisfaction that the stares of the posh villagers had twisted into frowns. He swung the boat round sharply, holding his balance as it swerved and slowed, and waited for just a second as its shoreward momentum fought against the whining motor; then he flipped off the outboard, and, as the hull drifted inches away from the shore, vaulted out onto the shingle. There was not the tiniest scrape of fibreglass on stone, but the boat had come to rest close and still enough that he could push its stern back out and take hold of the painter without even getting the soles of his trainers wet.

With all the insolence he could muster, he looked straight up at the people on the road and took angry pleasure at the speed with which they averted their eyes.

No sign of the kid. He must have started walking up already. Horace looped the painter round the struts of the wooden footbridge that crossed the stream's mouth, then marched up the paved road towards the ridge. He approached each corner carefully in case the kid wasn't far ahead; he didn't want to give himself away. The road climbed steeply between the harbour and the hillside houses – all deserted for the winter; they were all rich people's second homes – and then curved round the shoulder of the hill. He couldn't risk going too fast. The only thing he had going for him was the element of surprise.

Course, there was the shortcut.

Horace stopped in the deserted road. He took his cap off again to run fingers through his hair.

No one knew their way around like he did. He hadn't been through the hole in the hedge for a while but he still remembered exactly where it was. All he had to do was jump off the road onto the footpath that ran past the farm, carry on till he got to the gap and then duck through and he'd be in the woods right near Miss Clifton's house. Cake. And he'd definitely get there before the other kid if he hurried.

His feet knew the way. He didn't have to think about where he was going at all. As he hurried along he fantasised about how impressed Marina would be. He rehearsed their conversation under his breath as he trotted past the farm with its ridiculous barking dogs and came up to the edge of the trees. When he reached the place, it was a simple matter to check quickly that no one was coming – no one ever was – and then slip between the sagging barbed wire in the spot where the undergrowth was thin, and into the bushes beyond, onto Pendurra land.

He'd been thinking about sneaking up through the woods to keep an eye on the gate so he could catch the kid coming in. But now he realised he wanted to see Marina straight away. He liked the way she always smiled to see him. She never saw any other boys, or not that she ever said anything about. Nobody ever seemed to come and go. There was something special about the place, there really was, or how come there weren't any cars or farm machines, and there were no wires leading to the house, like it was lost in time or something, and even though it was really really old and there was all that land around it nobody worked there except Caleb and Miss Clifton? There was something special about Marina too, not just her bright smile and being friendly and pretty. She was so different from the girls at school. It was like she wasn't even the same species, she was . . . she was so . . .

Sadly, Horace Jia was only twelve and hadn't yet learned a language to describe how Marina was unlike all the other children he knew, or why he liked thinking about her so much. He remembered how she hadn't listened to him properly last time they spoke, hadn't seemed to care about how worried he was, and then she'd gone off with that other boy. The liar. The fake.

He worked his way through the dense stands of wild rhododendron with the automatic deftness of a gymnast practising a routine. So perfectly did he know his trackless route, in any season of the year, that as he approached the place where the undergrowth thinned out near the driveway, he would surely have noticed the strangely shaped trunk that had never been there any other day, if it hadn't been for the turbulence of resentment and fantasy whirling through his head.

As it was, the first he knew of it was when, quite suddenly, it moved, its true shape becoming clear. By then he was too close, and it was too late.

Being a boy of twelve, and the only child of a fiercely strict mother, the very idea of naked femaleness was a thing of paralysing fascination and terror. It was the first thing he noticed and it stopped him in his tracks.

He didn't take in the rest of it, because he couldn't. It was impossible. It couldn't be there.

He saw a woman's form, a woman's face and breasts and hips, but all a dark shining green, except for the eyes and nipples which were blood-red. From the shoulders outwards and the thighs downwards the form became something else, no longer even the image of a person. Its legs and arms grew darker and rougher, streaked and mottled like bark. At the long arms' ends burst clusters of spiked leaves that could not possibly be hands, though they flexed and stretched, finger-like. The feet were knots of wood, rooting down into the litter of dead leaves. On its smooth head, a crown of tiny white flowers seemed to grow right out of its skull.

The feet lifted, lithe and pliant, trailing earth, and as they stepped towards Horace, the mouth opened and sang in a warm, clear alto:

The holly and the ivy, when they are both full grown
Of all the trees that are in the wood the holly bears the crown

One of the branch-arms extended and the leafy twigs at its tip rustled and crooked, beckoning.

'Come, mouse,' said the voice, a deliciously musical hum. 'Come, squirrel.' The root-feet slid closer. 'Come, little owl. Come and rest in my branches. Warm yourself in my thorny arms.'

Some self-preservation instinct triggered itself. Horace spun round and began to sprint. There was a commotion behind him as if a gale had struck the wood. He was tripped hard, and fell, scrambling onto his back as he dropped. He saw the green face, the ruby irises in the black eyes, bending towards him. More in dumb shock than terror, he fainted, and never felt the limb scoop him up, scores of prickles tearing at his clothes.

At that same moment Gawain was hurrying up the old green lane, where for centuries the people of the village by the river had walked to reach the church among the fields above. Its grey tower rose above the brow of the hill as he climbed out of the woods. The sky behind it had turned solid, a wall of cloud. He pulled the map out of his back pocket without stopping and crossed a rutted field to the lane at the top of the ridge. There was a village nearby, a few roofs poking over the hedges. He scrambled away from it, up towards the crossroads. Checking over his shoulder in case anyone was around on the road, he was halted by the view opening behind.

Down to the west and south the landscape had vanished completely into the colourless storm. The horizon had drawn in so close he felt like he could touch it. It looked like the end of the world. He pulled his jacket tighter around him and climbed on.

At the crossroads the sky opened out around him, the wind stinging. An old mud-crusted car was parked at an odd angle on the strip of grass beside the junction, nestled front first into the hedge. Gawain wondered who'd have left their car like that, and where they were now. Then he saw the crumples and dents behind the front bumper, and the marks of skidding tyres like fat brown brushstrokes in the grass. Another wreck.

He hurried on the eastward road towards the gate, feeling unpleasantly exposed here in the high lane, though the only things watching him were occasional crows. He tried not to think about Corbo's warning. Something more fearsome than itself didn't bear thinking about. All he had to do was get in, under cover somehow. Then he'd work out what to do next. Find Marina. She'd know. Or at least she'd know more than he did. The thought that he had become more helpless and ignorant than Marina was almost as dreadful as the crow-beast's threats.

He slowed down as he neared the dense laurel hedge and the two stone gateposts. The crows cawed at him from the pines, echoing the monstrosity's warning. *Go. Go.* But the advancing clouds had taken away any choice he might still have had. He didn't want to be out in the open when whatever it was that had eaten the middle distance caught up with him.

He peered surreptitiously round the near gatepost and watched the house for as long as he could hold still. Auntie Gwen's car was still parked beyond it. There were no signs of life.

Cautiously, he went up to the door and listened. Until that moment he hadn't realised that he was far, far more frightened that Auntie Gwen might be inside than that she might not be. But the house was as deserted as when he'd first arrived. The door was still unlocked, and when he cracked it open the silence behind it was blanket-thick.

He looked down at his feet, scratched, stained, soil between his toes. They told him how far he had come in a day, since he'd last stood here. He'd returned a different person. Rechristened.

He was squatting on the floor by his bag, changed into warmer clothes, when he heard a new sound outside. His head snapped up.

At first it was no more than a change in the timbre of the wind, its hollowness filling in, a moan becoming a murmur. As he scrambled to his feet, heart thudding, and held his breath to listen again, he realised that it was music.

A voice sang outside, the words becoming clear as it approached the house: a woman's voice.

> *O the rising of the sun and the running of the deer*
> *The playing of the merry organ, sweet singing in the choir*

In the next room, the clock began to chime.

> *The holly bears a prickle as sharp as any thorn*
> *And Mary bore sweet Jesus Christ on Christmas Day in the morn*

Gawain crossed to the window. Snowflakes had begun to fall. He looked out into the winter.

> *O the rising of the sun . . .*

Through the window its berry-red eyes met his. His knees gave way. He slumped backwards, a rabbit in an eagle's glare. There was no light in the eyes, no depth, no watery softness: they seemed blind. Yet the song stopped, and as its dark-lipped mouth curved into a smile, Gawain knew it had found what it was looking for.

It pointed a long arm-branch towards him, the cluster of leaves at its end straightening.

'Princeling!' it called out, clear and loud. 'I'm sent to fetch you. Come out. Follow!'

Desperate instinct made him think *fire*. Fire, the primal defence against the dark, the weapon against the wildwood. Gawain spun away from the window, seized the thinnest and longest log he could find from the basket by the fireplace and shoved its end into the ash.

The voice, outside: 'Where have you hid yourself, youngling? Come out to the cold.'

He bit his lip and stared into the dead hearth. 'Come on,' he whispered through gritted teeth. 'Come on, come on.' The window behind him scraped. Spike-leaved fingers caressed the panes. He couldn't stop himself looking over his shoulder. It was watching him, huge in the frame of the window, taller than any man. It stared for a moment and then stepped out of sight, towards the door.

'Come. On.' Fire, his last hope. The abomination outside could crush him like an insect. His shaking hands stirred futile clouds in the ash. Crows screeched and gargled outside, their racket echoing his nightmares, the plagues of dark wings shot through with seams of flame.

He took one deep breath to silence his panic and held it.

'Burn,' he whispered.

The end of the log flared. He felt the blast of warmth on his face even before his eyes opened to see it. He sprang up, clutching it tight in both hands. Sparks fell from it as he lunged towards the door.

There was an almighty crack. The door exploded inwards as if it had been hit by a battering ram. There under the porch stood the tree-creature, its huge arm swinging back. Gawain thrust the burning brand out in front of him.

With a hollow roar of wind the blizzard struck.

Part VI
Snow

Twenty-four

IN FRONT OF Horace's eyes a white fury danced. It was coming towards him, or he was falling into it. His first groggy thought was that he must be dead. His body felt detached. He couldn't place himself. He was nowhere.

A face appeared in the white. This was unexpected. Some sort of angel, maybe? He strained to make his eyes focus and found that he could actually lift his head a little. He was cold to his bones, and the skin of his face felt brittle as the crust of ice on a winter puddle.

If he wasn't dead, maybe he was as good as. That might explain the angel. It appeared to float above him – *above*, yes, he was (things began to arrange themselves) lying on his back on the ground – indifferent to the white chaos. It was shrouded, ominously. Dark hair fell across its face. He watched the way the whiteness twisted around it and realised that the white was snow, heavy snow, the same snow that was steadily burying him.

Hands appeared and reached to the angel's neck. Horace saw the shroud unfurl from its body. It bent down closer to him, coming into focus. The face became female.

'The right length for you,' she said. 'And I have no more use for it.'

She covered him with the shroud. It was like a thick blanket, slightly warm. She tucked the edges around his hands and legs. The lessening of the cold roused his nerves, making them tingle, then blaze. He gasped with pain.

She turned her head and met his eyes.

An unmistakable sadness filled her face.

'Oh,' she said. She reached a hand towards him, hesitated, then rested it on his shoulder. 'You have a long journey ahead.' She seemed to be about to add something, but thought better of it. Horace was still trying to work out whether what she'd said meant that he was about to die or that he wasn't – he felt hazily detached from either alternative, as if it really didn't make much difference – when she stood up again.

'Keep my cloak. It will do you some good, on your way.'

It was doing him good right now. His muscles were thawing, though they throbbed in protest when he tried to wiggle fingers and toes. He managed to twitch his head enough to shake away the film of snow from his hair and eyebrows. The scene became a little clearer. He'd always imagined angels (when he'd imagined them at all, which come to think of it was basically never) as being better dressed than this. They were supposed to be radiant, weren't they? Or at least tidy. Also a bit more cheerful. Still, with him being more or less dead and all, an angel she obviously was, since she stood barefoot and bareheaded in the snowstorm without a flicker of discomfort, looking down at him with a face like one of those old paintings on Christmas cards.

There was something about her voice too. It came untouched through the wind and snow like a bird's wing cutting the air. She had walked away a little, but when she looked back to speak again he heard the words perfectly clearly.

'Of all the men and women and their children, you are the last to see me alive. I'm glad I came across you, to leave my cloak.'

Then she vanished into the snow, and Horace began fighting to stir his sinking body back to life.

The monster swung one barbed arm in through the shattered doorway, swishing through the narrow space as if the storm had entered the house. Gawain jumped back, nearly tripping on the bottom stair behind him. The burning branch swayed crazily. Popping sparks smouldered against the walls.

'I'm to fetch you, fugitive,' it half sang, half said. The air between them rippled with heat, making its green face look like it was melting. 'I am the snare that catches boys. My barbs hook man-fry.' The arm stretched forward again, beckoning. 'Come close.'

'L-leave,' he croaked. He tried to think of the way the dog had stalled, constricted by his words. His throat was choked tight. He had to shout to clear it. 'Go away!' The shout became a scream. 'Get out!'

It slid one of the gnarled and splayed protrusions that served it for feet over the threshold. Where the woody tendrils touched, the earth beneath the floor buckled upwards. Cracks shivered through the slate tiles, adding their sharp *tchak* to the fizzing of the log and the deep rush of the wind outside. It bent its flower-crowned head to duck through the doorway.

'No!' Gawain yelled.

But it kept coming. The frame of the door warped and split as the tree-thing stepped across it, as if its wood was being sucked into the advancing roots. Gav stumbled back, sick with panic, retreating through the green curtain into the living room.

'Wrong boy, right boy.' It was inside the house, inside Auntie Gwen's house. The last barrier was down; the nightmares had come indoors. 'Right boy, wrong boy. You're the one I'm commanded to catch.' Here he was, in the midst of all the stuff, the piles of paper, the mounds of books, the everyday mess, and in among it the huge green thing strode, tearing the curtain aside with a ripple of one long limb. 'No good saying no, princeling. We both must as we must.'

There was no escape, but Gawain kept going back anyway, deeper into the room. His hands shook uncontrollably. As he backed round the sofa the end of the branch dipped too close to a blanket. There was a sudden bitter smell of burning. The room was too small, and, he realised, it was full of paper, scraps scattered everywhere. He couldn't swing his fire-brand, or drop it, or anything. And still the thing pursued him. It watched the smoking branch, swaying away from its tip, but on it came as he retreated, with ghastly hypnotic grace.

'Fear me, flee me, follow me in the end.' Its lips were the black of wet bark, and a black tongue moved in its mouth. 'Find the right child and Holly will be free. And the right is you.' It slid closer, marking each step with a singsong word. 'And. The. End.' He was backed in a corner. 'Is. Here.'

His heels prodded behind him and met the wall. He gripped the log tighter and tried one last time to drive this thing out. He was near tears.

Abject terror had turned his limbs to wax. His lips quivered as badly as his hands. 'Go,' he tried to shout, but it came out more like a sob. 'Go.'

It closed its mouth, paused its advance for a moment and then smiled and slowly shook its head.

'No. Don't.' Its next steps would bring him in range of the bristled limbs. 'I'll . . .' He held the fire out towards it.

It sang:

The holly bears a bark as bitter as any gall
And Mary bore sweet Jesus Christ

One limb whipped upwards, swift as an uncoiling spring, and struck Gawain's hands. The burning branch spun away across the room as he cried out. The blow felt like it must have shattered bones. He slumped to the floor, hugging his fingers under his arms, defenceless, watching through a film of tears as the grotesque feet slid closer, the carpet ripping open and the floor heaving under them. The long body bent as if bowing to the wind. He looked up into opaque vermilion eyes.

'Greenwood fears fire,' it murmured, voice warm as a caress, 'but, I fear, you fear me more.'

With a roar the room erupted in heat and smoke.

The blazing log had fallen at the entrance, beneath the green curtain, which had abruptly caught fire. The monstrosity sprang straight, twisting round. Its arms thrashed, throwing a picture off the wall, knocking over the fire irons, smashing the glass front of a cabinet, sending a high shelf of books raining down on Gawain's head. A foul-smelling layer of grey-black smoke began drowning the room from the top, filled with scattered sparks. Gawain crawled away from the cascade of books and saw that the tree-thing had fled. Smoke already stung his eyes, but he made out its huge shape rushing past the burning curtain, furniture scattering like shipwreck behind it. Its flight unbuckled the appalling fear that had paralysed him. His brain was suddenly racing. There was paper everywhere and it would all burn, in moments, and him with it. It happened that he'd crawled beside the very stack of paper he'd rested his tea on, that other morning which now seemed unthinkably long ago: right in front of his face he saw *GAVIN*, doubly underlined, the tea stain circling it. The envelope was already spotting with heat.

Smoke trickled into his lungs. He flattened himself on the floor, coughing. He felt the fire like a solid thing, an embrace. He recognised it from somewhere: its patient hunger. His thoughts flashed back again to the other morning, when he'd stirred the ashes and woken embers. The fire had answered him then. It had known him.

Now he knew it.

When roused, it ate; he understood that, all at once, as though it was obvious, a thing he'd always known. He couldn't make it stop. That wasn't in its nature. But, outside, he also knew the snow, stilling, light-fingered, inexorable.

Flares of brilliant yellow surrounded him in the smoke. Scraps of paper rose on the boiling air and went tumbling around the room. Even as the backs of his hands began to scorch, Gawain slowed his breath, closed his eyes and curled into a ball on the floor.

He reached past the fire, out into the open air. There he felt the snow falling, blanketing everything it touched. Its vast silence was something he understood. He found where that knowledge was in him. Hush, he told the fire.

Hush, hush.

Hussshh, came a sound in his ears, a deafening hiss that faded into a long whisper. *Shhhhhhh.*

He opened his eyes.

Smoke drifted in a glistening grey cloud above a glistening grey room. The glister above came from beads of steam. Below, it was ice.

The fire was gone.

Every object in the room was lined with a delicate mantle of frost. The blackened edges of half-consumed books were tiered with it; the broken remnants of upended chairs sparkled with it, like the spars and rigging of a clipper ship abandoned in a polar sea. Some stray fibres of the curtain were still threaded limply together. The sudden frost had made a spider's web of them, dewy with ice.

Gawain stared. He wasn't sure whether he'd saved the house or ruined it. He did know, however, that it was him who'd done it.

There was neither sight nor sound of the tree-thing. Perhaps he'd destroyed it, or driven it away. He stayed crouched in the corner, listening to the moan of the wind, watching the entrance to the room, just in case. Nothing.

There beside him was his old name, scribbled on the back of an envelope. The paper was glazed with a transparent film of frost, like a leaf on a hard winter morning. Beneath it he saw Auntie Gwen's letter, the one he'd stolen from Mum's desk and read on the train. Where sparks had fallen the letter was charred, his aunt's writing defaced as if by black raindrops. He brushed at the spots, remembering quite suddenly something Miss Grey had chanted in the carriage. *His mother's sister is flown. His mother's sister is gone.* A hole had burned through the paper in the place where Aunt Gwen had sketched herself smiling.

This is the kind of place, it said at the bottom of the sheet, *that really might be perfect for him.*

He folded the letter away into his back pocket, and the envelope with her scribblings as well. Two small fragments of her life, saved from the glistening ruin. His handiwork.

He thought, Who am I?

Horace knew he was tough. He'd always been the little kid, and on top of that he'd always been the Chinese kid, so pretty much the first thing he'd learned in school was that he was tougher than he looked. Nobody picked on him for very long. This was what he kept telling himself as he squirmed his freezing limbs, forcing them into motion. I'm tough. I'm not like the soft kids. It's just a snowstorm. I can do this.

He rolled over onto his side and got his arms and legs chafing against each other. Moving his fingers was like trying to operate a clumsy puppet. He wedged them down between his thighs to get some warmth into them, though the pins and needles made it feel like he'd stuck them into a pan of boiling water. Once he could work his hands properly, he sat up and tugged out the hood of his coat. The snow was a patient roar around him. The blanket the angel had given him slid off. He saw a glint of metal inside it, like a button, and fumbled around with it, puffing on his hands, until he worked out that it had a clasp on two of its corners. Oh yeah; she'd said. *My cloak.* He worked out which way round the cloak went and draped it over himself, fitting the clasp at his neck. It was warm and thick, made of some sort of dark wool. On the inside it was more or less dry. Pretty stupid-looking, but he wasn't going to worry about that now.

His memories were fuzzy. He'd been in a hurry. Had to find Marina before some other boy did, that was it. He'd knocked himself out somehow and had a bad dream. Anyway none of that mattered yet.

He'd never seen snow like this. You couldn't see five metres. But he wasn't going to panic, no way. All he had to do was figure out where he was. Crazy how you couldn't even guess. But he had to be around Pendurra somewhere.

It couldn't even have been snowing for all that long, because in the patch where he'd been lying you could still see the tops of blades of grass. Come to think of it . . .

He scuffed a patch of snow away with his foot. Then he cleared a bigger area.

Weird. The ground was flat and even, the grass smooth. Not like being in a field at all, fields were always lumpy and tussocky. It was more like . . .

A lawn. The lawn! Now that he pictured it, it was obvious. He was in Marina's garden, he must be. There was nowhere else with even ground. He pushed himself up to his feet, legs wobbling and stinging. It was hard to keep his balance with the crazy wind swirling around and the snowflakes like tiny bullets. He braced himself and shielded his eyes. He knew his way around this garden like his own house. All he had to do was work out which bit of it he was in. Maybe he could go and check on Marina. Maybe her dad would even invite him in the house, let him see the inside. In this weather and the state he was in. Stupid of me to get knocked out, he thought. Must have banged my head on a tree or something.

A tree. Or something.

Just a nasty dream, he told himself, shuddering. Let's get moving.

There were small shallow footprints nearby, already filling in. He couldn't really tell which way was which, but it didn't matter much, come to think of it. The garden wasn't that big. If he just picked a direction he'd hit something he recognised soon enough. Might as well follow the footprints.

A shiver of doubt assailed him as he started. Who, he wondered, goes wandering around barefoot in the snow? That bit hadn't been a dream. What was it the angel said to him, something about a long journey? What was an angel doing here anyway? There were no such things.

At once he was far less sure of where he was. The snow was coming down really hard; he could have been anywhere, or nowhere. I know what I'm doing, he told himself stubbornly, but even so he felt a huge flood of relief when a shape appeared ahead and he saw what it was: an apple tree. One of the old, twisty, tangle-branched ones that were dotted around the garden. Many times he'd snuck across the lawn to pocket their surprisingly sweet fruit, or watched from the edge of the trees as Marina clambered around comically in their branches. With a surge of inward triumph he recognised this particular tree. I know exactly where I am, he thought. It's like I have a sixth sense.

Quite suddenly he heard an angry voice, not far away. It jolted the self-satisfaction out of him at once. He ducked instinctively behind the trunk.

As he did so, it was as if a soundless wind swept past him, clearing the snow away like a brush going through dust, leaving perfectly clear air. Inexplicably, magically, he found himself inside a scene like a reversed snowglobe; the whirling flakes were all on the outside of an invisible bubble. Within the dome everything was impossibly sharp and still: the bare tree with its crooked branches, and he, cloaked and hooded and crouching behind it, and, in the snowy plain beyond, the two women.

It was something out of a dream, but this time Horace knew for sure he wasn't dreaming, and, what was worse, he also knew all at once that his bad dream earlier hadn't been a dream. His courage collapsed. Terrified, he clutched the bark and prayed he was out of sight. But he couldn't stop himself inching his head to the side until he could stare with a single fear-widened eye at the women beyond.

One had her back to him, but he knew her at once by her bare feet and the untidy rags she wore. The other, taller, head to toe in black as usual, staring at the dishevelled angel with a look that dried Horace's mouth and withered his heart, was Miss Clifton.

It was her, but it wasn't. Horace was too numb with shock to work it out. All he could see was that Guinivere Clifton was standing there in her black boots and her baggy black skirt and her rumpled black leather jacket with the silvery patterns on it, but in her face was an expression that was never hers: hard, hunted. She had some kind of big stick too, and she was holding it like a club.

Every detail was crystal clear. The weird bubble they were in was illuminated by an unaccountable radiance. The air almost shone. Horace could hear every word too, but – and he'd had dreams before where this had happened – none of the words made any sense.

This was because they spoke to each other, as they always had, in Latin.

'*I am who I always was, Johannes. Perhaps I forgot for a time, thanks to you. But thanks to this woman, I have remembered again. She brought you back and so she brought me back. See, I have waited for you again.*'

At least the angel *sounded* like an angel, Horace thought. He had no idea what she was saying, but the tone was solemn and calm. She stepped a bit further away from the tree and Miss Clifton turned to keep facing her. Now he could see them both in profile: the angel with her curtained head tilted up, the other wearing her own face like a death mask.

Miss Clifton's voice was even worse. It was barely her own voice at all. It was like she'd forgotten how to use her tongue and her lips, and had to force the nonsense sound out from somewhere in the back of her throat.

'*The woman knew nothing of what she did. There is no wisdom here. The world has emptied of it. Your time is finished. You are long forgotten. You know it yourself.*'

'*What of you, then, Johannes? Do you imagine you belong here?*'

Horace saw Miss Clifton gesture widely, a sweep of her arms. It seemed to cost her a lot of effort, as if her own body was too heavy for her to move properly. She'd never been the most graceful person, but now she looked as if she was half crippled. He shrunk tighter against the bark.

'*I will learn. I will teach! I am magister, the wise man. It is my fate to bring wisdom back to this world. As it is yours to be forgotten.*'

The angel paused for what seemed like an age before answering. Time had stopped for Horace anyway, except for the rapid pounding of his pulse in his ears. None of this could be happening, none of it. He watched it like a film, like something behind a screen, not really true at all.

'*You deceive yourself at last, as people always do.*'

'*I have nothing more to say to you. You should have died twice a thousand years ago. You are an unquiet spirit. What have you waited for so long?*'

'*For you to return what you took.*'

Miss Clifton twitched, and her left hand went to her breast. Horace saw that instead of her usual pendant, the little black-and-white yin-yang symbol she always wore, something different dangled from her silver chain: a plain brown hoop. She spoke sharply. '*You gave it! You gave it freely.*'

'*You mistook it, Johannes. You desire the gift and not the burden, but the gift and the burden are the same. In your heart you know it is so. It is a heavy burden, to be both mortal and spirit, to see truth, not to die. Heavier than you know. It will fall hard on you.*'

'*Do not prophesy, witch!*' The horrible alien expression in Miss Clifton's face turned to anger. Her mouth could have been dripping poison. '*Do not prophesy to me! You are no prophetess here. Your temples were ruined centuries ago. You know nothing of this world! You have long outlived your fate. Do not presume to tell me mine!*'

'*It is a fearful fate, Johannes.*'

Miss Clifton bared her teeth and snarled.

'*Then be grateful to me!*' She spat out the gibberish words like daggers. '*I deliver you to your fate now, a mercy!*'

'*Yourself, Johannes? You will strike the blow yourself?*'

To this, whatever it was, Miss Clifton could answer nothing. The angel spoke again.

'*I do not remember what made me wait for you those thousand winters, but I waited. Remember that, as you strike the blow.*'

Miss Clifton winced and shuddered. When she spoke again, there was a dreadful bitterness in her voice.

'*I loved you. I do not deny it. But look.*' She spread her hands at her sides. '*Now I have a woman's flesh. I cannot tell how this woman unbound my wards. No woman could be so great a thaumaturge. Perhaps time did the work for her. Yet the woman has given me an unthought-of gift with her womanhood.*' The voice chilled Horace to his bones. '*She has taken away a man's love. And a man's restraint. And a man's reason.*'

'*Your fury is all yours, Johannes. None of it is hers.*' The angel's voice had changed too: colder, sharper. Though she was a head shorter than Miss Clifton, she suddenly seemed twice the other's size. '*Your pride is all yours too. Yet whatever you say, you must return my gift. It is mine to bear still, and mine to bequeath. You knew that, once. Why else did you try to conceal it?*'

Miss Clifton drew herself up stiffly. '*You have never understood what you bore. Not in all that legion of years.*'

The angel woman spoke quietly. '*No. No, I have not.*'

'*I am wiser. I know this ring's worth.*' Miss Clifton folded a hand over the pendant. '*Do you know what I will do with the ring?*'

'*I do, Johannes.*'

'*I will restore to this world everything it has lost. I will throw open the doors and welcome the life of creation back to this withered corpse. I . . .*' Miss Clifton coughed, heaved in a breath, straightened herself. '*I am the resurrection and the life. That is your gift to me.*'

'*I spurned the god and this is how he cursed me. You cannot heal the world with a curse, Johannes.*'

'*Those gods fell long ago. They are nothing but empty words now. And you, Cassandra, should have died with them. Why do you go on?*'

'*I never chose my burden.*'

'*Then rejoice that I bear it instead.*'

'*You cannot.*'

The hand covering the plain brown pendant shook. Whatever crazy language they were talking in, it was obvious they were arguing about it.

'*I have and I hold.*'

'*No. You do not. You never had the strength to bear it.*'

Miss Clifton gestured angrily with the stick. '*Shall we have a trial of my strength, witch?*'

'*You must give it back to me.*'

Horace gripped the trunk tighter as the angel unfolded an arm and held out an open hand, palm raised. His breath dried up. He saw what she wanted: the thing that was strung on the silver chain round Miss Clifton's neck. It was like the film had reached its climax. He knew some terrible significance hung on what would happen next. The taller woman still clutched the ring with her free hand, covering it. The angel kept her palm out, unflinching, perfectly still.

There was a very long silence.

Miss Clifton said something slowly. '*You put it in my hands. Yourself, long ago.*'

'*Because you loved me, Johannes.*'

Maybe it was a trick of the weird impossible watery light, but for a moment it looked to Horace like Miss Clifton was crying.

The angel spoke again. Her tone became intensely commanding and Horace found himself urgently taking her side. Horrible things would happen if the wrong person won.

'*The door is open again and the world will suffer for it, but that burden is still mine to carry. Give me my burden, Johannes.*'

Miss Clifton spasmed visibly at these last words, then sagged.

'*You must know what I have decided.*' It was a broken whisper.

'*Will you do it yourself?*' said the angel. Her outstretched hand had still not wavered. '*Will you end me by your own hand?*'

Miss Clifton heaved the stick up over her head to strike. Horace almost cried out, saved only by the terrorised astonishment locking his tongue. But the stick wavered in the air. It was too big and heavy for her to swing. Her arm wobbled clumsily. She lowered it back to her side, leaning on it, gasping. Horace felt an almost unbearable relief as he watched her other hand lift the chain off her neck. It's going to be OK now, he told himself. It's going to be OK! The angel won! He felt like cheering as he saw Miss Clifton hold out the ring on the chain.

Her eyes were closed as she dropped it in the angel's hand.

When they opened again, the fury had reappeared in them. She stepped back as the angel's fingers closed over the ring.

She spoke with dreadful menace. '*Not by my own hand. Nor will I stay to see it done. But what I have decided is decided. Call it prophecy, Cassandra. Call it fate.*'

The angel only lowered her arm and looked away.

Miss Clifton twisted round and shouted something into the air, some kind of wild command or curse, or maybe just a scream of defeat. But it doesn't matter, Horace thought; she lost; it's over. And sure enough, she walked away – not her proper walk, but a weird gait, as if she was going on artificial legs, using the stick to balance. She shambled right out of the bubble of clear air, passing through its invisible wall without a pause, disappearing into the snow.

Horace sunk to his knees. Without realising it, he'd been holding himself rigid while he'd spied on the exchange. It was OK now, he could breathe. The angel – he really had to stop thinking of her like that, it wasn't right for her at all: she was more like a cross between a homeless person and a Zen monk – was cradling the ring in both hands, her head bowed. She looked at peace. It was OK. It was finished.

For some reason he remembered now what she'd said: *Of all the men and women and their children, you are the very last . . .*

The prophetess was looking towards the tree. She'd seen him, surely. It was the first time he'd seen her face properly. The look in it was so old, so old. Old as the hills.

A dark shape appeared in the snow at the far edge of the bubble.

A dog walked into the clearing. A massive black dog. Horace froze.

The woman knelt down in the snow and bent her head.

The dog stared at her and bared hideous jaws. Its mouth burned like the gate of hell. It leaned back a little, muscles bunching, legs bending to spring.

Horace's hands flew over his face. He curled himself into a tight and quivering ball at the base of the tree.

There was an awful, brittle snap.

Twenty-five

At the moment his unsought inheritance came to him, Gawain was creeping through the wreckage of what had once been his aunt's living room. He'd just about persuaded himself that the tree-woman was definitely either burned or gone when a wild wordless cry came from outside.

He threw himself into the dining room, rolled across the floor, grabbed another length of wood and jammed it into the fire. But there was no second cry. No one came in. Breathing hard, he got to his feet, holding the burning brand beside him, and looked out of the house.

Snow already lay thick enough to cover everything, and when he stepped over the splintered remains of the door to peer out, the flakes lashed at him as if the wind was using them for a weapon. He shielded his eyes from the assault and looked for something to see, but the whole world had vanished. He couldn't even see the roof of the house.

Then the blizzard hesitated for a moment, as if drawing breath, and in that small respite he glimpsed a looming shadow further out from the door.

It didn't move.

He took three steps towards it. His bare feet sank into the powder without pain, without feeling anything except crushed geometries of ice. The shadow was forked and branched. He stopped, heart pounding, and realised there was nowhere to flee to. Ten steps in any direction and he'd be lost.

But the cry had sounded like a death.

Had he slain the monster? Was that who he was? Gawain, conqueror of beasts? He edged towards the bulky silhouette. Already its windward side was coated with a long stripe of snow. Now he saw the spots of red, the only colour in a monochrome world. Its mouth was open in a frozen scream.

It didn't look burned, but it wasn't moving at all. Gawain edged closer, fascinated despite himself. The snow covered enough of it that you could almost believe it was only a tree after all, one of those weird lopped and rotting stumps that looks like a person from the wrong angle.

He got too close, and then the head moved.

'Your day has a bad beginning, little lord,' it said.

The shock made him drop the smoking branch. It hissed as it flumped down into the snow. He didn't even think of bending to pick it up again. There was no escape. He was in reach of the lashing arms.

The head watched him, tilting. A tumble of snow shook loose from its crown of flowers and was whisked away into the blizzard.

'No need for dread.' Its voice carried above the surge and moan of the wind. 'Right boy, wrong boy. No longer the boy I'm sent to fetch. You have a more fearful enemy now, White Hawk.'

His heart was going like it would explode at any minute, but for some reason Gawain found it impossible to be as afraid as he ought to be. There was something different about it. It wasn't attacking him for a start, but no, that wasn't the real difference. Something about its voice.

It sounded sad.

He said, 'What did you call me?'

'By your name, once-boy. White Hawk. Hawk of May. Take to your wings and flee.'

Its voice was so beautiful that you couldn't be frightened when it was sad. There was a music in it that washed away any feelings that didn't harmonise.

'You're Holly,' he said, edging closer, and then yelped as the raised limbs stirred. They curled round in a graceful wide arc to meet at its hips, where the green woman's torso met the mottled bark-skin below. It bent over them. A bow, he realised, amazed. It was making a courtly bow.

'Holly of the bright berries. Holly of the white flower. Wintergreen Holly, queen of all the trees that are in the wood. And you, the unbelieved, you marvel at your own name. You frown at my greeting. Get you gone, while yet you can.'

Somewhere far in the back of his mind he recognised this as good advice. Get away from it all: the snow, the wind, the impossible creatures, the terrors and the threats. Find somewhere to hide, wait till it blows over. Wake up in the morning and everything will be back to normal.

Never again, he thought. No going back.

'What are you doing here?'

'Warning. Will you flee yet?'

'You were trying . . .' He came a little closer. 'In the house. You tried to hurt me. Now you want me to run away.'

'I am bound. I was commanded. Fetch the boy, the witch's ward. So, I sought you. But now you are unwarded, and I warn you away. And you delay, and delay. The once-woman will find you, if you stay.'

A metallic chill struck through him at these last words.

'Who?'

'Names neither help nor harm. Go while you can.'

'I . . .' Even the wind with its white freight seemed to be trying to push him back to the gate. He bent his knees to balance, resisting. 'I can't. I won't.'

Holly laughed, a single peal of disbelief. 'Such valour, once-boy? So bold, little lord? So quick to forget your fear?'

'Where can I go anyway?' he whispered, half to himself.

'Who can say? Who can say?' Holly's singsong voice rose into a weird carol. 'Not Holly, not I. Holly cannot prophesy. Holly cannot guess or lie. Ask me not how time may go. Words are not tools for such as I. We speak only as we know.'

He gaped at it, mesmerised by the sweet urgency of its song, unable not to notice the green swell of its breasts as it stretched its head up to serenade the storm. It was the most appalling and the most beautiful thing he had ever seen.

It slid towards him, ploughing furrows in the snow. He flinched, but there was no point running; he'd seen what those thorn-fisted limbs could do. It came to within an arm's reach and leaned down close.

Each tiny white flower in the cluster that circled its skull was pronged, four-petalled, blushed with the faintest pink. What should have been skin looked like polished stone, the kind of surface you find on a river pebble, so smooth that its hardness feels soft. There was a shape like a cheekbone, but no bone made it. The lips moved and changed the contours of the face, but the motion was more like flowing water than the stretching of muscles and skin. Its mouth opened wide and for a moment it was perfectly still, as if drinking the frosty cloud of his rapid breath.

'My master rules me,' it murmured slowly, measuring its words as though explaining something very simple to someone very stupid. 'He will punish. He will cleave me to this tree. I will be unfree. But you, once-boy, he will slay. Murder is done already.'

'Your master?' Gawain stammered, in a daze. 'Who—'

A distant howl fetched over the wind. Iron dread twisted in his stomach. Muffled though it was, he recognised the sound.

The black dog was somewhere near, and it was hunting.

He stared around wildly, his trance broken. Into the house? But the door was smashed, there was no refuge there. In every other direction he saw nothing but a grey-white curtain. He thought Holly was humming, *Flee, flee, flee*, but maybe it was only the surge of the wind, the flakes whistling past his ear. Dizzy with fear, disoriented, he lurched a few hurried steps away from where the howl had come from. Almost at once he found himself with no bearings at all. He might be running into the beast's jaws. It could be anywhere, screened by the blizzard. He'd never see it until it was on top of him.

A strangled squeal came from behind. He twisted round and saw a blurry shape falling into the snow near Holly's trunk-feet, flailing, yelping. 'Small boy, wrong boy,' the tree sang, and as the shape righted itself Gawain saw that it was indeed a child, arms thrashing, shrieking out incomprehensible words from a throat constricted by terror. Fighting to scramble through the thickening drifts, the boy backed away from Holly, then spun round, tripped over his strange long coat and fell into the snow again right beside Gawain. At once he pushed himself up and rammed his head blindly into Gav's chest, sending them both sprawling.

The howl came again, much closer.

'Wait!' Gawain shouted, as the boy tried to scramble away on all fours. To his astonishment he saw it was the Chinese kid, Horace, almost unrecognisable with his hair caked with snow and his face bloodless and terror-slack. Limbs windmilling, he shrieked as if the furies were at his heels.

Gawain had time for no more than that instant's astonishment before a rippling black shape appeared at the edge of visibility. With impossible speed it grew and gathered and became the massive dog, hurtling towards them, white spray flying up from its paws, eyes bright as headlamps, fiery spittle trailing from its open mouth like sparks struck from flint. There was a sound like a rattle of stiff leaves, and Gav, whose mouth had opened for a scream he never had time to utter, sensed rather than saw something huge come falling out of the blizzard to his left. The dog sprang. He fell backwards. The thing whistled in front of him and struck the beast down as if it had run into a wall.

It was Holly. Its other limb was already sweeping down as the dog tried to rise to its feet, thudding into its flank and knocking it sideways.

'Get you gone, make haste, run,' Holly sang. The limb pressed down on the furious animal, pinning it in the snow. 'Maybe you'll return. Go!'

'I—'

The face with the blood-red eyes swung towards him and shrieked, a single wordless note with a force like a fist. Gawain spun away, lost his footing, fell again. He'd tripped over the kid, who was sprawled in the snow, motionless as if he'd been shot. Without thinking what he was doing, Gav wrestled his arms under the body and hauled Horace onto his shoulder. One glimpse of the unmanning terror on the boy's face had been enough for him to know he couldn't leave him there. Horace had passed out completely, a dead sodden weight, but he was a small and wiry kid and Gav managed to lift him. There was a continuous grunting and gnashing behind, the sound of the dog's struggle. He staggered away as fast as he could. By sheer luck he ran into the driveway after only a few steps. His bare feet felt the pitted road under the snow instead of grass, and though his head was spinning with panic and the snowfall still blanked his view in every direction he could at least work out which way was uphill, towards the gate. Carrying Horace in a wet tangle over his shoulder, he forced himself up the slope, keeping the buried track under his feet. The inert body bumped and banged against him, and after only twenty steps the weight felt as if it might pop his shoulder out of its socket. He ploughed on, away from the snarling and thrashing. Abruptly a grey wall rose in front like a silent wave: the laurel hedge. There were the gateposts, and a ribbed pattern in the carpet of snow that had to be where the cattle grid was. He turned round the gatepost into the lane and the south-west wind struck him full in the face.

The snow tried to burrow inside him, into his panting mouth, his ears, stinging his eyes, finding every crevice in his clothes. He strained his ears for any sound from behind, terrified that some pursuer was following through the murk, but it was impossible to hear anything else now. There was no sign of the road at all. There was no sign of anything except stems and twigs in the hedge, fractured inches not yet blanketed. He dragged his legs through a heavy sheet of nothing. He told himself it wasn't far to the crossroads, and just below where the roads met he'd seen the outermost houses of some village. Anywhere safe, anywhere normal.

The barrier between him and madness felt thin as a sheet of ice. Each step became its own odyssey. Hauling one leg up, swinging forward, the dead weight on his left shoulder a fraction heavier each time, like a rack turning by inches, then staggering down into the snow again, fighting the impulse to fall. Only desperation kept him going. Anything could be coming through the blizzard. He'd never hear it or see it till it was on him. The agonising passage, step after step after step, seemed to make no difference. The sea of white stretched ahead and waited patiently for him to sink. He began to doubt the crossroads still existed, or the village he thought he'd seen. The storm might have wiped it all away, erasing the world, leaving only hideous impossible things. He was in a nightmare of clutching urgency and slow motion. He'd had bad dreams like this many times, when you had to get somewhere but couldn't and the more you struggled the heavier the invisible manacles became. Those dreams had come true now, like the other ones. Fire and blackness and the end of the world. The fire and blackness were close behind, snarling, raging.

He thought about dropping Horace so he could run, but it couldn't be much further, surely it couldn't, and despite the burning ache all down his left side he didn't have it in him to leave the kid to be buried alive in a blizzard, or worse. If he was even alive. Horace flopped on Gawain's shoulder like a sack of potatoes. His weird long coat kept bunching up in Gav's face and dislodging snow into his eyes. It didn't matter; he could hardly have been more blind anyway. There was nothing to see even when he managed to raise his head against the relentless wind. Even the broken spackle of twigs in the hedge was close to vanishing now. He panicked when he saw that; once there was only unbroken grey-white in every direction, what would he do? There'd be nothing to do, nothing but stop where he was and fall to his knees and wait to die.

A shape coalesced out of the spinning chaos. An object, some indication of an enduring world. He struggled the last few paces towards it, no longer caring what it might be. Each breath burned more than the last. He knew that unless he found something other than the blizzard there would soon be no more breath at all.

The object stuck out from the hedge like a low wall. Two more excruciating steps and it turned into a car, motionless in the road, already caked on the windward side with a deep layer of snow. Collapsing in the tiny patch of shelter it gave, Gawain remembered passing the crashed car at the crossroads on his way towards the gate. He'd reached the junction, then. The village wasn't far away, but he was finished. He couldn't raise his head into the wind again, and now he'd dropped Horace at last, his arms and shoulders were perfectly clear that they wouldn't be picking him back up. Anyway, how could he go where people were, ordinary people? If there were any left? And there was a refuge right here.

He hooked freezing fingers around a handle and wrenched. The car door came open, sending a sheet of snow down onto Horace. The kid was limp as a corpse. Gav tried to feel his neck, but his own fingers were so numb they'd never have been able to detect a pulse. There was something there, though, a metallic touch, a silky movement and a thin gleam. Blinking, he saw the silver chain of a necklace tucked inside the comatose boy's jumper.

Gav got his arms under his shoulders and shoved him up into the back seat of the car, then slid him all the way along the seat, into a strangely quiet haven of cold blue twilight. The windows on the other side were completely blanked by snow. There was no warmth, but being sheltered from the wind was almost as good. Gav brushed snow away from the kid and examined his slack and colourless face. Air stirred weakly around the open mouth. Not dead yet.

For the first time Gav wondered what Horace had been doing at Pendurra.

Reminded of what had been chasing him, he backed out of the car, slammed the rear door shut and crawled into the front seat, closing the two of them in. It was an old and battered machine, smelling of rubber and cheap plastic. He locked all the doors. The key was still in the ignition but nothing happened when he turned it. He wriggled across to the passenger seat, leaned back and was still.

The only sound was his hoarse breath. The storm was almost entirely muffled. The snow that had battered him now shielded him, making a blanket against wind and cold. He squeezed his hands between his thighs. Even that much effort was almost more than he could sustain. Through half-closed eyes he looked at his bare feet, pink-white and blotched with sickly veins. His trousers were stiff with damp. Between breaths he listened to the tenuous flutter of his heart.

He tried to think, but there was nothing for his thoughts to latch on to. *Lost in whiteness.* The words floated in his head like skywriting, fraying into mere cloud. He'd forgotten where they came from. There were lots of words drifting around with them, other words, equally meaningless, blank as snowflakes. *White Hawk.* He'd reached his limit of incomprehension. The world within him was as blank, as silent and erased, as the world outside.

Spent, rudderless, he sat in the defunct box of metal and plastic, a senseless child stretched out across the seat behind, while the snow went about its work of burying him, burying them both, them and everything else.

His breath quieted. Its rhythm became thin and soft like sleep. Idly, he wondered whether it wouldn't be a better idea to keep moving. There was something he had to do, something that still wasn't a dream, though it seemed like everything else was. But that would require energy, and his was all gone, and also it would require having somewhere to go, and he didn't, he had nowhere. No home and no hope.

The cold didn't sting as bitterly as it had. Now it spread through him like an embrace. Don't go to sleep, he told himself. You weren't supposed to go to sleep; that was bad. You got too cold, you went to sleep, you never woke up. Gone, like Miss Grey. Don't go to sleep. He wiggled feebly in the seat. The weight of his eyelids was unbearable. Don't go to sleep. The sibilant murmur of the word was like a lullaby hush. Don't sleep, sleep.

* * *

Less than half a mile away, Owen Jeffrey sat alone in the front pew of a village church, staring at the altar. The church was quiet.

It was always quiet. Even when he conducted the parish mass here every other Sunday, even when it was warmed by its dogged complement of the faithful echoing the responses and singing the hymns with their slightly embarrassed conviction, there was an underlying silence that wouldn't be shaken. All these old country churches had it. It was packed in among the timbers of their ceilings; it seeped out of their memorial tablets and bell towers and lady chapels. It was a thousand times deeper and more persistent than any congregation's reflex devotions. Nothing dented it: no children's services, no support group meetings, no midnight masses or Advent carols. The silence flowed back and drowned them.

The silence of the missing voice, it was. The absent ghost haunting every church. The silence that listened to their hymns and liturgies and prayers and entreaties, and answered – nothing. Nothing, ever.

It sang in Owen's ears. *There's no one here. There's never been anyone here. The church is empty, the altar deserted. There will be no reply. No one's coming.*

No one was going to answer him. Not even today.

He'd been alternately sitting and kneeling there all morning, since before the snow. The clock above had struck ten, eleven, twelve. No sign yet, not even a still small voice. No light from above.

He'd entered the church in brilliant sunshine. Now it was twilight-dim inside and the wind hummed around the tower. He ought to be getting going, he thought, though it wasn't clear where, or why.

He'd very much hoped that someone would tell him what to do now that the end of the world had arrived. But God was keeping his counsel, same as always. Everything else had changed, but not that.

Or maybe he'd already had all the instructions he was going to get. They'd been clear enough. Unmistakable, delivered by that exquisite voice, and painfully simple.

Go. Do not return.

Was that it? Was that all he needed to know, at the end of the world? Just to get out of the way?

Of course – Owen closed his eyes and shivered – that wasn't all he'd heard. Before he'd reached the gate, before it had seen him and turned to him and told him to leave, he'd heard the singing.

His lips opened and he chanted in a small cracked voice:

Rorate coeli desuper et nubes pluant iustum.
Rorate coeli desuper et nubes pluant iustum.

He wanted to recall the music of the chant as he'd heard it that morning, carolling over the sunlit fields like a blessing. It was like trying to remember a dream of flying.

That was when he'd known the end of the world had come. When he'd heard a voice no human creature could possess, singing the Advent antiphon inside the gates of Pendurra. Really there'd been no need to go any further, no need to look in at the gate and see the . . . the creature planted by the lodge.

He knew the song, of course. He'd warbled it himself in his services just that Sunday. The Advent invocation, pleading for the descent of heaven to earth.

Drop down, ye heavens, from above, and let the skies pour down righteousness.
Drop down, ye heavens, from above, and let the skies pour down righteousness.

And here were the heavens falling, the sky pouring down its relentless embrace. Owen looked out of tall windows and saw the torrent of snow.

That's the justice we've earned, he thought. Cold, silent, deadly.

Same as always.

He stood up wearily and made his way back to the door.

'Still nothing to say for yourself, eh?' His voice came with the faintest stony echo, as it did when he delivered his sermons. He'd come to think of it as the sound of the church swallowing his words, the way it had swallowed generations and centuries of sermons before him, absorbing all their pieties into granite. 'Not a word? Nothing? Not even today?'

The night before, he'd been assailed by a fragment of the darkness, whirring like a storm and croaking like a death rattle. And then in the morning, in the sunlight, when he'd finally plucked up courage to go back to Pendurra, he'd passed his wrecked car, turned in the gate and seen . . .

The end of the world.

No more than a mile up the road there was a thing eight feet tall with arms and legs of knotted wood and an evergreen face and a voice of liquid gold.

It had looked at him. It spoke to him. It told him to go away. And still God wouldn't answer his prayers. Not so much as a shuffle of His feet or a clearing of His throat.

He sighed and headed for the door. There was no point praying any longer. 'All right, then. Have it your way.'

Outside, the storm assailed him. No letters of fire were appearing in the heavens. No grim horsemen rode by, thundering out the good or bad news. The dead stayed safely tucked up in their coffins. Judgement was descending as obscure and characterless as the snow.

One more try, he thought. He'd head up there one more time. Tristram and Marina and Caleb and Gwen were his friends, after all. He wasn't sure how much that mattered any more. But what else was there to hold on to?

Rorate coeli desuper. He hummed it to himself breathlessly. *Et nubes pluant iustum.* He went home for his coat and scarf and wellies, and then back out to endure the falling sky.

Gawain dreamed of a forest.

It was a huge, airy, mossy forest of cedar and hemlock and ferns, lush with the moisture of a grey ocean nearby. The smell was of ankle-deep pockets of pine needles and rotting bark, gathered in the hollows of lichen-spotted boulders. At first, in his dream, he had not himself been in the forest, observing it instead as if it was a picture. Then, gradually, it gathered him in. He grew aware of its clouds of mosquitoes, its damp air, its undergrowth of saplings striving for light. Then he was trying to pass through it, out to the shore. There was a strong and disturbing feeling of familiarity, which grew and grew until it seemed to be the whole point of the dream, and he heard himself saying out loud, 'Is this where I came from?' He knew it couldn't be so, because of the tall straight trees and the nearby ocean, but nevertheless he shouted out the question in fear. Miss Grey answered him: *It's where you're going.* He was tremendously relieved to hear her voice in his dreams again, because for some reason he'd been afraid she was dead. He couldn't see her, though, so he began searching through the forest. He came out onto a long strand of smooth round pebbles beside an ocean inlet, littered with bleached dead wood, and there she was, sitting on the stones, her back to him. In the dream he thought how strange it was to see her somewhere so unlike anywhere he had been before. The name of the place came to him: *Tsaxis*. He came over the shore towards her, but now it wasn't her after all. It wasn't even a dream; it was an actual woman sitting on a real shore, the shore of Tsaxis, looking out seawards. She turned when he called. She was a young Eskimo woman in a furred hood. Miss Grey had said her last goodbye.

He woke up thinking he was still stranded on that shore, with the cold of the ocean all around him. He was a boulder, curved and hard. He wondered where the ocean girl was. She could turn him back to flesh.

The ocean girl was far away. He felt strongly that he needed to find her. Only when that feeling came over him, carrying its charge of urgency, did he wake up properly. He jerked upright in the seat of the car, looking around in confusion for the thing that was missing. Gradually he remembered where he was, alone in the cold little box of blue-grey light.

Alone.

He sat still for twenty seconds, piecing together what he thought he remembered, filtering out the vivid intensity of the dream, making quite sure that he was right about the fact that there should have been someone with him. Then he turned round slowly and looked into the back seat.

Horace was gone.

Twenty-six

THE WOMAN WHO was no woman leaned on her staff, pulled her strange garments tighter around her strange skin and looked down pensively at the other woman, the one who was dead.

Snow had all but submerged the corpse. Only one stiff arm stuck out, rigid fingers open, the hand that had taken the ring mockingly empty.

The wind had calmed in the last few minutes. Snow fell thinly and perfectly straight. Still, the woman who was no woman would rather have waited inside the house. Her clothes were inadequate to the winter, though in the absence of the wind the cold had abated. But she could not bear any more waiting.

She faced the snow and shouted a word.

'Corbo!'

Around the edge of the garden, trees crooked black fingers at the invisible sky. She scanned them, brushing smears of wet hair away from her eyes, until the shadow appeared. It angled towards her, growing huge, and landed, raising puffs of snow to glitter on its feathered thighs.

Foul as it was, the woman felt a horrible lurch of envy. It swept along the air with such dark grace, where her own flesh was cumbersome and weak. It eyed her, head swivelling. She thought she detected resentment in the animal gaze.

'Acknowledge me,' she commanded.

'Master.'

She swallowed, cleared her throat. When she had been a man, it had never occurred to her that speaking was an action of muscles and flesh, like walking. The woman's voice was as hard for her to use as the woman's limbs. She loathed the sound of it. A woman's voice. How could that be suited to command? (*Johannes, turn.* She shivered, but not with cold, and thrust the memory away.)

'You have not found the thief, then.'

'No no.'

'One child, alone in this storm, and you cannot find him.'

'Never saw.'

The woman lurched closer to where Corbo stood. 'You try to evade me again, puka.'

'No no.'

'You do. Your tongue is as filthy as the rest of the flesh I gave you.'

'Hungry.'

'Do you think I care for your carrion appetites?' It ruffled feathers, loosening a white dusting from its impenetrable black. She thrust her chin angrily toward it. 'If I have no use for you, I will let you starve.'

'*Wraaak,*' it cawed, bobbing its head.

'Do you understand me?'

'Yes yes.'

'There are torments worse than hunger, puka. I can summon them with a word.' She brandished her staff as she made the threat. 'Answer me without evasion, plainly. Where is the boy who fled here with the witch's ring?'

'Never saw. Saw track.'

'His track in the snow?'

'Yes yes.'

'So you know where he has fled?'

'Out. Past gate.'

'Then why did you not pursue?'

'In box.'

'Box?' she echoed, before she could stop herself.

'Big box. Dead thing. Track to it. Not past.'

She straightened her shoulders as best she could. She would not allow her confusion to show. 'Why do you not watch this . . . this box?'

'You called.'

Most of all she hated its voice, the inflectionless grating croak that always sounded as if it hid contempt. She regretted having conjured such a thing into existence. But she had been alone and helpless, ignorant as a newborn, her staff not yet recalled from the sea; the mistake was pardonable.

'You watched it until I called? Just these last minutes?'

'Cold. Cruel wind. Long watch.'

'And saw nothing?'

'Nothing in. Nothing out. Only snow, *kkraaaa*.'

'Then why—' She pressed her lips closed, swallowed, coughed. She must not ask weak questions, as though she were helpless without it and the dryad. She must not let it think that. Know that.

She began again, choosing her question carefully. 'What of my familiar?'

'Stuck,' it said.

She shook snowflakes from the lank tangle of her hair. The beast stared back at her, passionless. *Stuck?*

'Repeat yourself.'

'Stuck.'

'Explain yourself!'

'Stuck. Can't go.'

'The familiar?'

'Yes yes.'

'What has halted it?'

'Holly.'

'What?' she blurted. Her foolish woman's mouth. She bit her lip, anger rising, as it repeated its answer.

'Holly.' As though she were deaf, or stupid.

'You tell me the dryad has . . .'

Impeded her. Betrayed her. She could scarcely believe it. She would have suspected the puka of some trick, but it was not capable of lying, and both question and answer had been without ambiguity. She stared at it with loathing.

These abortions. These spirits forced, at her will, through the passage she commanded, by the virtue of the ring, into substantial flesh; these miscreations whose only reason for existence was to do her bidding, how had they so much as conceived of defiance, let alone dared to defy her?

'Where,' she croaked, 'is the dryad?'

'Gate.'

It had been a bad mistake. Awaking from death, in a dark chamber of a dying world, she had reached out with the power of the ring and acted on an impulse of fear instead of wisdom. The servants she had conjured were poorly chosen. Puka and dryad, lesser spirits, mere exhalations of the crude earth. They should have been as far beneath the notice of the greatest magus in the world as the filth of a midden. She should have left them insubstantial.

It was past time to show them what obedience meant.

'Follow,' she ordered. The puka ought to witness what she would do. When the ring had been recovered from the Cathay brat, there would be ample time to look around and choose her attendants more wisely. And meanwhile the familiar at least would obey, as that fiery spirit always had, bound to the staff she had summoned back from the seabed. Though it had found flesh without her knowledge or her choosing, it was the same spirit and served her still. It had dedicated itself to her service long ago. It had not even named its payment.

(Unaccountably, she shuddered. Corbo let out a soft rattle behind her, *krkrkrrr.*)

The crow-beast stalked behind her as she staggered to the woods. Perhaps she should have ordered the old man to clear a path through the snow, but he appeared even feebler than she was, good for nothing but slumping in his chair with his dead eyes, only animated when he wept for the girl he called his daughter or appealed to the once-woman with a name that was not now hers and pleaded for things she could not understand. She struggled along until she gained the cover of the trees. There the way became somewhat easier and she could raise her head and stride more purposefully up towards the gate, or at least as purposefully as her woman's flesh allowed. The puka's silence behind her was like a laugh behind a raised hand.

She thought, I must regain the ring. Only let me be the keeper of the doorway to the eternally living realm and all obstructions will melt away as easily as these snowflakes on the back of my hand.

But as she ploughed through the deeper snow towards the house by the gate, the sight and sound she met there drove all assurance away.

The sound came first, a muffled thrashing and a stifled rolling growl like faraway thunder. She saw the gruesome outline of the form the dryad inhabited, one of its limbs pressed to the whitened ground. Beneath that limb writhed a snarling black blur.

'Stuck,' Corbo explained behind her, unnecessarily. 'Strong arm.'

The woman who was no woman was for a few moments speechless and motionless with astonished rage.

'A boy,' the dryad sang out. She heard it easily though it was facing away. 'A small boy, and out of his way. Your beast bared its teeth, Master. Must more necks be broken?'

Its wheedling unlocked the anger that had frozen her tongue. 'Release it!' she screeched. At once the limb curled up and the black dog sprang out of its cavity in the snow like shot from an arquebus, scattering white spray.

'Master—'

'Do not speak! Do not move! I forbid—' She gagged on her fury and bent, coughing. The dog let out a brutish growl, shaking snow from its head. Its legs sank deep. It came to her in short leaps. She gathered her breath, almost as furious at the weakness that left her spluttering and crouching in front of these inferior things as she was at their treachery. Her familiar twisted its sleek muscled bulk around her legs, flame like drops of orange quicksilver spilling from its mouth and leaving dark stains in the snow.

'Saved a life,' Corbo muttered.

She turned to it, slowly. Her breath was racing.

'What do you know,' she began, 'of human life?'

'Short,' it began. 'Hungry—'

'Silence!'

The beak-mouth snapped shut.

It deserved nothing from her except commands, yet she could not help herself. She spoke slowly, tightly, her shoulders shaking. 'You.' She pointed a thin finger at the puka, then jabbed it at the dryad behind. 'You . . . creatures. Are nothing. Dirt. In the great order of creation you stand scant rungs above mere vacuum. I raised you. I gave you body.' The finger curled to her own chest, where the ring had hung. 'I did! I gave you mouth and limbs. I elevated you to substance and speech. You may not—' Her voice rose to a horrible squawk; she choked it, forcing herself to maintain the dignity of a master before his servants. 'You may not question me. You may not judge what I do, nor presume to speak of life to me. Silence!' The jutting mouth had opened. 'Listen!'

Gathering herself, she approached the dryad through the churned snow. Its two long limbs trembled and flexed, then swung suddenly, so fast that Corbo shuffled back with a startled caw. But they could not strike the once-woman. They swept up at her sides and came to rest above, barbed shadows against the sky.

'A mere boy.' Holly's whisper might have melted ice. 'An innocent.'

The woman who was no woman had expected wheedling and pleading. Long experience had taught her how such beings would beg for the things they had forfeited, or avoid the things they promised. She was becoming colder by the minute. She had no time for it.

She spoke the word that named the dryad, which she had learned as she wore the ring on her finger, and would not now forget. The tree wavered as if the earth it stood in had quaked.

'Hear your punishment.' She hated her tongue's clumsiness. Her man's mouth would have delivered the judgement with august finality. She sounded instead like a cackling witch in a stroller's play. 'I gave you those arms and that mouth. You used them to defy me.'

'Holly hauled down the hunter. Never you said—'

'Be still!' It came out as a bark. By what corruption of the natural order did this mannequin think it had the right to argue with its maker? 'You know the familiar serves me. You were not free to let the boy escape it. I will remind you of it for ever. You will not leave the spot where you chose insurrection. Your roots sink, now, and fasten you here.' Holly quivered again, stretched its neck up, the mouth working in silent agony. 'You will see, and speak, and raise your abominable limbs to the heavens. The earth will feed this body I gave you. You will live for ever within it and never move. You will remain always what you are now.'

A long, bitter groan came from behind her, *kraaaaa*. The sentence enacted, she turned to go.

Holly's voice rang out at her back.

'As will you, man-woman, as will you. The unsuckled breasts. The blood in the bed. The itch in the loins, the itch! Do you feel it, man-woman? Does the tender flesh there flame with it?'

Fury exploded within her, so hot it almost made her blind. She spun round, but her clumsiness betrayed her, and she slipped and fell face down in the snow, landing at Corbo's feet. Panting, she pushed herself to her knees, trying to shake the long hair away from her face. Wet snow plastered it to her cheeks and eyes. It clogged her mouth; she spat and coughed. Intolerable humiliation thickened her tongue. She couldn't speak the command to silence Holly's mockery. It sang on as she struggled to her feet.

'Woman unknit all your wards. Woman woke your talisman. Woman found the mirror of your vanity, where your old soul hid. Woman welcomed it, warlock. Are you not grateful?'

She managed at last to paw the stringy hair off her lips. 'Silence!' she tried to shout, but it came out as a choked squeal. She felt her temples throbbing as she limped towards it, leaning heavily on her staff. She wet her lips, reached her free hand out and held it in front of the green face, spreading her fingers.

'It is,' she began, deliberately slowly to prevent herself screaming like a harridan, 'a woman's hand.' She drew in a long breath. 'It did not understand what it did, when it unsealed the great enchantment by which I overcame death. It was ignorant. Weak, reckless. This whole world has fallen into ignorance and decrepitude.' She leaned closer, her breath hissing between clenched teeth. She knew she ought not to waste words on the dryad, but fury boiled inside her and spilled out.

'Since I woke in it I have heard the sky roar with a noise like a thousand furnaces. I have seen the near horizon lit at night as though hellmouth were open beneath it. I have seen comets riding the lower sky. They pulse like hearts. Monstrous leviathans rear misshapen backs above the waves. The air itself is tainted. This world is a stinking marsh. Its woods and fields are shorn of life as if the plague had visited them. I thought only the wisest and worthiest master of the latter days would be able to find what I safeguarded. Yes, it was this woman instead.' She waved her hand in front of the green face. 'A mere woman. Mock me for it, then.' She could not stop her voice rising. 'Mock this hand, but it still masters you.' She clenched her open palm into a fist. 'Taunt and rail as you will, you will never stir an inch from this place, and the spirit that you are will rant and weep in its wooden prison until the world itself is gathered for the last judgement. You will have time enough to remember my power. The world may have forgotten it, but my art endures.' She lowered her fist, her rage cooling. 'I am its master, and yours.'

The dryad had not moved. Pleased at having quelled its insubordination, she was beginning to regain her proper magisterial calm when Holly spoke again and shattered it.

'Not so.'

Raw with cold, her hands began to shake. She thought she must have misheard, and before she could control herself, she grunted out, 'What?' like the dullest apprentice.

'Not so. It is not so.'

The world was mad. She must not have awoken in the true world at all; that was the only explanation. She was in some degraded copy of it, blemished by incomprehensible sounds and sights and lifeless simulacra of living things, a purgatory of lost virtues and decayed powers. A place where lesser spirits contradicted their master. That it had been capable of disobedience at all was startling enough, but she put that down to her own pardonable carelessness. She had known nothing of what was around her, barely even known herself, when she had bound it and the puka to serve her, to protect her from her ignorance of the place and time to which she had come. But to hear it speak against her from its own mouth . . . She was so astounded that she almost forgot to be enraged.

There was another thing, a thing she could not forget; but she refused to remember it, she would not even entertain the thought. *The spirits cannot lie.* She would not think of that. She would not.

'Not your master?' Her voice quaked with the effort of not shrieking. 'Move, then, if you can. Strike me. Drag yourself out of the earth I have fixed you in. Let us see whether I command you or not.'

'You mistook your mastery. It is not yours.'

Tchok-tchok, muttered Corbo, behind. The magus was frozen with sudden doubt. *It cannot lie, it cannot lie.*

'What do you mean?' She was horrified to hear her mouth say the words. What was this spirit, to be interrogated by such as her? 'Answer me!'

'Mistaken, mistaken,' it sang, sounding gleeful. 'It flees you, Master.'

'The ring?' She blurted it out like a threatened child. 'Answer! Do you speak of the ring?'

The silhouette moved at last, limbs twisting and waving like a pair of giant serpents coiling over her. 'Holly sings the beggar's ring, the living gift, the stolen thing.' And it was indeed a kind of song, a threnody of sweet despair. 'Holly saw it come to light, but stolen still, still unrequite.' It swayed towards her and she shrank back, fearing that it would topple, but its roots were deep. 'Another owns it now, by right.'

The chill had eaten inside her. *It cannot lie.* Now it touched her heart. She felt as if her soul had withered again to a hand's breadth of cold metal.

'It is mine,' she said in a halting whisper. 'No other is worthy of such a talisman. It was offered to me and I accepted it.'

'Not! So!' Holly's voice pealed with triumph.

To be interrupted was more than she could bear. Her scream of inarticulate fury silenced the dryad. Meeting its vermilion eyes, she began to croak the spell that would send her fiery minions like an insatiable flame inside the living heartwood and make the dryad suffer the torment of damned souls. But her borrowed mouth betrayed her. Gagging on her own words, she choked like a slaughtered animal, struggling for breath, bending double, clutching her staff for support. As she tottered in the snow, the picture of her utter humiliation suddenly shone clear to her. She saw herself, a stumbling, gaping, bedraggled, female wreck, an object of scorn to her own servants. The rage shrivelled into despair.

Miserably, she thought: I must learn what it knows. I must endure its taunting. So begins my penitence for what I had to do.

She was spared the shame of having to ask the dryad to explain itself. While she hauled herself straight, wiping the dirty hair away from her face, Holly spoke again, now in a gentle murmur.

'The gift passed to another, Master. Today, as the bells struck twelve. A new day begins. You it was, Master, who made the old day dark. You broke your word and you broke your world. But now the stolen gift belongs to a boy-child. Kin of the flesh you bear. Did you not know him when you saw him?'

'Stupid boy,' Corbo added.

Defeated, unable to muster any answer at all, the magus stared at the mocking green face.

In her mind's eye she was seeing again the body in the snow. Had she ended the prophetess's inconceivably ancient existence for nothing? She remembered how she had loved her with a man's body, a man's love: the splendour of it, the marvel. The magus had never shrunk from the endless pursuit of knowledge, nor ever feared to take any step that led higher into the regions of hidden wisdom, no matter what the cost; but surely she had never done a greater and more awful thing than casting down her once-beloved. Could it really be possible that she had been somehow thwarted?

And yet, she thought with a shudder, the spirit cannot lie.

'The ward,' she whispered hoarsely. 'You mean the ward, the ward of . . .'

'The ward of her your hunter slew. The boy, a sister's son, a simpleton.'

Her anger and her humiliation had spent themselves together. Something worse was taking hold now. A cold, dull feeling, murderous as a blade.

'Where is this boy now?' The abomination appeared to hesitate. 'Answer!'

'Can't say,' croaked the dark voice behind. 'Don't know.'

She turned carefully. Corbo looked back at her sidelong.

'The boy you allowed to go from the well,' she said. Slowly she was beginning to grasp the depth of the disobedience these vile miscreations had practised. 'Though you knew I wished him kept there.' She turned back to Holly and pointed her staff. 'The boy I commanded you to watch for and bring to me, though you brought another child instead, the Cathay brat whom I left for dead.' Thwarted, thwarted by children and monsters. Oh, how they would all suffer. 'The brat who stole the ring and fled from here, with your help.' The chill inside her hardened into determination. 'This is the boy you mean?'

Neither of them answered.

'Speak. Is that the boy to whom you say the talisman's power has passed?'

'No power,' Corbo said, and at the same time Holly began reproachfully, 'Only truth lives in the tree-tongue. Holly—'

'Answer, slave! Is that the boy you spoke of? Yes or no?'

'Yes.'

'Yes yes,' Corbo echoed, fluffing its folded wings.

She gazed at the hideous things she had made until the cold made her eyes water. Deep inside, she was wondering where exactly everything had gone wrong, and how it had come to this, but those thoughts were buried like leaves at the bottom of a frozen pond.

'Then,' she said at last, 'I will destroy him too.'

Snow fell placidly around them.

'More necks,' Corbo muttered.

'Yes.' She rounded on it. 'Yes, puka. More necks will be broken. Man or woman or child. They will die in the snow and be left for carrion like the witch. Perhaps you will tear their flesh yourself, if I permit you to eat. Or perhaps I will starve you until this loathsome flesh you wear withers and rots. You and all others who obstruct me will learn what it is to oppose me. Do you understand?'

'No no,' muttered the puka.

'No,' hummed the dryad.

She rode over their soft answers as if they had not spoken. 'I alone can bring life back to the world. I alone. I will not be denied. I will not.'

The black dog had made its way to the entrance of the lodge, among the splintered remains of Guinivere Clifton's front door. It broke the silence that followed the once-woman's speech, raising its head and spitting out a bark.

She turned to it with relief. She still did not know how the fiery spirit had found this dire form to wear. There was a magic in it she did not recognise, something ancient, earthbound and godless, dark as the northern forests, reeking of death. But she saw that the familiar obeyed her in its new flesh. Without prevarication or hesitation, it followed her will. That was her only concern now. That, she saw, was the essence of magic: mastery. Nothing mattered in the end but command and submission.

The dog was nosing around the wreckage inside the house. There was something there, a black satchel strangely marked. Growling, the dog lunged as though it had spotted a rat. It came up with a piece of fabric in its jaws. Foggy with the aftermath of her fury, the once-woman took a while to understand what it had found.

'Puka.'

'Yes yes.'

She gestured towards the dog. 'Is that a garment?'

'Blue thing.'

'Yes! Is it a garment?'

'Yes yes.'

The dog dropped the shirt it had snatched from Gav's bag, which was still right where he'd dropped it the first time he'd entered the house, just inside the doorway. It sniffed at it, then stepped over the bag and leaned out of the house, swaying, tasting the air.

'To whom does it belong?'

'Stupid boy.'

'What? Answer clearly!'

'Boy. Ward. What Holly said.'

The woman gripped her staff and took a moment to compose herself. Her lips felt rigid with cold and despair. When she was sure she could trust her woman's mouth, she spoke the beast's name, the word that named the black puka she had conjured into the bird. With brutal pleasure she felt it pulled into her grip, as if the syllables were a cord she had jerked tight round its neck.

'Fly,' she ordered. 'Go at once. Search again for each boy, the thief and the ward. Do not touch the earth or anything that grows in it until you can bring me news that you have seen one child or the other, or until you are called. Keep searching even if you must fly until your flesh starves.' She turned away. 'Go.'

She heard the rustle, and then the great thuds as its unfolded wings battered the air, quickly fading high and to her right.

Holly keened softly, so she addressed it next.

'Be silent,' she said. The gentle groan died instantly. 'After I leave you here, you will not open your lips in my presence again. Not another word. Not another sound.' She did not even look at it. 'Acknowledge it.'

'Master,' Holly whispered.

Last, she turned to the dog.

'Pursue the boy who stole the ring. The Cathay boy. Find him first.'

'Small boy,' Holly murmured. 'Wrong boy. A sapling merely. Ignorant, innocent.'

The woman did not even trouble herself with its complaint. She went on as if its words were no more than perfumed air. 'Bring me back the talisman. Then you may pursue this other scent.' The dog stabbed its muzzle at Gawain's shirt, pawed the cloth. 'Hunt it. Kill it.'

Holly wailed wordlessly. The woman who was no woman raised her voice to drown it out.

'I will not,' she said, 'be denied.'

Twenty-seven

ALL AROUND the river, things had come to a stop.

To the west and north, snowploughs were out on the main roads. Trails of headlights crawled along behind them. People stuttered and slid their way indoors. Below, in the valleys that twisted down to the river's sheltered creekheads, the blizzard was impassable. Vehicles had been abandoned. Livestock knelt with their heads down, waiting for the grass to come back.

Surely, everyone thought, it wouldn't stay like this much longer, although no one had predicted it and for some reason the weather people weren't able to say when they thought it would stop. In fact they didn't seem to be able to say anything about it at all, other than talking about a 'freak storm', as if that turned their bafflement into expert assessment. In the house neighbouring the Jias's, Myrtle Pascoe tutted as she and the nice man from the newspaper listened to the latest bulletin on the wireless.

'Well now, that isn't much help is it?' he said, in his pleasant Irish brogue, as she switched off the set. (For Myrtle Pascoe, any Irish accent was a 'pleasant Irish brogue', the same way any country vicar was a 'dear old thing' and any three-year-old a 'cheeky little monkey'.)

He sipped the extraordinarily weak tea she'd provided him, marvelling at the speed with which its tepid warmth radiated out through the paper-thin china, leaving the drink with the overall character of a half-hour-old bath run from a rusty tap.

'Looks like I might have to book myself into the Red Lion for the night.' They'd have coffee at the pub, he thought. In mugs. He'd have to quarry some kind of story out of the trip so the paper would let him expense it, of course. But even if the mad prof next door wouldn't talk to him, he'd have no trouble coming up with something. Weather emergencies were always reliable that way. Come to that, if this old biddy kept going as she was, he wouldn't even have to get his shoes wet. It felt like she'd already told him the life stories of half the people in the village. He'd covered six pages of his notebook in doodles while she banged on.

'Dear, oh dear,' she twittered, leaning forward in her chair. 'Oh goodness me. Look at it coming down. There'll be dreadful trouble on the roads. Oh I do wish Hester would get back. She had hardly a stitch on when she went out this morning. I mean,' she added hurriedly, 'not for this weather anyway, though it was fine this morning, wasn't it. That's what's so peculiar. Glorious. They said it was going to be fine all day, I'm quite sure. I listened to the early bulletin. I don't always sleep as well as I used to, you see, Mr Moss . . .'

Take cover, he thought. Here comes the stream of feckin' consciousness again.

'. . . It's one of those things when you get old like me . . .'

Almost time for emergency-exit procedures. He was pretty confident the stream wasn't going to throw up anything more about the prof next door. He'd never thought there was much of a story there anyway. It had all been his editor's idea. Professor H. Lightfoot's mad as a box of frogs, she got the sack, so what? Feckin' typical of Vicky to send him off to try and squeeze an interview out of a lunatic.

He was saved from having to make a run for the door by the ringing of Mrs Pascoe's phone. Spotting his chance, J.P. Moss set down the saucer and began ostentatious preparations for departure: hand-rubbing, briefcase-packing, the works. He had his coat on and his hat in his hand by the time he realised the call was something to do with his quarry next door.

'Well, this is the terrible thing, you see,' Mrs Pascoe was saying, making eyes at the phone as if it could transmit some digital impression of immense sorrow. 'I've been trying myself, all day. I've tried and tried, oh, I don't know how many times, but you see, I think she must have unplugged her phone. Poor dear, you can understand it, can't you – after all the . . . Oh yes. All right. Yes, all right, Mrs Jia – you needn't worry. I'll get a message to her.' She nodded meaningfully towards J.P., or at least he supposed it was meant to be meaningful. 'Yes, of course . . . No. No one could possibly expect you to be there in this dreadful weather. Dreadful! You think of the money they pay those weathergirls on the telly nowadays. Honestly I don't know what's happened to the BBC, I really don't . . . No. Shocking. Ever since that lovely old fellow retired, what was his name, you know the chap, he always used to wear those cardigans . . . Oh. Yes. All right then, Mrs Jia. Yes, I'll take care of everything . . . Yes . . . Goodbye, then. Bye. That's Mrs Jia from next door.' The flow changed course from the phone to J.P. without interruption. 'Such a dear. Chinese, you know. I can't think how she manages. She called to say she's stuck in Falmouth and won't be able to come to Hester's house this afternoon. She does some cleaning in the village, it helps her keep body and soul together. I don't know that Hester needs the help, really, now that she's . . . Well, anyway, it's a kindness, isn't it? Not having the stress of work on top of—'

'It surely is, Mrs Pascoe, it surely is. Can I help at all?'

Flustered by the interruption, Myrtle Pascoe lost her thread. Her hands groped inexpressively. 'Oh. Ah. Well, you see, Mrs Jia asked if I could just go over with a note to let Hester know she won't be coming after all. We've all been trying the phone but she must have switched it off. But with my old legs in this snow, you see, I wonder, perhaps . . . if you wouldn't mind terribly . . .'

'Not at all,' J.P. said, with his most accommodating smile. 'Why don't you just write that note and I'll pop round and ring the doorbell.' He was already late for lunch. The pub might well stop serving early in this weather and then he'd be royally buggered. He extracted his notebook from the briefcase, tore a page from it and handed Myrtle a pen. 'It'd be a pleasure.'

'Oh, thank you. Thank you so much. Oh yes, now where did I leave my specs? Oh dear . . .'

J.P. kept the smile in place while she fussed. Concentrate on the bright side, he told himself. His car would be buried and the roads were hopeless anyway. There was every chance he'd be overnighting at the pub. A couple of pints out of his own pocket to get him through the afternoon, and the rest of his bed and board courtesy of that fine organ the *Western Cornishman*, God bless it.

He got out of the house without being further delayed by Mrs Pascoe's increasingly chaotic mix of apologies and farewells. Prodding carefully in the snow, he made his way across the lane to the mad prof's house. He rapped on the door a few times just in case, but though Mrs Pascoe was far from the most lucid of witnesses, she'd been very clear about the fact that she'd seen her neighbour heading off out of town before the blizzard arrived. There couldn't be any chance now that she'd have made it back. She'd be hiding out somewhere warm and dry if she had any sense at all. Just like he should be.

He poked the letterbox open and slotted in the piece of paper. It occurred to him that he couldn't remember repacking his notebook after tearing the page off for the old baggage's message, but the very last thing he was going to do was expose himself to another ten minutes of the Pascoe Monologues. He'd go back later if he had to. After he'd fortified himself with a couple of rounds of something a lot stronger than her abomination of the name of tea. Though thankfully that wind had let up. At least a fellow could see where he was going now.

The pub turned out to be more or less empty, which meant he could pick his spot by the blissfully authentic fire. He was just about dry and relaxed and content when a tinny rendition of the Darth Vader march struck up inside his briefcase.

The boss. He dug out his mobile, giving it a doleful stare before answering.

'Your wish is my command,' he said into the phone, and then a moment later, 'Ah, I felt sure you would, Victoria my dear. So what have you got for me?' He listened for quite a while and then began miming eye-rolling despair in the direction of the ceiling. 'Well now,' he told the phone, 'it is indeed not too far, but there's the small matter of the Helford River between here and there. Plus, as your finely honed editorial instincts will have noted, there's a feckin' blizzard out there.' More listening, with his eyebrows raised. 'Of course, send it along. I'll take a look . . . Is it? . . . Sorry, run this past me again. What is this fellow saying? . . . Right. And how drunk was he at the time? . . . Yes, yes, all right. So since we can't find lunatic number one, this bloke will do as a back-up, is that it?' Ah, humour. He ought to know better by now. He sighed while the phone chattered crossly, wondering what terrible childhood accident had got the broom handle wedged so far up Miss Victoria's backside that she made even average everyday English uptightness seem positively mellow. 'All right . . . Yes, I'll have a look at it and then see if I can track the fellow down.' Right after the steak and ale pie, that is. 'Send it along. I'll let you know.'

He snapped the phone shut and took a moody swig from his pint. As promised, the phone beeped again, this time with the chime that indicated the arrival of a message. He flicked the tiny screen up and watched the photo assemble itself. All right, he thought wearily. Let's have a look at whatever's got Vicky straining at her lead. There's a path and some trees – that's all clear enough – and someone standing on the path, a young fellow it looks like, back to the camera. And the other thing, the thing the young fellow's facing, is . . .

Is . . .

He cradled the phone and bent over it, then shifted a couple of seats along so that he was next to a lamp at the end of the bar. He stared at the tiny image for a long time.

The black shape stared back at him until he could no longer bear its gaze. He turned the phone face down onto the counter of the bar, his hands shaking.

Struggling down a track of virgin snow, Horace tried to push every idea out of his head except one: getting home to his mother.

Other thoughts kept trying to break in, terrible ones. Mum would make them go away. Mum would sort everything out.

He went as fast as he could, but it was hard going, even for him. Trying to run through the deep snow was like wading in chest-deep water. Still, at least he was going downhill now, and at least he knew the way. When he'd come round, he'd had no idea at all where he was, except that someone had knocked him out and tossed him in the back of a car. He'd lain very still for a long time, afraid to move. When nothing happened, he began lifting his head just inches at a time, listening hard, and that was how he saw that other kid slumped in the front seat. It looked like he was dead. Through the gap between the seats he could see bare feet like a corpse's.

He knew right then he had to get away. He couldn't remember what was going on, but he knew it was crazy and bad and he had to get out of it. He slithered along the back seat and reached for the door. He noticed he was covered in the cloak thing, which meant that bit at least couldn't have been a dream, but forget all that, he told himself, forget all that, just get out of here. Leg it.

The door had opened with a scrape of dislodged snow. He tipped himself out almost soundlessly. He was groggy with cold and confusion and his head throbbed but he still knew how to move without making much noise, especially now he was escaping from kidnappers. It was a conspiracy, he remembered that much. He wasn't worried about what Mum would say any more. She'd just be glad to have him home. He wrapped the cloak around him once he was out of the car. As he fastened it round his neck he touched a silver chain. The thing he'd taken from the angel's dead hand, the ring on its chain, it was still tucked inside his jumper. So some of that hadn't been dreams either, though they couldn't have been anything else. The snow made everything confusing. It fell straight and soft, like static in the air. Forget it. Get going. None of it could be right. Mum would sort it all out.

But which way was home? The car he'd just crawled out of had crashed into a hedge. Made sense. That kid had kidnapped him, crashed in the snow, killed himself. And thank God he'd crashed at a junction because there was a signpost and Horace had been able to work out where he was.

He pressed on faster, down the clogged road.

He made it to the village at last. No one was about. His boat was still there, right where he'd left it. The sight of it almost made him feel himself again. It sat on the whitened shingle, tilted over. The rising tide was maybe ten minutes away from tickling its stern. He jogged down towards the bridge and the mouth of the stream. The screen of snow was by now not quite thick enough to hide the opposite shore. He could just about see the moored boats, the pub, the ferry landing. Long familiarity with the tides told him it was around two in the afternoon, give or take an hour. He was nearly away. Whoever or whatever had done this to him, he'd almost escaped them. Forget about all of it, he told himself. Forget about ever bothering with that freaky place again.

He was kneeling on the foreshore, scooping armfuls of snow out of his boat, when a guttural howl ripped through the air.

In that one moment Horace's tenuous determination blew away like dust. He looked wildly around the harbour. Up on the road above he caught a glimpse of a blurry black shape, moving. That was enough to set him heaving and dragging the boat down the few feet towards open water, gasping, swearing. His bladder loosened and soaked his crotch. The hull scraped the stones with a noise like grinding teeth, and the howl answered, closer. His hands shuddered and slipped and his legs lost their footing, but terror also gave him a frantic strength and at last he forced the stern into the shallows. He splashed after it, pushed and ran until he was knee-deep in the river and flung himself into the boat. His relief at discovering he'd forgotten to lock the outboard was so intense he almost fainted. His hands were shaking like a drunkard's, but it was only a moment's work to fumble out the pin and tip the propeller down into the water.

His head swivelled madly from the outboard to the foreshore and back again. Tears stung his eyes; he couldn't see properly. The terror was like a living thing inside him, a squirming maggoty knot. He managed to get hold of the throttle and twist it, but the handle of the starter cord kept slipping out of his grasp. He swore in a constant choked whisper, keening in agonised frustration each time his fingers failed him. On the fourth or fifth attempt, he got his fist around it. He yanked.

There wasn't even the slightest cough from the motor.

He pulled the starter again, ferociously, and then again, so hard that his hand flew free and he lost his footing. The boat yawed wildly. He got up on his knees, shaking snow off his face, and saw a black stain spotted with firelight on the bridge above the mouth of the stream.

Hope, desperation, everything, drained out of him. His face was smeared with tears as he crawled back to the outboard. He hunched over it as if it held the world's last warmth. Pulling the starter again and again, he looked back at the shore, and whispered, 'Please,' a pinched and dry whisper, as if the jaws were already closing on his throat. 'Please. Please.' But the outboard was silent. Something was wrong with it, it had died completely. He heard the scrunch of pebbles. The blackness had taken shape. He watched its burning eyes, and its unhurried steps, standing out against the snow. He wanted not to look at it, but it was impossible. The boat was drifting serenely, held near the shore by the tide. Horace imagined jumping into the river and swimming, or screaming at the silent village for help, or heaving the outboard off its hinge and using it to club the dog, but he did none of those things. His will had forsaken him; he was powerless as a baby.

The dog came down to the edge of the water.

Its lips twisted into a snarl. Fiery saliva flowed over them, spilled, slicked on the surface of the river. It stared, measuring the distance for its leap. Then it paced backwards, steadily, deliberately. Its hind legs tensed and began to quiver. The boat was drifting further away from the shore. The dog sidled after it, keeping the shortest distance, and pawed at the snow for a better grip on the shingle beneath. It coiled and crouched.

But the boat's idle drift had become a steady impulse. Smoothly, without current or engine or paddle, it was sliding out into the harbour, among the empty buoys and the few tethered vessels, carrying its shaking, weeping cargo towards the open river. The dog skittered forward, but the gap had become too wide and it pulled up short as it reached the water. It hesitated, then dashed into the river, only to stop again when it was up to its chin. Now Horace's boat was gliding soundlessly away, a widening arrowhead of silver ripples in its trail. Already it had passed the moorings. Daring to lift his head, Horace slowly released his death grip on the useless engine.

The dog shook itself as it came out of the river. It stared after the boat and then planted its feet, threw up its head and with a gush of oily flame from its mouth howled its thwarted rage.

There were neat indentations in the white plain outside the car. Gawain crouched to examine them. Fat flakes tumbled down noiselessly, already eroding the traces of Horace's passage. He didn't know how long he'd slept. The kid had vanished as quietly as if he'd never been there, leaving only the line of small vacancies. Gawain's dream shimmered behind the white landscape, like a mirage. Waking up hadn't banished it. He felt half asleep still, not sure which of the things he thought he remembered might also have only happened in his sleep. Only the lingering soreness in his shoulder confirmed that he'd actually carried Horace to this directionless crossroads. Now the kid was—

Lost in whiteness.

The words appeared inside him as if spoken by another voice. In his dream there'd been a voice at his ear, invisible. Miss Grey.

But Miss Grey was gone, wasn't she?

Lost in whiteness. You will bear it on your back.

What was the voice talking about?

You will lose it.

He put his hands over his ears. There was no one there. No one was talking to him. Miss Grey had never whispered over his shoulder.

Then, startlingly, he did hear something. The crunch and squeeze of footsteps in deep snow. He stood up, alarmed, remembering all of a sudden that he had an enemy.

A thickly wrapped figure was struggling up to the crossroads from the south. Gawain was about to duck out of sight behind the high snowbank piled against the car when it stopped for breath, raised its head and saw him. Gloved hands reached to wipe snow from its glasses, then pulled down the scarf wrapped over the lower half of its face.

'Gavin?' it said.

The combination of mildly perplexed voice and squinting scrutiny jogged Gawain's memory: Owen Jeffrey, the priest, the first person he'd seen at Pendurra, unless you counted Marina disguised as a corpse.

It was just the two of them, the white nothing all around. Gav thought he could still smell the pines, soft bark rich with rot.

'Not really,' he answered.

Padded in layers of clothing, Owen waddled up to him like an outsized toddler. His eyes travelled down to Gav's rolled-up trouser legs and bare feet, then back to his face. He frowned thoughtfully, as if an interesting possibility had just occurred to him.

'You're not God,' he asked, 'are you?'

'No.'

The priest shrugged, apparently a little deflated. 'Oh well.'

Gawain waited for him to go away. Owen was peculiarly passive, though. There was that inexplicable tranquillity about him that occasionally comes over mad people.

'I don't suppose,' he began after a moment, 'you'd be able to explain' – his cocooned arms spread – 'this?'

'No,' Gav repeated, and then, seeing the wrinkle of disappointment, 'Sorry.'

Owen looked up. The snow went on around them, quietly relentless.

'Do you know what the word "apocalypse" actually means?'

'No,' Gav said a third time. 'I don't.'

'It's Greek. It means "unveiling". Literally, taking a cover away. Lifting the lid. That's what's happening, isn't it?'

Gav thought about what was happening. 'I'm getting cold,' he said.

Owen's eyes refocused. 'Oh yes. Sorry. Is this . . .' He waved at the car. 'Have you been . . .'

Gawain stepped round to its sheltered side. If he closed his eyes for even a moment, if he so much as blinked, he could feel the atmosphere of the ocean-fringed forest. He was light-headed with exhaustion and cold and something else, something that had scooped him out hollow inside and unmoored him from the world.

'I came up past here this morning,' Owen said, as Gawain climbed in the back seat. He spoke in a mildly conversational tone, as if neither of them should be at all surprised to see the other, as if nothing had particularly changed since their first encounter. 'On my way to . . . Ahh. There.'

Gav folded his arms and tucked his chin down. The priest leaned on the open door, looking around irresolutely.

'I got as far as the gate. This morning. I just thought I'd stop in and let them know what . . . Anyway, I looked in the gate, you see. Where. It.'

Gawain could almost see the sentence curl up and die in his mouth.

'It told me to go away. It had a voice like an angel. It sang.'

When Gav didn't answer, Owen sighed, came to a decision and got himself in the driver's seat, wiggling awkwardly as he loosened a couple of his layers. 'Do you mind?' he said to Gav's reflection in the rear-view mirror.

Gawain didn't mind anything at all. That was part of the light-headedness. Everything was fading away from him, going out of focus. He wondered whether he ought to be going after Horace to make sure the kid was OK, while there were still tracks to follow, but then he didn't know how long ago the kid had snuck out of the car. *Lost in whiteness.*

'The thing is, I know the words. Of the song.' Peeling off a scarf, he chanted something churchy-sounding in a wavering voice. 'It's an antiphon. That's a piece for a choir, sort of a call and answer. It's the one for Advent. We had it last Sunday in fact. It's about God coming. "Drop down, ye heavens, from above and let the skies pour down righteousness." She sung those words. They're from the Bible. Isaiah. A prophecy about when God comes back to the earth. That's why I, er . . .' He twisted round and looked hopefully at Gawain. 'Anyway. I'm sorry if it seemed a weird question.'

Gav was trying to hear another voice. *It will come to you today*. He rubbed his forehead. He felt he ought to be able to make Owen disappear just by blinking. Gone in the blink of an eye, like Miss Grey.

Owen shrugged, wiggled in the seat. 'I always knew, you know.' He glanced at Gav in the rear-view mirror. 'About . . . there.' Finding no encouragement, the glance slid away again. 'Pendurra. I've always known it was . . . different. The one place God forgot to turn off the miracles. Well, I don't know. Perhaps there are others. You read about marvellous cures and children who see the Virgin. Perhaps there are lots, but people don't talk about them either. You keep the lid on. No uncovering, no Apocalypse.' He made the motion with his hands, pressing down. 'They trusted me to keep their secret; that why I'm their friend. But I've always known. I think really I knew even before Swanny came, when it was just Tristram by himself in that extraordinary house.'

Something tugged Gawain's thoughts, a nudge back towards the here and now.

'Swanny?'

Owen twisted round again, perhaps surprised that Gav had even been listening. 'You don't know about Swanny?'

'I don't know anything.'

'I thought maybe you . . .' Owen turned away again to contemplate the nothing in the windscreen. 'Swanny. Marina's mother. She . . . she wasn't like anyone else.'

Gav sat a little straighter.

'Marina said her mother died.'

Owen winced. 'What else could we tell her? How else could you say it? She was only a toddler, she couldn't understand anyway. It would have been all right telling her her mother was a mermaid. Any small child could accept that quite easily. But we couldn't tell her her mother had abandoned her.'

The dream was fading away at last, the day coming back into focus.

'A mermaid?'

Owen shrugged. 'It's just a word. Who knows what the proper name is? If there even is one. She came from the sea and went back to the sea. I don't know what she was. We don't have that sort of knowing. She was something amazing. We all loved her. Gwen loved her almost desperately.'

'Auntie Gwen?'

'So you are her nephew? That's who you are?'

Gawain didn't answer. A series of images gathered in his mind's eye, coming together. The white face rising from the water, silk married with stone. A black-and-white photo in a frame on a desk. Marina's face, with its elfin changes of mood. The three faces whispered to him together, barely audible but urgent. *Find my child.*

The creature in the water was Marina's mother.

She'd come to plead with him. She'd known something terrible had happened, and she'd beckoned him down to the water's edge and strained her airless throat to beg him to help.

A plucking tension tightened in the bottom of his stomach.

Swanny.

He shifted in his seat and reached into the back pocket of his trousers. Owen watched as he drew out the envelope and unfolded it, flipping it over. Auntie Gwen's scribblings were blotched but still legible, surviving fire and snow. Even the tea stain round what had once been his name was still visible.

Jess!!
chap girl?
(O.J.)
key chap Joshua Acres

well
Swanny's O?

GAVIN

Swanny.

'What's that?'

Gawain looked over the list again and then handed it to the priest.

'Is this . . . ?' Owen furrowed his brows.

'Auntie Gwen's writing. This was in her house. She wrote it right before she disappeared.'

Owen's lips moved silently as he read the notes down to the bottom. He glanced up at Gawain quizzically.

'Swanny's ring?' he said.

Twenty-eight

HORACE JIA WAS not a particularly imaginative child. In his inner landscape the sense of wonder amounted to little more than an occasional fuzzy intuition that maybe not everything would always turn out to look exactly as he expected. Since he preferred to think of himself as being right about everything, he tended to ignore it. Now, shattered and astonished, and having given himself up for dead – a feeling he could only recall with an odd sort of curiosity (*Oh yeah?*) as if it must all have been a confusing mistake – and then finding himself alive and apparently being carried home across the river, he'd passed so far beyond his limited capacity for amazement that all he could do was sit in uncomprehending silence in the stern of his boat and wait for whatever might happen next.

It was perfectly obvious that something was moving the boat.

At first he thought maybe a freakish current had appeared like the answer to a prayer and drawn him away from the shingle. But he was enough of a waterman to know there weren't currents like that in by the shore, and he'd discounted the idea completely once the boat had spun round at the harbour entrance and started moving with the same steady ease towards the far bank.

What happened next was a splash like a fish jumping, very close to the boat. It came from somewhere under the bows. Since the river was otherwise perfectly silent, he crept forward and leaned over the side to see.

A white arm reached out of the water.

With a stifled yelp, he shrank back from it and began clawing away the snow in the bottom of the hull where the paddle was stowed. He found the wooden shaft and pulled it out, raising it like a club.

He stood there, knees braced, panting, the boat still yawing drunkenly. Snowflakes spiralled round him and died silently on the river surface.

'Help me up,' came a liquid whisper from below.

Horace could not begin to guess who had spoken, but he didn't like the idea that there was someone near him he couldn't see. Paddle raised and ready, he leaned over the side.

Another arm had joined the first, and below them, half obscured by a waving mass of green weed, was a face, just breaking the surface of the water. The arms were slender, oily-smooth and bone-white. Their fingers fanned towards him.

'Give me your hand,' said the voice.

'Wha-what d'you want?' said Horace. What was going through his head was something like, I'm not putting up with this. They can't make me. I've had enough.

'Your hand,' it replied. 'Help me.'

'Why should I?'

The boat rocked violently. Horace dropped the paddle, windmilling his arms as he struggled to keep his balance. He failed, collapsing onto the thwart and knocking the paddle overboard. He flung himself half out of the boat trying to recover it, instinctively terrified of ending up with no oar and a dead outboard, but it bobbed just inches beyond his reach. Then as if sucked down by an invisible whirlpool it vanished beneath the surface. He stared wide-eyed at the fizz of bubbles where it had been. The head appeared there, sodden tendrils floating around it. He tried to draw back but he was too slow. Two hands shot up from the water and clasped one of his.

'Pull me up,' said the snow-soft voice, 'or I'll pull you down.'

The hands were cold. They felt more like scales than skin. They also felt strong. Thinking of his sunken paddle, Horace braced his other hand against the gunwale and heaved.

A pale body rose, accompanied by a silky rush of water flowing back into the river. For a moment he thought the weight was going to drag him back and drown him. Then its feet appeared on the gunwale, and with a peculiar swift twist he couldn't follow it – or rather she, as he now couldn't avoid noticing – flipped herself over the side and, releasing his hand, perched on the bows.

Horace squirmed inwardly at her nakedness, half revolted by her fish-white flesh, half mesmerised by its unblemished and glistening sheen. Hair like the trailing fringe of a jellyfish snaked down to her waist, making her a coral-patterned patchwork of pale and dark. She reached her bloodless arms forward and clasped her fingers together.

'Find my child,' she said.

Horace's mouth fell open.

He said, 'You what?'

'My child.' The voice wasn't actually a whisper. It had no breath in it. It was like a stream over rocks, sibilant and narrow. 'I've seen you with her. I saved your life so you can find her. I beg you.' With a slither of long limbs she came forward from the bows and knelt in the bottom of the boat, clasped hands raised to him. Her face tilted up, and Horace saw its wave-sculpted smoothness, and recognised it.

'You're . . .' It was unmistakable, but it sounded impossibly stupid. 'You're Marina's mum?'

'I was. I am. Help me.'

His cheeks burned despite the cold. He was acutely aware of her marmoreal shoulders, her flat breasts draped with curling fronds of hair, and a smell like the metallic tang of a pebble in a brook.

'Marina says her mum died.' He didn't want any of this to be right. He wanted this to be another thing he could run away from and forget as soon as he got home, another thing that would turn out to have been only a dream.

'To her I am dead. I still watch her, though. I watch for her every day. When she sits in sight of the water I weep with joy and pain. Now there is danger, she has not come and I can do nothing. You must help me.'

The steady snow didn't melt where it touched her skin. Her body gathered its flecks like sequins. Her eyes were milky, with a pearlescent glow of their own. Her hands unclasped and stretched tentatively towards his. 'I heard the hunter come down to the river, seeking my wedding ring. I slid under your keel and took you to safety. Haven't I earned your help?' The chill fingertips touched his sleeve. Horace flinched his arm away. He saw a ripple of anguish flow over the face. It reminded him instantly of Marina, how easily crushed she was.

'OK, OK,' he said hurriedly. 'Just—' He was about to ask her to stop begging and get up, but he imagined her body straightening in front of him and his mouth dried up. He looked away.

'If you were a grown man, you'd not sleep or have an hour's rest until you had done what I ask.'

He felt insulted, but he also felt utterly at sea. He wanted to retort that he wasn't a child any more, but he couldn't say it. He didn't know how to argue with a thing like this.

'Do you love my daughter?'

'Huh?'

'Would you die for her? I would. If I could become a woman again, I would let the warlock's servants rip my flesh only to set eyes on her now. Her birth was agony to me, but I would suffer ten times that pain every sunrise if that was the price that bought her happiness only as long as noon. Do you love her that much?'

Horace, beyond astonishment, could only think about his own mother. Did she want him to be happy? Did she love him? Why was she old and boring and on her own and too busy all the time and always bossing him around?

'Can't you just take me home?' he said, tears rising.

'You must promise first. Promise to return and find my daughter.'

Horace wiped his nose. 'Yeah. OK.'

'Promise it.'

'OK. Yeah. I will, I'll come back. Just let me go home now, please.'

'The world has changed and I'm strong again. I'll watch for you if those are empty words, and when you come to sea I'll find you and drown you.'

Horace stared desperately at the shore. It looked so close, but they were getting no nearer. 'I told you, didn't I? I will!'

'Say it. Say, "I promise."'

'All right!' Despite his half-stifled tears, Horace reacted the same way he always did when anyone tried to bully him. He lost his temper. 'All right, all right! I promise. OK? I promise!'

He turned away from her and started fiddling ostentatiously with the outboard. No one was going to threaten him. (He tried not to think about the paddle, swallowed as if the river was a grey crevasse.) He didn't care who it was, if someone wanted his help they better not talk to him like that. He yanked the starter uselessly a couple of times and swore. Out of the corner of his eye he saw her rising gracefully. He tried not to look, not to see her naked, not to notice the face that was so strangely like Marina's watching him.

'Only bring her to the river. Bring her where I can reach her and she will be safe. I'll bless you as long as you live, and the sea will never hurt you. Promise again.'

He was going to give some snarky retort, but instead . . . 'I promise,' he said, meaning it this time.

'You are mortal flesh. The warlock has no power over you. And you carry my wedding ring. Keep it close. Wear it if you must. Maybe it will protect you. Do you understand?'

'Yeah, course,' he lied. His fragile pride was all he had to go on now.

'Are you afraid?'

'Course not!'

'Good.' She stepped up onto the thwart, arched like the crescent moon – for a heart-stopping instant Horace knew he had never seen anything so beautiful – and dived into the water with a tiny splash. The boat swung round purposefully and set itself for the opposite shore, weaving through the moored boats, the snow falling lightly all around. He heard the soft swish of the bow-wave and mistook it at first for her voice: *Find my child, find my child.*

Owen handed the envelope back.

'Gwen was totally mesmerised by her,' he said. 'I think for your aunt Swanny was living proof that she was right about everything. You know, that the world really is full of mysteries. I think she loved Swanny almost as much as Tristram did. I sometimes think we all did. It was almost like you had to. You couldn't help yourself.'

Gav looked at the envelope in his hands, its few scrawled lines, so full of secrets. Marina's mother. Had Auntie Gwen known? She must have. She'd kept that photo on her desk. But she'd never told Marina. None of them had. All Marina knew was that she sometimes saw a white woman with green hair, watching her from the river. She was as ignorant of herself as Gav was.

He couldn't put the pieces together, but he was beginning to see that all of the seemingly indecipherable nonsensical words had meant something to Auntie Gwen. Something that had led her to the chapel with its evil light and its voice like dead leaves.

He traced the stain left by his mug of tea with a fingertip. Round and round, circling his old name. He tried to conjure a pattern out of the scribbles above, but nothing would come. He frowned and examined the top of the list.

Jess!!

'"Jess"? What's that?'

'A who, not a what, I think.' Owen sounded relieved to have something to talk about. Soon I'll go, Gav thought. A little while longer and then I'll go and I'll find her. 'Gwen was talking about her just this last weekend, so I assume that's who she means. I hadn't thought about it for ages. A woman who showed up on the estate, years ago. Happens occasionally. People take a wrong turn from the footpath, or perhaps they get curious. Usually Caleb just escorts them out. This one was different. She had an infant with her.' Owen blinked, remembering. 'Tiny, a newborn. They were both in a terrible state. God knows what she thought she was doing. I think she belonged to some religious commune up the valley and they'd thrown her out when she showed up pregnant. I'm not sure. It's a long time ago. She was homeless anyway, and she hadn't had anyone to look after her properly at the birth, that was obvious. She'd started bleeding. They got hold of me and we got her to the chapel, her and the baby.'

'The chapel?'

Owen took off his glasses and massaged his eyes. 'There's a tiny old private chapel off in the woods at Pendurra. Sixteenth century, I think. It ought to be a ruin by now, but it's not. Anyway. They built it over the site of a spring, and there's a well inside, or a sort of pool. They say the water from the spring is blessed. It's supposed to have healing powers.'

The water that makes you well. Gav winced. Marina had told him that already, but he hadn't listened. He looked out through the smudged window, wondering if the day was getting dark. Time to get going soon, he thought. Time to find out where she is.

'The baby survived. Amazingly. The mother did too, though she was in a pretty bad way. I wanted to get her safe somewhere but she disappeared with her boy. I've no idea what happened to them. No one seemed to know. I'd forgotten all about it . . . This was all before Marina was born. I don't know what suddenly got Gwen interested in it. Can I see that list again?'

Gav passed it forwards. Owen tapped the envelope. 'That must be me in the next line, in brackets: "O.J." See?' Owen Jeffrey: Gav had to concentrate to remember the priest's name. The fragments of old stories tumbled around him like snowflakes. 'I've no idea who that next person is.' Owen tilted the paper so Gav could see. '"Joshua Acres." If he's anyone. But "key chap" must be the key to the chapel. She's obviously thinking about the chapel anyway, isn't she. The "well" must mean the water there, the pool. And then something about Swanny. I'm not sure why the "O" made me think of the ring she used to wear. Maybe it's a name instead, I don't know.' Owen's look travelled down to the end of the list. 'And then.' He looked up at Gawain. 'You.'

Me, Gav thought.

Something had made Auntie Gwen think of the old chapel in the woods, locked because there was something important hidden in it. She sent Caleb away. She made her plan to fetch the key. And all somehow because of him.

He was afraid he might sit in the car until he fell asleep again if he didn't get started soon. He looked at the scarved and muffled man with his shell-shocked face and saw a member of a different species, a creature more strange to him than Holly.

He stretched his legs, aching with tiredness and deep-rooted cold. 'I have to go.'

'Oh right. Yes.' Owen looked embarrassed, an unwanted guest. He handed back the envelope and began tussling with the zips and Velcro of his coat. 'Me too. Though God knows where.' He pulled gloves out of a pocket. 'And he's not telling. Look, my house is just down at the edge of the village. Why don't you head there? It's not locked. You can get out of the cold, warm up.'

'No,' Gawain said. 'Thanks.'

'Really? It's only a little—'

'There's something I need to do.'

Owen watched him in the mirror for a while, then nodded. 'Yes, I suppose there would be.'

'I don't think you should go back there.'

Owen paused his clumsy battle with the zip of his coat. 'You don't?'

'No.'

His glasses had fogged. He looked suddenly helpless.

'Are they going to be OK?' he said. 'Tristram and Marina?'

Gawain saw the answer the priest wanted. He opened his mouth to give it, or something like it, but it wouldn't come out.

'I doubt it.'

Owen shrugged weakly and turned away. 'Silly question.' He opened the car door. 'Oh look, it's stopped. More or less.'

The lead sky had disburdened itself of all but a few laggardly flakes. A world of featureless white opened out at the top of the ridge. 'How about if I leave you my phone? If you need help or anything, you can just . . . call.' He withdrew a mobile from inside his puffy coat, offered it hesitantly to Gav and then put it on the dashboard with an apologetic shrug. 'You never know,' he said, as he swung himself out.

He surveyed the obliterated landscape for a while, then ducked his head back in through the door.

'If I ask just one question,' he said, 'will you give me an honest answer?'

Gav blinked out of his trance. 'OK.'

'Is this the end of the world?'

Gawain studied the man. He thought about it.

'The beginning, I think,' he finally said.

A shadow of pain crossed Owen's face. He nodded wearily and straightened.

'All right. Thank you.' He rubbed his gloved hands indecisively. 'Good luck, then.' And he was gone, scrunching back down the way he had come.

Gawain waited for the sound to die away. He flipped the envelope back and forth in his hands, looking out at the snowfield, wondering again what time of day it was.

The light seemed no less dim although the snow had cleared. Late in the afternoon, maybe. Dusk would come early under this covering of cloud, and the night would be dark as the inside of the locked chapel. He should have left before, he thought, instead of squatting dumbly in this dead metal box listening to the priest. He had things to do. He had to go and find Marina. This time he had to do it, come what may, hellhounds or living trees or worse.

He glanced down again at Aunt Gwen's hasty jottings, flipping the paper distractedly in his hands. The jotted words on the back, telling some story he couldn't understand, a story that had ended in disaster; on the front the typed address, looking so innocent. A stamp, a London postmark. The envelope had been neatly slit; he noticed the thin sheets within.

A letter. He frowned. Well, of course it was a letter; that's what envelopes were for.

A letter to Aunt Gwen, from London.

Uppermost in the stacked pile beside her chair. The first piece of paper to hand when she'd got whatever crazy idea had got hold of her and made her figure out how to get rid of Caleb and then go and get the key to the chapel. It must have just arrived.

He looked again at the neat brown ring circling his name.

He could almost see Auntie Gwen making her notes. It was something about the haste of the scribbles, the exclamation marks, the underlinings. It was so like the way he remembered her, haring off after her weird enthusiasms like an excitable dog after a squirrel. As if in a dream he saw her sitting in her armchair, the stack of paper beside, some sudden impulse sending her rushing for a pencil. Some train of thought that had ended in him.

But where had it started? What had set her off?

Jess!!
chap girl?
(O.J.)
key chap Joshua Acres

Gav could feel the tumble of her thoughts, one after another. She sees someone called Jess, or hears the name, or remembers the story. Jess, the girl who came to the chapel once, years ago. Owen Jeffrey knew about it. He'll be able to tell her. There he is: O.J. And in the meanwhile she wants to go to the chapel, so she reminds herself where they key is hidden. And then . . .

He thought of the figure in the poisoned firelight and shivered again. He couldn't bring himself to think of what happened after that. But what about whatever had happened before? What had got her going?

He looked around the back of the car as if Horace was still there. He was going to ask him to repeat what he'd told Gav and Marina in the woods. Gav hadn't really paid attention at the time. Too busy feeling sorry for himself. But he did remember something about Horace going and fetching a letter for Auntie Gwen. And after she'd read it, she'd been crazily overexcited.

A letter.

He was holding it. This was it. The top piece of paper, just arrived. The thing that had got her going, that had made her think of the woman with the baby and the key to the chapel and Swanny and (underlined twice, all capitals) Gavin.

He blew on his fingers to try and loosen them a little, then worked them between the sides of the envelope.

A handwritten letter. Gawain's fingers went still. He thought his heart did too; for a few seconds it seemed that everything stopped and the snow outside hung suspended like tinsel.

The handwriting was his mother's.

He took the letter out and unfolded it. There was the date, at the top. Last Thursday. *Thursday 24 November.* Mum was always so anal about including that stuff. That was the day Auntie Gwen's letter had arrived, the one he'd stolen from Mum's desk and read on the train. So this was his mother's reply. Posted Thursday. It would have arrived at the post-office box in Falmouth on Saturday, just like Horace said.

Dear Gwen

Thank you so much for coming to the rescue. I've been at my wits' end wondering what to do. This couldn't have come at a worse time for me. I feel like the worst mother in the world but I'm going to take you up on your offer. We had a friend all arranged for the evenings and overnight but she can't manage days as well and I can't bring myself to leave Gav at home by himself. I know I ought to cancel the holiday but we booked ages ago and you know how Nigel gets. He and Gav aren't getting along very well at the moment I'm afraid. It wouldn't have been a very happy week for anyone if we'd stayed. Gav will be on that train on Monday.

I'm sure he'll be fine for the journey. Really I don't see why he wouldn't have been fine at school. Given the amount we pay them I would have thought they could at least have kept him there while they talked to us. Of course he won't tell me anything about what he said to the teacher but he seems no different from always. Just please make sure he leaves messages occasionally. I made him promise but I doubt that means anything to him. I'll check the phone whenever I can.

You know, he'll be happier with you. You can never tell with him but I think he's really looking forward to spending a week down there. I hope the two of you have a lovely time together.

Gwen, I lay awake all last night thinking about this and I'm going to ask you a big favour. It's a terrible thing to ask but I'm at the end of my tether, I really am. Gav won't talk to me at all and Nigel's the proverbial brick wall when it comes to anything like this. I'm sure that must be why Gav talked to the teacher. He can see it's a dead end at home. He doesn't trust us any more. Why should he? When Nigel and I agreed to bring him up after Iggy died we never thought about the fact that we were agreeing to lie to him for ever, but that's what it comes down to. I just have this feeling now that I can't begin to be any sort of mother to him until I stop pretending to be the mother I'm not.

Of their own accord Gawain's eyes stopped moving. For forty heartbeats they dwelled on that one full stop. Then he read on.

Can you see what I'm asking? I swore I'd never tell him but I never swore not to ask someone else to. I'm such a coward. I know, I ought to sit down with him myself. But I promised Nigel. And – this isn't easy to write, Gwen – it will be better coming from you. Gav has so much of Iggy in him. They're supposed to be my genes too but you and Iggy were always much more alike. Gav would have been so much better off with you than with me. I really think it's time he knew the truth.

(*Truth hurts*, whispered a voice somewhere, a lost voice.)

Would you find a quiet evening to sit down and tell him? And tell him I asked you to. Tell him I want to try and start again. I don't know if it will help. But you're the only person I'd ever trust to be with him when he finds out.

I'm sure he'll want to know about his father too but Iggy never said anything about him. All I know is she was with some Christian place at the time. Funnily enough it was somewhere down near where you are now. Maybe I should have moved to darkest Cornwall too instead of being the sensible one who stayed in London and got the job and the husband. She was calling herself Jess, I remember that. You know how she always said Ygraine was too posh and Iggy was too silly. She wanted the baby to be Gawain though so she must have liked the Arthurian business more than she ever let on. After she died Nigel put his foot down and said it was a stupid name and made me change it. Like he makes me tell everyone my name's Isabel. I don't know if you want to tell Gav that as well. It seems fair somehow. I doubt his relationship with Nigel can get any worse so I can't see it doing any extra harm. I should have stood up to Nigel but getting him to agree to bring up Iggy's baby was such a battle I didn't have the strength for anything else. Gav can blame me if he likes. I deserve it.

Can you do this for me? Please do. You'll have to, because I'm going to tell Nigel you've done it. I truly don't know how he'll react but that's my problem. He hasn't hit me yet so I suppose I'll survive.

Oh and that reminds me of a small but horrible thing I should tell you. Nigel wouldn't let Gav see any of the postcards you sent. He intercepted them and threw them away. I won't try and explain why or I'll go mad. But just so you know, if Gav looks blank when you mention them. There. Now you know what my life is like. Funny isn't it, when we were growing up the story always was that Iggy was the evil twin and I was the good one. Little did they know.

Sorry for all the misery. This is what comes of not getting any sleep. I'll put Gav on that train and then at least I can spend my week thinking of him being happy. I'm so sorry to put this burden on you without being able to talk beforehand. Get a phone for God's sake.

Your failure of a sister

Iz

Twenty-nine

THE BOY WAS the only moving thing in a world suspended by winter. Bunched in the trees, crows watched him as he struggled up the lanes, bearing round his neck the door to all the magic in the world. They saw he was too small to carry such a burden and cawed their eager disapproval.

It was little more than a mile from the beach where he kept the boat to his house, but the steep rise from the river and the high lane clogged with snow would have made it a hard mile for anyone, let alone a numbed, freezing, unravelling child. By the time Horace reached the village his eyes were stinging with tears. The clamminess in his crotch had turned icy; his shoes were full of melting snow; he stank of sweat and misery. He put his head down so no one would stop him or talk to him. He counted his steps through the village to keep him going, twenty, then another twenty.

No one saw him but the crows. People were stranded far from their houses, or huddled inside them, barricaded against the storm. The half-daylight was beginning to fail. Wrapped in the prophetess's cloak, Horace passed their windows like a ragged shadow. Around him rose the white humps of buried cars, barrow-mounds of an arctic necropolis.

The crows murmured to each other in their roosts. A thought spread among them, a restless discontent mixed with excitement. In twos and threes they shuffled from their branches and dropped into the air, following the boy.

At the place where the roads met they rested on a roof of thatch. They passed their thought among each other in soft harsh trills. Under that roof, in the pub, John Patrick Moss cocked an ear, shook his head, flipped his phone up again for maybe the fiftieth time and made his fiftieth attempt to see in the picture it displayed something other than what was there. After a while he opened his briefcase to get out his notebook.

He couldn't find it. He remembered worrying he'd left it at the nosy neighbour's house. No choice but to go back out in the cold and knock on her door again before it got too dark. He stared unhappily at the last third of his pint and held his head in his hands.

The carrion birds waited for Horace to reach the joining of the roads. Their numbers grew. Their thought amplified. A memory was mixed in with it, a memory five hundred years old. They smelled it like a change in the wind.

The boy struggled past the pub, crossing the road so he wouldn't pass under its windows. Faint with exhaustion and hunger and disarray, he dragged himself down the lane, past Myrtle Pascoe's house and up to his own front door. He pushed a trembling hand inside the cloak, inside his school blazer, looking for the pocket where he kept his keys. His fingers felt like frozen meat.

The keys were not there.

Snivelling tears came faster. They dribbled into his mouth. He patted all his pockets, turned them inside out. His keys lay where they'd fallen, in a crevice between the back seat and the door of a crashed car on the other side of the haunted river, for ever lost. Horace bent double and gritted his teeth.

The house was dark.

He rang the bell but he knew his mother wasn't there. She'd gone out that morning. Working all day, like usual.

'Mum,' he whispered. 'Mum.' A crow sneered at him from the roof.

He tried to be brave. He tried to think. It was impossible. Horrible things had got into his head. He needed Mum to tuck him into bed the way she used to when he was little, light the nightlight and sit by his bed until the bad dreams went away.

She was never there when he wanted her any more. She was always too busy. Cleaning houses, helping people. Other people.

A small flicker of hope twitched beneath the weight of misery. Hadn't she said she was going to come back in the afternoon to help the professor with her unpacking?

Through the crystals of dirty tears clogging his eyelids he blinked at the house opposite. She might just have got back before the snow started. He tried to think when the blizzard had begun, but he couldn't remember a time before the snow any more, before the angels and the demons. It was his only chance anyway.

He dragged himself over the barriers of snow in the lane, squeezed himself past Hester's car and stood on the doorstep looking for the bell. The carrion birds wheeled silent and unnoticed above, a black and hungry cloud, waiting to break.

No bell. He knocked, hesitantly at first, then louder. No answer. Of course not. No one could have got anywhere in this snow.

He crumpled to his knees on the doorstep, his shoulders shaking. The little voice inside him that he'd always thought of as being his own was carrying on its usual boastful litany. *I'm brave*, it said. *I'm tough. I won't let anything beat me*. But he didn't believe it any more. He was just an abandoned child. He'd got so scared he'd wet his pants. He was freezing and soaked and terrified and he wanted his mother. He pulled the edges of Cassandra's cloak tight around him, wrapping his fists in it, and began to sob, while the expectant crows flitted down to the gutters above. He cried in little gulps of freezing air, each one stinging his parched throat. He wished the angel had let him die in the snow. He wished the nightmare dog had snapped his neck too. He wished the mermaid had drowned him.

Curling himself tighter and tighter, trying to clutch up inside himself like a snail in its shell, his fists pushed against the little lump hanging at his chest.

Keep it close. Wear it if you must.

His hands were so cold. He tunnelled them up inside his jumper. They felt the smooth circle looped on the silver chain.

Wear it if you must. Maybe it will protect you.

He remembered lifting the chain out of the dead angel's hand. Her palm had still felt slightly warm. He couldn't remember why he'd done it, except that she'd been kind to him somehow, and he didn't want that other woman to get the thing they'd argued over. Then he'd run, and then the dog thing had come after him.

Maybe it will protect you.

Under his jumper he curled the fourth finger of his left hand alongside the slender silver chain and slipped it into the ring.

The crows stirred on the roof, ruffling out their feathers and shivering. Horace

heard their harsh excited chatter, felt the forty pairs of glassy eyes on him, knew their eager thought. He heard the wind sough around them, heavy with approaching snow, threaded through with the influence of the hidden stars. He heard the caged and buried winter earth mumble in its half-sleep, ground bass to the whole concord of the coming twilight

He stood up.

There were other voices. Nearer. Single voices, together making a deep turbulent murmur. He wasn't alone any more. He was in company.

Come in, they said. *The door is open.*

The boy turned the handle of Hester Lightfoot's front door and swung it inwards. The slow-moving throng of voices spread around him. Behind its tightly closed blinds the room was almost dark, but that was all right. He stepped inside, among the masks, bearing the open door.

By a light that was not the grey remnant of the winter afternoon he saw the speakers of the voices. One of them seemed to single itself out and turn to him. It addressed him.

Water-child.

The sound of its unspoken words was deep, placid, without echo.

Bring me home. Take my way.

At once the boy knew the way it meant: a great, endless, open expanse, in which a tender and beautiful light was suspended, azure-gold above, indigo below; vast and free. His heart leaped at it. He strove to answer the invitation, seeking the one that had offered it. It turned to him, and

ma'chinu'ch

in the darkness he saw its oval-eyed, high-snouted wooden face, every curve and line the shape of an ocean wave.

Home.

Gawain sat with his legs outside the car. The letter lay open on the seat behind him. He stared out across a wide white emptiness.

The glow of Owen's phone on the dashboard was growing luminous. It was beginning to get dark.

Time to go home, he thought.

But before that there was one last goodbye to deal with.

His fingers were unsteady as he reached for the phone, though that might not have been because of the cold.

Each of the many times he'd fantasised about this moment, he'd rehearsed a quick, gleeful, perhaps even vengeful goodbye, succinct as a punch. Now that the time had actually come, he wasn't sure what to say.

He dialled the number, listened to the message, waited for the beep.

'Mum, Dad. It's . . .' He couldn't use the name they'd given him, but he didn't want to say the true one. 'Me.' He stopped, listening to the phone's soft echoing hiss, wondering if it was the sound of the hundreds of miles through which his voice was travelling, dissolved and beamed through the air, reassembled as a spectral sound in an empty house, a speaking machine. 'Nigel and Iz, I mean. Not Mum and Dad.' He felt the vindictive bitterness rising and swallowed it down. 'So. I found out who I am. Or at least who I'm not.' A few more seconds of the ghostly hiss. 'Anyway. Mum, you'll be the one who hears this. Don't worry about me, OK? I'll come and find you someday.' These words astonished him. He'd only meant to tell them that he was never coming home. 'It may be a while. Just try not to worry, OK?'

He started to picture his mother listening to this message, dialling in from some crappy anonymous hotel in whatever ski resort it was, like she'd probably been doing every hour she could get away from Dad, getting more and more anxious as yesterday passed without a word from him, and most of today, and now listening to this, her relief at finally getting a message turning so quickly into bafflement and shock and then a permanent hurt.

'You'll soon see why I left. Everyone will. You won't understand it, but . . .'

He closed his eyes. 'Anyway. Forget that. Just remember what I said, OK? I'm not coming back, but one day I'll find you. OK? OK Mum.' But he wasn't talking to Mum. He was talking to an artefact of plastic and circuitry. She wasn't his mother, anyway. She was his mother's twin sister; his mother was dead. Her grave was far to the east. *The sun rises on your mother's grave.* Miss Grey never lied, never. It was just that he'd never believed her.

'OK, bye then.' He took a breath, then said the word more gently, with care. 'Bye.'

When he brought the phone round to look for the button that would hang it up, he saw that its bland light had begun to dim of its own accord. The numbers faded. The little screen went dark. It had gone dead in his grip. He prodded some of the keys to make sure, but there was nothing in them. It had always been dead; it had just taken a minute to accept the truth from his hands.

There'd be no calling for help. There was no connection. The last tether anchoring him to his old life had been slipped. He tossed the phone onto the floor of the ruined car, down with Horace's keys and other bits and pieces, rags and junk, possessions and accessories and detritus, the graveyard of things.

On his way back to Mrs Pascoe's house to retrieve his notebook, this is what J.P. saw:

The sky came suddenly alive with a welter of black birds, swarming together. The air shuddered with massed wing-beats. Under their shadow a small thing with legs and arms and a huge misshapen empty-eyed head was disgorged from one of the houses and came barrelling out into the lane, flurries of snow sheeting up around its feet. It paused in the middle of the road, monstrous head swaying, long enough for everything J.P. thought he was sure of in the world to dissolve, and then it crouched and loped away.

Then all he saw was a village lane in deep snow. When he looked around himself to check that the world was still standing as it had a moment before, he noticed a disapproving elderly face peering at him from a window.

His feet were damp. J.P. tried to remember why he was standing there, the cold of the grave crawling up from his legs.

After a while it struck him that he probably ought to do something.

He thought about going back to the pub. His room was all arranged.

The radiator clanked and the back of the cupboard smelled of piss. Could be worse. A few more drinks and a night's sleep and in the morning he could start again. Tomorrow is another day.

But he knew, all of a sudden, that there'd be no sleep for him that night, and he knew that tomorrow would be nothing like today, nothing like yesterday, nothing like all the days he'd known up until that one. Not unless he turned on his phone and discovered that the picture was gone and in fact had never been there at all. Not until he could persuade himself that his own eyes hadn't seen what had just appeared in the street, right here, right in front of him.

He tried the second tactic. (The first hadn't been working very well, all afternoon long.) He walked up to where the thing had appeared and studied the snow.

There were footprints. They were small, a child's, and deep. They were fresh. He knelt down and touched the delicate rim of flakes at their edges, feeling the tiny stings of cold on his fingertips.

The footprints came out of the crazy woman's house. He looked across and saw its door swinging open.

It would have been easier to bear if it hadn't been for those prints. Then maybe he'd have blamed it on the pint he'd had with his lunch, or maybe the other one, or the stress of work, or a trick of the light. But there they were, neat, clear, deeper at the toes to show someone was running, perfect hollows of shadow in the silk ribbon of the lane. They stretched out ahead of him like an invitation.

'Ah Christ,' he muttered aloud. 'You're going to regret this, J.P.'

He balled his hands in his pockets and set off in reluctant pursuit.

On a white page, Gawain was a speck of spilled ink. The cold had penetrated him so deeply it had become an irrelevance. He went barefoot through the snow, keeping his eyes mostly on the sky. The birds had abandoned it. Eastwards, ahead of him, its murk faded to iron-grey. Dusk was coming.

He wondered whether his mother had walked down this same road, fifteen years, a month and fourteen days ago, carrying him, bleeding. He wondered what had driven her into the woods. He wondered what she'd known, what she'd hoped for.

He ought to have been afraid, but he wasn't. He thought about that too. It occurred to him that the perpetual swamp of low-level fear in which he'd passed his life for almost as long as he could remember was, when you got down to it, the fear of being wrong, of having his incurable galloping wrongness exposed to the world. Now that was gone. Terrifying as Holly was, as the hell-dog was, terrifying as was his utter ignorance in the face of whatever he was heading towards, none of them were as frightening as the old habitual fear that he'd accidentally made it all up.

But he wasn't wrong. It was the rest of the world that had been in error, all this time. Who'd have thought?

He wasn't even Mum and Dad's child. He'd never been that person.

Gawain. *The name your mother gave you.* Miss Grey never lied. It was his parents who lied. No, not his parents. Nigel and Isabel whose name they all had to pretend wasn't really Iseult. Fifteen years of lying. Fifteen years of trying to force on him the difference between what was real and what wasn't, and all the time having it exactly backwards.

The landscape was utterly transformed. Snow lay over it like another language. It might have been starting again from nothing, like him.

A faint sound occurred, drifting from the east. Gav stopped to listen. When he held his breath, the sound became the only noise in the whole white world. It rose and fell, suspension and cadence.

Holly, singing. In the wintry desertion the sound of it was like the promise of warmth, so beautiful Gav found himself blinking away tears. He strode on as best he could until he was near enough the gate to make out the words of the carol.

Now the holly bears a berry as blood is it red
Then trust we our Saviour who rose from the dead
And Mary bore Jesus Christ our Saviour for to be
And the first tree in the greenwood it was the holly
Holly, holly
And the first tree in the greenwood it was the holly

When he came to the entrance the song stopped. The thin rails of the iron fence stuck out of the snow, marking the line of the driveway as it curved down into the screen of trees. Their branches were black and motionless as the iron. To the left was what had three days earlier been Aunt Gwen's house. In the barren monochrome the thing outside the ruined door stood out like a desert flower, burnished green studded with its two pairs of blood-red circles.

Gawain went in, under the gaze of the red eyes.

'Don't stop,' he said, when he was almost close enough for the limbs to swing out and crush him. 'That was beautiful.'

The head inclined, loosening a breath of snow. When it spoke, Gawain felt a peculiar stab of joy.

'You hear, then? Men have ears, after all?'

Smiling foolishly, he spread his arms, indicating the surrounding silence. 'Couldn't really miss it.'

'I warned and am ignored. Why, White Hawk? I bid you run, yet here you are again.'

Gawain glanced around, but the landscape was perfectly, immaculately still. 'This is my home,' he said. 'I don't belong anywhere else.'

The tree-woman's bulk stirred, a colossal statue coming alive.

'Your death is commanded.'

He made himself remember that he wasn't afraid of it any more. 'You're going to kill me, then?'

'Not I. Not I.' Its limbs flexed, descended. He stood his ground as they circled behind him. 'But the hunter has your scent. Your path is marked.'

'OK,' he said, more bravely than he felt. 'I'll just have to hurry up.'

'He will break you. Rake and rip and leave you to rot. He—'

'Yeah, I get the idea.'

'Then get you gone.'

Gawain shrugged and shook his head. His decision was made. Like he'd said to Owen, there was a thing he had to do. Now that everything else in his life was gone, it didn't even feel brave, or complicated, or surprising. It was just all there was.

'I'm going to find Marina.'

'You will find murder.'

'You're not much help, you know.'

'Help?' It managed to fill the one syllable with bitter laughter and tender grief all at once. 'Holly, help? I am haled here, cleaved to this tree, and my roots riven earthwards. I am weaker than a word of yours. Do you believe it? A day-old boy-child is a greater thing than Holly. Did not your kind make ghosts of us merely by forgetting? Am I not less than a trick of your thought?'

He shrugged again and glanced towards the darkening horizon. 'I have no idea, to be honest. I don't know what you are. I'm just going to try and find my friend.'

'The changeling child.'

Gawain remembered standing in shock at the door of the chapel, hearing the dry rustling voice. *The girl, a changeling. The boy, an orphan, and ward of her you seek.* Perfectly simple, though even then – even just yesterday – he hadn't been able to so much as take in the words.

'Holly?' He tried to meet its look, tried to talk to it the way he'd have talked to anyone. 'What does that mean, "changeling"?'

Holly swayed sinuously, impossibly graceful. 'Ah, May Hawk. I would tell you tales, had we time. I would sing you stories. Fairy-children, cradle-theft. Ballads of the otherborn. You would lean on my trunk through the night and listen. But your trail grows warmer. You would never see the dawn.' It bent closer, shaking its head. 'Nor will you see dusk, if you tarry. Go, boy, before you are found. Go.'

There was a powerful temptation to make it talk again. While he had its attention, nothing seemed to matter except keeping it. He forced himself to notice the gathering dark. 'Can you at least tell me where she is?'

'The half-girl?'

'Marina, yeah.'

The limbs spun lazily outwards. 'Holly sees only this. Little enough. The child went in and never came out.'

In the silence that followed Gawain stared into the pupilless red eyes. Their impassive stillness was like a repetition of the word. *Never.*

'Went in where,' he said.

'My master's dwelling. Take your way elsewhere.'

'What do you mean, she didn't come out?'

'We are not men. What we say we mean. Now be gone.'

'No. Listen.' He breathed deeply. It could have meant anything, he told himself. *Never.* A voice so beautiful couldn't have told him what for a stupid moment he thought it was telling him. 'I have to go. I'm going to find her.'

'Where my master dwells?' Holly managed to sound amused and horrified at once. 'You would hurry to your own massacre?'

'You've really got a way with words, don't you?'

'It is all the ways I have, now.'

'Yeah. Well, I can't go anywhere else either. I can't run away any more.' This was true; he fastened on the truth and tried to speak with more conviction. 'I mean it. I just can't.'

'Is it so hard for men to live?'

'Marina.' *An ocean girl tends it.* 'She's got something I need.'

Again the long humming exhalation, and now a shape like a smile bent the black lips. Its branch-arms lifted slowly.

'Man's desires,' it sighed. 'Mystery, mystery.'

Gav felt himself blushing under his chapped and frozen skin. 'It's not like that.'

'Love and death.' The gorgeous voice was a warm whisper. 'Death and love. Man's day-star and night-star. Your kind lives and dies and never learns which is which. You seek one here and will find the other.'

'I'm not in love.'

'Touch me.'

'What?'

'Touch me, White Hawk. Lay your hand on Holly.'

You're kidding, he was going to say, but didn't. Instead he took two steps forward, towards the ashy mottling on the bark of its limbs, the tiny caps of snow on the sleek berries of its nipples. He reached out his fingers to the green waist.

'Mortal warmth,' it whispered, somewhere just above.

He let his hand spread over the surface. Cold and smooth. His fingers recognised the wood, the wild fecund holly. But he felt the other life as well, inside the tree, something belonging to a world or a way of being he'd always thought (or been told) he was only imagining, a life he had no word to describe.

'You are not altogether the child I chased away.' The part of it he touched moved a little. 'Though your hand is a human hand still.'

'Yeah.' He felt absurdly uncomfortable about its breasts being at the level of his face. He stared fixedly at his fingers. 'I think I figured some things out.'

'Go on, then, White Hawk.'

Reluctantly he withdrew his hand and stepped back. 'I'm Gawain,' he said, inexplicably shy.

'White Hawk. Hawk of May. Live to see another day.'

'I'll do my best,' he said. Far enough away that he felt he could look up at its snow-crusted head again, he surprised himself by adding, 'If I can figure out a way to release you, I will.'

'Your will weighs nothing beside the warlock's.' Gawain twitched and looked around. 'Pay Holly no heed. Go warily.'

Warlock? All at once it seemed like a good idea to hurry up, before he decided to run away after all.

'And the hunter will return. Do not be seen, once-boy. Do not be seen.'

Thirty

HE HURRIED DOWN towards the wood, not looking back until the trees closed around him. Holly's jagged shape stood out against the skyline. He couldn't tell whether it was still watching him.

In the shelter of the wood the snow was thinner and he walked through it quickly, a cage of knotted shadows appearing to move with him. His first glimpse of the house brought him up short, heart racing, guts churning. Through bars of intervening branches he saw light in upper windows, the unsteady radiance of firelight. Its shimmer made the house look like it had half-open eyes, flickering across the garden, watching for him. The fear he'd been ignoring asserted itself with a vengeance, all in one sick rush. Holly had as good as told him he was going to his death. He squeezed against the bark of a tree and tried to get a grip on himself. Ridiculous, he thought to himself. This is stupid. There's someone in there who can turn crows and trees into people and make dogs breathe fire. How am I supposed to face that? Turn round and go. Now.

He stayed tight to the trunk.

You seek one here and will find the other.

It could have meant anything, he told himself again. Or nothing. Just another song, just a hum of sweet words. There was no reason at all to think Marina might be . . .

He squeezed his eyes shut and gritted his teeth. It didn't matter how frightened he was. He had to go and find her.

He edged round the tree and started through the undergrowth. Powder fell around him, shaken loose by tiny motions in the canopy. He trod carefully around thorny stems, all furred white. Soon he could see the front doors with their bands of metal. Between them and the edge of the wood stretched the unkempt avenues and borders of the garden. Anyone moving across that open ground would stand out as obviously as Holly outside the lodge. And even if he reached the doors unnoticed, what then?

He stared at the house's irregular grey outline, feeling increasingly desperate. He wasn't even sure he could remember his way around inside. How was he going to find one person when he couldn't even guess what else might be in there with her? If only he could get inside secretly, with time to look around. If only . . .

If only there was another way in.

But there was. Of course there was. She'd shown him the very door. And he was the one who'd noticed that it was unbarred.

The door in the old office. The one Auntie Gwen had gone out of after taking the key. After reading his mother's – no, Iz's – letter, and realising that Gav was the child born in the woods all those years ago and deciding to break into the chapel to try and find the secret of Pendurra before going to pick him up from the station, so she could tell him everything: who he was, his name, his story, why he was *special in a good way, the best.*

Marina had told him that door led to the stables and then outside. No one ever went there, she said. The old office was even hidden by a secret door. A hidden door. It opened from the landing at the top of the rickety stairs in the office to the gallery around the hall. And the gallery led to the warren of upstairs rooms.

A different kind of cold settled on him. He began circling through the woods, towards the side of the house where the hall was. Its vaulted and crenellated roof stood out like a grey and mossy shipwreck foundering on the rest of the building. The tall windows were empty, dark as stone in the fading light. Beyond them a clutch of low haphazard buildings enclosed a cobbled courtyard adjacent to the house. The stables, surely. The edge of the wood came up close behind them. Gawain looked across fifteen paces of open ground. A quick dash across and he'd be able to work his way along the walls out of sight of any windows.

It only looked like a quick dash until he'd reached the limit of the trees. Then suddenly it yawned before him like a white abyss. He crouched, fear battling with the strange queasy cold determination. It felt like his last chance to turn back. Corbo had warned him to stay away; Holly told him to run. If things like that were afraid on his behalf, what business did he have ignoring them?

Find my child.

He was halfway to the stable wall before he even thought about what he was doing, and by then it was too late. Now he had to move, and keep moving, no choice; he was on his way in. Adrenaline terror flooded over him. He felt it squeeze his lungs. He flattened himself against the outer wall of the stable block, gasping, appalled by the glaring track he'd left behind him in the snow. Someone would surely notice it. Something. Hurry, then! But now he had no idea where the door into the house would be. Back tight against the stone, he edged sideways until he came to a corner. Peering round with one eye, he saw the house, terrifyingly close. It looked different for some reason. He panicked, convinced he'd lost his bearings and was trapped in completely the wrong place. Then with a dizzying swell of relief he realised what it was that looked different: the sash windows, the perpendicular angles, the dressed stone. The old office. Marina had told him it wasn't as old as the rest of the house. Suddenly it all fit together: he saw how the newer extension abutted the ancient hall, and where the stable block was joined to it. He'd stood with Marina looking down at those windows and the unbarred door beside them. That door must be . . . there.

He'd have to run again, across the courtyard. More tracks. No help for it, and no time to worry about it. He raced across the snow and squeezed under the lintel of a barn door, fumbling at its latch. It clattered horribly but opened, inwards, into a chill dark space that smelled of mud and leather. The dread was so intense it was all he could do to stay upright, but he slipped inside and closed the door behind him.

For a few seconds there was nothing but the feeling of stone around him. Then his eyes adjusted to the dimness and he saw thick wooden trestles, low beams hung with brackets and hooks, and everywhere objects whose names and uses were completely obscure to him, things of straps and ropes and brass loops and strange-shaped metal blades.

A wide wooden door was set in the far wall.

Maybe it's barred now, he thought. Or there could be someone behind it, waiting. But his feet kept going. It was a nightmare again, inevitable motion even as the brain screamed to stop. His knees felt weak as water. He put his hand out to the door to steady himself. There was a handle on it, a ring of iron like a manacle.

He held his breath, put his ear to the wood, listened.

An odd thing happened then. There was no sound at all, nothing where he was and nothing coming through the heavy door, and yet in the silence he heard something. At first it seemed like the faintest, most distant snatches of Holly's music, up beyond the wood, but it wasn't that. It wasn't a song, or even a sound at all. It vibrated in some other air, different from the air he breathed. It was infinitely quiet.

It had a source, a shadowed corner beside the door. He was looking straight at it.

There was a stick there. A walking stick, slightly curved, smoothed by craft and use. It had a voice.

Gawain thought of the faraway murmuring of Hester's masks and remembered how they'd come into focus when he'd touched the faces. There was something about this other music that felt like a glimmer of reassurance. It might not be a bad idea to carry a stick, he reasoned. It would make a good companion, and though he doubted it would do him any good in a fight, he thought he'd still rather not have empty hands, should he come across anything that tried to stop him.

He picked it up.

Quickbeam, it whispered. *Lightning tree. Rowan, sovereign against enchantment.* These were not words. It was knowledge, known the way he knew his face in a mirror. He recalled the boughs with slender leaves and bunches of orange berries tacked above the doors and windows of Auntie Gwen's house. It was the same wood, the same faded magic. He gripped the staff more comfortably. *Whispertree, witchbane.* The names were not names but textures in his hand.

He turned the handle. The door hadn't been barred. It creaked, whined, opened a sliver of musty grey. Through the crack Gawain saw the piled boxes and the faded ledgers shelved from floor to ceiling, exactly as he remembered.

He slipped in, bringing the rowan staff with him, and slowly, slowly closed the door behind him, until with an apologetic click it shut him in the house.

For a few seconds he stood looking up at the landing as if Marina was still there, nervous and fidgety and very much alive, wrapping the baggy sleeves of her sweater around and around her hands. As if he'd never seen the telltale marks in the dust and the name on the label of a drawer, as if none of the last day had happened at all and he was still wearing shoes and socks and spending a week in the country visiting his scatty, silly aunt while his parents (still his parents) went on their skiing holiday.

Then somewhere deeper in the house a door banged.

The shock almost toppled Gawain over. The only thing he could think was that someone wanted to kill him, here in this house, behind these walls. Move, he told himself desperately, move. Upstairs, that was it. The secret door, the gallery, the passageway. Find Marina. He started up the flimsy stairs. Their timbers popped and groaned. He felt each noise in his gut like the jab of a knife. His feet looked like they belonged in a morgue, stained and bruised out of any resemblance to living flesh. Another noise in the house: a metallic clang, closer. He cringed, overbalanced and had to clutch the railing to stop himself falling. The staff knocked clumsily on the treads. He swore between clenched teeth, shut his eyes and waited for the enemy to come and massacre him as Holly had promised, but everything went quiet. He resumed the ascent, another tread, another, soft creaks announcing every step like denunciations. He reached the landing and leaned against the wall, clammy with fear. The only way to mitigate the racket of his panting breath was opening his mouth wide, as if readying a scream. He listened again. Now the silence was horribly unnerving. He wiped his hands on his filthy clothes and gave the handle of the landing door the tiniest twist.

Silence still. The drapes concealing the door on the other side muffled light and noise. Gav pushed and felt their weight pushing back. He eased through the door on tiptoes, doing his best to disturb the fabric as little as possible. The hall seemed empty. He poked shaky fingers into the gap between the tapestries and put his eye to the crack.

Again everything was exactly as he remembered it, except that instead of the dreary and frosty mid-morning light a cloudy gloom hung thick in the hall. The old glass in its windows sapped the expiring afternoon's remaining strength. Among the beams of the ceiling it was already dark. Gav looked across to the far end of the gallery, the branching stonework and the arched door just visible in the shadows. Tenuous determination gripped him. He was inside. No one had seen him. The house was big and full of obscure corners. Suddenly it seemed plausible that Marina was waiting for him somewhere, that he could steal unnoticed through its shadows and find her. He stepped between the drapes and started along the gallery, lifting each foot high and lowering it heel to toe, testing the boards for discretion.

He glanced down at the long table below as he passed along the gallery. When Marina had shown him through the room the morning before, there'd been nothing on it, he was sure. Now five thick candles were arranged there in a circle, unlit. Between them, in the centre, was a wide shallow bowl, gleaming like old silver. He slowed involuntarily. The symmetry of it seemed disturbingly purposeful and strange. He shivered again, tightening his grip on the stick, and then, without warning, the dread became real.

Muffled footsteps sounded below, approaching. He was in the middle of the long side of the gallery, at the furthest possible extreme from either door, completely exposed. The steps came on. He dropped to his hands and knees, behind the thin posts that railed the gallery, and pushed himself back into inadequate shadows. Appallingly loud and close, a door scraped directly beneath him.

The steps came in. Paralysed, he could only watch, eyes fixed on the space below. There was nowhere to hide or run; he could not so much as shift his weight without making a sound. He was trapped. Sparks danced in his vision, and all he could think was, Please let it be Tristram. Please let it be Marina. Please let it not be . . .

The person who'd entered the hall shuffled into view, directly beneath him, carrying something awkward to the table.

It was neither Tristram nor Marina. It was, as Gawain had by some awful insight known it would be, Aunt Gwen.

It was and it was not.

Gav had faced things more hideous than nightmares that day, but this was the worst moment of all, the moment when a knowledge so unspeakable that it couldn't be admitted finally showed its face. Though he was looking down on her back from high above, in the last light of a grim day, he knew her immediately. His old ally, his childhood friend, his beloved comical aunt, the only person who'd ever shown any sympathy at all for the catastrophe that was his life: how could he not know her? But at the same time something – no, everything – was grotesquely wrong. She was hunched, concentrated, slow and uncomfortable and heavy, moving as if each motion required an effort to remember how it was done, and as if the continuous effort of it had turned her bitterly angry. Gawain saw all this in the two or three steps it took her to come to the table and set down the thing she carried. The one emotion he couldn't imagine infecting his kind, enthusiastic, naïve aunt was bitterness. Now she reeked of it, even in the mere twist and strain of her arms.

It was as well she didn't turn round, because Gav thought that if he saw her face he'd probably die. As it was, the horror of watching her held him still as death. Only an instinct of self-preservation kept him clinging to the walking stick, or it would have clattered onto the gallery floor and given him away. The thing she'd carried was a jug, a wide-bellied earthenware jug; he'd seen one like it in the kitchen. Full, as was obvious from the way she'd wrestled with the weight of it. Now she bent over its handle, grunted as she heaved and poured its contents into the silver bowl between the candles.

The splash of running water broke Gav out of his paralysis. He looked around, trying to think, wondering how to keep himself alive. He didn't know what had happened to his aunt, he didn't even want to begin to try and imagine it, but he knew with utter certainty that if he met her eyes – if she saw him – Holly's worst predictions would come true. The horror would stop his heart. This, here, was the enemy, the thing that was wrong. Marina's mother (mother!) had somehow known the truth and begged him to help; now he would. *Find my child*, the mermaid said. *You must*, Miss Grey said. It was simple, like turning left or right. Escape or die.

Placing the staff on the timbers beside him with breathless care, he shifted his weight onto his knees and palms and slid one leg just an inch towards the far door, then the other. The pouring noise stopped; he stopped with it. He looked across the room. If he could even get as far as the next corner that might be enough. Beyond that the gallery was raised on stone columns and railed with a thick carved screen. The stone would hide him and wouldn't creak when he moved. He focused on the distance between him and the corner and the series of infinitesimal movements that would get him there: palm up, fingers splayed, forward an inch, down again, then the legs, the other hand, reaching back to pick up the stick, move it on, lower it gently as a feather falling to earth.

Impossible. He couldn't turn his head away from the person crouched over the table below. She held his eyes like a disfigurement.

A feeble yellow light appeared under her body. She had lit a sort of long match, though he'd heard nothing strike. She reached it out towards the five candles. Light spread upwards, her face turned a fraction, and Gawain got his first glimpse of her profile.

His eyelids flickered shut and his heart almost stalled. Holly's strange word rang in his head like a slamming bolt. *Warlock.*

Escape. Escape. He lifted a hand, held it, put it down as slowly as his trembling arm allowed.

The hall was growing brighter. There was nothing he could do about it. Aunt Gwen was lighting the candles, one by one. The cloaking dimness under the beams melted away. Gawain saw the soft blur of his own shadow on the whitewashed wall behind him. If she even turned sideways now, if she glanced round for any reason, she'd see him. He couldn't risk the slightest movement. All he could do was watch.

By the candlelight he saw a design chalked on the table, a five-pointed star. The candles were set at its points, and the silver bowl was contained in the centre of the pentagram.

Despite himself Gawain felt a quiver of fascination. This, here, now, was the power that made impossible things happen, the stranger that had walked beside him all his life. This was magic. When he was younger, Auntie Gwen had sometimes let him watch her doing things a bit like this, but what was happening down in the room was no more like those pantomimes than the person below was like the aunt he'd loved, no matter how similar they looked.

She began to speak, half-voiced syllables that barely sounded like language at all. It was like a snake had coiled up inside her mouth. Gawain clenched his teeth, but there was nothing he could do except listen to the horrible alien sounds trickling out. The longer he listened, the more, despite himself, he understood.

The warlock was calling to someone. No, *something.* The water had become a channel. Something was on the other side.

It was answering.

The room was suddenly very cold. Though the candles didn't waver, Gawain felt a sharp and odourless wind circling the hall. Over Gwen's shoulder he saw in the bowl a grey-blue nothingness, like looking up through a porthole to an ocean sky. Gwen crouched forward, her voice rising. The intensity of her concentration was obvious and now Gawain saw a chance to get out of the room. He seized the stick in one hand and started crawling as quickly as he dared, crouching low as if the rails of the gallery might screen him, though it was all too obvious that they wouldn't.

'*What do you want?*'

The voice came from nowhere. It seemed to be in the intangible wind. Gawain flinched and pushed himself tight against the wall, staring into the shadows of the room. There was no one there. Gwen bent lower over the bowl, knuckles resting on the table. A noise had come into the hall as if the phantom wind were rising. It masked the tiny sounds he made. He sped up his progress to a reckless creep.

'To question you,' the warlock said, in her grating voice.

'*Who are you?*'

'Gawain,' he whispered, before he could stop himself. The voice was so close, right at his shoulder like the angel in Hester's picture. There was a pitiful loneliness in it.

Gwen spoke at the same time: 'Do you not know me?'

'*I hardly know myself.*'

'Answer me, then, and I will answer you in turn.'

'*Who am I?*' The question was tinged with pain. Gawain stopped, inexplicably touched.

'You must answer me first.'

'*Must I?*'

'No,' Gawain whispered, and, 'Yes,' said Gwen. He shook his head and forced himself to keep moving. This was the time to find Marina, now, while Gwen's energies were absorbed in the battle of wills.

'*I am obscured,*' the nowhere voice complained. '*I am wronged. Is it you who wronged me?*'

'You must answer me first, but because I have power to choose, I choose to tell you this. I have done you no harm. You suffer because all things have fallen into decay. I have come to restore the world. I will right you. I am your saviour as well as your master. You knew me once, an age ago, though you have forgotten.'

'*Forgotten . . .*' it sighed.

Edging further down the gallery's long side, Gawain was now far enough along to see round Gwen's back to her profile. He made the mistake of looking once. He shuddered, sweating, then fixed his eyes on the arched door at the far end of the gallery and swore to himself that he wouldn't look aside until he was through it.

'Now, sky spirit, answer me in turn.' Her awful mockery of a voice filled the hall. 'You roam wherever the wind blows. I seek a thing a man-child carries. It is a thing I must hold to right all the wrongs that have been done, and reappoint all the things that have been forgotten. It is a thing of potency. You will recognise it. It is close to the place where I stand on the earth. Search and you may see it. Do you see it?'

In the pause that followed, Gav froze mid-crawl, fearing her concentration might break and she would look up.

'*Yes,*' the voice said, at last.

'A boy carries it?'

'*Yes.*'

'Where is he?'

'Don't tell her,' Gawain said. It was barely louder than a breath, but still he clapped his hand over his mouth, horrified that he'd again spoken aloud.

The voice said, '*Who is the other?*'

Gawain didn't dare move a muscle. What had he been thinking? What did he think he was doing?

'Answer me!' Gwen rasped.

'*Across the drowned valley, seeking the ocean. Or where you are, but in a place I cannot see, though I hear him. Now tell me who I was.*'

'Where I . . . ?'

Gawain heard the abrupt uncertainty in her tone, felt the spell weakening and knew he might not have much longer. Eyes fast on the door, he made himself press on. It was coming tantalisingly close, so much so that it was all he could do not to jump to his feet and bolt.

'*Tell me who I was,*' the voice repeated, and its hollowness had a deeper resonance now, as if it had grown.

'You are what you always were.' Gwen sounded impatient. 'You are of the order of essences called *genii*, and your place is the air. You—'

'*Not that.*' The room grew colder, and the strange whistling sound raised its pitch. The thing that spoke with the voice seemed to be prowling the invisible wind, circling its cage. '*Tell me what I have lost. Restore my station.*'

'Spirit!' Gwen had to raise her voice. 'You spoke of two places, not one. I am not yet fairly answered. Where is the boy with the ring?'

'*The other tells me not to answer.*' The voice was unmistakably larger now.

'Other? What other?'

'No, don't, please,' Gawain mouthed. It was no more than ten strides to the door, but if Gwen so much as flicked her glance to her left, she'd surely see him. His resolution broke and he stole a glance back, saw the mounting fury in the dreadful face and recoiled from it.

'*Will you tell me what I once was?*' demanded the wind.

'Yes,' Gawain breathed, 'I'll try,' at the same time as Gwen shrieked, 'Nothing! And you will remain nothing unless I find what I seek! Tell me! What other forbids you to answer me?'

'You were free,' Gawain whispered to it. A phrase had popped into his head, a stupid cliché; it was the first thing he could think of. 'Free as air.'

As soon as the words had left his mouth he knew he was right. The presence was going. He'd answered its question truthfully and released it. He jumped to his feet and began to run.

'No. No!' The warlock's screech sounded barely human at all.

The phantom wind swept wildly around the room, and now shadows danced crazily, though the air itself was not stirred. The candles guttered. Shadow cloaked the gallery where Gawain ran, five steps, eight. There was a splash, and a dull clang: the bowl being overturned. Calm returned to the hall just as Gav pulled the door, squirmed through the crack he'd opened and drew up in the passage beyond, breathless, filmed with sweat.

Now he was deep inside, and suddenly the rules of the game were starkly obvious. He knew what he had to avoid. He'd seen it. The knowledge was unbearable, but on the knife-edge of the moment it was better to know than not. All he had to do was whatever it took to stay out of her way. Hide behind doors, in cupboards, under beds, anything, anywhere, as long as she didn't know he was there, until he found Marina, and then they had to get out and away as fast as they could. That was it. That was all. The simplicity of it gave him a surge of unexpected confidence. He'd made it this far and not been seen. Quick, then, quick! There were noises from downstairs, but that didn't matter, downstairs was fine. Anywhere not near him was OK. He looked hard at the doors, trying to keep his head clear of the fog of panic. Marina's room first. (Footsteps: he froze, staring at the nearest door, but the steps faded.) Which one was it? Which way had he come, the day before? (He remembered the shape of the house downstairs. The main staircase, which was just ahead round a crooked corner; the steps he heard were going away from it, down the panelled hallway towards the front door. She was leaving!) He reached for the nearest door and was about to try it when he realised it wasn't right. Something about its shape, or the pattern of fat nail heads; not that one. The next one.

From downstairs came a grinding scrape. The front door, opening. Gav almost laughed with relief. She was going outside, out of the house. She wouldn't find him after all—

His relief expired like the flame of a match.

Tracks. He'd left tracks. If she went towards that side of the garden she'd see them. In the virgin snow they were plain as print. She'd know someone was in the house.

He grabbed the handle of the door to Marina's room, then made himself stop and listen for a second before he tried it, though fresh panic was knotting his guts. Not a sound beyond the percussion of his own blood in his ears. The handle shrieked horribly when he turned it.

The curtains had been drawn in the bedroom.

'Marina?'

He stepped in, closing the door behind him very carefully. The room was cold and cobweb-grey in the veiled dusk. He thought he saw a lumpy outline on the four-poster bed.

'Marina!'

Probably just a pile of pillows. He chewed his lip. Any moment now Gwen might see his footprints. Where else could Marina be? He'd have to search all the upstairs rooms.

That odd-shaped unmoving shadow on the bed couldn't be her.

It couldn't be. Never.

He remembered something else Holly had said, something he'd been trying hard not to remember at all.

Murder is done already.

His eyes were adjusting to the near-dark. The thing on the bed wasn't a pile of pillows.

He felt his way across the floor, trying to avoid the stuff scattered around. The boards grunted and sighed but he'd stopped noticing the noises. A dreadful shock was preparing itself inside him; he could feel himself trying to wall himself off from it, empty himself out, feel nothing. The thing on the bed was now definitely a body, a child's body, gangly limbs draped at odd angles, absolutely motionless.

He leaned over the bed. A little metallic drum was going *no no no no no no* in his head, faster and faster. He prodded the body gently. Nothing.

He shook harder, tipped it over onto its back. It was Marina, limp and lifeless as a rag doll.

The first time he'd seen her, he'd thought she was dead. It was his fault, all his fault. His stupid mistake had killed her in the end, a black prophecy.

A bruised hand dangled over the edge of the bed. He remembered holding it, how alive it had felt. He tried to think of something to whisper as he reached out to touch it again, but there was nothing there, not even *goodbye*.

The hand was warm.

He put the rowan staff down and felt her face with both hands to make sure. Unmistakably warm. Around her lips he felt the tiniest whisper of breath.

He blinked. He hadn't noticed he'd been crying. For a brief and extraordinary moment he realised he didn't care what happened now. The worst had shown its face to him and then turned away and passed by. He put his mouth right to her ear and hissed into it as loud as he dared, 'Marina!'

Not a twitch, not a mumble. She was asleep, but as if in a coma. He shook her again, vigorously. Her head flopped around as if it might come off.

As he bent over the pillow, a crazy thought occurred to him. It made him blush. If he hadn't been so delirious with relief, he'd never have let it in.

An enchanted sleep. A daughter, hidden away in a weird and forgotten and grand and ancient house, imprisoned by a warlock . . . He didn't really think it would work, but then what did he know about magic?

With his fingers he found where her mouth was. He leaned forward and kissed.

The spell didn't break. It didn't even waver. But as soon as his lips touched hers he could taste it. The taste was acrid, smoky and sweet all together. It came so vividly to his mouth that he forgot what he'd just done (although he would remember it many, many times later, the furtive downy touch). He recognised it as magic first, by that same unnameable sixth sense that had heard the hum of the rowan staff and spoken to the *genius* of the air. But his other senses knew it too. His flesh felt it: tiny hard spots of it.

Poppy seeds.

He ran his fingers over her face until they touched her lips again. There were seeds stuck in the corners of her mouth. He poked a finger between her slightly opened lips and felt them on her tongue.

He wiped his mouth with the back of his hand. Each dot was like a miniature whirlpool, a vortex opening into perfumed darkness. He began brushing them off her lips. He knew, without knowing how he knew, that the seeds were the heart of the spell. But they weren't just on her lips and tongue. She'd swallowed some too.

A shout outside, in front of the house. Two syllables, scraping like the back and forth of a saw: 'Corbo!'

Gawain snapped his head up. He'd forgotten what he was doing, who was out there. He shook the body frantically. 'Marina! Wake up! Wake up!' No use at all.

There was, he saw, only one thing for it. He'd already carried Horace. Marina was quite a bit taller, but thin as a rake. He'd manage.

He grabbed her round the torso, heaved her upright and tipped her over his shoulder. She was in her pyjamas. The pink ones, he guessed, though it was too dark to know. The limp body wasn't heavy, but it was utterly uncooperative. It was impossible to lift her up without producing a cacophony of cracking in the floorboards and bumping against the furniture. He staggered to his feet.

The hoarse call came again: 'Corbo!' A passing shadow seemed to darken the room, or perhaps he only imagined it. He grabbed the staff again, hooked the other arm round Marina's hips and started for the door. Her chin jabbed his ribs, her droopy arms swayed and threatened to catch on every object he tried to steer around, and he had to grip fiercely to prevent her hips sliding right off his shoulder. He thought he heard the voice outside, speaking low.

He'd got as far as managing the handle and letting himself back out into the passageway when he heard the front door open and shut again. The noise was right underneath him. She'd come back in the house. Thinking only of the distance between him and the open air, he tightened his grip on the absurdly limp body slung over his shoulder and took a step.

The old timbers of the floor gave a sharp pop as his weight shifted. He froze.

For a moment of deathly suspense he stood still, hoping that if he didn't move, everything would just go away.

He heard a call from downstairs. 'Old man?'

Then he knew he'd been heard. The game was finished. Now there was only one thing to do, and that was to run, and hope he could run fast enough. No more thinking or guessing or sneaking. Time to run for his life.

It was hard to believe anyone else could move clumsily enough to be heard over the racket he and his cargo made as they careered down the corridor, but nevertheless he heard the sounds of pursuit all too clearly. She was coming. Uneven steps thumped up the staircase.

For some reason he'd been imagining a romantically surreptitious escape from the house: he and Marina hand in hand and on tiptoes, fleeing into the dark, blending among shadows like the ghosts they both perhaps were. Now he had no idea what to do except run, and keep running, hauling the dead weight for as long as he could stand. The load seemed to double with each step. His day had drained him; only mortal desperation kept him going. If his legs gave out now he was dead. Behind him the ragged steps reached the top of the stairs and began coming down the passageway. He gritted his teeth and crashed through the arched door into the hall, kicking it shut behind him. The tapestries at the far end looked impossibly far away, but he forced himself along, one step after another, fighting for his balance. Either Marina was a lot heavier than she looked or he was a lot weaker than he thought he was. He had to crouch to run along the gallery, and it seemed like her weight was always about to pull him over the railings. His arm shook and burned with the effort of holding on.

The door banged open behind him.

'Boy!'

He tasted bile. Her eyes on my back, he thought. Auntie Gwen, shouting at me, not knowing me.

'Stop!'

He turned the corner. On his left shoulder Marina's body shielded him from seeing his pursuer. He heard the stumbling steps, the clatter of boots on wood. Faster than him. She was going to catch him, it was hopeless. For the briefest instant he thought about dropping Marina and bolting, but he couldn't. He couldn't even let go of the rowan staff in his other hand. It clumped along beside him like a crutch. All he could do was keep going until he was caught. He wondered if he'd be able to swing the stick in anger, if it came to it, but that would mean looking Aunt Gwen in the face, and somehow he knew death would be better. He shoved the stick between the heavy fabric to open the way to the hidden door.

From the keyhole, a black bar protruded.

He'd left the door ajar. He stuck his toes in the gap, prised it open, threw Marina and the staff down on the landing – she landed with a horrible dead thump – then reached back and yanked the iron key from the lock. The pursuing footsteps sounded as close as the hammering in his ears. He slammed the door shut behind him and jabbed frantically around the handle with the key. He couldn't see: salt stung his eyes, and the old office was in deep twilight. Two agonisingly futile seconds stretched out like the end of time, and then by sheer luck the teeth of the key found the hole. He got it in, twisted, heard the bolt slide. An instant later the handle rattled.

Hands thumped the other side of the door. The handle twisted again, left, right.

There he was, bent double, his own breath like smoke in his lungs, the enchanted changeling girl and the rowan staff lying at his feet, and no more than the thickness of a plank of wood between him and something that made an appalling mockery of all names.

'Are you there, boy?'

He thought he could feel her breath. Her mouth might have been touching the other side of the door. Auntie Gwen's mouth.

'Shall I tell you how I punish thieving?'

He crouched into a hunched ball, tears dribbling into the corners of his mouth.

'The penalty is death, boy. Do you think me incapable of that?'

No, he mouthed, an O of pain. It was her voice. He'd known it as long as he could remember. But it had cracked and split like earth in a drought.

'Unlock the door, boy. Return the girl and you will have done no wrong. Spare yourself.'

No no no.

'Boy?'

There below him was the unbarred door. The escape route. He focused on it, blinking away the tears. He had no answer but to keep on running, away from that voice. There was power in him somewhere, he knew that. He'd saved himself from burning. He'd forced the black dog away. He felt the magic around him, the enchantments and the compulsions. But he didn't know what the power was, or where. He knew nothing about it. If this was his day, like Holly said it was, he'd spent the day cold, terrified, bewildered and now hunted. He had nothing to go on. He couldn't face the person on the other side of the door, the ghastly ruin of someone he'd clung to since childhood as his only living friend.

She twisted the handle again.

'Turn the lock, boy. Do as I command.'

'No.'

He hadn't meant to say it aloud. It came out as a croak. Loud enough, though.

The door clattered. She'd struck it again. When she spoke it was with tangible menace, a tone so alien to anything Auntie Gwen could ever have managed that it dried up his drizzle of tears. This wasn't his aunt. Auntie Gwen was gone, like Miss Grey. Everyone he'd loved was gone.

'My servants are as swift as the wind. They will have you soon.' The handle shook again. Gawain knelt down, feeling for the sprawled body. He grunted with effort as he got his arms under hers and sat her up. It was like wrestling. She toppled into him. Her head lolled and cracked painfully against his ear.

'You are the ward of the prophetess?'

With a groan he heaved his back straight, lifting Marina off the floor. He scrabbled around for the staff.

'I slew her, boy.'

He stopped. His right hand clutched the walking stick tight.

Murder is done already.

'She lies unhallowed in the snow outside. My servant broke her neck. That will be your inheritance from her. You and she will rot together. Do you understand me?'

In place of the gruesome fear, a new feeling began to spread through him. Anger, hard as the frozen ground.

'Unlock the door now or die.'

So Miss Grey was dead. He'd known it, somehow. In a way it was better than thinking of her leaving him by choice. She'd known she was going to die. She'd come to say her goodbyes.

The prophetess. Well then. Dead and gone she might be, but she'd left him with a prophecy. She'd given him a future. So he wasn't going to let himself be hunted down by the horrible thing that boasted of killing her. No matter how exhausted and cornered he was, he wasn't going to let it happen.

The way out was below him. He'd have a head start if he hurried.

The handle rattled furiously behind him as he manoeuvered his load down the awkward stairs. He heard a screech of inarticulate rage. Footsteps started away. She'd go through the hall, along the passage to the stairs, down and out the front door and round the house to the stables. He guessed he had maybe two minutes. Maybe one.

Marina's head jolted against the banister. No time to worry about that. He clumped down to the door, yanked it open and limped as fast as he could through the stable.

Outside, the light had faded to a deep sullen grey. The snow was turning ghostly. He gulped in the clean air and hesitated a second. He hadn't quite believed he'd ever see the outside world again, but he'd done it, he was out, he'd got her out. He'd never got as far as thinking about what to do next. It was easy, though, because there was only one thing to do.

Keep running. Keep running. Not uphill: his legs wouldn't make it. Not into the woods: he'd never be able to work through the tangle of wild rhododendron with Marina slung over his shoulder. Down, then.

. . . her to the river . . .

He pitched himself forward and ran.

He ran under the long windows of the hall, the oak and beech crowns arching above, almost touching its parapets. His lungs felt like they were on fire, but what did pain matter now? *Truth hurts.* He reached a corner of the building. Out beyond the sloping field of unblemished snow and the lower woods he saw the coming night, the eastern horizon turning black as his dreams. He loped down the virgin field in long disjointed strides, battling the weight that threatened to tip him forward each time he planted a foot. It was desperately slow, but the wood was desperately close; he saw the opening in the trees marking the path Marina had led him along.

There was a furious cry behind him. He faced the smothered dusk and made himself go faster, though the strain cost him tears of agony. Beyond and below was the river. If he could only get her that far he could die in peace. He thought he heard a different voice shouting from the house. It might have been her father's. It didn't matter. Nothing mattered at all except staying upright until his legs gave way. The cleft in the trees came closer even as the deep snow clutched and dragged at his heels. Twice, three times, he stumbled badly and had to jam the staff ahead of him to brace against a fall, screeching at the pain that shot through his arms. The darkness under the trees beckoned him on like sanctuary. Someone was shouting Marina's name, but if he stopped he'd be caught. He tumbled in under the branches. The path through the old wood stretched ahead of him. Another entrance reached and they hadn't got him yet. He risked a look over his shoulder.

For an instant the scene was perfectly still, as if winter had frozen them all. A silhouette was framed in the window of the corner room, looking out, the unmistakable tall wild-haired outline of Tristram Uren. Another silhouette was outlined against the snowfield, descending clumsily after Gawain: the thing that had once been Aunt Gwen. She'd struggled a little way down from the house but had gained no ground on him in the heavy snow, and now stood, arms wide.

Her hands lifted slowly to the sky.

The shout chilled Gawain to the heart. Not a scream of anger or frustration, this time; no empty threat. Its three words held no meaning he knew and yet somehow he understood them immediately for a summons.

With a stab of terror he knew she was bringing the black dog.

Two miles or so to the south, an elderly couple looked out of the picture window of a bungalow towards a stony beach.

The husband said, 'Don't much like the look of that.'

He took off his glasses to wipe them on his sweater and replaced them, studying the thing that had washed up on the shore.

'Don't do that, George. It only makes them worse. Do you recognise her?' The wife, whose eyesight was (to her good fortune) worse, nosed closer to the glass. 'Should we call the lifeboat?'

'Bit late now,' the husband sniffed.

The bungalow was one of a shabby row on a low rise overlooking the beach, testament to a species of seaside holiday that was already nearing extinction when they'd been built. The tide, turned now to the ebb, had exposed a grey rim at the edge of the crescent of snow. A battered sailing dinghy was tilted at a forlorn angle on the stones, its creased white sail shuddering weakly.

'Dan Frye's boat,' the man said. His wife tutted as if the name itself was unlucky.

'Oh dear.' She peered again. 'Are you sure? I don't know how you can see anything, it's almost dark.'

'You know you can't see anything. Of course I'm sure.'

'Dear me. Poor old fellow. Isn't he the one who—'

'Always took his boat out, in all weather.'

'But wasn't it because he . . . Oh you know, George. He went a bit mad. That chap. His wife left him because of it. Myrtle knows her. She—'

'Hello,' the man interrupted, cupping a hand over his eyes against the glass of the window. 'Look at that old fellow.'

'Look at what?'

'There.' He pointed. 'Look at the size of him. He must be half a wolf.'

The wife nudged against him. 'Is that a dog?'

'I don't know why you don't just put your specs on.'

'It can't be out by itself in this weather? Honestly, some people. The poor old chap must be half dead with— Oh! I see him! He is a big . . .'

A huge coal-black creature had come padding with eerie purposefulness over the shingle at the very edge of the sea. The reason the wife hadn't finished her sentence was that she'd noticed its eyes.

It was impossible not to. Against the uniform grey of sea and sky, they shone like beacon fires.

'What on earth . . . ?'

The massive dog stalked closer, its blunt wedge of a head lowered slightly as if to follow a scent. It never stopped, looked around, fidgeted. There was nothing animal about it except its brute form. It loped up to the dinghy and sprang inside it. They lost sight of it behind the sail, but heard a violent clatter as it began to ransack the hull.

'George?'

The black dog emerged with a small, grey, limp-looking thing in its mouth. For a horrible moment the husband thought it was someone's foot, as if the beast had found Dan Frye's corpse down there in the bottom of his boat and torn it to shreds. But when it bounded down onto the pebbly strand and released the object, he saw it was just a shoe.

The dog bent down, turned it over with its nose, sniffed it.

It bared its teeth.

The man clutched at his heart as flame spewed over the beast's jaws. Its lips curled back, back, releasing rivulets of ghastly fire, and then it snarled and lunged. He fell. He didn't see the dog stab one paw into the shoe and rip it apart, shred it, snap wildly at the fragments it tossed in the air, shake and claw them again. The last thing he heard before the veil closed his ears and eyes and everything was its gigantic, dismal howl.

Everyone in the village heard it too, whatever they were doing – everyday things, ordinary things, things they'd later look back on with a helpless nostalgia, as one looks back from the far side of a catastrophe on the vanished happiness that preceded it and wonders how one forgot to notice how happy it was – and stopped. Some of them knew it at once, instinctively, for what it was: a black portent, a warning siren.

The howl was all the valediction drowned Dan Frye received. The sea-creatures he had longed to see again – longed unbearably, incurably – had not even noticed him as he threw himself overboard and sank, nor had they helped his empty boat to shore. Only the tide and a faint wind had washed it up, Gawain's shoes still tucked in the bows.

The dog was staring over the water that had a second time denied it its prey when it heard its master's last summons. At once it turned to the north and began to run, vanishing with deadly speed into the gathering dark.

Thirty-one

When he reached the spot where the path crossed the streamlet and divided, Gawain made the mistake of stopping. It was only for a second, but a second was long enough. The burning muscles in his legs cramped up. He collapsed into muddy snow, howling, Marina pitching off his shoulder and sprawling uselessly beside him. When he could move again, he hauled the dead weight back towards him. Spasms of excruciating pain shot through his legs, but he couldn't stop: the dog was coming, and this time its command would be to kill him as Holly's had been to fetch him, and no word of his would hold it back. He made a couple of agonising attempts to lift Marina again. Both times his legs tightened to iron and then gave way. 'Jesus, Marina,' he whispered fiercely, 'can't you . . . just' – he heaved again – 'wake' – another heave – 'up?' No good. On all fours, bare hands and feet deep in the icy slush, he shifted her until she was slung over his back like a sodden pink sack, but that was the most he could manage.

The darkness was closing in. He remembered Marina telling him the downhill path led to the river, but he couldn't see anything that way. It couldn't be far, but the best he could manage now was an aching crawl, and the hunter was coming. *Swift as the wind.*

The other path led up to the chapel, to the well that had saved him and his mother.

He thought of how one mouthful of its water had cleared the pain away before. He had another idea too. There was no way of knowing whether it would work, but the chapel wasn't too far, and the racking pains shooting through his calves and thighs told him he wasn't going to make it much further the way he was.

He shuffled his back and pulled Marina's arms round his neck, gripping them tight with one arm. The other hand held the rowan staff. He bent his forearm, propped himself on it, gritted his teeth and forced himself to crawl up the slope.

Up and on, over the gentle crest, towards the hollow where the chapel was, trying not to think of his pursuers, one slow but remorseless, one deadly quick. Beneath the layer of snow the flints and roots shredded his shirt and trousers. He looked like a tortoise struggling under a dirty pink and blonde shell. Not far, he kept telling himself, expecting at every moment to hear the howl that would mean he'd failed, he was dead. Not far. The last steep little slope, where he'd once watched Marina scramble unthinkingly towards her capture, was an unspeakable torture, but he managed it. The ancient building appeared in the gloom. He scraped and gasped his way through the straggly hollies and found the door still open.

He dragged himself to the edge of the pool and with a final heave of his shoulders tipped Marina off his back. It was all but pitch black inside, and utterly silent beyond the heaving rattle of his breath. He reached down and cupped water into his mouth.

He often thought later that if he could have bottled one instant of his life to keep for ever that would have been it, despite the hammering terror and the desperate ignorance. The pain washed out of his legs and arms as if it had been no more than dust, rinsed away. Where I began, he thought, and for a blissful moment he felt like he'd sloughed off his aching and scratched and battered skin and emerged new-born, pristine.

It was only a moment. There was no time. He grabbed Marina and turned her over until her head dangled over the stone lip. 'Last chance,' he muttered. He was still breathing hard; even the effort of kneeling up beside her made him suck air. 'If y'don't . . . wake up . . . now' – he reached down to the pool – 'I'm . . . leaving you . . . here.' He tipped her head up and splashed the handful of water into her mouth.

He'd become so used to the sprawled, awkward weight of her that he almost dropped her head when it twitched in his hands.

He knelt closer, whispering urgently, 'That's right. Wake up.' There was no time. The dog was coming, there was no time. 'Come on. Come on.' He scooped another trickling fistful between her lips. She quivered again. 'Got to drink some.' He cradled her head in the crook of his elbow. She squirmed reluctantly. He guided his cupped palm to her mouth. 'Drink up.' He tipped the water onto her tongue. 'Do you good. There you go.' He felt her swallow. 'And another . . . There.'

At the third mouthful she spasmed like a struggling animal. He held on, waited for her to relax. Her head turned, and though it was too dim to see her face he was sure her eyes had opened.

'Mummy?'

It was the small clear voice he remembered.

'Marina!'

'Hello,' she said. She hadn't moved. She seemed suddenly quite comfortable, propped against him. 'I think I might be asleep.'

'Marina. We need to go. Right now.' But he couldn't let go of her. It would have been like dropping a baby.

'You aren't my mother, are you.'

'Jesus.' He straightened and felt the gnaw of frustration as she adjusted herself to settle back against his arm. 'No you don't. Come on. Get up.' The seconds were ticking away.

'I don't want to, I'm comfy.'

'For fuck's sake!' Her head dropped back with a squeak of indignant surprise. 'Stand up. Now.' He tugged her upright with him. She wobbled, clutching his arm.

'Wait. What . . .' The sleepiness had gone, replaced by anxious alarm. 'Where—'

He took advantage of her hands on his arm to pull her towards the threshold. 'Just come with me. Fuck's sake, hurry!'

He drew her out into the scraps and shreds of dying light. She stumbled next to him, looking around in confusion.

'This is the chapel,' she said, sounding more and more panicky. 'And you're . . . you're—'

He held her shoulders to make her look straight at him. Her sallow, beaky face had lost all its elfin animation. She was deeply frightened.

'Marina, listen. You have to come with me. OK? Now. Fast.'

'But what—'

'Now!' He tugged her and set off down the path, clinging fiercely to her wrist as if she was a child having a tantrum.

'Gavin? What's— Ow! Stop! What's happening?'

'Can't stop to explain. We have to get away.'

'Away?'

'Right now.'

'But— no, stop!' She planted her feet and tried to hold him back. He was stronger. 'Ow!' she yelped again, pitching forward behind him.

'Just come on.'

'Ow, no!'

'Yes, Marina, yes.'

'What about— No! Stop! Daddy!'

They were slipping together down the steep incline. He wished she'd be quieter. He wished she'd hurry. He had the prickling, shivering, distracting certainty that something was coming closer. They'd been far too slow already. They'd never had a chance. The hunter was almost on them.

'Come on!' he urged, and his tone was almost as panicky as hers.

'I can't leave Daddy! He was crying!'

'We have to. Please, just—'

'No. No! Caleb disappeared and then she . . . she . . .'

She was slowing him down. He was too tired to battle her, too weak to drag her along. 'We'll go back afterwards,' he said. He was seeing black shadows everywhere in the deep darkness under the trees, closing in. 'We've just got to—'

'Afterwards? After what?'

'We have to get you away.'

'Where?'

'Down to the river. Quick! For fuck's sake, please, hurry!'

'The . . . No! I can't! Stop!' Her voice rose to a shriek, and she tried with both hands to haul him back. 'I'll die!'

'Marina—'

'Not like winter. I won't come back. I'll die properly. For ever!'

'Marina!' He whirled round. They had passed the dip in the path and stood at the top of the long slope that descended to the river. 'I swear, if we don't hurry up, right now, we'll both be dead in five minutes. OK?'

And without loosening his grip on her wrist he turned back down the path; but they didn't have five minutes, after all. They didn't have one.

They had no time at all, none.

The black dog was there, standing on the bridge. Its eyes were two dying stars in the near-night of the wood.

Too late, Gawain thought to himself, with a strangely empty sigh. Oh well. I almost made it.

It growled like distant thunder and stepped towards them.

My death.

To his surprise, he found himself thinking of the promise he'd made his mother. Not his mother. Iz. The one he hadn't meant to make until he said it. Telling her he'd come back some day and find her. How long would she hang on to that promise? When, he wondered, would she give in and admit to herself that he'd lied to her, that he wasn't coming back, while he rotted away among the discarded leaves with his neck broken and his throat torn out? Never?

'That's not a real animal.' Marina's voice behind him was a tiny frightened whisper. For a couple of paces the dog trotted, gathering itself. Then it was charging.

This must be what they mean by one's life flashing before one's eyes, Gawain decided, as he released Marina's wrist and took the rowan staff in both hands. It was as if he was standing to one side of himself, watching himself having these thoughts, his last thoughts, with a curious kind of detachment. It wasn't that he suddenly remembered everything all at once; it was that the few seconds remaining to him seemed to be happening incredibly slowly, while his mind raced at light speed. How come he had time to find Marina's remark so comically ridiculous? *Not a real animal.* Hmm, you think? With fire trailing from its onrushing mouth and the blazing fury in its eyes? No, not exactly the pooch next door. Although given that it's been sent to kill me, excuse me for not caring too much whether or not it's a fake. He was swinging the staff up in front of him to make a barrier, though it was perfectly obvious he might as well be trying to stop a cannonball with a chopstick.

The dog's mouth was opening soundlessly. No howl, no growl, just the soft percussion of its paws in the snow and the jaws readying. But in the strange slow-motion silence he thought he heard and remembered its dark and hungry voice, its litany of hunt and kill. Hello, my death, he thought. My death. *Through the door you left open walks my end.* Miss Grey's voice drifted dreamily into his head. He saw the cruel teeth bared in the long muzzle. *It's to do with maintaining a relationship with the spirit world.* Hester's mild voice joined in. Now his life was flashing before his ears instead of his eyes. *The mask is a sort of vehicle for a spirit. Or a dwelling place. Or a mouth.* Some other mouth was screaming, a tight-throated, half-choked scream. Maybe it was him.

Voices around him. He remembered the room swimming with voices. The way they'd seemed to turn towards him when his hands touched the mask. Maybe it was him.

The fiery eyes were close. *Through the door you left open.* It *was* him. The mask was a door. His hands had opened it and the fire had flowed in. That was the kind of door Miss Grey was talking about.

Close the door, he thought, as the widening mouth leaped, the twin stars filled his vision, and the blackness blotted everything else out. Close the door. The scream was definitely Marina. His own eyes twisted shut. The curtain coming down. End of story.

He felt the door against his fingers.

He closed it.

Marina finished screaming. Something clattered in front of them. Gawain's heart finished its beat. He opened his eyes.

The only sound was a weird soft hiss in the air, disembodied. A flare of red-gold light spiralled up and faded away into the sleeping trees.

The mask that had gone missing from Hester's house lay on the path at Gawain's feet, tipped sideways, propped on its blunt snout.

As if someone had pressed the fast-forward button, the usual ratio of thought to time reasserted itself. A hundred things went through Gawain's head, but now they were all in one great confused babbling crowd. The only thing he was aware of thinking was that now he'd be keeping his promise, after all.

'What is that?' Marina said. She sounded as if she was in shock. She'd gone ghost-white, as bloodless as her mother. She prodded the mask with her toe hesitantly, as if it might still bite.

Among the many things rushing through Gawain's mind was that he thought he knew the answer to that question, and that it was because he knew the answer that he'd been able to do what he'd done, closed the door through the mask as he'd unintentionally opened it before, and that was why he wasn't now dead, and that discovering the answer to questions like that was maybe the most important thing about who he now was, who he was destined to be, Gawain, White Hawk, Hawk of May, the stupid boy, the prophetess's heir.

'Don't touch it,' he said. She jerked her foot back at once. 'It's a mask. I saw it before. You were right, something was wearing it, something that didn't belong. It's gone now. Come on, let's go. Quickly.'

She edged nervously around it and broke into a half-run to catch up with him.

'Where did it go?'

'I don't know.'

'It was going to kill you.'

'Yeah. I told you, we have to get away.'

She kept glancing back up the path to where the mask lay, then having to hurry along again. Shock had made her pliant. She scurried behind Gawain as if the worst thing that could happen to her was being left alone in the near-darkness.

'Are you taking me away from—'

'Yes.'

'But what about Daddy?'

'I don't know. We'll think about that later. We have to hurry, she wasn't far behind.'

Marina's voice shrank to an awful whisper. 'She?'

'Auntie Gwen. But it's not really her. Quick, this way.'

They reached the place where the stream flowed under the path. A skin of ice had formed in its tiny pools, catching the last of the light. Gawain set off on the side path, downhill, towards the river.

'Gwenny's gone wrong.'

'I told you, it's not really her.'

'She told us what to do. It was like a dream. Even if we didn't want to. It hurt when I tried to do anything else.'

'Please, Marina. Please hurry up. She wasn't far behind.'

She clutched his arm with a death grip. 'Not this way.'

He yanked her along beside him. It was getting hard to see the path at all. 'No choice. Come on.'

'But this is a dead end.'

'You told me it went down to the river.'

'Yes, but that's beyond the wall.'

'OK, then—'

'No. I can't.'

'Marina—'

'I can't. I can't!'

'You can't stay. You know that.'

'No, you don't understand. There's something wrong with me. I'm different from you. I'll die if I go away from here. I will, I mean it.'

'You won't. There's—'

'No, please. I went once. I snuck away.' She spoke like she walked, the words coming out in a skipping trot. 'I trod on the road outside. It hurt so much. Gwen— They heard me screaming down at the house. Then another time—'

'Didn't you see what that thing was trying to do?'

A shimmer of dusky purple appeared through the trees ahead. She began to resist more desperately as the view of the water grew clearer. 'No. No, stop.'

'Just come on.'

'No!' she moaned, and sagged her knees, almost toppling him over. He didn't have the strength for it any more. He could barely force himself along, let alone the two of them. But the river was so close now, so tantalisingly close.

He halted and hauled her straight, rounded on her in desperation.

'Marina. Your mum sent me to fetch you.'

It was as if he'd slapped her.

'What?'

'I saw her. She spoke to me. For fuck's sake, keep going!'

But he'd stopped her dead. He might as well have shot her in the heart. He had to grab her shoulders again before she'd move, and he had to steer her down what he could see of the path as if she was blind. They came down into a flatter area of scrubby undergrowth, nettles and sprawling ivy and hazel saplings. He saw the outline of the low wall beyond, the border of the estate. Beyond it was the footpath, and beyond that a small sandy cove.

'Mummy died,' Marina whispered.

'No. I promise. And you won't either. She wants to see you.'

'But . . .' His tactic had worked in one sense: she'd completely lost interest in what might happen to her. Unfortunately she'd also apparently forgotten where she was. He had to push her towards the low earth wall.

'Is that her name?'

'What?'

'Fux. You keep saying it. For her sake.'

'Jesus wept,' he whispered to himself, and decided to concentrate on keeping her moving.

Beyond an overgrown bank of earth and piled stones that marked the boundary, the woods thinned out to become a small glade at the back of the shingly cove notched into the shore. He worried Marina would resist once he started trying to pull her up onto the wall, but she let him half help, half drag her down onto a riverside footpath. A disturbingly insistent feeling was nagging at him: What now? He'd never expected to get this far. He'd never expected anything. He had no idea what to expect. For the moment the woods seemed quiet, but the thing that had once been his aunt was still out there, surely still looking for him, and there wasn't any further to run except into the freezing dark water itself. Well, maybe that's what they'd do if it came to it. He led her carefully down to the cove, until they stood by the smear of heaped pebbles and driftwood marking the height of the last tide. Across the river, wide here near its mouth, the fields with their hedge borders were a white quilt laid over the coast. At the top of one round hill a church tower rose above flat-topped pines.

The fields, the church, the winter evening. For a few moments, while the boy and girl stood with nowhere to go, it was passive, it was content, it was much as it had been for five centuries: the undisturbed empty world.

Then a furious shout came from behind them, muffled among the trees: 'Corbo!'

She's found the mask, Gav thought to himself. Another, fainter cry in a different voice followed it quickly: '. . . ina?'

'That's Daddy!' Marina started and twisted round. But it was the first shout that had stung Gawain into motion. Before Marina could protest or resist he pulled her towards the water's edge: no other choice.

'Daddy!' she shouted, and pawed frantically at Gav's hand on her wrist. 'Daddy!'

Gav gritted his teeth and kept his eyes on the far bank, wondering how cold it would be, whether the currents would drag them out into the sea, how far they'd get. That was why he saw, distant but unmistakable, a huge black stain unfurl from the trees below the church on the opposite bank, its wings spreading, gliding across to answer the call, and then, only a moment later, much closer, just out in the slow-ebbing water beyond the cove, a pale shadow gathering and becoming a shape rising from the river, a glistening white head under trailing fronds of green.

The thing like a gigantic deformed bird had been wheeling over the valley, back and forth in the dismal twilight, scanning the north shore. It traced its wide gyres in the air, while people at their windows below gaped, went for binoculars, regretted using them.

Two things drove it. There was the command it could not disobey: watch for the boy who carried the ring, across the river from the house, where the sky spirit said he might be found. Just as imperative, just as unbreakable, there was hunger.

The hunger was like a chain wrapped round it, tightening with every hour. Hunger was the bolt and bars of the body it had been enclosed in. As it flew, it looked for carrion.

It circled over the mouth of the river, where the coast bent like a wing. Beating its way back above the northern shore, it saw the church tucked on its promontory in the wing's crook. A grey speck under the walls of the building caught its eye. It felt for the air differently, unstiffened its wingtips and plunged, cawing greedily. The speck became a heap, then a body. Fallen flesh.

Corbo was forbidden from touching the earth or anything that grew in it, so it landed atop a tombstone, folding its wings, swaying, clenching its talons on slate. The body was crumpled in the snow beneath.

Hester hadn't made it far from the porch. Out that morning, looking for Gawain after he'd vanished without warning from her house, she had been caught by the blizzard on an exposed stretch of the coast path. She'd eventually struggled her way to the church porch, the only shelter she could reach, but by the time she'd got there the clothes she'd hurriedly put on for a bright morning had been soaked through, sweat and melting snow turning icy in the first fierce wind. She'd waited in the porch, getting colder and weaker and more desperate, until as the evening grew dark she'd panicked and tried to summon the strength to battle out through the snow to the road. She'd slipped almost as soon as she'd started out from the porch, and fallen, and not been able to get up again.

The tumult of Corbo's landing and the raking of its claws on the upright stone stirred her from her deathly faint. To the beast's bitter disappointment, the slumped body twitched and let out a feeble moan.

'Not dead yet,' it grumbled. The pang ratcheted tighter.

The woman inched her head round. Some instinct told her, perhaps, that a shadow loomed over her, the creeping certainty of being watched. Her half-frozen eyelids struggled to open, then became narrow slits in a face grey as the snow. She looked up to see what had blocked the dying light.

Her eyes opened a little more and watered. She blinked.

She tried to scream.

'Back later,' Corbo muttered.

The shock had roused Hester's chilled heart, but only for a moment. Her head sagged back down. Her bloodless lips opened and struggled with a word. It took a long time.

'Help,' she said, in a dry and tiny whisper.

'Over soon,' Corbo croaked, but then cocked its head and ruffled its wings. Another smell had caught its attention.

'Man coming,' it said. 'Lucky you.'

On the other side of the church, J.P. Moss heard a guttural mutter.

If he'd thought there was any chance it was a sound made by the thing whose small wide-spaced steps he'd followed from the village, he'd have turned right round and gone back to the pub.

He'd actually been about to give up anyway. The lane down to the church had been OK, it had a few streetlights, but everything beyond was rapidly darkening. And at the end of the lane the footsteps quite clearly carried on into the wood beside the church, passing over a wooden stile and heading down the footpath that led through a pine glade to the river shore below. It was as good as night down that way.

Fortunately the sound had definitely come from the other direction, somewhere round in the graveyard. It had sounded like a choked sort of voice. Maybe someone in trouble. He hesitated for a second and then squeezed through the lychgate into the churchyard.

It was at that moment that Corbo felt the summons. J.P. came round the west end of the building just in time to see the monstrous man-crow spread its wings and thrash the air into a brief typhoon. The noise of its flight drowned his strangled shriek. It bore itself up to surmount the tops of the pines, so that for a moment it appeared to him as a baleful black angel suspended against the lesser dark of the sky. Then it swooped south, across the river, to where its furious master demanded its aid.

We are sought no longer, said the deep, spacious voice in Horace's thoughts.

He thought it himself. The voice was his; he and it were the same. It wove among the hundreds of other voices all around him. He was part of a chorus, the perpetual choir of things.

The bird is flown. Go.

The boy rose from where he had been sitting, under the cover of the pines—

The pines! The music they made was a faraway harmony, resonant with a different air, belonging to a distant forest, a place where he and the other him wanted to go. It felt like home. Far away, immensely far, along great currents that stirred the world and the skies. Far away from . . .

Go.

On his left hand he wore the plain brown ring that looked as if it was made of wood, though it was not. On his head was a whale mask. He was not merely wearing it, the way it had been made to be worn over on the other side of the world, in that other forest, among the fern-green moss and the wet hemlocks and the cold ocean inlets. More than that: its great oval eyes were his eyes, its long mouth his mouth, its voice his voice.

He went down to the rocks. The trees behind him were thick with crows. They broke their silence all at once, the shore echoing with their chafing uproar. When his feet entered the river he felt an inexpressibly huge joy. He kept going, losing his footing as the tide nudged him.

Amid the welter of life and sound around him the touch of water recalled a liquid whisper, *Find my child, find my child, find my child.*

I made a promise, he remembered.

Then keep it, he answered with his other voice, as his head slipped under the water and the boy began to drown.

The mermaid rose from the river, sinuous as an eel, ghost-pale, a nacreous sheen glistening where water slid away. Lank and weedy tendrils clung to her. Gawain and Marina stood at the very edge of the tide. The girl's fingers were still on the boy's hand where she'd been trying to prise herself out of his grip. They went limp. Her lopsided mouth fell open.

This time Gawain saw in the flesh what he'd guessed at before: the family resemblance. Though one face belonged to a terrified and overwhelmed child, and the other was as inhuman as a marble statue dredged up from a thousand forgotten and submerged years, they were mother and daughter.

The mother knew it. She reached her white arms forward as she came higher up the beach.

The daughter had not yet understood.

'Go on,' Gawain said. 'That's her.' He let go of Marina's wrist.

'But . . .' Marina stammered. 'I . . .'

She took two hesitant steps into the river, towards the embrace. Then they heard the hoarse and desperate call from the woods again. '. . . Marina!' The mermaid froze, and the boy and the girl spun round. None of them could yet see Tristram Uren, though he was coming down the path from the house in a wild delirium, heedless of his old limbs and wheezing lungs.

But they did see Gwen.

She stood unsteadily atop the earth wall bordering the footpath, staff planted in the snow. A burning radiance writhed around its tip. At the sight of her Marina clutched Gawain's arm in absolute terror. 'It's OK,' he told her, though his jaw was clenched and his heart thudding. 'Go to your mum. Go on. She can't come much closer, she belongs in the sea. Quick!'

Gwen began descending towards them, undergrowth snapping as she forced herself along.

'Daddy—' Marina began.

'Now!' Gawain said, and shoved her into the water.

It was his aunt. He could see her clearly enough now despite the twilight, face on, for the first time. Her face was all wrong. Or rather it was exactly the same face, but wrong on the inside, or put together wrongly; he couldn't figure out exactly where the wrongness was, but it was so horrific to look at that he wasn't sure how much longer he could stand in place watching it approach, and he refused to collapse or run away or die of horror until he knew Marina was safe; he *refused.*

Alas, Marina had known very little fear and stress in her thirteen hidden years. Being pulled so hard in so many directions was too much for her. She sank to her knees in the shallows, whimpering, clinging with one wet fist to the hem of Gawain's trousers, squeezing her eyes shut. He knew he ought to kick her away, do anything to get her out into the icy river, but she was holding on to him as if he was the last tether stopping her from sinking, and he couldn't do it. Her desperate grip anchored him; all he could do was watch as the mermaid and the warlock approached, one from the shore, one from the sea.

Swanny beckoned urgently as she rose higher. Gawain could feel what it cost her to come so far up into the air. Unlike when she'd leaped into Horace's boat, or when fifteen years before she'd seen Tristram walking by this very cove in moonlight, the ring was not nearby, and without the passage it opened she could not be truly a woman rather than the sea-image of one. She dropped to a crawl and forced herself up the strand, straining the fingers of one hand towards her terrified child. Her mouth was working, but the watery whisper Gawain remembered was inaudible against the clamour of the crows on the far bank. She mouthed her child's name. Marina couldn't hear or see it; head bent, hands over her face, she moaned wordlessly to herself, over and over again.

'Go on,' Gav begged her. 'Please. It's her. Please go.'

The mermaid's hand, trembling, stretched out and touched her cheek.

Marina stopped shuddering and opened her eyes. Her skin remembered the mother's touch, perhaps. The memory worked its way gradually inwards, towards her heart.

Above them, on the beach, the warlock steadied herself, raised her staff to her lips and spoke three words. The spell was barely more than a laboured whisper, but Gawain heard it and recoiled in dread. To his ears the words carved through the air like stones from a sling, and in the passage they made he felt fiery presences thronging. The glow at the end of her staff blazed up. She raised it with both hands and pointed it down towards where the mermaid and her daughter knelt together in ankle-deep water.

Swanny twisted and stiffened as if struck by lightning. She fell on her back, her head tossed up on the sand. Her legs thrashed in the shallows.

'Mummy!' Marina screamed. 'Mummy!' She clung to the shuddering white shoulders. Swanny's arms tried to curl over the child, but the agony gripped them again and they pounded on the sand. She was drowning in air, while the invisible tormentors pinned and racked her.

Gawain's head was buzzing. Everything was a chaos of noise. The distant cawing, shouts from the trees, the girl's anguished cries, the air thrumming and burning, his own desperate rage. 'Stop it!' he shouted, not knowing which part of the cacophony he wanted silent. He couldn't think. 'Stop it!' That was it: he had to stop her. Consumed with horror and fury, he forgot to be afraid. 'Stop!' He gripped the rowan stick so hard it hurt his numbed hands and started up the beach. He didn't see his aunt any more. No one could have. The merciless bitterness in the warlock's face had transformed it. He saw only a thin hunched woman who had no power over him. He yelled and broke into a run, raising the stick over his head.

A whirring shadow swamped the last light. Vast black wings swooped over Gawain's head. Then Corbo was standing in front of him, blocking his way.

The horrible broken voice behind it said, 'Kill the boy.'

Gawain stared into its obsidian eyes.

The hooked mouth opened.

Kaaaark

'Corbo?'

It took a step forward. Its talons raked deep marks in the sand.

'Run,' it said.

A gurgling, choking sound had begun behind him. Swanny fought to speak, while the tide ebbed further from her. Marina sobbed over her dying mother, shouting and crying all at once, her hands looking for some part of the pale wet flesh to hold.

'Let me past, Corbo,' Gawain said, as steadily as he could.

'Not now. Told to kill. Run.'

The crow-thing stepped closer again, then suddenly threw back its head and screeched. 'Run. Run. Run run run.'

It came at him, a blur of wings and claws. Gawain swung the walking stick reflexively. A fast and angry blow might have hurt it, but he'd never learned to fight. Corbo swayed away from the rowan staff with implausible grace, wings spreading, and lifted itself into the air. One foot swept out and clutched the stick, and with the next huge thrust of the wings wrenched it out of Gawain's grasp. He stumbled backwards, hands stinging. 'Run run,' Corbo cawed again, neck stretching. It dropped the stick and landed, hopping closer. 'Run. Dive.' Gawain scrambled back into the water. 'Go, *wraaaaak*. Go.' It bounced forward and beat the great wings again. Its talons flashed out with grotesque speed. He flung himself to one side, landed with salt water drenching his face, righted himself, spluttering and gasping. He was quite certain now that he was going to die, but, unbearably, that certainty was less tormenting than the girl's pitiful cries and her mother's final agony, the knowledge that he'd failed them.

Corbo alit on the shore, balancing itself. Beside it the mermaid shivered weakly, her thrashing reduced to spasmodic quivers. The glimpse of Marina's grief-struck face shredded Gawain's heart.

'Kill him now!' another voice shrieked. 'Now!'

Even Corbo's expressionless cries sounded like a roar of misery. '*Rrraaaak*,' it groaned. 'Flee, flee, *wraaaa*.' It launched itself, wings pounding air, gaining purchase, rising.

Gawain pushed himself upright, splashed three steps towards the open river and threw himself down as the hideous shadow spread over him and plummeted. This time he felt talons tearing his back. His mouth filled, drowning his scream. Salt burned in the wounds as if the claws had stuck to him and were burrowing down to his bones. He thrust his head up to gulp air and howl in torment. The whole twilit scene began to swim and blur. Hazily, he saw the monstrous bird rising above him again, screeching as bitterly as he was, preparing to lunge. He saw the warlock hobbling out onto exposed rocks that jutted out into the falling tide, looking for a better view while her servant tore him apart. Scrabbling desperately against the muddy seabed, he took a huge breath and shoved himself down, the sky darkening above him again as Corbo swooped.

The water seemed to embrace him, not dense and sluggish but easy as air; he slipped right down to the submerged rock, shaping himself low and flat like a diving cormorant. There was a bubbling commotion on the surface above, and maybe the plunging claws didn't reach him, though the torture of the open wounds in his back was so fierce he could feel nothing else there anyway. Through eyes misting with grief and pain he saw the impenetrable murk ahead, the weed-covered depths where the drowned valley sank away below the lowest tides. It seemed like a peaceful, mercifully silent darkness, like death. He swam down towards it, kicking.

The water dimmed and then swirled again, with a strangely inert sound. Gawain rolled as he swam and, looking upwards, saw small whirlpools where Corbo's claws had pierced the surface and withdrawn. Ribbons of blood fanned out in the agitated water. He kicked up quickly. His head broke into air and he found himself screaming; when the pain had emptied his lungs he gasped to refill them. The warlock had picked her way out to a shelf of kelp-draped rock far out from the shore. She stood as if on a tiny island, as far as she could go, on the brink of deep water, pointing to where Gawain had surfaced, shouting something in a voice as harsh and almost as inhuman as Corbo's racking cries. Above, the wings beat, wheeled, tipped as it plunged once more.

He twisted to dive. His back felt like it must have broken. He couldn't tell whether the darkness gathering around his vision was the falling shadow above or the silted mud below or the coming night or just his own life bleeding out of him. He sank, welcoming the bite of the cold. It damped the fire in his gouged back. He was shrinking inside himself. Soon he'd contract to nothing. The splash of Corbo's feet scything through the surface above sounded dull, almost gentle. He was down among the swaying weeds, where everything was slow and placid. Only his lungs were still protesting, burning as the last draught of air expired. They would calm too, once he filled them with water. Everything would go quiet. Quiet as Miss Grey.

He felt the deep, enduring plenitude, above and beneath. His memory filled with her goodbye kiss. The last kiss, she'd told him. Earth and sky had opened as her lips touched his, the world going on without her, without him.

There was a hum in the water.

It was a deep, wonderful sound, a homecoming sound. It rushed towards him, joyfully swift. His consciousness of things fading, beaten down and completely spent at long last, Gawain ceased his struggle and let it come for him. He sank slowly as it swelled closer. For a strangely blissful moment it drowned out the agony in his back and the crushing weight on his lungs, and he knew it; he remembered its hymn of blood and sustenance, the song of the untrammelled ocean. He remembered its name: *ma'chinu'ch, ma'chinu'ch.* He opened his throat to welcome it. In the darkness of the water he saw the singer, a huge slick blackness surging towards him as if the sea itself had taken flesh.

A great welling current in the river came ahead of it like a second tide. It thrust him up. Noise and chaos returned in a rush as his head came out. There was Corbo, wheeling high above, cawing its grim cry. He'd surfaced far out from the shore and the winged beast had lost track of him for the moment. Through the sting of salt and the sparks of pain in his eyes he saw the warlock still perched at the extremity of her low spur of rock, bending forward, scanning the river.

'There!' she shouted. 'There!' She stretched out her staff towards him. 'Finish him!' Corbo was already pitching down, a black bolt from the sullen clouds.

The surface of the river trembled, then roiled, and then light and darkness breached it and surged up, massive and swift and irresistible.

Corbo screeched, but now it was shouting the name of the thing that had leaped from the water: '*Orca! Orca!*' A whale, black-backed and white-bellied, a slick titanic bullet cannoned from the river, so swift that Gawain only saw it for the second of its deadly arc through the air. But that second was long enough for it to sweep alongside the isthmus of rock where the warlock stood. The glancing blow of its fin tossed her up like winnowed chaff.

Talons rushed at Gawain's face. He lifted his arms weakly and sank straight back down to the silence below. He didn't see his aunt's body crash into the water, limp as a sack, or the warlock's staff bobbing away, already in the grip of the seaward tide. He didn't see Corbo's wings snap stiff, carrying the suddenly quiet crow-beast away in a long glide. All he saw was the featureless dark expanse stretching away from him, and himself fading into it, ebbing, vanishing oceanwards.

He sank slowly, his last strength gone.

Then he was rising again. He felt himself lifted, but was past knowing or caring how, though there might have been white arms. He was flotsam.

He came to the surface. The sky was barren and peaceful as the depths. Water dribbled from his nose and mouth.

Something washed him up on the coarse sand. He lay there, belly down, up to his chest in the icy river, a piece of sodden driftwood. Fragments of shells pricked his cheek. He tasted blood and seawater.

Slow feet scrunched down the beach. Wheezing breath accompanied them. Gawain didn't think to try and move his head to see who it was. He felt peacefully insensible, like a stone.

'Oh my love,' said the voice that went with the wheezing and the footsteps. 'Oh God. Oh my dear love.'

From somewhere beyond his feet another voice whispered very softly 'Fetch him water.'

This struck Gawain as a wonderful idea. He noticed how unbearably thirsty he was. The salt in his mouth made it feel like it was being scoured and baked.

'From the well.' If everything else hadn't been so quiet all of a sudden, he doubted he'd have heard the rippling whisper. No one moved.

'Marina,' said the same voice.

More scrunching, and he heard Marina now, sounding very trembly and very young.

'Where's . . . What happened to—'

'The warlock is broken. You're safe now. The well, quickly, or the boy will die.'

'Yes, sorry. Sorry.' Poor Marina, Gawain thought distantly. Always does as she's told. 'I'll go.' Her steps started away hesitantly at first, then sped into a run and were silenced as she clambered up to snow-covered ground.

He hoped she'd hurry. Dying didn't seem too bad now that he was three-quarters of the way there already, but he was really desperate for that drink.

The voice beyond his feet whispered something so quietly that only a ghost like him could have heard it.

'Go safely. My heart. My second heart. Be always safe.'

Shoes appeared in his line of sight. Wet brown shoes, with wet brown trouser cuffs above them. He would have had to turn his neck to see more, and he had the vague feeling that any attempt to move would start a volcanic eruption of pain in his back, but he didn't need to bother, since he'd figured out that this was Tristram Uren. Something about the shoes. Funny the things you notice, he thought.

'Swanny. Oh God, Swanny. Oh thank God. Thank God.'

Now he couldn't hear what she said. It was obscured by the sound of Tristram's feet shuffling into the water, and his hoarse gasp at the cold.

'I can't let you go again,' he said. 'Not again. Oh, Swanny. This has to be the end.'

He must have stopped splashing around, because this time he heard her. 'Then come to me. Quickly, before she returns.'

The steps struggled further into the water, halted.

'How can we leave her? Oh my love, my love!' Between joy and grief his voice cracked apart.

'I watched her for these many years. I will watch her still. And the boy is kind, and brave.'

I wonder what boy she's talking about, Gawain thought.

'Eleven years.' Tristram's whisper was almost as soft as the mermaid's. 'There hasn't been a single minute when I didn't think of you. Not one.' His voice rose. 'Not one. Swanny, Swanny! God forgive me, this is all I ever wanted. To be yours again. To die happy.'

Dictionary definition, another ghost said in Gawain's head, hazily. *A state of rapture, supposedly inspired in men by nymphs. Hence, a frenzy of emotion inspired by something unattainable.* He remembered stories. Odysseus and the sirens. When sailors saw mermaids they'd throw themselves into the sea and drown.

'I'm here,' Swanny said. 'Come now. If our child sees you go, her heart will break.'

Gawain felt something trickle along his nose. It was a tear. He hoped it would drip into his mouth.

'Tell her—' Tristram began, and his heavy breath choked. 'Tell her—' he tried again. He made a small noise that might have been clearing his throat.

'Tell her . . . she has been the light in my life all these years. Tell her I couldn't have borne losing her mother again. No more than she could have borne it herself. Tell her I love her more than . . . more than . . .'

The mermaid's whisper broke the silence, remote as a wisp of mountain cloud. 'Come and love me.'

The shoes and trousers went further into the river and out of Gawain's sight. He had gone back to contemplating the bleached shards of shell in front of his eyes when it slowly occurred to him that Tristram's last words had probably been addressed to him. Wait a minute, he thought. Tell her what? Tell who? Why?

There was some agitation about the question that broke through his dullness. It suddenly seemed important to see what was going on. With enormous effort, he inched his chin a little closer to his shoulder, angling his head just enough to look down past his own slumped body and out into the river. It took nearly as much effort to get his eyes to focus. There was an awful, throbbing pain. He'd somehow managed to avoid noticing it before, but now it interfered, making his eyes water and fill with shooting stars. He squinted through them.

The mermaid was waist deep in the river, arms out, a luminous smile on her glistening face. Tristram Uren, his hair white as winter, waded out towards her through the shallows. She seemed to glide back a little as he approached, and a little further again, until it looked as if he might stumble and sink before he reached her embrace. Then in one joyous movement she surged forward, clasping him, lifting both of them up. They held each other as tight as if they had grown together, she the white column and he the clinging vine, and it seemed to Gawain's imperfect sight that they shone for a moment as they kissed, the sheen of water catching whatever final radiance the expiring day had to give them. Then they sank together and the river settled over them. After that there was nothing to see.

Part VII
Omens

Thirty-two

FOR THE FIRST time the greatest magus in the world knew what it truly meant to face death.

Her ribs had cracked when the whale struck up at her, and all the breath had been driven from her body when she fell to the river, and her clothes, filled with freezing water, weighed on her like the chains of the condemned, but none of the agonies of the body even began to compare to the livid terror of knowing she would now die. She'd drowned once before, but now there was no enchanted microcosm of her soul given in immortal safekeeping, no assurance with which to defy the hideous indifference of the sea. This was the end, the unthinkable terminus.

And beyond the end, judgement waited.

No plumb could have sounded the depths of horror the magus knew in those few stretched seconds of her drowning as the prospect of a final reckoning opened before her. Johann Faust had thought himself one of the holiest of men. He had been the devoted and selfless servant of wisdom, that most precious of virtues. He had reverenced the fingerprints left by the Maker's hand. Even when he was wrecked with the English mariners in the guise of Master John Fiste, and sunk to his first death, the horrible animal fear and solitude of drowning had been warmed by a comforting conscience; for although he had already then dreamed of stealing immortality for himself, he had – the certainty of it was bedrock under the tossing storm – done no harm. Had that been the day of his true death, he would have gone down among the cursing sailors like a prince among peasants, calmly enduring the brutality of the waves for what it was, a mere instant of suffering before an endless journey into glory.

But now – she could not deny it to herself, even in her most desperate need – she had descended to cruelty.

Unforgivable cruelty. The dryad locked for ever in its tomb of wood, the screaming boy bleeding in the water, the half-girl watching her own mother die. And – this was the sight that overwhelmed her mind's eye, in those few seconds of wasted struggle – the beggar prophetess, the princess of Troy, the bearer of the gift of magic itself, lying with her neck broken like scythed stubble. She, the deepest marvel of the world; she, who had waited twice a thousand years for his love; she, flushed out and killed like a barn rat, and left unmourned in the snow.

The magus knew, with the iron certainty that arrives as the ingenious subtleties of self-deception finally expire, that she was damned.

Damned.

And to compound the awful, absolute horror of this certainty, she knew – as surely no other mortal ever had, not the penitents nor the church doctors nor the raving visionaries – what damnation might mean. She knew some fraction of it: a drop from the unquenchable Phlegethon had already fallen in her cup. For the blank-eyed servant whose obedience she had won so long ago, the fiery phantom whom she had made her messenger and viceroy in the realms of spirit, was a being of the lower spheres. Not a demon, no. Not that. She could no more command demons than angels. But (how could she have denied it to herself all those years? How could she have been so seduced by its willingness to serve that she had never once asked herself what it truly was she had admitted to her company?) it was the most despised companion of demons, denizen of the outermost suburbs of Pandemonium. It ranked among the worms and the mayflies of hell.

Hell's great brass gates yawned open to receive her. Its welcome was prepared.

So the great and fallen magus lamented as she sank to her death, the river darkness thicker around her inch by inch, foot by foot.

Then the murk was lit as if by a burnished aurora. Hollow voices and lidless eyes thronged around her.

You die the final death, Magister.

Under the choking weight of the river, her eyes were twisted shut and her mouth open in a drowned scream.

Give us flesh again, Magister. Give us body. Admit us and be saved.

The gates were wide. She was on the very threshold. Her poor battered husk was empty of air.

We have served you, Magister. Now accept us and live. Share our being.

Better to die, the magus knew. Better to die. The judge was merciful. He had atoned for all sins. There might be forgiveness still, if she refused the last temptation and denied them.

The final instant is here. Permit us to do you our last service. Give us your flesh and live with us.

The magus had once, triumphantly, believed herself ready to assume immortality. She had let herself be touched by the prospect of something beyond life, love, death, something no longer part of the commonwealth of humanity. Once cursed by that desire, she could not surrender it. For all her wisdom, all the patience and study and humility to which she had once dedicated herself, she could not, in the end, bear to die.

I accept, she said in her heart; and so, at the very last, Johann Faust sold his soul.

The drenched and ruined body jerked, tensed, filled with strength. Eyes blazing underwater like the furnaces of a sunken city, it stretched out its limbs and swam powerfully away.

Thirty-three

MOTHER OF GOD, J.P. thought, looking around the professor's front room. No wonder she lost her feckin' marbles.

None of them could stop themselves from stealing glances over their shoulders at the faces on the walls, even as they pushed the furniture around and squeezed past each other and fussed over the business of getting lead-grey, semi-comatose Hester Lightfoot into her house. The masks quelled the useless hubbub of conflicting instructions that had been pouring out of the small crowd ever since it had assembled in answer to J.P.'s call for help. This at least was a relief. One of the women was close to hysteria herself, and between her wavering on the outskirts of a screaming fit and the others trying to shut her up while arguing over what to do with Hester, he thought he'd have been mad himself in another minute.

If he wasn't already.

He'd be back in the pub right now, so help him, with a glass of something a lot stiffer than stout, were it not for the fact that other people had seen it too, watched it gliding along the sky. *It.* Come on now, J.P., you're a journalist, make an effort. *It.* The black thing, the black flying thing, rising up before his own two eyes like death's feckin' messenger.

It's the end, he thought. It's finally come. Who'd have thought? Turns out Ma was right after all, God rest her. Hands up everyone who'd guessed he should have paid more attention to Sister Beata and the feckin' nuns. Some of it stuck in your head, mind. Some of the words had a way of getting in there and never coming out. The poetry of them. *And I saw an angel standing in the sun; and he cried with a loud voice, saying to all the fowls that fly in the midst of heaven, Come and gather yourselves together unto the supper of the great God; that ye may eat the flesh of kings, and the flesh of captains, and the flesh of mighty men, and the flesh of horses, and of them that sit on them, and the flesh of all men, both free and bond, both small and great.*

His phone vibrated in his pocket.

'Excuse me a sec.' He left the others attending to Hester and went out to the front steps. She'd be all right now if she was going to be, the others would see to that, and he urgently needed to reduce his exposure to her version of interior decoration.

It had started snowing again. Of course it had. The old Vikings had a name for it, he remembered. *Fimbulwinter.* The last winter, when the world got ready to die. Three unbroken years, was it supposed to last? Now that was just a story, though.

Just a story.

He wrestled the phone out of his pocket. The message from Vicky blinked up: *bbc on line, want ur story.*

He stared at it for a long while.

Well well well, he thought sardonically. My big break. In the right place at the right time. Just what every provincial hack dreams of: getting to do a report for the Beeb.

He imagined how it would sound. The crisp, uncommitted, inoffensively regional voice of the studio anchor. 'John Patrick Moss of the *Western Cornishman* sent us this report.'

This report. What would he say? What would he tell the country, and the world? There was a BBC way of doing these things. Detached, wry, just a tad sceptical. Don't worry, nation of Britain. Don't worry, people beside your retro radios or in front of your shiny flat-screen televisions. Your man in the field won't ask you to think anything you don't want to think.

He called in.

'Vicky? J.P. . . . Not so great, since you ask, but— . . . Yes, of course. Now? . . . OK.' He puffed a cloud of breath into the chill air. 'No . . . What? . . . Is there a story?' He tucked the phone closer to his chin. 'Is there a feckin' story? Is that what you're asking me, Victoria dear?' He let the silence stretch a little. 'The end of the world. How's that grab you, Vicky? Think it'll do for the front page? . . . No. No, you listen to me. I'm here. No one else is going to get here until the weather changes, and that could be a while, eh?' Three unbroken years. 'I know what I've seen. And I'm not the only one. Put them through.'

He heard beeps in the office and Vicky's exasperated sigh before he hung up. He fiddled with the phone, blowing on his fingers. It rang again almost at once.

The urban voice. Slightly bored. Techie. He imagined the bloke in his studio, surrounded by all the equipment. Probably finishing his shift. Coffee, the kind that came with extra adjectives, in a paper cup.

'Yes, I'm ready,' he said. 'OK . . . Got it . . . Yes.'

Silence. The machines were waiting to record him.

Ah, feck it, he thought to himself. Like Ma used to say, always tell the truth; it's the easiest thing to remember.

He told the truth.

Gawain had to hold her hand every step of the way. If he let go even for a second, she stopped dead, as dead as when he'd first seen her, sleep-walking in the rain. But he held it gently this time and led her without hurrying. This was partly because she'd gone so numb he knew there was no point trying to make her speed up, and partly because it gave him more time to think of something to say.

In his other hand he held the little wooden box with its tarnished silver clasp, which she'd used to bring him water from the chapel.

The snow was falling again, countless millions of white silences descending. What was he supposed to say?

In the first violence of her grief, once she'd at last understood what had happened, she'd clung to him with a stricken intensity to which he had no answer at all. He'd never seen what anguish like that did to a person before. She gripped him so tightly her nails made him bleed and yet she might as well have been a thousand miles away, so powerless was he to reach across the abysm of misery that separated them. *Daddy, Daddy, Daddy,* she'd cried, again and again, until it stopped sounding like a word and became the scream of a gull. How could he answer that? And when at last the cries had emptied themselves and she'd shrivelled into a limp stillness that was if anything worse to witness than the paroxysms of grief, none of his clumsy words had touched her at all.

'Marina.' Nothing. 'Come on then.' Nothing. 'Let's get you warm, come on.' Nothing. 'Marina, I'm so sorry. I'm so sorry.' Nothing.

The first time he'd set eyes on her he'd thought she was dead. It was a bad omen. She was getting colder. Dying from the inside out.

So he'd lifted her to her feet then, thinking at least he should get her inside somewhere, out of the snow. The chapel was closest, but he couldn't take her back there, not now, and anyway, she needed warmth. He could find something in the house, maybe. Some clothes. A fire.

She'd stood up unprotestingly, face vacant. But now as she followed him along the paths under the trees again, mute as a beast of burden, Gawain admitted to himself that it wasn't shelter she needed, or fire, or dry clothes, or even the attention of someone who knew what they were doing. What she needed was a speck of light in the emptiness, some tiny thing to hold on to. Something as small as a word, even.

He stopped when they came out of the woods, at the bottom of the field below the house. Awkwardly, he put the box down and took her hand in both of his. Her eyes looked straight through him into nothing. It was almost full night now.

'Marina.'

Not a flicker. It was like trying to address a waxwork.

'OK. Marina. Before he . . . Before your dad . . .'

In the shadow of her face he thought he saw her eyes slide round and look at him, hopelessly.

'Before he . . .'

Tristram hadn't known what to say either. How could he have? What last message could possibly be adequate to the pain he'd handed down to her? How could he even have dared open his mouth? Gawain wondered: maybe speech runs out where magic takes over. Maybe that's what magic will turn out to be: the things we don't have words for. And it's just that there turns out to be so, so much more of that than we all thought.

He took a deep breath.

'Your dad told me to tell you something. Before he . . . went to your mum. He told me to tell you that . . .' He swallowed, closed his eyes. It was just like he'd been doing all along since he got here: keeping going. No turning back. Just keep on. 'That you kept him going. That he loved you so much, that you were everything to him. That without you he couldn't have held on even as long as he did.' Her lips trembled and opened. He knew what they were going to say: *Stop. Stop torturing me.* But he blundered on, wading through her misery like he'd forced his bare feet through the snow. 'He couldn't say it himself, because . . . He could never. Not face to face. He was stuck between . . . between . . .' Her eyes glistened, then overflowed. Appallingly, her face stayed perfectly still as the fat tears coursed down, like a weeping statue, or a weeping corpse. 'Marina, I'm so sorry. But I know. The thing is, he didn't have a choice. It's . . .'

He grimaced, then let go of her hand and took her shoulders. Say the truth, he told himself. Just say it. Don't try to hide it. *Truth hurts.* You'd think words would be the easy bit, the bit that didn't need courage, but oh no, oh God no.

'Marina, please. Listen. I lost my mum and dad too. Today. I didn't even know who they were. I still don't. All I know is they're gone, I don't have anyone either.' She was weeping with her eyes wide open, completely silently, staring at him all the while. It was unbearable, but he had to go on. 'It's like you catch something. Or it catches you. And after that things just can't keep going like they used to. That's what I mean, there's no choice. Your dad loved you so much, Marina, I know he did. But after . . .' He shrugged helplessly. 'This. After all this, he couldn't go on living here, being your dad. Your mum too, I know she loves you.' *My second heart.* The tears washed scars in the dirt and sand on her cheeks. 'I know she'd do anything to just come and be your mum, if she could. But she can't. It doesn't matter how much she wants it. What we want doesn't make any difference at all. I used to have my life too, Marina. I used to have somewhere to go and stuff to do. But after today all of that . . .' He mimed releasing a handful of dust into the wind. 'I'm sorry. I don't know what I'm trying to say. All I know is, at least . . . at least . . .' He swallowed thickly, tasting salt. 'At least there's two of us, Marina. It's not just you. It's not just me. At least—'

He only stopped because she flung her arms round his neck. 'Stay here for ever,' she was saying, in a voice worn soft by grief. 'Stay here with me for ever. Stay here.' She buried her nose in the hollow of his shoulder. 'Stay with me. For ever, for ever.'

For a moment he had no idea what to do with his hands. They hung stupidly in the air. Then he folded them around her, with a tenderness no one had ever taught him.

'OK,' he said, and patted her hair gingerly. 'OK. For ever.'

Corbo flew until it was almost out of sight of land, tracking the demon in the water, but it dared not go on further. It gave up the chase with a despairing cry, wheeling low over the swell and turning back to the northwest, loathing each condemned wing-beat that propelled it back towards solid ground. Hunger might sink it before it got there. If it could not be free, it must feed the flesh it was shackled to. Already it felt itself weakening. Its wings wrestled with the air, hammered it instead of stroking it.

There was death in the sky. Somewhere over land, things that were not alive rose up and flew, growling and roaring with dead voices. They had the smell that fouled the world, the poison-smoke smell. Corbo could not see them, but it feared their approach. Battling the agony of its craving, it flew faster, making for the shore and the sheltering woods.

As it neared, it felt the rustle of a crow-thought. *Meat!*

Spurred, it beat harder and rose as it crossed the cliffs, the upwelling air carrying it high. It glided noiselessly over the house. It saw the half-girl and the once-boy below. They embraced, a little shivering huddle of persistent life, and went in under the roof.

Turning as it met the current of the southwest wind, it smelled its fellow prisoner Holly below. Her limbs stretched up. She sang out her greeting.

Rorate coeli desuper et nubes pluant iustum
Rorate coeli desuper et nubes pluant iustum

From the canopy beyond the house came the sweet stench of the crow-thought, gathering strength as more birds arrived to share it. Now Corbo too found the scent of fresh death and rejoiced.

Among the trees the chorus of crows drowned out Holly's antiphon. From generation to generation the crow-mind had preserved its memories of the old feasting fields, tapestries of slaughter garlanded with smoke. In their roosts they hoarded dreams of their centuries of plenty, the long golden age when the earthbound had been too impatient to wait for death and killed each other instead, legions of them, in numbers that made a mockery of burial. Now they smelled the crow-banquet coming again. A new wind was rising, rich with plenty. They called from valley to valley, spreading the word.

They scattered as Corbo descended. The corpse was too fresh for them anyway. Their hunger was visionary; Corbo's was urgent. It did not care about the coming feast. It ravened now. All it saw in its future was bondage to the misshapen body, its cravings, its ecstasies, its sufferings – that, and the labour of watching over the once-boy, who would need all its care, if the crow-thought saw the coming months and years rightly.

But that could wait. It stamped down undergrowth with its splayed talons and bent over the body.

Madness had descended on Caleb as a kind of mercy, numbing the torment of his thoughts. He had thrown off the last of his clothes as he crawled among the nettles and thorns. The winter night had judged him with kindness, quieting him slowly, inexorably, irrevocably, until he was silenced for good.

Talons gripped and dug.

When Corbo finally straightened itself, its hooked mouth was smeared and dripping, and its feet too were stained crimson. It was transformed: a horrific incarnation of the chough, the Cornish crow, black all over but for its red beak and legs, a blazon of night and fire and blood. The carrion birds cawed the chough's name in welcome, *Pyrrhocorax, Pyrrhocorax*. Their grim revels shook the wood.

On the other side of the world, across land and water, in a place once called Tsaxis, a teenage girl zipped her coat up higher and burrowed down under the blanket.

She always slept with her coat on. When it got cold, like tonight, she put the hood up too. Its thick, furry trimming gave her a nice animal feeling, snuggling up to something warm while she went to sleep, like being a raccoon kit.

Not tonight, though. She couldn't get comfortable. Mom wasn't back yet, which wasn't a good sign.

She checked the clock with the glow-in-the-dark Mickey Mouse hands. Two in the morning, they said. Mickey pointed up like he was doing a cheesy disco number. Over in the proper bed, Carl was doing that snore that was like a panting dog mixed with a stalling engine. The excuse was that he got the proper bed because he was the biggest. Actually he got the bed because he said so, even though she was older. He got plenty of use out of it too. Not just sleeping, though he was lazy as a piece of wood. Whenever Mom flipped the TV around to her channels instead of his, up he'd come and in he'd go, and if it wasn't to sleep, then he'd push Jen and Cody out and shut the door and do whatever it was he did on his own. Playing with himself. He left the magazines lying around. Some of the pages stuck together. Jen tried to stuff them back under the mattress before Cody saw them. It was the only mattress in the room – she slept on an old couch – and she didn't think it was going to last much longer, what with Carl getting almost too fat to put his own shoes on.

Cody slept noiselessly on a camp bed near the windows. He'd built his barricade next to it, as usual, between him and the door. It was only piled blankets and clothes and some other crap, cast-off hockey pads and empty cigarette boxes and things like that, but he built it up anyway, every night. He waited for Carl to fall asleep before making his little wall and then woke up before him so he could take it down again secretly. He was learning to hide his weaknesses, though Jen thought it was kind of a bit late for that.

As well as her two brothers there was baby Crystal, asleep in the folding cot. If she woke up, it would be Jen who'd have to try to keep her quiet. Or if Cody woke up with one of his screaming fits, it would be Jen who'd hold his hand and curl up with him until he stopped, and then walk him all around the house to show him Andy wasn't home, and then take him outside whatever time of night it was to prove that Andy's truck wasn't anywhere near the house and he really didn't live with them any more. If they both woke up at the same time, it would be up to Jen to combine the two jobs, crooking the baby in one arm while she led Cody around with the other. If Mom came back late and happened to be in one of her moods when she wanted to talk, it would be Jen who'd have to intercept her at the door before she set Cody off, and steer her to her own room and listen to the weeping and mumbling for however long it took that particular night until her bloodshot eyes went glassy and she tipped over and passed out.

Between one thing and another, Jen spent a lot of time awake in the night.

To make matters worse, she'd developed a pretty good sense of when these things were likely to happen. She'd learned to read the signs. These days she even had an idea of when the baby was gearing up for a bad night. Not so surprising, since she was the one who kept an eye on Crystal every afternoon and evening. When Mom got going she liked to whine about how hard it was looking after all the kids. Jen thought that was pretty funny, since she usually came back from school to find Mom downstairs with beer and smokes and the TV on loud and Crystal cooped up in a playpen in a different room with a big wet diaper. Come to that, Jen thought it was pretty hilarious that any of them complained to her about anything. They were the ones who dropped their burdens on her like she was paid to carry them. She made half an exception for Cody, who'd had a bad time when Andy'd lived with them, but she still reckoned she'd been in more trouble than he had, in the last few months of Andy's stay. She'd seen that new look on his face each time he barged in the bedroom to take it out on Cody. Those wolf eyes of his would roam over her way. Taking a long hard look, before he got started on her little brother. She was sixteen; she was getting her boobs; the way they were coming along, she'd end up fitted out like the pink-fleshed girls in the magazines. That was why Mom had finally kicked Andy out. Not because he bullied and hurt Cody – she pretended not to notice that – but because she got jealous. She couldn't stand him looking at someone else.

Jen had got into the habit of going to bed with her coat on and zippered up anyway. But the rest of the time she was actually pretty happy about the boobs. They were her ticket out. Mom would never let her go away, so her only chance was to get someone to take her. There'd be a white guy in town someday with a stack of cash, an address way down island and an eye for the boobs. Wham, bang, see ya later. All the girls at school agreed she'd be the first to make it.

There was a loud crash outside.

Jen's eyes opened very wide.

It sounded like someone had gone through the woodpile. If Mom was so drunk she'd missed the house by that much, she'd probably crash out as soon as she got in the door. She'd still be in the chair in front of the TV when the kids went down in the morning. That was good; it meant a quiet night was more likely. But – Jen's eyes flicked nervously from side to side, though her head stayed still, nestled in the hood – she hadn't heard the sound of the truck coming back. She was sure of it.

Another clatter. They called it the woodpile because a guy up the road came three or four times a year and cleared out dead wood behind their lot for them, split it and stacked it neatly and covered it with a tarp. He did it just to be helpful. Jen liked watching him work. He took his shirt off when he was busy with the axe, even in winter. He had muscles all over his back and shoulders, not boy-muscles, not puffy gym-muscles like the jock kids at school, but man-muscles, stringy and supple and useful-looking. Mom tried to get him to come in for a beer but he always smiled and said no. It was never the nice guys who fell for Mom. Funny, that.

Jen wondered why he bothered coming back anyway, since all they ever did after he'd gone was toss their own sad ugly garbage around his craftsman-like stack. Their yard was an arrangement of junk heaps. You left anything out there more than a week, it became the bottom of a new pile. Mom kept everything. She had this idea that time would turn it all into money. 'We could sell that someday,' she always said. 'Someone's going to want that someday.' Empty canisters, lengths of pipe, mower parts, fishing nets, old toys, a broken fridge, window frames, a boat trailer, tyres, outgrown bikes. All time ever did was rot it or rust it, whatever it was.

Something was climbing around in it. She heard glass breaking. Not Mom; it couldn't be. Not drunk kids screwing around or she'd be hearing voices too. An animal?

A thunderous clang: something must have been knocked over against the old truck. Could an animal have come down out of the woods and got tangled in the junk? It sounded like a big one, elk or bear. But animals didn't clatter around in people garbage unless there was food involved, and even Mom wasn't stupid enough to leave anything out there that smelled. There was a lolling, clumsy rhythm to the sound of the thing's progress through the yard. Animals didn't get drunk, did they?

Her breath caught.

Andy?

She'd have heard a truck; surely she'd have heard a truck. Unless he'd got some scary idea about sneaking up along the road on foot. Maybe he knew Mom was still out.

The baby squirmed. That baby could be half a Carney, Jen thought, as she pushed back the blankets. Could be Andy's child. We could be rearing a wolf cub right in this room.

She tiptoed to the bathroom and looked out of the window.

She thought at first it *was* a bear. Something dark and shambling was pushing through the scattered junk. Then she saw that the dark was some kind of big coat, and the shambling was two-legged. In the shadows cast by the single outside light it looked like a moving tent.

Noises came from it, smothered wheezy grumbling sounds. It got clear of the pile and shuffled towards the house.

It stopped. There was a shaggy head on top, which till then had been bent like it was rooting through garbage bags. The head lifted, twisted round and then looked straight up at the bathroom window.

Jen felt a queasy mix of relief and fear. She'd been so sure it was Andy sneaking back, wasted or high, a thirst for revenge boiling behind his hard eyes, that she couldn't help smirking at the sight of some old bum blundering out of the woods and getting caught up in the woodpile. But this one seemed to have brought the woods with him. He was big, really big, wide like a bear, a big head hunched on heavy shoulders. And the coat was . . . She squinted. The coat was covered in stuff. Like leaves and twigs, except they clinked, and bits reflected the light.

The face was completely hidden in shadow.

A voice called out to the window where Jen watched. A crabbed voice, an angry old woman voice. She shrank back into the bathroom.

Now she was only frightened.

She could cope with Mom, pathetic as her mother was. She could cope with her brothers and her baby sister. She could even cope with Andy drooling over her boobs like a dog in heat. What frightened her – really frightened her – was new stuff. When things changed they got worse.

The front door shook.

Crystal began to grizzle, but Jen ignored the baby. She headed for the phone in Mom's room, trying to remember whether she'd seen Mom using it recently, which would mean the bill had been paid.

There was a tinkle of glass and the porch light went out.

The house was suddenly pitch dark. Panicking, Jen grabbed for the phone. She knocked some stuff over onto the floor. The phone went down with it. She knelt and scrabbled around. The door downstairs banged hard, and there was a rough shout.

In the kids' bedroom Cody began screaming.

Jen swept her arms over the floor, scattering empty cans. She found a cord and hauled on it. A shape that felt like half the phone came into her hands.

The bum was kicking the door. Each kick made the whole house shake. Window screens rattled. Cody's screaming drilled through her head like a car alarm. She fumbled at the thing that might have been the phone and dropped it.

There was a mighty crack from downstairs, the sound of the door breaking open. Jen cringed on the floor. Carl was awake now too. Through the wall she heard him yell at Cody to shut the fuck up. Get the phone, just get the phone, Jen thought, though now the shouting and the screaming and the banging made it too loud to think straight. The crotchety old voice was shouting as well, shouting up the stairs. Things crashed around in the front hall like a moose was stuck in there. The whole house was coming down around her ears.

She gagged as an unbelievable reek flowed into the room, a stench of rotting fish and sea-filth. The bum was shambling up the stairs and the fouled air flowed in front like a bow-wave. Next door Carl was yelling at Cody. 'Shut up, you fuckin' freak!' He always tried to shout louder than the other kids could scream, as if that would stop them. 'Jen!' She heard him roll out of bed. Her hands were twisting round and round the cord that might have been attached to the phone.

'Hey fat boy!' croaked the stranger's voice, mean and mocking, at the same time as Jen heard Carl open their bedroom door and holler, 'Mom! What the fuck are you doing down there? Jen!' She put her hands over her ears and curled up on the floor. The smell was like sharing the hood of her coat with a dead bird.

'You! Fat kid! You listening? You got ears on you?'

It was a woman's voice for sure, a big, bullying cackle. It had a husky, old-fashioned accent to it. Somehow Carl was totally ignoring it, all of it, the smell, the rattle, the huge thing in the stairway, he didn't seem to know it was happening. She heard him go into the bathroom, still shouting for her, looking for her to clean up the mess, to get everything straight, but this time she couldn't. She was holding the phone to her chest like a doll. She no longer had any idea what it was for.

'You deaf, asshole?' the voice spat. 'You!' It was upstairs now, right outside the bedroom door. Carl came thumping to the top of the stairs and yelled, 'Jen! What the fuck! Jen!'

'Asshole's deaf as a brick,' growled the voice, and then shouted, 'Who's listening? Someone here's listening. Hey! Out of my way, asshole.' Carl's shouts changed to a screech, and with a sound like the roof falling in he tumbled down the stairs. Jen couldn't stop herself letting out a horrified cry.

'Who's that?' the voice barked. Cody went on screaming. Jen could picture him, sitting up, knees hugged to his chest, banging his head with his hand, screeching, screeching, while the baby squalled beside him. She curled tighter.

Slats of light swung through the room. Headlights turning into the yard. They let Jen see that the bedroom door was opening.

'Oho!' A massive shadow filled the doorway. 'Oho! Hey! Look what I found.'

From outside, Mom's shout, shrill with stupid panic: 'Jen!'

The shadow mumbled. Its coat clicked and rustled as if it were alive, like rats in the roof. A sharp hiss, a flare. It had struck a match.

The invader was a huge old woman with sneaky little eyes like a whale's set in a cracked face the colour of mahogany. Her cheeks were chalked a smudgy white. She rattled as she moved because her coat was sewn all over with beads, bones, feathers, copper discs, knots of deer hooves bunched like tassels; so were her stiff hide leggings. A ring of bone pierced her nose. The miasma radiated out from her, rancid, blubbery, unspeakably foul. She hunched, holding the match out in fingers so filthy they looked completely black.

'This one's not deaf and blind, huh? Hey? Oho! A girlie!' She grinned, exposing brown teeth tumbled around as if there'd been a landslide in her mouth.

'Jen!' Mom cried out from downstairs. Then she shrieked. She must have seen where Carl had fallen. The chorus of screaming vibrated in Jen's head.

'Wasn't looking for a girlie,' the crone cackled, apparently pleased. 'But I guess the girlie come looking for me! Come up off there, girlie.' She motioned. 'You found what you looking for.'

'Jen! Cody!'

Jen found her tongue. 'Mom! I'm here!'

The crone pushed further into the room, reached out and slammed the door shut behind her.

'Just you and me, girlie,' she said, backing against the door. The match had burned right down to her fingers. She hissed in surprise and spat on them, then scraped around somewhere in the flaps of her coat and lit another.

'Jen!' Mom was running up the stairs.

'Mom!'

The bedroom door shook, but the crone had got her bulk against it. 'Let me in!' Mom cried. She slapped on the door. 'Open it!'

'You gonna listen to me, or you gonna listen to that?' the old woman said, her eyes glinting. 'Hmm?'

'I can't, Mom!' Jen shouted.

'What's going on? Open up! Jen!'

'You gonna crawl around here an' let these assholes keep you down, girlie? You gonna live your days eating up their shit? Or you gonna learn killer-whale dance and go dancing away? Get on your feet!'

'Jen!' Both palms pounding on the other side of the door. 'Jen!'

'You got white-girl name, girlie? You got white-girl spirit? You wanna go deaf and blind like the fat asshole?' Her face creased with disgust. 'Up!' she barked.

Jen stood up.

'Gotta stand on your feet for killer-whale dance.' The reek and the shouting and banging chaos made Jen's head swim. The second match burned out and in the darkness she thought the shape blocking the door had become a whale, a massive domed whale head thrusting up from the floor. She staggered to one side.

'Gotta open your mouth to sing killer-whale song. Open your mouth, girlie.'

'Huh?' she said.

'Open your other mouth, girlie. Not the one you use for eating shit. Open it. Gotta say my name. What's my name, girlie?' Everyone was shouting; everything was shouting. She squeezed her hands over her ears but none of it would stop. 'What's my name? You know it, girlie. I don' come here otherwise. I don' come out to your shithole unless there's killer-whale dancer here. Firs' time in a hundred years! What's my name?'

'*Ma'chinu'ch!*' Jen screamed, her ears ringing.

The shadow screeched delightedly. 'Killer-whale girlie!' It swayed, waking the skeletal music in its coat. 'You own the clan house! You gonna dance the dance!' The dried hooves clacked, the strings of beads skittered together. 'You better learn it quick, girlie!'

'*Ma'chinu'ch!*' Jen shouted. People were shouting back at her from the other side of the door, but she couldn't hear them. '*Ma'chinu'ch!*'

The vast shadow whooped. 'Not anyone sees me but you! Not anyone hears me but you! You finished eating shit, girlie. Killer-whale song come down your mouth. You gonna tell them all what's coming.'

'It's coming!' Jen cried. 'It's coming!'

The blind darkness filled with dead things chattering. 'Orca boy coming! Coming the long way round. Orca boy got oceans to cross. But he's coming, and he's bringing the world.'

'Orca boy's coming!' The ocean girl threw back her head and ululated to the stained ceiling. 'Orca boy's bringing us the world!' Her mother and her brother heaved at the door, crying and hammering. The prophecy soared above their pandemonium, an eagle over a churning sea. 'He's finding his way home. Light the hearth. Open the door of the house. Let the ancestors in. The world's coming back! The world, the world!'

Author's Note

LIKE THE TALE of King Arthur, the Faust legend is one of those stories that exists mostly in outline. All they need are a few essentials: in Arthur's case, the sword in the stone and the Round Table and Guinevere and Lancelot and Merlin. The bones of the Faust legend are even simpler: the bargain, the interval, the final payment coming due. All the rest is flexible, which is why Arthur stories range from *Le Morte d'Arthur* to *Excalibur*, and why the two best-known Fausts – Goethe's and Marlowe's – are likewise about as spectacularly different-looking as Malory's romance and John Boorman's film.

One of the few details we know for sure about the magician's adventures is that he once demanded to see Helen of Troy, renowned for centuries for her beauty. We know this because it's the only inessential narrative detail that Marlowe and Goethe agree on. Their source is the cheerfully sensationalist sixteenth-century biography called (in its English translation) *The Historie of the Damnable Life and Deserved Death of Doctor Iohn Faustus*. From chapter 55:

> . . . wherefore he called his Spirit *Mephostophiles*, commanding him to bring him the fair *Helena* of *Greece*, which he also did: Whereupon he fell in love with her, and made her his common Concubine and Bed-fellow; for she was so beautiful and delightful a piece, that he could not be one hour from her, if he should therefore have suffered Death, she had stolen away his Heart . . .

Goethe, of course, knows there's more at stake in this relationship than celebrity sex, and has Helen stand for an ideal of pure classicism against which the magus has to measure his Romantic ambitions. Marlowe's Faust, much less wise, gets nothing from the encounter at all, unless you count two of the best pentameters in English:

Was this the face that launched a thousand ships,
And burnt the topless towers of Ilium?

In the shadow of those towers, Cassandra's legend is appropriately elusive as well. She's a marginal figure in the *Iliad*, and Homer stays tactfully silent about her prophetic burden. It's left to a dramatist some two or three centuries later to flesh her out. Aeschylus sends her onstage in his *Agamemnon* as a prisoner of war, dragged from Troy to Argos among the rest of the victorious king's spoils. The play makes her a silent witness to the scene where Agamemnon's wife Clytemnestra welcomes him back to the palace after his ten-year campaign. Her silence, in fact, is all we're allowed to know about her at first. She doesn't speak even when Clytemnestra invites her to follow them inside. Perhaps she doesn't understand, Clytemnestra says; she's a foreigner after all, her language no better than a swallow's twittering. The watching men of Argos think she looks like a captured animal new to its cage. Or just mad, Clytemnestra retorts, but the bridle of slavery will cure her of that, once it's made her bleed. With that parting insult the queen goes in, leaving Cassandra alone onstage with the chorus.

Then – while, unseen inside, Clytemnestra throws a net over her husband and hacks him to death in the bath – Apollo stings her into speech at last. *Otototoi*, she cries, words that mean nothing but pain:

Otototoi popoi da
Ôpollon Ôpollon

She knows what's happening inside, and she knows it's her turn for slaughter next. I'm glad to have spared her that much at least, though in the *Agamemnon* prophecy is a worse pain to her than murder, and she won't escape that burden until Gawain comes along.

The corner of England he'll arrive in already exists and, allowing for the differences you'd expect between a world still without magic and a world under the pressure of its imminent return, can be found on the maps. Three or four of the locations in the story have pre-emptively managed to escape disenchantment and, especially in the winter months, appear nowadays exactly as Gawain will see them. Anyone can visit the station where Hester leaves her car or the cove where Tristram will drown. (Out-of-the-way beaches and train stations are potent magical places, as small children might tell you.) The ferry lands on the south side of the river at the same steps where Gav will disembark, and the footpath from there up to the crossroads goes through the same woods beside the same stream. According to an old guidebook I once found on the shelves of a holiday cottage, that stream is called *dhu ra*, though only one of those words appears to be properly Cornish, and I never found the name again.

Pendurra itself – the house – did not exist when I started writing Gawain's story. An altogether different building stands in its place, the relatively modest remnant of a vanished manor. However, by the time the early versions of *Advent* were finished, it turned out that I'd conjured the house into being. (No one was more surprised than me.) It appeared in the wrong place, about ten miles off, and the architectural details didn't come out quite right either, but I had the garden almost perfect, and the atmosphere – the hush of granite and suspended ruin, the feeling of stepping onto a shoal in the river of time – is exact. Anyone who can find it can go there as well. Winter, as always, would be best.